SHATTERED BONDS

A Jane Yellowrock Novel

Faith Hunter

ACE
New York

ACE
Published by Berkley
An imprint of Penguin Random House LLC
penguinrandomhouse.com

Copyright © 2019 by Faith Hunter
Excerpt from *Blood of the Earth* © 2016 by Faith Hunter
Penguin Random House supports copyright. Copyright fuels creativity, encourages
diverse voices, promotes free speech, and creates a vibrant culture. Thank you for buying
an authorized edition of this book and for complying with copyright laws by not
reproducing, scanning, or distributing any part of it in any form without permission.
You are supporting writers and allowing Penguin Random House to continue to
publish books for every reader.

ACE is a registered trademark and the A colophon is a trademark of
Penguin Random House LLC.

ISBN: 9780399587986

First Edition: October 2019

Printed in the United States of America
1   3   5   7   9   10   8   6   4   2

Cover art by Cliff Nielsen
Cover design by Katie Anderson

To my Renaissance Man.

*Thank you for all the rivers, all the laughter,
all the joy, and all the love.*

Life without you would be a very dark place indeed.

ACKNOWLEDGMENTS

Teri Lee, Timeline and Continuity Editor Extraordinaire, for all the changes.

Mindy "Mud" Mymudes, Beta Reader and PR.

David B. Coe for raptors and feathers.

Let's Talk Promotions at ltpromos.com, for managing my blog tours and the Beast Claws fan club.

Lee Williams Watts for being the best travel companion and PA a girl can have!

Beast Claws! Best Street Team Evah!

Carol Malcolm for the timeline update in *The Jane Yellowrock Companion*.

Mike Pruette at celticleatherworks.com for all the fabo merch!

Joe Nassise for putting me in touch with VIPs about older helicopters.

KC for helicopter info.

Larry Correia for contacts and info.

Lucienne Diver of The Knight Agency, as always, for guiding my career, being a font of wisdom, and career guidance.

Cliff Nielsen for all the work and talent that goes into the covers.

Poet and writer Sarah Speith for giving me Jane's medicine bag. It's still perfect!

Copy Editor Eileen Chetti.

As always, a huge thank-you to Jessica Wade of Penguin Random House. Without you there would be no book at all!

CHAPTER 1

He Ate Her Body While She Was Still Alive, Piece by Piece

Beast *pawpawpawed*, slow, across ridge of rock over creek. Silent. Good predator. Moving back paw into front paw track, paw prints overlapping in fresh layer of snow. Beast lifted snout and sniffed, breath in two white clouds in icy air. Wind blew own scent back, along path. Wind filled nose with musk of three male deer, upwind. Bucks did not see or smell Beast. *Beast is best hunter.*

But.

Biggest buck raised head. Sniffing. Pawing dirt. Eyes on tree bark where Beast had left mark before last pregnant moon. Where Beast had sharpened claws to mark territory. Old spoor. Beast had hunted along creek then. Was best hunter's old spoor still strong with threat? Had Beast made stupid kit mistake?

No. Beast is good hunter. Want big deer. Has much meat. Will have good blood and good organs and good belly fat. Beast hungers. Big buck is strong and healthy.

Pawed closer. Crouched. Eyes on other creek bank and deer below. Watching.

Snow covered ground, deep as Beast paw. Wet rocks

were black, sharp as knife blade in hands of human
hunter. Sunlight was low, angled. Reflection in pool of
water below did not show Beast. Did not show deer. Was
good hunting spot. Water splashed from small falls, crisp,
like breaking sticks. Would cover Beast sounds.

Smaller male in male deer herd finished drinking.
Leaped up bank to flat ground beneath Beast's perch. Beast
waited. Finally, big deer dropped head. And drank.

Beast tightened crouch, pulling all body onto paws,
shoulders high. Leaped. Shoved off with back legs.
Stretched out front legs. Claws extending. Falling. Thick
tail rotated for balance. Scent of buck rushed up. Heavy.
Pungent.

Deer flinched. Hooves left ground. Buck leaped high.
Away from other deer. Beast snarled. Not expecting
jump. Whipped tail, swiveling body. Reaching.

Buck splashed into deep water. Beast missed.

Buck leaped again. Splashed hard. Hooves driving up
far bank. White tail held high.

Beast fell.

Landed half in water.

Front paws missed rock just under surface.

Paws, legs, shoulders, head, slapped into water. And
under it. Nose flaps closed, but not before water went up
nose.

Front feet hit bottom, back feet hit bank.

Wrenched body back. Rear paws and claws dug deep
into half-frozen muddy bank. Body twisted. Out of water.
Blew water out of nose in loud snort. Spat and shook.
Loose coat slid around muscular body. Flinging water
droplets into snow. Blowing.

Beast whirled, searching for two smaller deer. They
had vanished. Beast snarled at world. Screamed. Big deer
must have heard or smelled Beast.

I hunger! Screamed again, sound echoing in hills.
Chuffed in anger. Pounced up and down, paws sinking
into half-frozen mud.

Deer did not come back. Prey was smart.

Shook again. Water had not penetrated into deep coat.
Had not washed into paw pads. Beast would not freeze.

Pulled in air over tongue and over scent sacs in roof of mouth. What Jane called flehmen response, but Beast called scenting. Stopped. Held muzzle into air and smelled again. Caught stink of cat on air. Sucked in air again, hard and long, showing fangs, smelling with nose and part of brain that Beast had stolen from ugly dog, good nose, what Jane called bloodhound.

Smelled cat. Was male. Did not smell like lynx or bobcat. Was not small feral cat humans used as mousers. Was different. Was . . . bigger. Scent was old and no tracks showed in snow. But cat had been on Beast's territory. Back feet landing in prints of front feet, Beast stalked scent. Followed old cat smell many short steps, body in crouch, to tree on edge of hunting territory. Male cat had left spoor near tree. Old scat. Male cat was healthy. Strong. Bigger than lynx. Beast sucked in scent through nose and mouth. Cat was not lion from Africa. Cat was not leopard. Not puma. Was not werecat. Beast knew those smells. Did not know this cat. Beast pawed scat and saw bones of rabbit in scat. But. Cat was gone.

Beast clawed tree, shredding bark. Clawed and clawed, marking territory. *This is Beast territory. This is Beast hunting ground.* Snarled again. Shook more water out of pelt. Left spoor at ground under tree, on top of male cat scat. This said, *Beast place.* All who hunted here would know it was Beast place. Went back to pool of water and drank. *Beast water. And when Beast sees deer again, Beast deer. Beast food.*

Beast screamed, mountain lion cry bouncing up hills like human ball on walls. Beast shook, flinging more water, and shoved off with all four feet. Straight-up jump, what Jane would say was too high, but *Puma concolor* knew was good jump. Landed on top of rock ridge. Raced into trees and down top of hill toward house that was human home.

Snow began to fall. Ran through snowflakes, slinky and lithe and lissome. Good words for Beast. Each leap covered more than Beast body and tail, body and tail, and part of body again. Was long run steps.

Sun dipped behind western ridge. Dusk fell. Beast

eyes saw world as green and silver and gray and many
shades of black. Cold air and snow kept Beast cool. Felt
good on strong body. But Beast still hungered. Was
skinny.

Thought of humans and vampires and witches. *Want
to hunt bison in Edmund car. Edmund is gone. Want to
sit on Leo and rub jaw on Leo to scent mark. But Leo is
gone. Want to curl around Angie Baby and Little Evan
and new kit and keep kits safe. But kits are gone. Beast is
hungry. Beast is sad.*

Thought about big-cat spoor. *Beast is lonely.*

Felt/saw/smelled change. Beast stopped. Crouched.
Thought was another deer, but . . . vibration beneath
Beast's paws was too big for running deer. Was like stone
on stone, not deer hooves. Beast quivered in reaction,
sniffing, dropping belly to snow. Thinking. Vibration got
stronger. Claws extruded and sank into leaves on ground
beneath snow. Vibration got stronger again. *Earth moves,*
Beast thought. *Earth is alive.*

Snow fell from quivering branches overhead. Large
globs landed on snow with soft plops. Dollop of snow
splatted onto Beast's back. Beast hissed. Leaped high
and to side, into trees, hissing, spitting, hissing, growling.
Raced up tall tree into branches. Hunched tight. Smelling for enemy. But tree was shaking too.

Earth settled. Night fell darker beneath heavy clouds.
Faint light came from place where sun set. Beast turned
to stare at it. Sun was gone. Was too light there now. Had
been darker there when sun set last time Beast hunted.
More white man's lights? Hate white man's lights.

When Beast was satisfied that Earth was staying still,
Beast dropped from limb, loped toward house. Smelled
wood smoke on air. Smelled Brute spoor stink. Smelled
Bruiser and Eli and stink of gunfire from new shooting
range. Family. Saw snow fall, felt snow landing on coat.
Trotted out of tree line, along row of grapevines, branches
showing hints of green from warmer weather, now gone
again. Bruiser said Mother Nature was fickle. Beast did
not understand fickle. Trotted past unfinished cottages.
Past finished cottages. Up to house that Jane called inn.

Beast did not need lights, but security lights were on. Alex and Eli trusted Beast to know if Beast was safe, but did not trust Jane to live, so littermates had come. They had put up cameras. Beast was on camera and motion sensors. Beast thought about spraying spoor on cameras and chuffed with laughter. But Bruiser was here. Eli and Alex. Family. Beast did not spray cameras.

Beast was nearing front steps when something in mind tore with harsh sound. Beast stopped. Stumbled. Fell to snow. In head, deep in mind, Edmund screamed, "My mistress! *Dange—*" The sound of his cry was cut off. Was sound of agony. Beast froze, lying in snow.

Edmund cry waked Jane.

Beast? Was that Ed?

Beast whirled body and spun to feet. Raced for door, sprinting, leaping, covering twenty feet in a bound.

Ed? Jane whispered in my/our mind.

Edmund screamed. Sound as if heart was being torn out with claws.

Oh no. Oh nonononono, Jane thought. *He's being . . . He's being tortured.*

Pain and vertigo and the scent of blood flooded through me. Beast's paws overlapped and we stumbled, falling hard to our side. Rolled back to our feet. *Ed?* I screamed for him.

There was nothing. A blank dark hole where the connection to Ed used to reside. I hadn't even noticed the bond was there, a real, tangible thing. Nor had I noticed the shield between us until it tore, that horrible ripping sound in Beast's mind. But the absence of the bond, the absence of Ed, was glaring, screaming, like night terrors and drowning and being sucked into a deep, dark hole in an underground river.

I/we staggered, raced up the stairs and inside, through the huge rubber-flapped cat door Eli had installed to the side of the human one. The silver-bell chimes announced our arrival. We raced across the thick Oriental rug of the foyer. Dry heat, artificial light, and the sound of a game on the huge TV screen over the fireplace were like being smacked in the senses, and we skidded on snow-damp paws across the marble flooring as we raced into the noisy office/TV/living area.

Beast had hunter eyes on Alex, sitting at the antique two-sided desk that took up the entire far end of the room. We leaped to cross the space, cat eyes seeing what he was working on while in midair. On three of his screens were files and research about the Dark Queen, and on two others were e-mails from witches about methods to treat magically induced cancer. We landed, slipping again on the slick floor, banging into the splayed feet of Alex's desk chair. Sending him rolling.

The Kid grunted, pulled himself back into place, and tried to wave us away. Beast reached up and took his hand in her teeth.

The game went silent.

The room went still. Sweat smell of surprise came from Alex. He slowly turned his head and looked at us, long curls sliding across his dark-skinned forehead and cheek. "Jane?"

Eli was standing behind us, weapon drawn.

They think I died and you went feral, I thought at Beast.

She snorted at that thought and let go of Alex's hand. It tasted of sweat and soot and coffee and an odd chemical under-tang. Beast rose to her back feet, placing her right paw on the desk near the keyboard.

Alex said, "Oh." He opened the file drawer to the side and pulled out the specially made, heavy-duty, oversized keyboard, placing it in front of us. Behind us, Eli relaxed and we heard the sound of a weapon click back into the Kydex holster.

Beast extruded her claws and turned over the use of the paw to me. Carefully, slowly, I typed. Letter by letter, the words appeared on the small designated screen to Alex's far left. 'ed n trouble. where ed?'

Eli grunted in worry, propped a hip on the large oak desk, and pulled out his phone, probably to text Bruiser to get back to the house. My honeybunch was out in the vineyard, checking the youngest vines and the new trellis and the stability of the terraces down the hill from the house. Beast had smelled him on the wind as we raced inside and located him reliably. Bruiser wasn't alone. He was with Brute, the white werewolf, and Pea, the grindylow. Not things I had consciously noted until I needed to.

Alex slanted sharp eyes at us and went to work, minimizing two of his screens, searching through private vampire sites he was able to access because of my position in Mithran hierarchy, and other sites that were open to the public. Beast dropped to the floor as he worked and pulled the ceramic water bowl to her with a paw. There were water bowls placed strategically throughout the house, all ceramic, since she refused to drink out of metal bowls, preferring toilet water to the taste of steel. Which had been *gack* until I was able to explain to the humans what was wrong. She lapped water.

The house had been an inn and vineyard that I bought before I left New Orleans. I'd needed a place to lie low while either my human body died from magically induced cancer or I decided to stay in Beast's form forever. I hadn't known what I was buying, not exactly. I was just hunting for acreage and I bought a property that had gone into foreclosure after the original owners' costly divorce. Now it was territory for Beast and a house big enough for my family and clan to live with me. If I survived.

Eli asked. "Did you hear Ed psychically through the binding?"

Beast stopped drinking and looked up at him. I/we nodded once. Deep inside, my thoughts plundered the empty place where Ed had been, a place that was now raw and bleeding and broken. He had been here, inside of us, all this time, bound to me as his mistress. Now he was gone. I needed to help him. I needed to help him *now*. And I couldn't.

Beast will hunt for Ed, she thought.

Ed is far away, I thought back.

"You're all wet," Eli said. "What'd you do, fall in the creek?"

Beast snarled.

Eli's face seemed permanently creased with mixed emotions, complex weavings of fury, despair, anger, grief. He seldom laughed these days, and I was the problem. If he could heal me by shooting something, I'd be healthy and happy, because he was going through ammo as if it grew on trees, in the outdoor shooting range he had set up. But he was helpless in the face of a magical disease that no one knew how to treat. A rare moment of amusement lit his face. "You did," Eli said. "You fell in."

Beast snarled at him and thought at me, *Do not like water. Hate water. Hate cold water. Water helped deer get away. Water stole deer.*

I let my thoughts riffle through Beast's memory and saw her landing in the icy water, plunging beneath. Inside, I laughed but said nothing.

Beast is best hunter. Water stole deer, she insisted.

Okay, I thought.

I hunger. Want to hunt bison in Edmund car.

There were at least three bison ranches within driving distance of Asheville, and we had this conversation multiple times a week. I figured that this time it was to cheer me up, to put my fear for Edmund to the side, but it was more distraction than comfort. I mentally counted to ten.

Ten is more than five. Hunt in Ed's car, Beast thought, observant and yet cat-adamant all at once.

Ed's in trouble. Ed's in danger. So no, that ain't happening.

Beast hungers. Will Eli give dead cow?

I'm sure he will.

My cell chimed. Beast and I followed Eli to my gobag in the mudroom, the small bag hanging on the rack with other winter gear. He swiped the screen, tapped in my security code, and started back to the office, saying, "Molly, it's Eli—"

Angie Baby screamed, "My Eddie is in trouble! My Eddie! No! No!"

Beast growled, showing killing teeth. My/our heart did a fearful, arrhythmic bump-and-pause, and then raced too fast. Again, I searched for the connection to Edmund. Gone. Severed. As if it had been cut out with a knife. It was a strange sensation, as if a part of my own body had been instantly amputated and I kept searching for it, feeling something but . . . not the missing part. Ed was mine. Ed was gone.

Molly's voice came over the phone and my attention swept to the cell. "Sorry, Jane. Angie woke up screaming from a bad dream about Ed. We've been trying to calm her down, but she grabbed my cell and called." In the background, we heard the sound of Angie Baby's screams diminish in volume and the crooning of her father's flute magic, soothing her.

"Eli here. Jane's big-cat at the moment. Angie may not be having a dream."

"What's happening with Ed?" Molly asked, a trace of fear in her tone.

"We don't know, except that Jane heard Ed through the vamp-binding. Alex is searching for him."

In the background Angie's screams crescendoed, the pitch so high it hurt Beast's ears. She turned her ear tabs down against the noise and thought, *Kits . . . Kits in trouble. Ed in trouble.*

"Eli, I—This is . . . Has Ed been killed? He and Angie have a blood bond. I don't know what to do if . . . ?" Molly's voice trailed away, uncertainly.

I/we nodded Beast's head up and down, then back and forth, an uncertain yes/no gesture. We stared at Eli, snarling and licking our jaw, hoping he would understand that this was really not right.

"Jane and Beast are upset too," he said.

"I think we'll come visit," Molly said.

"We have the room," Eli said.

"Yeah. I've seen the sales brochures," she said wryly.

In the background, the screaming stopped. Evan said, "She's asleep. Pack fast. More snow is coming."

Into the cell, Molly said, "We'll probably have to keep her in magically induced sleep, but expect us after nine tonight."

"The county brined the street but the drive is frozen," Eli said. "Call if you get stuck."

"Will do." The call ended.

From the office, I heard the Kid's voice in quiet conversation with Grégoire, Blondie's and Alex's voices barely loud enough to pick out, even with Beast's ears. Grégoire was in France with Edmund. Good. That meant up-to-date info. I/we trotted to him.

"Send me everything you have," Alex said.

"*Oui*. My people do so now. *Dieu vous garde en sécurité.*"

"You too, dude."

I heard a connection end and felt a smile tug at my puma lips. Only Alex would call a royal-born, centuries-old, powerful vamp *dude*.

"Do the Everhart-Truebloods know how sick you are?" Eli asked me as we reentered the office.

Beast snorted. Louder, Alex said, "Yeah. They know." The younger Younger had been putting out the word, asking about magical treatments or cures for magical cancers. That meant talking to witches and revealing everything to Molly, my BFF, and her husband, air witch Big Evan. Witch boy children got magic-induced cancers often. Fighting the cancers meant a lot of study had gone into the magical and mundane cures. However, I wasn't a witch. My cancer was different.

Molly had mostly given up on finding a cure for me. She wanted me to drink a lot of vampire blood and cross my fingers that the healing of vamps would work on me. The only problem with that cancer treatment was that Ed was my first choice, my only safe choice, and he was in Europe. Any other vamp would see how sick I am and might challenge me to a blood duel on the spot to get my lands. And besides. I knew in my heart, no amount of vamp blood was going to heal me. My DNA had doubled, folded, multiplied, shredded, and knotted itself when I bubbled time. Vamp blood wasn't going to fix that.

My partners and I had been looking for a permanent cure. I wasn't dead. Yet. We still had options. Sort of.

Eli placed my cell phone on the big desk. His face was intent, the expression he wore when he was strategizing, ideas coming, undergoing scrutiny, being filed or discarded. To Alex, he said, "Yeah. Okay. We can do this. A house full of magic-using kids." He smiled slightly as if he was anticipating it. "This will be interesting."

Alex tapped keys, scanned screens, grunted, and swiveled to us. "I got something," he said.

Beast and I sat beside his chair and wrapped her long tail around our feet. The tail was warm with strong blood flow, thick, deeply furred, heavy, and cozy on our paws.

Alex leaned forward and propped his elbows on his knees. That made us eye-to-eye level and brought his scent strongly to our nose. He smelled of testosterone and garlic and coffee and aftershave and worry. Beast butted his hands, which were laced and hanging between his knees in a posture that was very Eli-like. Alex's mouth twisted into a parody of a smile and he scratched Beast behind her ears. "I've been in FaceTime conversation with Grégoire. Things have been happening fast in France, and there're things Grégoire hasn't told us, not wanting to worry you."

Beast snarled. So did I. Blondie knew I was sick. Blondie had been keeping secrets.

"Ed," Alex said gently, scratching, smoothing our lips back over our teeth. He looked into our eyes as if he was about to break my heart, "Was stolen from his lair in France at midday, five days ago."

My heart stuttered.

Ed? Beast asked.

Eli's lips twitched. On another man it would have been a scowl like thunderclouds. "We weren't notified," Eli said. "Why?"

"There was a fight," Alex said, even more gently, "in a farmhouse in the wine country of France. Four of Ed's people were killed. The house where they were laired burned to the ground."

Ed? Our lips moved but no sound came out. Our eyes burned. But Alex didn't appear to be grieved or as if he was about to tell me—

"His surviving people thought Ed had burrowed under the hearth, into a small safe-room lair, with three others. His vamps had been sharing blood and so they knew he was alive, but that was all they knew until they

got the safe room excavated." Alex sounded so grown up.
So adult. So much like Eli in his delivery, but with his
own touch, that gentleness I would never have expected
when I first met him. His fingers scratched deep and
Beast closed our eyes in bliss. "Because of the heat of the
fire and the presence of the local law," he said, "that rescue took place only a few hours past. Ed wasn't in the safe
room. Grégoire now assumes that Ed was taken by the
attackers the day of the assault."

Ed in cage? Beast thought, opening our eyes.

"Once his people started looking, they discovered that
Pellissier Clan's Bombardier Learjet 85 flew out of Paris
four days ago with Ed and four other vampires aboard—
none of them Ed's. The aircraft landed in the Bahamas
and Ed's passport was marked. Then he disappeared. They
were getting ready to inform us when I called them first."

Beast hissed deep inside me.

We pulled away from Alex and turned to face Eli
when he took up the narrative. "What we haven't discussed with you is that there's been a vamp war in Europe
and in other parts of the world between several Naturaleza and the Mithran factions. It's been simmering for
centuries and the emperor had controlled the violence
with an iron hand, but with Titus gone and Ed not yet
having a loyal base, things were getting dicey. With Ed
gone, I'm sure they've gotten worse."

Alex said, "According to Grégoire, the local fangheads are rising and fighting between themselves." Alex
captured my attention with his eyes.

Beast didn't like the direct stare. I held her still,
waiting.

Slowly, he said, "There is no emperor. No Dark Queen.
And you aren't in any shape to fight duels. Getting you
well has been and still is the goal, not fighting duels or
dealing with fanghead politics. So this is not your fault.
In any way. You got that?"

The Kid knew I had a guilt complex a mile wide, but
I'd been working on demolishing it. Since I got sick, I
hadn't felt guilty about anything at all. Except being sick.

And that was totally my fault, even if I hadn't known I was doing it to myself at the time. I snorted in disgust.

"What's happened?" Bruiser called from the front door. He was taking off his peacoat and pulling off snow-covered boots. Eli filled him in as my honeybunch crossed the wide space, as succinct as the former ranger could be. Three sentences, max.

"Which faction burned the house where Ed was staying?" Bruiser asked, his eyes lighting up. The former primo would know all about the political problems in Europe, and if the gleam in his eyes was an indication, he was already engrossed.

Alex said, "Things are bad over there. From what Grégoire was saying there are five key European factions, major infighting, and some of the European Mithrans have begun looking for new land to conquer. Two factions headed west, including the one that stole Ed and the Bombardier. That means that things are about to get bad in this hemisphere."

They've been hiding things from us, I thought to Beast. *Jane is sick. Jane cannot help. Why tell Jane?*

I'm still interested. They should have told me.

Jane is Dark Queen still? No. Jane gave up alpha among vampires. Walked away to find new territory to hunt. Jane is silly kit who does not know what she wants. Does not even know if she wants to live or die.

It isn't that I want to die. I just don't think I can live. And I'm nosy.

Beast swiveled her ear tabs back in disgust. She was disgusted a lot these days.

Alex said, "Grégoire debriefed me. Most of it's bad." Alex made eye contact with each of us, one by one, staring through the ringlets across his forehead before continuing. "Shimon Bar-Ioudas's faction is one that headed west. His passport shows he entered the British Virgin Islands two weeks ago, with an entourage, and then disappeared. But Grégoire thinks Shimon's people may have spearheaded the attack on Ed. He thinks Ed is now in the hands of Bar-Ioudas."

"Bar-Ioudas? Jane killed him and fed him to the were-wolf," Eli said, frowning.

"Shimon Bar-Ioudas," Bruiser said, "Shimon Bar-Judas, if we use the modern vernacular, is the name of the younger Son of Darkness, and according to what I know from my time as Leo's primo, he is far worse than his older brother." His voice was toneless and yet somehow still full of dread. "He's gone by many titles over the years. Flayer of Mithrans, Son of Shadows, Son of Night, Soul of Darkness, Son of Deception, among others. It's said that he was the brother who personally sacrificed his younger sister on the wood of the crosses of Calvary in the act of black magic that brought their father back from the dead and created the first of the blood drinkers." He hesitated. "The records suggest that he ate her body while she was still alive, piece by piece, while she screamed."

CHAPTER 2

Grégoire's More a Lover and a Dueler Than a Politician

Beast growled. I went very, *very* still inside. Among my kind that was the blackest of black magic. Even hearing about it made my pelt rise in hackles. Alex's hands went dead still and I backed away from the Kid.

"Yeah," he said to me. "Okay. So here's what we have on Shimon Bar-Judas," Alex said, spinning back to his computers, his fingers flying over the keys as he accessed the files amassed by Yellowrock Securities. "The SOD Two. For a thousand years, his traditional territory was Western Europe, the Middle East, North Africa, and India. With all the political unrest everywhere, he's had to move around, and indications are he isn't happy about that. With Leo in the grave and Titus true-dead and mostly eaten, he had two choices: challenge Grégoire and Edmund for Europe—and they might actually be better with edged weapons than he is, considering the fact that he hasn't actively dueled in centuries—or come here and take over Leo's lands from a woman who hasn't forcefully claimed them."

"Kidnapping Ed and coming here was not a strategy I expected. Or even understand," Eli mused.

"The Dark Queen *has* been silent," Bruiser said, thinking it through. "She hasn't raised an army or claimed more territory. She hasn't made a show of strength. It might appear that she's injured from the Sangre Duello and healing human-slow. Therefore, she may look like the easier conquest. He may think she is still licking her wounds, making it easier to claim her lands." He propped his chin on a hand, the beard hair making a soft scrunch, a sound that was new in our relationship. I loved his beard. So did Beast.

"If Jane looks weak . . . Alex," Eli said, "what's the MOC of New York doing?"

New York had been paying tribute to Europe for centuries. If he was part of the attack in some way—

"New York lost a challenge from Rosanne Romanello of Sedona," Alex said, glee lacing his tone. "He's headless. Rosanne is composing formal letters of fealty to Jane, writing as the MOC of Sedona and New York. The letters will be hand delivered by messenger in a week or so, according to proper Mithran protocol."

And no one told me. I had walked away from my responsibilities and they had let me. Eli should have slapped me upside the head and forced me back to work.

Bruiser's brows drew together, making vertical lines on his forehead. "Once Shimon has the Americas and Edmund firmly in control, then he could turn his attention back to Europe, which by then would be headed by Grégoire. But a Grégoire without a Dark Queen backing him would be easy prey. Grégoire, for all his grace and charm and fighting ability, is not a ruler. His grief over Leo's passing has made him into a dueling, fighting machine. Creating alliances takes a heart of stone, and Grégoire's more a lover and a dueler than a politician."

I'd seen Blondie duel when his emotions were involved. There was no mercy. He'd strip the flesh from his opponent before he'd stand and talk.

Alex stared at Beast. "Jane? You listening?"

The last Son of Darkness is in this hemisphere, I thought.

Ed in cage. Taken, Beast thought, thinking with me instead of thinking about deer and bison.

And if the SOD Two is in this hemisphere, he'll be attacking my people. People that I left in the lurch when I abdicated. I nodded Beast's head and she sat again, wrapping her tail around her paws. I remembered the sound of my primo's shields tearing. The sound of his voice as he screamed. The silky feel of his blood as it ran across his flesh. As he was ripped away from me. That had been a psychic attack on Ed. It would take a megastrong vamp to rip him away from me.

Alex said, "I'm still looking but I haven't found SOD Two entering the U.S. Not anywhere. And it's hard to hide a large contingent of bloodsuckers."

"The SOD's numbers?" Eli asked from the fireplace, where he had taken up his usual position.

"Grégoire estimated fourteen fangheads. Forty-five humans. Fifty-nine bodies."

I noted that he didn't say warm bodies.

Alex pounded the keys some more. "Okay," he said. His voice rising in pitch. "Yes. A ship called *The Scarlet Dragon* was found floating off of Palm Beach in Florida yesterday. Abandoned. The Coast Guard boarded and found a crime scene to beat all crime scenes. Fourteen people were found drained of blood in the galley freezer, stacked up like firewood. The crew and all of the staff were among those in the freezer."

"Assuming that Grégoire is correct," Bruiser said, the words coming slowly, "then Shimon took the ship from wherever the Bombardier landed, and sailed here." His syntax changed, becoming the formal, measured phraseology and tone I had heard when Bruiser was primo to the Master of the City of New Orleans, the tone he'd used when he made official pronouncements in the court. "Unless we are much mistaken, Shimon Bar-Ioudas, the Flayer of Mithrans, the younger Son of Darkness, is in the States."

Even in Beast form, my heart froze. I had thought I was done with all this. I was an idiot. There had *always* been two Sons of Darkness. Two sons of Ioudas Issachar—Judas Iscariot—two fathers of all vamps, two black witches who had used the wood and iron spikes of Golgotha to bring their father back from the dead, and who had been the first blood drinkers. No way was I going to be allowed to avoid him. *Shimon Bar-Judas. Holy crap.*

"ICE and PsyLED believe an upper-level vamp came ashore in Florida, but they don't know who they're looking for or where he is," Alex said, fingers clacking keys. "Every alphabet agency in the U.S. is a week behind. Looks like they're acting on the assumption that the fangheads are headed to New Orleans. If they're right, that gives us time to prepare and to warn your people."

I remembered Sabina, the outclan priestess of the U.S. Mithrans, saying, once, of the elder Son of Darkness—Shimon's older brother—Joseph Santana, aka Joses Bar-Judas, aka Yosace Bar-Ioudas, *"He cannot be brought to true-death, Jane Yellowrock. He is all that we have to bargain with. He is all that we have to keep his brother, Shimon Bar-Judas, at bay. And Shimon has always been the more dangerous of the two."*

So of course I beheaded Joseph and fed his true-dead head and body to Brute. In hindsight? *Crap.* I'd do it again.

I needed to be human. It was night, dark enough for me to shift. I could shift into Beast day or night, but shifting back to my human form was a problem until after dark.

Beast wants cow. Beast hungers.

Later. I stood and trotted up the stairs and along the hallway to the suite I shared with Bruiser, through the soothing tall-ceilinged bedroom, decorated in cream and stone and soft green, into the cream-and-stone bath and the doorless shower. Sat. And thought about being human.

Pain sliced along my bones like obsidian knives. Shifting was never the same way twice. Sometimes more pain. Sometimes less pain. Either way, it wasn't a piece of cake. Bones snapped and joints tore. I screamed.

*   *   *

I woke on the cool tile of the shower. Naked. Clean. Dying.

All the strength and energy I'd experienced as Beast were gone, leaving me exhausted and in pain. My skin was pale, my bloodless fingers almost white on the gray tile instead of their previous golden tones. I pressed on my middle, feeling the hard, pointed ends of the tumor in my belly. It was star-shaped, like my own, new, blended power. And like the new magics, it was deadly. The tumor was stealing all my circulation, using all my muscle protein to feed itself. My hair was a black tangle of lusterless shadow. I was a mess.

The only positive thing in all this was that while I was in Beast shape—which was healthy—the tumor didn't grow. Beast's body was just dandy. Staying *Puma concolor* gave my clan time to search for cures that might work on a two-souled Cherokee skinwalker. Chemo was out. Traditional and tribal forms of medicine hadn't worked so far. The tumor was magic-based, and my pals the Everhart-Trueblood clan were compiling possibilities. But so far? Nada. Nothing. Zip. The star-shaped magic constantly fed the tumor it had created, and it was growing as if it was on steroids.

I pushed myself to my knees and pulled up on the tiled half wall until I was standing. Woozy. Weak. I straightened my spine, forced air in and out of my lungs, and went to the sink and the small tray where the CBD oil and hemp oil were kept. Both oils came from the cannabis plant, but the hemp oil was made from seeds and the CBD oil was made from a single strain of flowers and leaves. Eli had found a supplier who was top-notch, and the quality of the oils was too, making it the most expensive body oil I'd ever used. I took a CBD dose orally—a little bitter, a hint of turpentine—and rubbed more CBD oil on my body, applying it to my belly and the bottoms of my feet to decrease pain. I used the hemp oil on the parts of my back I could reach, shoulders, arms, and legs, to combat dry skin.

I moved out of the frigid bathroom and pulled on

warm velour sweats and wool socks. The clothing was baggy and hid some of my weight loss. Having cancer sucked.

I took a peek in the tall mirror and saw a skinny, sick woman whose odd amber eyes were hollowed out in her sallow-skinned face. Again I put my shoulders back and walked out of the suite. And into Bruiser's waiting arms. He had been standing in the hallway, giving me privacy to dress. He did that all the time now—gave me privacy. As if he knew what it took to psych myself up to face the world in human form. I leaned into him. He cradled me gently enough that my middle didn't ache where we touched. I breathed against his down-filled vest, smelling the feathers, the clean outdoors, the slightly citrusy, slightly spicy Onorio scent.

"I love you," he said, his tone fierce. His arms tightened on me, restrained yet claiming.

Turning my head, I rested my forehead against his cheek and jaw. The beard was long enough to be soft on my skin. "I love you too. Can't wait to see the beard grown in full."

"I have a robust and manly beard," he agreed. "It is a wonderful thing to behold."

"I have no doubt." I was smiling when I pulled away. He picked up a milkshake from the hall table and circled my hands around the insulated tumbler. The shake was the purplish blue of blueberries, bilberries, and tart cherries. I hated the cold, but the ice cream was the easiest thing my human form could digest, and the berries were full of antioxidants and minerals and stuff Eli thought was important. I took a slow pull through the oversized metal straw, needing the calories to pay for the energy I'd used in the shift. Because I wasn't on chemo, I didn't have as much nausea as other cancer patients, but the first food on my stomach was still not easy. Bruiser took my free hand and laced our fingers together. Slowly we ambled down the hall.

"How is your vineyard?" I asked, seeking a moment of normalcy before the battle to come. The youngest grapevines had been planted just prior to the nasty divorce that culminated in my buying the property for such a great price. Most of them had survived the winter well enough, but we'd had two weeks of springlike weather and some of them had begun to leaf out. The late freeze had stressed the young vines.

"Remarkably well. And now that an earth witch is on the way, I can hope for a boost in growing power for the vines." I was drinking down the shake and didn't reply. He asked, "Are you okay, love, if they stay in the big house with us? If the last Son of Darkness is out and about, I'd like to keep us all close."

"Why wouldn't I be?"

"Let's see. Two adult witches, one who has imperfect control over death magics, one precocious, dangerous, out-of-control double-X-gene witch girl-child, one male witch child, also already exhibiting early magical ability, one infant still at the breast, said death-magic witch lactating and hormonal, her husband trying to hold it all together while still hiding in the male-witch-sorcerer closet, all running around screaming and making a mess, both physical and magical. And they might accidently kill us all. That?"

I chuckled. What he described sounded like heaven. And by his tone, Bruiser wasn't against the idea of company. My sweetcheeks had been quiet for several weeks, maybe even a little depressed, not that he had said so, but it was there in his tone, in his body language, in his scent. I figured he was dejected because Leo was gone and I was dying, but maybe also because he didn't have a job, a purpose, anymore. He was a type A personality and had been gainfully employed for a century, handling social and political situations with powerful paras and managing a powerful vamp's clan, businesses, servants, and money. He had made life-and-death decisions daily and nightly for VIVs (very important vampires) and their blood-dinners, dealing with human and vamp politics and high-stakes business. Now? He was my nursemaid. Maybe he needed this crisis. "I'm happy they're coming," I said.

"Good. I've given them the Thomas Wolfe Suite and the Charles Frazier Suite. They have a connecting door so Molly and Evan can keep eyes on the little ones. I've ordered in supplies and food, to be delivered at eight in the morning. And extra ammo. I've already put linens on the beds and in the baths."

I swung my eyes his way. My honeybunch had mad skills for social niceties, courtesy of an English boyhood and a hundred years or so as the primo to the former MOC of New Orleans. And he was doing linen? Yeah. He needed a purpose. I had been spending the majority of my time as Beast, so I hadn't noticed who had what jobs around the inn, but we hadn't brought servants. So someone had to be taking care of laundry and dishes and household things. Usually that meant Eli, but he'd been upgrading security measures everywhere and making himself useful with a hammer and nails on the unfinished cottages. "Sounds good," I said, pressing the elevator button. "Let's see where we stand with Shimon and his merry band of blood drinkers. We may have to travel once we find him."

"Love."

I tilted my head back at him as the doors closed on us.

"We could call in some other monster hunters. Nomad and his cohorts." Nomad was my first boyfriend and he taught me all about fighting vampires, then deserted me when I got in trouble. Nomad had also been bitten by werewolves, not that I'd told Bruiser that story. Maybe someday. My face must have shown my reaction to Nomad's name.

"Rick LaFleur?" he suggested. Another former boyfriend, no less annoying, but not a bad guy. In fact, he had been pretty great during the recent unpleasantness. And I needed to have a talk with him, one-on-one, and clear the air, now that I had a better grip on what magic did to people's will. But later. If I lived through this.

"Ayatas?" he proposed when I remained silent, pushing, making it clear that we needed backup. Ayatas FireWind was my brother, and though things were better between us, they weren't so great that I wanted to call him for support. He worked for PsyLED, the senior Special Agent in Charge of the eastern U.S. In the past, he had put his job first, before family, or at least before me. I wasn't at war with him, but I was a long way from trust.

Yeah, we'd need help of some sort, but I shrugged, noncommittal yet unimpressed with Bruiser's recommendations. Ed was in trouble. The last remaining Son of Darkness was nearby, probably planning revenge on me for feeding his brother to the dogs, so to speak. We needed to warn all the law enforcement agencies, and we had to warn my people in New Orleans to be ready. That was my political home base. That was where the attack would come because almost no one knew we were no longer in NOLA.

"Your clan Mithrans and Shaddock's Mithrans?" he suggested, pushing just enough that I knew he was worried.

Lincoln Shaddock was the newly promoted local Master of the City of Asheville, and the protector of the most valuable vampire in the world, Amy Lynn Brown—the only vampire whose blood could shorten the time a newly turned vamp spent in the devoveo—the ten years of nutsocrazies vamps went through before they "cured," like bacon, and found reason again. If they found their sanity at all. Many did not, or had not before Amy Lynn had come along. Any attacker would want to obtain Amy Lynn pronto, meaning she was in danger. The MOC owed me favors and loyalty since I'd made him master of his own territories and hunting grounds.

"Sure," I said. "We're in Shaddock's territory, and any invading vamps might look me up eventually, so we should notify Shaddock and get his advice, but only call in an army if we need to."

Bruiser gently squeezed my hand. The doors opened. Shoulder to shoulder, we stepped from the elevator to the main level and the central living area.

The winery part of Yellowrock Clan Home in the mountains, what I called Yellowrock Appalachia, was a big building off to the side of the inn, with a grape press, colossal stainless steel wine tanks and fermenters, and a Borelli bottling line, whatever that was. It was all top-of-the-line stuff that had made Bruiser's eyes go wide when he first saw it.

The inn was designed in a large, wide-mouthed, blunt-nosed V-shape, with the entrance and main public area in the blunted point of the V and the two V wings containing five suites each, on two stories. When he first saw the place, Alex had called it a "humongous, freaking big house." He was right. With a stone façade and four massive, wood, unshaped timbers that rose from the entry-level floor to the top of the second-story domed ceiling, actual trunks all twisted and golden and gorgeous. The trunks were the kind of logs one might expect to see in a Hobbit home, but bigger, and had been blasted with corn-cob grit to polish them, making them shimmer softly.

Besides the five family bedrooms and five guest suites, there were twelve one- and two-bedroom cottages, with entrances on both the inn and the gorge/creek sides. Three of the cottages were finished and set up as vamp lairs; nine of the more outlying units were unfinished, barely dried in. The previous owners had big aspirations.

The inn's central main rooms had been designed with weddings, tours, and other public events in mind and had originally consisted of a public tasting room, wine shop, gift shop, bakery, two half-finished kitchens, and summer café. In the last months, all that had been converted, giving us a chef's kitchen with commercial fridges and freezer, and a baker's kitchen with three commercial ovens, a real brick pizza oven, and commercial mixers. We had three dining spaces, multiple sitting areas, and a game room with space for a future pool table, all currently unfurnished.

The TV lounge and office space was located against the outer wall and walled off from the rest of the living areas. In it, Eli had installed an egress access in the floor, leading to a ladder and a wide tunnel that the previous owners had hoped one day would be a personal wine cellar and a doomsday bunker with its own outside entrance.

We entered the central part of the inn. The two-story, vaulted, tongue and groove, natural wood ceilings and marble floors meant the air was always just a little chilly in winter and the audio ambience was bright, sharp, and echoing. Even with the four polished golden timbers and the warm cream color of the two-story wallboard walls, even with the fans pushing warmer air down into the living space, even with the heated floors in some rooms, it wasn't homey. Not yet. Not even with fires burning in the three fireplaces. It still looked like a public space for weddings. Bruiser had ordered furniture and rugs to turn it into a home, but they hadn't arrived, nor had most of the furnishings beyond the bedroom furniture for the suites. The main area was open and empty, so we lived in the kitchens and the TV lounge/office, where we ended up now.

I placed the empty insulated shake cup in Bruiser's hand and sat gingerly on the comfy recliner. Bruiser had purchased the chair just for me, and it had a push-button mechanism that laid me back and raised my feet. Bruiser covered me with a soft, fuzzy blanket and turned the chair's warmer up. I sighed in relief. I was always cold these days. A game was on the big screen, as usual, muted, the score and team names on the bottom banner. I ignored it and gave my attention to Alex. Bruiser disappeared with my empty tumbler and returned to position a cup of ginger-honey green tea on the small table at my elbow.

"What do we have?" Bruiser asked. He took an oversized pillow off the sofa, dropped it beside my chair, and sat on it, resting one arm across my raised foot stand.

Eli told the house system—which Alex had named Merlin—to turn on the lights, and the hidden fixtures in the ceiling and along the walls came on. They threw dark gold highlights across Bruiser's dark hair and caught lighter tones in his beard. In jeans and flannel shirts, he looked nothing like the primo to the Master of the City of New Orleans he had been when we first met. Eli, wearing jeans and layered T-shirts, took his position at the stone-faced fireplace, facing the room and all the entrances. It was the location that allowed him to see the foyer, out a front window and a back window, and into the kitchens and mudroom. He was armed, a double thigh rig and a shoulder holster, nine-mils in each. He was always armed, but the in-your-face abundance was a new addition. He was worried and I wasn't sure why.

Alex spun in his office chair, facing us, and glanced at his brother. Eli nodded. They had been talking. Or hiding something. From the sick and dying me, too weak to deal with troubles. I glowered at them. Hurting, feeling the winter chill, I pulled the fuzzy blanket over my shoulders and watched the guys settle in. Inside me, Beast thought, *Littermates. Mate. Strong den, safe against predators. Beast is . . . what Jane calls happy.*

Yeah, I thought, surprised, especially in light of what I'd planned when I discovered I had cancer and had run away to die. *Me too. Even with still being the Dark Queen, it hasn't been bad. Not bad at all.*

Other than the Dark Queen, I'd abdicated my titles in favor of Ed, my primo, who was now Master of the City of New Orleans and most of the southeast U.S., with loyal but independent masters of various cities owing him allegiance. He was also the titular emperor of Europe if he could take it and hold on to power. Or he had been before he was kidnapped. "Out with it," I said, as my body settled into some semblance of comfort.

Alex said, "You abdicated the emperorship of the EuroVamps. We know that. But apparently no one in Europe knows that. If Ed ever got the papers, he never said anything."

I had sent my abdication letter to Edmund and Sabina, the outclan priestess of the Mithrans. I hadn't heard back from either of them. But . . . Sabina was old enough to take a decade to reply to correspondence. Ed was sneaky. Ed played the long game. What had Ed done? Maybe more important, what had he *not* done? "That little sneak," I said, trying to sound calm and not mad enough to chew nails. Lying by tone. Before they could reply I added, "And what is Grégoire doing? Is he safe or is he in as much danger as Ed?"

"Grégoire is fighting duels and battles in France, challenging the Mithrans who are killing humans, and trying to hold his own lands," Bruiser said. "He is scheduled to fight Titus's former heir this week." He turned his head and gave me a cheeky grin. "At each duel, he declares that he is fighting as the proxy of the emperor—Edmund—and for the Dark Queen, holding her up as some sort of King Arthur, and her reign as some sort of Camelot."

"Oh . . . *crap*," I said, incredulity and laughter lacing my words.

"He is gathering an army that he doesn't intend to use, planning to gift it to you." Bruiser's smile faded and he touched my ankle through the blanket as if to reassure himself I was still here. "Brandon and Brian keep me in the loop."

Brandon and Brian were Onorios, like Bruiser. They would talk. And no one was talking to me because what good was I? "Why not keep the land himself? Become the next emperor. I'd let him have it if Edmund . . ." *If Ed dies,* but I didn't say that. ". . . doesn't want it."

"Grégoire once told Leo that ruling is *tedious*," Bruiser said.

I breathed out a soft laugh. Yeah. That sounded like Blondie. The gorgeous diminutive fanghead would rather seduce his way through France and fight battles in a might-makes-right bloodsucking world than rule. And he was still grieving for Leo, so that meant he was geared for violence, not politics.

I sipped the green tea, thinking. The tea was very sweet, with strong notes of ginger, lemon, and mint, soothing my stomach; the mug warmed my cold hands. The chair heated beneath me and micromuscle cramps I hadn't consciously noticed eased. I fought to keep the relief off my face. My brothers hated it when they saw my pain. "I need to make some calls. May I have my cell?" I asked. I didn't have the energy to get it off the desk only feet away.

Eli crossed the room and placed it in my hand. "Charged."

"I'll be making calls too," Bruiser said, "to the Master of the City of Asheville and checking on things in New

Orleans." He kissed my forehead and I suddenly wished he wasn't so . . . *solicitous*. That was the word. I needed to hit something, not be coddled. "You'd break bones," Bruiser said, his grin returning. When I scowled at him he chuckled and said, "It was in your eyes. You can spar with all of us when you're well."

I grunted. He had a point. And at least he no longer sounded so despondent. We had allies to warn and favors to call in, possibly a trip to New Orleans to plan, and a battle to strategize. Bruiser should be in his element. "Hey," I said, trying to offer up a positive, "Europe may be going to hell in a handbasket, but we have our allies and our land."

"Our?" Bruiser asked, a strange sort of triumphant delight on his face. As if he'd jump at the chance to do important primo things again, and hearing me slip in such an obvious way was a happy-happy-joy-joy moment for him.

Glaring at him, I said, "Ed's. Ed's allies and Ed's land." But it was too late. Everyone had heard my claim and the three guys were grinning, even tightly wired Eli. Fine. Maybe I wasn't as uninvolved as I had thought. I scrunched up my nose at them and tapped in my cell's security code. It was old-fashioned security, but facial recognition or other biometric reader methods wouldn't work on a multiform being.

I scrolled to Soul's number. Soul was the assistant director of the Psychometric Law Enforcement Division of Homeland Security. Also an arcenciel, a rainbow dragon. Also a friend of sorts. For a chick who once had only one friend, I'd managed to make a lot of them. And then seen some die. That had sucked. A lot.

The call went to voice mail. I left a message to call me about the fanghead mess in Europe and heading this way. Then I called my . . . my brother. Ayatas FireWind, senior SAIC, PsyLED, working directly under Soul. I wasn't calling my brother for help, but to warn him and his PsyLED teams. I left the same message on his cell. Then I called Rick. Ditto on the message. "No one answers calls anymore," I grouched.

I got through to Sloan Rosen and Jodi Richoux, who were both in the WooWoo room at New Orleans Police Department. I filled them in and told them they were welcome at Chez Jane anytime. They didn't laugh, which told me things were less than stellar in New Orleans. I didn't want to go back, even if I managed to get healed. But if my people were in danger . . . And there it was again. A possessive word I shouldn't be entitled to. Disgusted with myself, I signed off.

I was still holding my cell when it buzzed. With Edmund's number. I sat up fast, the footrest flapping down with a bang and my stomach twinging with pain. "Alex. Trace the call!" I said, too loudly. The words echoed through the inn.

Alex didn't bother with questions; he just leaned in to his equipment and went to work. He had an energy drink at his elbow. I had thought he was off those things, but I'd been wrong. That explained the chemical taste in his skin from earlier. *Gack*. Eli glanced at the screen of my cell phone and moved to check the perimeter through the windows, while staying close enough to hear everything. Bruiser came back into the doorway, ending his call, waiting, watching.

I accepted the call, put it on speaker, and went on the attack. "Edmund," I said. "I assume you're in the presence of a kidnapper fanghead."

"Mistress," he said. He sounded like crap, but I was so relieved he was still alive—undead—I hardly heard the pain in his voice.

"Jane Yellowrock. *Tribal woman* of the Americas." It was still Ed's voice, but the inflection was odd, the words sounding different. And the tone dripping with distaste.

Fear snaked up my spine like a dozen baby rattlers. "This is the Dark Queen," I said, all vamp-formal, the blanket sliding to the floor at my feet as I stood. "You will address me by my proper title."

Ed's voice said, "You speak with the Flayer of Mithrans, woman. The Son of Shadows, Soul of Darkness. Shall you address me by my titles? They are many and varied."

"What do you want, bloodsucker?"

The laugh was low, mesmerizing, and demanding, even over the cell connection. Ed's voice, but not Ed. "I require your presence. We shall meet and parley in New Orleans."

"No."

Edmund screamed. My hand clenched on the phone. Bruiser, suddenly at my side, took the phone before I accidently disconnected or dropped it. He held it away, but not far enough away. Edmund screamed again. The sound was full of agony, and the empty place in my soul, where the bond with him had once been, thrummed with his pain. I thought I might throw up at the sound. It was . . . It was my friend being tortured. The Flayer of Mithrans had Edmund. Boneless, I dropped back to the chair.

I gestured for the cell. Started to beg for Ed.

Brute raced into the room, skidded, whirled, and stopped beside me, his head almost in my lap, his nose almost touching the cell. Brute was a huge werewolf, and his face wore a snarl I had never seen before, full of menace and hatred. I shut my mouth. If I begged, Ed was dead. I knew it, somehow, deep inside at a cellular level. It was there in Brute's eyes. In the emptiness of my soul. I forced myself to breathe. Gripped the arm of the recliner. Steadied my thoughts. Pulled a hard-learned formality around me like an insulated cloak.

Ed's suffering trailed away, to leave only the sound of my vampire gasping for breath. I knew what kind of punishment it took for a powerful vamp to need to gasp like that. *Ed. My Ed. The enemy was hurting my Ed. He would die for that.*

CHAPTER 3

Acting Enforcer to the Dark Queen

Brute's growl was a rumbling vibration of threat. Slowly, I placed a hand on the white werewolf's head. His fur was cold. He had been outside in the night air and had come running. Brute fell silent, but his eyes never left the phone in Bruiser's hand, a crystal blue gaze of death. The grindylow crawled up his spine and sat on Brute's neck, holding on, gripping tufts of white fur. The neon green creature chittered softly, watching me. I was pretty sure it was Pea, but all the magical critters in the U.S. came from the same litter and were identical. I scratched Brute's head and behind his ears. He whined softly and pressed against my hand.

When Ed could speak again, his voice was rough but still held the stilted tones of the one who was . . . what? Possessing him? "Your servant means so little to you?" the caller asked, sounding amused.

Bruiser said, "The Dark Queen has retired for the season. She will consider your . . . *invitation*"—his tone making it clear he didn't consider it such—"and return your call." Bruiser ended the call.

My heart hammered against my ribs, an uneven cadence. All my energy drained away in a gushing flood of defeat. Closing my eyes, I drooped back into the chair. Hugging my middle. Rocking slightly. Pain thrummed through me with my pulse.

Alex said, "The call originated in Jacksonville, Florida. Running search-and-location programs, checking cameras near his GPS coordinates." His fingers were flying across the keys, staccato, relentless.

Someone, I assumed Bruiser, covered me with the blanket. The room was silent except for Alex's ubiquitous tapping. When I got the guts to open my eyes, it was to see Bruiser and Eli standing at my chair, watching me. "The Flayer of Mithrans has Ed," I said, redundant. Useless. But I needed to say the words.

"Yes," Bruiser said.

"Do you want to go back to NOLA to deal with this, Janie?" Eli asked.

"No." I sat up and looked around, unfocused, thinking. "In New Orleans, there's thousands of people to be collateral damage. A city full of them." I looked at Eli. "What about here, at the inn?"

"Strategically and tactically, against an old-world fanghead with fifty followers, traveling in stealth, unlikely to have the means to transport modern warfare on this continent, or to know how to obtain it on foreign soil, this location is as good as any." His tone was cool, his words clipped, analyzing, offering no opinion or personal input. Battle face. Battle persona. "Unlikely doesn't mean impossible, however. Here, we have high ground, easy exit through the tunnel, off-the-grid options for power and water, sufficient supplies, good positions for shooters and cameras, and no collateral liability. You can warn Molly away."

"Shimon Bar-Judas is a powerful sorcerer," Bruiser said. "We could use magical assistance and Molly could use the protection. She hasn't hidden her light and power under a basket, and her name was quite public at the Sangre Duello. Finding her would be within the ability of almost anyone. She should have the option of staying here and fighting with us, versus her family being alone in their hilltop home."

"Here then," I said. "Issue the invitation to the fang-heads. Then let's get ready to whoop some undead ass."

No one laughed at the idea of me—all hundred and twenty pounds of cancer-ridden me—kicking ass. Eli grinned at me, all teeth. Alex whispered, "Yessss." Bruiser hit RECALL and the rings sounded in the quiet room.

"This is the telephone speaker for the Flayer of Mithrans, the Darkness of Souls," a heavily accented voice answered Ed's cell.

"This is Onorio, George Dumas, formerly primo to Leo Pellissier of New Orleans. I speak for the Dark Queen. She is in Asheville, in the state called North Carolina. The Dark Queen is willing to receive Shimon Bar-Judas. Here, in this town."

"One moment." The phone went muted. We waited. Then Ed came on. "Tell the tribal woman that I shall progress to her. We will be in the Ashe Ville in two days. Secure rooms for our coterie and servants." The connection ended. Bruiser put the blanket back in place and settled the cell on my blanketed lap. Brute growled again and licked his muzzle as if remembering the taste of vampire flesh. He backed two steps and sat, his eyes on me. The grindy peeked over his head between his ears.

I said softly, "Two days to get a place for Shimon to lay his evil head, bring in enough people to deal with the SOD Two, and for me to get well. Easy peasy." I dropped back my head onto the recliner. I had been putting off the more risky methods of attempting to get well. It seemed as if the slow and methodical way was out now, however. I'd be jumping off the cliff of improbable remedies, mystical mumbo jumbo, and prayer. My get-well-or-die vacay was over.

"I need more painkillers and another shake," I said. "I need to know where we stand." The guys went to work, leaving me to worry. I dialed Molly and she answered, road noise and the sound of wipers in the background. I told her about the presence of undesirable vamps in the U.S. and headed this way. Her response was, "Vamps hate witches and we aren't exactly flying under the radar these days. We can be found. We're coming. Safety in numbers and all that jazz. Besides, weather reports say the storm is heading north and away. Once the snow stops, home isn't that far away, Big-Cat. See you soon." She ended the call, and a tiny flame of happiness danced in my chest.

Kitsss, Beast thought.

A shake was placed into my palm and a handful of pills rattled into the other.

Painkillers didn't help me much, not even the stuff Eli had gotten for me, but they were better than nothing and took the sharpest edge off the pain. I didn't ask what the meds were or how he'd gotten them. Probably a vamp doctor, somewhere, had owed me allegiance and written me a script. My name was on the bottle. Eli had added the hemp and CBD oil I was using, and, taken together with high doses of OTC drugs, the strong stuff had better effect. Sadly, there was no way to maintain the meds or the oils in my bloodstream between shape-shifts, and it took time to get the medicine and natural pain relief levels up high enough to do a good job. After the shake, I took another dose of oils, this one followed by hot chocolate so sweet it made my teeth ache. Eli was trying to keep my weight up. It wasn't working.

At some point, the elder Younger put homemade pizza in the oven, and the smell was garlic-cheese heaven, not that I could stomach more than a bite or two, even after the meds kicked in. We all gathered around the bar in the baker's kitchen, me close by the radiant heat of the pizza oven in my comfy bar chair, and talked the nuts and bolts of the security business as they applied to the new house: infrared and low-light security cameras run through enhancement computer programs, perimeter alarms, laser trip wires, and how well or poorly they worked in heavy snowfall. We also discussed lines of sight and ammo and weapons placement and snipers' hides and potential retreat into the woods and the hills. All the fun stuff of the vamp-fighting life. I hoped it would take Eli's attention off how little I was eating. My lack of appetite was making him crazy.

The pizza had taken a serious hurting and my chocolate was halfway gone when the alarms went off. It might be weird, but my only thought was, *Finally! No more sitting around*.

Beast thought, *Fun!*

Alex dove for his system and lit up everything on the main TV screen. "Molly?" I asked, jerking to follow Alex. Stopping. Forcing down the pain that movement brought on.

"No," the Kid said. All the screens showed that it was snowing hard outside, near enough to a whiteout. One screen showed something else as well. "Vehicle just turned in from the street. A brand-new Range Rover in what I think is lipstick red. Wait. Make that two of them. They pulled in to the drive and stopped."

The drive was a half mile of unpaved one-lane road. The former owners hadn't gotten around to paving it and the weather had been too unpredictable to put concrete down since we arrived. And it was stupid to plow when the snow was still falling, no matter how much Eli liked the new toys—including the spanking-new John Deere tractor with all the attachments.

"Conditions?" Eli asked, checking his weapons.

"Maybe four inches and falling steadily," Alex said. "Forecast is calling for eight inches and twenty-four degrees by morning, when the storm blows over. The drive is covered and no one's been out since the snow started."

I said, "If Bar-Judas's fangheads were tracking the call on Ed's phone—"

"Too soon for tracking by the call," Alex said. "It's been"—he touched his mouse to check the time—"forty-five minutes. Even if they knew we were holed up here, near Asheville, and not in New Orleans, it would take them ninety minutes, maybe longer, to reach us in this weather from the city itself."

"Unless the phone call was a ruse and they already knew where we are," Eli said grimly to Alex and Bruiser. "Check in at NOLA HQ in case it's a two-pronged attack. I'm on recon."

Bruiser tapped his cell screen, saying, "Calling New Orleans HQ," which meant Leo's headquarters, still and always, though Leo was gone and buried. The phone was on speaker.

As it rang, Eli swiftly secured his weapons, grabbed a pale gray jacket from the back of a chair, slung a gobag over his shoulder, and vanished into the night. Brute, the grindy riding on his shoulder, followed him out, working the lever that locked the cat door for security with his paws. The massive werewolf was silent and deadly backup.

"New Orleans Mithran Council Chambers," Wrassler answered.

"George Dumas here. Anything odd happening? Anything on the security cameras?"

The silence on the line was acute; then there was the sound of keys tapping, and Wrassler said, "Checking cameras. And good evening to you too, Consort."

Consort? I thought.

Bruiser is Jane's mate, Beast thought. *Jane is Dark Queen.*

Bruiser laughed easily. "Forgive me. Good evening. I hope you are well."

Keys kept tapping. "Tolerable. Winter's over, so that's always good. Keeps an old man's bones from aching so bad."

"We have snow here," Bruiser said, the two men indulging in the common Southern niceties while I gritted my teeth, waiting for information on what problems were taking place in NOLA. On the screen, the Range Rovers just sat at the entrance to the inn's driveway, snow accumulating on the vehicles, headlights illuminating the falling snow, the expanse of snow, and the dark trunks of trees striping the snow. Clouds of vapor gathered around and under the vehicles from the tailpipes.

"Nothing showing anywhere. No suspicious activity. No more people missing."

"*More* people missing? What?" I muttered, moving closer to the office desk.

Alex said, "Oops."

I realized my housemates knew things I didn't. Things

they were keeping from me because I was too sick to do anything good about anything awful. I wanted to hit something but I was so weak my fist would be little more than a love tap. "Go on," I ground out the two words.

"Ronald Roland left Bouvier Clan Home Tuesday last, to pick up supplies, and never returned," Wrassler said.

Ronald was heir of Clan Bouvier and he wore jeans and six-shooters at his hips. He could rapid fire the pistols faster than a nine-mil semiautomatic and hit any target he could see. I got a knot in my stomach thinking about a Mithran missing. "Who else?" I asked.

"Cooper," Wrassler said. "Vanished about the same time. It's been suggested that he's on the way to see Janie and just didn't say so."

"Who's Cooper?" I demanded, a flash of anger heating me.

"Tex," Alex said softly.

Tex. I had claimed him. He was mine, part of Clan Yellowrock. Tex was a master vamp, as powerful as any master of the city I had ever known, but was content to do security at Vamp HQ. He was one of few vamps who had a dog, a big slavering mastiff who loved Tex better than peanut butter. "His dog?" I asked.

"We found him in Tex's house," Wrassler said.

"Tex would never leave his dog behind," I said. *Someone took Ed and Tex and Roland.*

Took kits, Beast thought. *Will kill taker of kits.*

But the Son of Darkness Number Two only hit the shores a few days ago. He's in Florida. So who else is here? Who has my people?

Without looking at me, Bruiser said, "If Cooper was coming here, he hasn't made it. Who else?"

Guilt on his face, Alex muttered, "I've been scanning all traffic and security cams for seventy hours on either side of Ronald's disappearance. Searching for Tex and Ronald." He raised his eyes to me, his curly hair tangling in his lashes. "I don't have a starting GPS so it's not gonna be fast."

"When did you first hear about all this?" I asked him.

He ducked his head away.

"One other Mithran hasn't checked in." Wrassler hesitated before going on, a strange break in words and tone. "Shiloh Stone, missing for a little over seventy-two hours."

My heart fell and shattered into a thousand pieces.

Shiloh. Molly Everhart's niece, my scion, also part of Clan Yellowrock, according to my claiming and according to vamp law. *This.* This is why they hadn't told me. They knew what this news would do to me. I closed my eyes to shut out the world. Shiloh was a witch as well as a vamp. If any vamp had her and figured out what she was, she'd be killed in a heartbeat. She was young and not well trained as a witch, not a powerful vamp. She was mine to protect. I had let her down. I had let all of them down.

The old familiar guilt wormed through me, telling me I wasn't good enough, wasn't strong enough, wasn't enough in any way. Especially now.

The more rational part of me suggested that if they were being held together, maybe Tex and Ronald could protect Shiloh. That part of me also suggested that if Shiloh was dead, Molly would kill me.

Alex murmured, "Janie knows about the missing vamps. Yeah. All of them. Tex Cooper, Ronald, the heir of Clan Bouvier, and Shiloh Stone." I realized he was updating Eli in the field, on comms.

"I've instituted new protocols since Derek Lee's car went off into a bayou and he went missing. And since Janie isn't here," Wrassler said.

"Derek's missing too?" I asked, louder. "When? How?" Heat flared through me, anger I hadn't experienced in months. "And why wasn't I told?" I demanded of Alex. Derek was the number one security guy at HQ now that I had other titles and responsibilities. "I should have been told."

"With all due respect, Legs," Wrassler said, his words clipped, his voice laced with anger, "you *left New Orleans.*"

My mouth opened in protest but I said nothing. What could I say? I was sick. Dying. I had abdicated. I stared at Alex. He was tapping away on one of the multiple keyboards and he had an old-fashioned mouse at each hand, a gaming stick, and two finger pads lined up within reach. Beneath his naturally dark skin, he was flushed with mortification. I looked at Bruiser who met my eyes with . . . was that *pity*?

Wrassler went on. "Ed was Leo's heir. And Ed was your heir, but everything came through the grapevine, not official notification, no ceremony, no pomp and circumstance, and you elected not to send a prefect or cede dominion of the city to another. With you out of the picture and Ed in Europe, we've done the best we could to protect New Orleans and keep the peace. Under the circumstances, the city is doing *outstanding*."

Unspoken was the sentiment *No thanks to you*.

My running away had resulted in a long and heated tirade by both Youngers that had included accusations like selfish, spoiled, dispassionate, nonaligned, and detached. And cruel. Their charge that I had been cruel in running away had been the one that hit home. I had thought I was saving them the torment of watching me die. Instead I had hurt them. They hadn't yet let me live it down, and this thing with Wrassler wouldn't help.

"Before Edmund Hartley *took off*," Wrassler said, his voice rising in pitch and tone, "he instructed us not to initiate contact with you unless *you* were in danger. *You* are not in danger. We know you're sick, but skinwalkers *live forever*, so what the *hell do you want me to do, Janie*?" he shouted.

"Holy crap on a cracker," I said. "I've got cancer; I'm not dead." And I felt, now that anger was coursing through me, more like myself.

"Cancer," Wrassler said, startled.

"Got it," Alex said, without taking his gaze from the screens. "I've pulled up the police report on Derek." His fingers had been tapping as Wrassler and I argued. "Derek Lee's vehicle was found in a bayou about twenty-five miles out of New Orleans after a hard rain. Official reading is that he tried to cross a bridge that was running deep with runoff and was swept off the road. But no body's been found. According to the written report, there was damage to the back panel that could suggest he was rammed. Here are the investigating officer's photos. They show a gray smear of contact paint. Sending all this to you at HQ."

Alex had obviously accessed official law enforcement records. Illegally. I should have stopped that, but . . . we needed the info.

"Cancer? What the hell do you mean you have cancer?" Wrassler said. Then, as he caught up on everything, "Rammed? I never got any photos. Let me look. I was assured by the sheriff—" He stopped. We waited. After several seconds, Wrassler cursed. "This was in Plaquemines Parish. I screwed up. I'm sorry, Empress."

Empress. Me. Wrassler was great at security and tactics but wasn't quite as competent on politics and law enforcement. He should have called me personally, no matter what, even against Ed's orders. But he was mad at me for disappearing, so he didn't. And the Youngers and Bruiser knew how sick I was so they didn't tell me. And the Plaquemines sheriff had reason to hate vamps. And me. I had, after all, helped Leo to muck up her current job, and had thrown her future political aspirations into the toilet.

I pushed my thoughts back to Derek Lee. Despite having each other's backs in some pretty hairy situations, he and I never really got along. Derek was afraid of vampires and the sexual stimulation that resulted from being a blood-meal to one of them. But Derek was under the protection of Edmund Hartley, so in a convoluted way, Derek was mine to protect, even if he himself didn't want to be. I had failed him too. My eyes burned, dry and aching.

Alex talked over my silent thoughts. "I'm sending a request from NOLA fanghead HQ up the law enforcement ladder to the governor. I'm requesting that the official investigation into the accident not be closed until someone has considered the possibility of a hit-and-run and kidnapping."

"Whose signature goes on that?" Eli asked his brother.

"Jane's, as Dark Queen."

"Who's Edmund's heir?" I asked, as a thought occurred to me. Last I'd heard, Ed had appointed Katie to manage things, but if he had an heir, that person could be my—what term had Wrassler used? My *prefect*. Yeah. Ducky!

"He didn't have one. All you have are the local Mithrans. Vamps need a leader, Legs, someone to rule the office of Master of the City. Edmund's office. *Your* office."

My office. Crap.

"You said something about protocols changing after Derek left. What protocols?" I asked.

Wrassler said, "No one leaves anywhere, anytime, without sending a text to HQ first, and then another when they return. Anyone missing is reported to HQ. We follow up every twenty-four hours. Most of the Blood Masters are complying." Which meant that some were not.

"Derek was the Pellissier Enforcer. Now he's missing. I need an Enforcer in NOLA," I said. "Someone everyone would obey. A vamp Enforcer."

"That . . ." Wrassler made a soft *hmmming* noise. "That would actually work. Someone to take names and break a few jaws."

Alex tapped a keyboard and the camera feeds at the entrance of the inn's driveway took center place on the TV screen. To its side was a series of smaller screens, most lit with pale green light. I walked closer and took in the feed from one infrared and a dozen low-light cameras mounted in the trees. One showed a very pale form moving through the snow, from camera to camera. Alex punched some buttons and the cameras changed to infrared, but Eli showed up no better. On other screens I followed Brute and his passenger. The werewolf was a hot, bright impression on infrared, the grindy even hotter.

"Hang on," I said to Wrassler and pointed at the screen. "Why is Eli showing cold?" I asked. I didn't add, *as a vamp*.

"Cold coat," Alex said, distracted. "So well insulated he won't show up if he drops into a crouch in the snow. Precautions against tech-savvy enemies."

Alex enlarged the video of the Range Rovers, creating a grainy mess as he initiated programs to clean up the feed. Blocks of black and white and color flashed all over and resolved into the video of a vamp emerging from the first vehicle. He moved with that sliding, easy grace of the vampire, something I had forgotten or gotten so accustomed to while living among them that I no longer noted it until now, when I had been away from them so long. He had a long, lean face and long pale hair, reminding me of Legolas in *The Lord of the Rings* movie, except cruel, hard. He wore slacks and a dress shirt and city shoes, with a long winter coat that made him appear even more broadshouldered and slim than he already was. The color sharpened, to show the lipstick red of the Range Rovers and the gray of the gorgeous coat.

Onscreen, the vamp lifted his head and sniffed the air. Snow pattered down onto his coat and hair, not melting. Cold-blooded for real. The other vehicle's front window lowered and Lego spoke to the other one, whose face was hidden. I regretted not having audio on the cameras.

"Eli has the driveway mined in two places," Alex said, "but farther up, not at the street."

"We don't know who is in the vehicles," I said. "We couldn't detonate anyway."

I returned my attention to my cell. Speaking slow, with a care for the meaning of each word, I said, "Wrassler, two groups of vamps have moved out of Europe. One group may have been in New Orleans for a while—long enough to snatch our missing people. Withdraw all of Clan Yellowrock into HQ and invite the other clans. Go on lockdown. Send word to Koun requesting that he accept the position of Acting Enforcer to the Dark Queen, New Orleans District, in addition to his position as chief strategist of Clan Yellowrock, until such time as Derek is able to resume his duties. If he isn't interested in the job, send me a list of candidates. Alex will send a letter instructing all blood clan masters to defer to Koun, Acting Enforcer to the Dark Queen. So speaks the Blood Master of Clan Yellowrock"—I took a breath, claiming my political power—"and the Dark Queen."

"Yes, my mistress," Wrassler said, with a breath of relief.

On the screen, the lone vamp standing in the snow turned toward the camera recording him, as if he knew it was there. Snow fell on his face. He was green-eyed and now I could see the nearly white platinum blond of his hair. He stretched out an arm and snapped his fingers. The back door to the second vehicle opened. A girl was shoved into the brightness of the headlights: she fell to her hip, skin white as the snow. Long, straight red hair slapped down. "No," I whispered, placing a hand on the screen. Lego grabbed the girl's arm and yanked her up, against his chest. Dark red smears were left in the white behind her. Blood. Her blouse had once been white. It was dull with brown stains.

She was still bleeding freely and there were vamp-bite marks in her throat.

He jerked her hair, pulling her face up, into the meager light. Snow fell on it, unmelting.

Shiloh Everhart Stone. Of course it was.

"He's got Shiloh. She's hurt bad," Alex said softly to Eli.

Wrassler cursed, hearing the words over our connection.

Sooo . . . one group of vamps or two? I had told the Flayer where I was. If a second group was, or had been, in NOLA and bleeding and reading my people, then they may have figured out where I was too. Either way, this was bad.

Eli put on a burst of speed. But the drive was uneven and unpredictable and he couldn't run flat out without risking a broken ankle. The snow suddenly fell harder as a sideways blast of wind shunted it horizontal. We weren't supposed to have wind at all. Brute put on a burst of speed, bounding high through the drifts.

Through the blustering snow, I watched as the vamp raised his hand and ripped out Shiloh's throat. Blood splatted and dribbled, bright in the whiteout. He didn't drink. He held her up by the neck and wasted the blood, a vamp insult. Lego dropped her to the snow and got back into his Rover. Sedately, the two vehicles backed out of the drive and pulled into the night.

"You are dead," I whispered to him.

Shiloh raised a hand. Gripped her throat. And squeezed. Shutting off the meager blood loss. Meager because she had already been drained so completely. Blood oozed through her fingers.

Brute dashed after the Rovers, a flash of white wolf on white snow, and out of camera range.

Eli fell to Shiloh's side and pulled a small blade. Without the headlights it was hard to see, and the snow grew thicker. Heavier. The night darker. Eli placed his wrist at Shiloh's mouth, but she pushed it away. She couldn't drink. She didn't have a throat. She needed vamp blood to heal. And we didn't have any. Brute raced back to Eli's side, panting, looking all wolf and furious, as if he would attack and destroy the world. He threw back his head and howled, the sound angry and demanding. Unanswered.

"Keep my people safe," I said to Wrassler. "That includes Jodi and Sloan." I ended the call. To Alex I said, "Call Big Evan. Tell him about the Range Rovers. Tell him to shield his vehicle."

"Roger that."

"Tell him that as soon as it's safe, they're to turn around and go back home. Nothing is safe here."

He didn't reply.

"You should have told me" I whispered to Bruiser.

"To what purpose," he whispered back. "We have done what you wanted us to do."

He was right. I had run away. And now, my world was falling apart, my friends were in danger, and I couldn't do a single freaking thing about it. I had sworn to protect all my people. I had failed. I needed to heal. Fast. Now. I needed to be everything I had walked away from. And more. And I couldn't.

Except . . .

"What?" Bruiser asked softly. I raised a hand to stop him, thoughts whirling through me, images, sensations, memories.

I had taken Leo's blood at the creation of Clan Yellowrock.

I had taken Gee's blood at the creation of Clan Yellowrock. I had taken Edmund's blood. I wasn't a vamp, and calling Ed hadn't worked before, but . . .

But *I wasn't a vamp*. Right. Not a vamp.

But I *was* the leader of Clan Yellowrock, through the blood of Leo. And I was the Dark Queen.

"I need the crown." Without thinking about it, I pulled on Beast-speed and raced up the stairs toward the bedroom. Pain forgotten, lost in the wash of blood spilled from Shiloh's throat.

I ripped open the closet door and dropped to my knees in front of the oversized plastic tub of magical trinkets and snapped the lid open. Everything I had brought from New Orleans and everything the Youngers had brought from NOLA when they joined us here was in the tub: charms Molly had made for me, the carved bone coyote that had appeared after a weird dream, the blue Anzu feather Beast had taken from a dead Anzu, lots of stuff in a jumbled mess. I grabbed up the Glob. The lightning-and-angel-created, multi-magical-item amulet was warm to my hand. The Glob absorbed magic. That was the Glob's magical power, to drain out magic, especially aggressive magic being used against me. It had once drained *le breloque* when the crown tried to take me over against my will. But it hadn't stopped the power merge when I had *chosen* to use the crown. *Le breloque* was somehow tied to the position and power of the Dark Queen, not that I knew how that worked. Yet. I stood and carried them both back down the stairs, feet tapping fast, passing Bruiser on the way up.

"Janie?" He whirled and followed me.

"I'm the Dark Queen. I'm the freaking *Dark Queen*," I ground out. "Not crowned by Leo, but a power chosen for *myself*. I put the crown on my *own* head. The magic in it claimed *me*. It has to mean something. It has to come with power of some sort. I took Leo's blood. I have this magical crap." I held out the two icons. "I have star-shaped scarlet energies in my body that I don't know how to use, and that are growing cancer, maybe because I can't use the magic and it has to go somewhere and do something so it settled on disease. Maybe I have to be able to *use* the power and the magic, or let its pressure off, like a steam valve. I need to be able to access it. I just don't freaking know how to do that!"

Bruiser's eyes went unfocused and his thoughts turned inward as we reached the landing. "The last Dark Queen didn't end so well. Alex found a record that suggested she vanished and was never seen again."

"She must have timewalked into danger and died. Or timewalked and caused herself to never be born."

"Impossible. If she was never born, then she was never the Dark Queen. Time-traveling paradoxes are likely multidimensional, creating new universes or interdimensional pockets, or even opening rifts between universes."

"Yeah," I said, crossing the central space, cool air drafts sweeping by, stirred up by the fans. "Like the rifts where the arcenciels fell through to Earth. But the office and power of DQ have to come with more than that. More than just timewalking."

"I agree. But it might require blood."

"Sweetcheeks, I don't care if it requires blood, sweat, and couple of fingers."

Bruiser burst out laughing. "You're still calling me sweetcheeks?"

I flushed red. I wasn't sure I had ever called him that out loud. "You have the best butt I've ever seen. Deal with it."

"Oh, my love. I deal with it every day. It's good to have you back."

"Yeah. Depression and grief and dying suck." We reached the TV room. To Alex, I said, "Update."

Alex looked relieved and happy instead of like the young, worried kid he had been for weeks. Interesting. All I had to do to restore balance in the house was be demanding. I'd remember that. He said, "Molly said she'd talk to you about the danger when she sees you. She and Big Evan pulled into the drive while you were upstairs. They took the sleep charm off Angie and put it on Shiloh. Then they did some kind of stasis spell on the vamp so she doesn't go bonkers with bloodlust. Eli put a stake in her belly, just in case, and he's with her in the back of the van."

The Kid had a familiar—and recently missing—mischief in his eyes. "Clan Yellowrock's in town and ready to fuck some shit up."

"Alex!" I said. And then I burst out laughing. My face felt weird, creased up with a grin instead of down with pain. And my belly didn't hurt nearly so bad.

On the main screen, the Everhart-Trueblood van pulled to a stop at the front of the inn and the side door opened. Angie Baby sprinted from the van and up the steps.

Because of the magic cancer, I no longer bent or bubbled time, but I made it to the front porch before Angie did and fell to my knees as she rushed into my arms. EJ—or Evan Junior or Little Evan, depending on who was talking—followed close behind, though my head was down and he probably didn't see whom he was hugging as his arms spread out. I had them both.

Kitssss, Beast whispered deep inside me.

"Yeah," I said aloud. "Kits."

Eli appeared from the van, still in his cold coat, but now it was bloody. He bounced a sleeping vamp up over a shoulder. Shiloh. She was even more bloody than my partner. Molly stepped out of the van and reached into the back seat, her hands busy with the straps on the car seat. Big Evan stepped out and the van rocked. Molly placed the baby in his arms. The infant looked like a toy against his bulk.

"Love you, Ant Jane," Angie said, drawing my attention back to them. "Is this your new house?" She pulled away to race into the middle of the inn. Stopped beneath the giant black wrought-iron chandelier in the vaulted high ceiling and turned in a circle, her head back, staring up, around, at the vast space. "I love this place, Ant Jane! It's magic, right here!"

"Wuv—*love*—you An' Jane," Little Evan said. He popped a slobbery kiss on my neck and rushed to his sister.

"Yes," I murmured to them, though they wouldn't hear me, and were now running to see Alex. I stood and walked out onto the steps. Snow was still falling hard and the cold made my bones ache, but I waited there as Eli entered with Shiloh in a fireman's carry. Dripping blood.

Climbing the steps behind him were Molly and Evan, the baby on his shoulder, bundled against the winter, asleep. My BFF was smaller than when I last saw her. She had lost a lot of the baby weight. Her red hair was longer and less curly. Snowflakes were melting in the waves.

"They were right," she said. "You look like shit."

I burst out laughing again—hadn't laughed this much in months—and held open my arms. Molly, decorated by snowflakes, stepped to me and I closed my arms around her. Breathed in the smells of Molly, baby, milk, diaper cream, baby urine, and French fries.

"Is Shiloh going to be okay?" she asked.

"Yes," I said. Vamps were destructible, but not by bloodletting or being staked in the belly.

"Good. But son of a witch on a switch," she whispered. "You're nothing but skin and bones. You can't be expected to fight a big bad ugly."

"It's okay. We have two days to get me well."

Molly made a grieving laughing sound. "Well, in that case, no problem."

I released her and led the way indoors, closing the big, well-balanced wooden door behind us. The door was carved with a grapevine heavy with bunches of wine grapes, the vine coiling on a wooden fence. I had fallen in love with the carving. I might be falling in love with the house now that the screams of children and the noisy stomping of running feet were echoing in the vaulted ceiling so far overhead.

Evan handed off the baby to Molly, and my BFF brought my namesake to me. Cassandra Evangeline Jane Yellowrock Everhart Trueblood was tiny. Cassandra for one great-great-grandmother, and Evangeline for another (not for her demon-calling aunt), and Jane for me. For all the weighty names, she was a little smidge of a baby.

Kitssss, Beast thought again.

Molly leaned in and snuggled the baby into my arms. "Say hi to your godmother, Cassy."

Holding a baby always felt awkward, but Beast reached out and encircled the bundled baby into my/our arms and against my/our chest. My eyes filled with tears. "Hey

there, Cassy," I whispered. The baby was redheaded like
her daddy, a bright copper-penny red, and her skin was
peaches-and-cream. She would be nothing like me, not in
looks or temperament, but I adored her and I adored that
she carried my name.

Cassy opened her eyes. Looked right at me and smacked
her lips. Something turned over inside me, something
warm and joyous and full of life. Something that had been
missing for a long time.

From the corner of one eye, I glimpsed Eli as he entered the elevator with Shiloh. I figured he was going to
place the vamp in a tub. The blood would have a nice
place to drain and no furniture would be ruined. And the
kids wouldn't see the body.

I grinned, holding the gaze of the infant. "Hey, beautiful," I crooned. "You got your mama's eyes and your
daddy's hair and . . . Well, I'm sure you got lots of something from them both." Molly's and Evan's witch X gene,
one from each side. I could see the witch magic coursing
through her and it was waaaay too early. I glanced at
Molly. "Really? Three of them? Three witches at once?"

Molly sighed. "Yeah. It's going to be challenging. So
we've agreed. No more ankle biters for me." The baby
made smacking motions again. "She's hungry. Anyplace
private where I can nurse?"

Bruiser said softly, "I put aside two suites for the
Everhart-Truebloods."

No more babies? Yeah, sure. That was never going to
last. I handed the baby back to her mama and leaned my
bony spine against the door, the cold shut out, watching
as Bruiser led Molly to their rooms. Alex had already
started the kids making s'mores at the biggest fireplace.
And this was . . . this was amazing. My clan gathering
under one roof. If we weren't all in danger, this might
be fun. Except that Molly and Evan needed to go back
home, out of danger.

Kitssss, Beast thought at me.

Yeah. Kits. Family. Clan.

Big Evan pulled off his coat and hung it on one of the
hooks by the front door. He walked to me, his eyes

studying me. I could tell he was using a *seeing* working and knew he'd be able to discern the shape of the magic in my middle. I let him look. He stopped in front of me and crossed his arms over his barrel chest, folding them over the tail of his bushy red beard. "Pentagram-shaped? When did that happen?"

"Not long ago. The cancer came shortly after I had been timewalking. I've been assured by Soul that time-walking is not an activity meant for a human body. Or a skinwalker's body."

"You working with a traditional healer?"

"An Elder of The People has been contacted and we're supposed to start sessions soon. Eli built a sweathouse. One of the first things he did when he got here."

"He was almighty pissed at you for running away."

"Yeah. We had that conversation. It wasn't pretty."

"Hmmm," Big Evan said, the vibration more like the rumble of boulders rubbing against each other than a human larynx. "Thanks for the warning about passing the bloodsuckers. We had just enough time to get pulled over and a *hedge* up. Two red SUVs, right?"

I nodded, not letting my thoughts travel to what might have happened had the vamps somehow seen and recognized the van and tried to stop my friends. The fangheads wouldn't have won, but it would have been messy and dangerous. I frowned. "Why did y'all come on? You drove up and found Shiloh, bleeding in the snow. You know about the danger. It's going to get worse around here, not better."

"Molly made the point that no place is truly safe. Plus . . ." He rubbed his face, the beard making a scratching sound. "I know it sounds improbable, but Angie said the house was a dangerous place to be right now. She said we needed to be with Aunt Jane."

"Your kid is scary."

"Yeah. We noticed." His tone was loving and gently possessive.

"Where's KitKit and George?"

KitKit was Molly's not-familiar, because witches do not have familiars. It's simply not done. Except for Molly. And George was Angie's bassett hound.

"Dropped 'em off at Bedelia's." Bedelia was Molly's mom, and I wondered why the kids weren't there too, except that Bedelia was getting on up there in age and might not be up to having the pets, Carmen's little one, and Molly's three around. "I'm hungry," Evan said, interrupting my thoughts. "Eli got food?"

"Pork shoulder and all the fixins in the fridge. Leftover pizza on the counter."

"Good." He didn't move away from me. I met his eyes, mine asking what was up. "Don't know if I ever said it. But I'm sorry I was an ass."

"I'm sorry your family was placed in danger just by being my friend."

"Life's a bitch, ain't it?" he said. "We've said all this before. Think we got it out of our systems this time?"

"I think if we say it any more we'll have to hug."

"God forbid." Moving like the boulder he sounded like, he rolled on toward the kitchens. Over his shoulder, he added, "Soon as I eat, you need to try to reach Edmund. As leader of your own fanghead clan, you should be able to touch his mind." He paused, his eyes scanning the floor and walls and high vault where his daughter had turned in a circle studying the inn. "This will do for a circle." Then he walked on.

Angie had stood in the center and said, *"Magic . . ."* *Precognition?* I crossed my arms and shivered.

Kitssss, Beast said.

So soft it was little more than a breath of air, I said, "Family."

CHAPTER 4

Beast Needs Ðead Cow for Magic

The kids ate enough pizza and sweets to have a sugar high, but crashed in the Charles Frazier Suite, two of them smelling of chocolate and marshmallows, all three on the king-sized bed, hemmed in by rows of pillows, what their mother called a bumper, with chairs pushed around the edge to keep the kiddos from falling off. The infant, my namesake, was at the foot of the big bed, sleeping like the angel she was, her bow-shaped mouth puffing with each breath. Their parents stood on either side of the bed, drawing protective workings over them, healing, warnings, love, and prayers. The magics they drew were blue and purple and golden and they shimmered like a holy net across the big bed. It was a magic anyone could see in the parents' eyes and it woke in me a longing I didn't understand as they closed the protective circle that placed the kids in safety. Molly and Evan met at the foot of the bed and clasped hands, bowing their heads in prayer. I left quietly, knowing I was intruding on a moment that was just for the two of them. And wondered where the nearest church was. It had been a long time for me.

In the open area of the main living space, Eli was un-rolling a rug he had carried in from one of the furnished bedrooms. It was thick, dark blue, and had buff fringe on two sides. Simple and manly enough to be a rug from his own room. He placed it directly beneath the wrought-iron lighting fixture. I assumed that Alex had overheard Big Evan's plans and not that Eli had ESP and mind-reading ability. He disappeared into the kitchen and came back with a beer, which usually meant that he was off guard duty, but tonight he was still wearing weapons, so maybe he was relaxed but not. The former Army Ranger was often a mystery to me.

I set *le breloque* and the Glob on the rug and wasn't surprised when Eli came back, toting oversized pillows from the TV room. "One of these is sticky with chocolate and marshmallow." He dropped three pillows and carried one off, saying, "The kids are charming but messy. Told you we'd need washable shams."

I vaguely remembered that. So maybe he did have ESP. "Where's Shiloh?" I called to him.

"In your tub."

"Oh. Yuck. You coulda put her in a guest bath."

"Babe." He stopped and looked back at me. Took a pull on his beer. There was an almost-smile on his mouth. "I certainly could have."

I stuck out my tongue at him, as if he was my big brother and I was a brat. And once again, I didn't hurt quite so much. I had family. I had clan. I had kits. Life could have been a lot worse.

Big Evan half fell, half rolled onto the pillow, his legs bent uncomfortably, and told Eli, "You know you're going to need a forklift to get me up, right, dude?"

Eli gave a faint smile. "I'll manage."

"I'm still weak from childbirth," Molly said, taking her seat. "If I can roll to my knees and get to my feet, you can, too. Stop whining."

Evan said to me, "She's been this way ever since she gave birth. Bossy."

"She's always bossy," I said.

"I'm sitting right here," she said. "In the room with you."

"When she was giving birth to Cassy, she ordered the nurses around, and when they refused to do every little thing she said, she knocked over the IV pole and broke things. Then she threatened to kill me if I ever touched her again."

"I knocked over the IV pole because I was in pain and no one would give me the good drugs. I threatened you for the same reason."

"Uh-huh. Bossy. And I love you for it."

Bruiser was hovering in the shadows of the opening to the back mudroom entry. He was half-hidden by the kitchen island and was watching me with such tenderness, my heart turned over and landed in a puddle of coronary mush. He raised his brows in a question and gestured at the big space. His lips moved soundlessly: *You okay?*

I nodded.

He blew a kiss my way. It was a sweetness I had never experienced before. My coronary mush was so syrupy it was like molasses and brown sugar and marshmallow cream. I smiled at him and eased down to the pillow placed for me. When I looked up again, Bruiser and Eli were exchanging hand signals. They were both weaponed up and wearing comms headgear and multi-ocular eye-pieces, ready to protect the inn while the rest of us were occupied trying to find and reach Ed.

Molly was watching me, wearing an expression I couldn't name. It was penetrating and affectionate and I turned my head away, uncomfortable. People loved me. It was weird.

The circle had been made by flour from the kitchen to represent Molly's earth magics and with five small wood flutes placed at the five points of the pentagram. The flutes would call to Evan's air magic. The two-foot-tall rosemary plant by Molly's knee was a call to life. I studied the plant, inhaling the rich herbal scent. Molly had brought a dead rosemary plant back to life once. . . . I looked my question at her and she gave me a saucy grin, as if she was saying, *Yeah. So what?* She was in control of her death magics, which was good. "I'm ready," I said.

Beast thought, *Beast needs dead cow for magic.*
No. You don't, I thought back.
She chuffed at me, cat laughter.

"And so are we," Moll said. "Put on the crown. Take up the Glob. And here's a lancet set." She tore open some sterile packets, arranged everything on a silver tray, and held it out to me. "Clean your finger with the alcohol, prick your finger, and let three drops of blood fall into the silver chalice."

I took the tray from her and fought laughter because this circle was supposed to be sacrosanct and laughing at her here seemed rude. "This isn't a chalice," I said, straight-faced, holding it up. "This is a silver shot glass."

"If I say it's a chalice, it's a chalice," Molly said, her eyes narrowing.

"Bossy," Evan said.

"Stop saying that."

"She's so sexy when she's bossy," Big Evan said to me.

"TMI," I said. "Waaay too much TMI." Molly glared at me and I flapped a hand at her. "Okay, fine. Whatever. Your shot glass is a chalice."

Inside the open circle, we were in a triangle, with Big Evan at north, his largest flute in his lap, Molly to his right with her plant, and me to his left with my Glob and *le breloque* at my knees. "Closing the circle," Evan said, his voice deep and sonorous in the empty room. He blew a single note on his flute, a basso sound that echoed in the ceilings and made my flesh quiver. The breathy tone felt potent and imperative, as if something deeply significant was happening. Magic swept across my skin as the circle closed and some version of a *hedge of thorns* rose over us.

I shook the strange sensation off and plopped *le breloque* onto my head. Its magics shivered through me. The crown seemed to adjust to my head size, as if it knew I was about to call on it, as if this was something more than trying on a hat. Maybe it had felt the circle closing and reacted to the power. Or maybe it was once again claiming me. I'd intended to give the thing to the NOLA witches, but with Lachish Dutillet spending time in a null-room prison, I'd never gotten around to it. Never thought about it again. Which was interesting, but a thought for another time.

The alcohol was cold on my fingertip and I squinted my eyes and made a face as I stabbed myself with the lancet. Which hurt *bad* for such a tiny wound. I dripped three drops of my blood into the silver shot—um—chalice. "Okay. What now?"

"This is your magic, Jane," Molly said. "Do your thing."

"My thing." *Crap.* Flying by the seat of my pants was how I got into this mess. But Moll was right. My magic wasn't witch magic. She couldn't help me. Carefully, I sought my skinwalker magics, the silver energies of the Gray Between, shot through with motes of darker power, now bound with the pentagram of witch magics inside of . . .

Inside of me.

Witch magics. Timewalking magics. *Le breloque* magics. Glob magics. Vampire priestess magic. My own magics. And the magic of an angel of the light. All bound together in a body with shredded DNA. I studied the red mote zipping along the star pattern of magics in my middle. And the silver and charcoal motes of my own power zooming along with it, adhering to the new pattern. And the faint, barely there shadow of black magic that had jumped into me.

Hayyel, the angel, had told me something about the pattern of my magics. What was it? I pulled the memory from the deeps of my mind, but it was half-formed, half-remembered. Something like, *The new configuration of energies within you is a new strength.* He said he had *healed my soul home.* And then he disappeared. Had Hayyel done this to me? Had he let my DNA get scrambled and let me get sick, so that I would . . . what? Die? A plan by the Almighty to get me to do something? If so, what? The disease within me had to do with timewalking. With changing time. So that meant . . . it had to do with fangheads and maybe the rainbow dragons, who wanted vamps to have never been. Yeah. That was a lot of help. Not.

I blew out a breath and tried again. Studying the magics.

Wondering what an angel might want. Hayyel had been partly responsible for the making of the Glob. Sooo . . . Well-worn thought paths trampled down again.

The Sons of Darkness had been trying to bring their father back from the dead and steal power that wasn't theirs when they dug up their father's body and gathered the iron spikes and the wood of the crosses of Golgotha. They were trying to be as powerful as Jehovah and raise someone from the dead. They hadn't known which implements of torture and death belonged to the murderer or the thief or the innocent, so they had used all of it. They had messed up. When they raised their father from the dead, he was a monster, whom they had been forced to kill and then chop into tiny bits to keep him dead. Hayyel knew all about the creation story of the vampires. Did he intend me to time-walk and fix something in the past? Or stop someone else from doing that and messing up the here and now? Or something else, even more obscure?

Surely an angel of the light, assuming he was one, wouldn't have done something without the direction of the Almighty. Except . . . doing things on their own is how angels supposedly fell from the light and entered the dark in the first place. Over and over. I'd been over this ground so often my mind knew the patterns and I was getting nothing new, except that maybe Hayyel didn't have a job for me. Maybe he hadn't been part of causing the cancer. Maybe it was all just timewalking, which actually made more sense than an angel needing me to do something for God. Yeah. Okay. That was a relief.

I picked up the Glob. It contained a splinter of the Blood Cross and the Blood Diamond, powered by the magic of sacrificed witch children, and some iron discs made from the melted-down spikes of Golgotha. I turned it over in my hands.

My finger, still smeared with my blood, touched it. I jerked it away almost instantly, but a faint quiver of electricity shocked through me. It reminded me to call Ed. *Edmund Killian Sebastian Hartley,* I called. The blood on the Glob sizzled with heat, spitting black motes of power.

My vision went sideways, and I was in a different place. In a room, dark and muggy and . . . moving. Vibrating engine noise. The bed of a truck or an RV. Metal beneath my cheek. The stench of diesel and rotting blood and death. The sound of sex, bodies hitting rhythmically. Pain rippled through my body as if every muscle were in spasm. *Hunger. Hungerhungerhunger* hammered me. I pushed it away, feeling the direction of the truck. He was headed north. Toward Asheville.

My mistress?

I was in Ed's mind. "Ed," I whispered. "Hang on. You'll be here soon. We can help you then."

My mistress, he thought back at me. *Stay away. The Darkness is within me.*

I turned from the sound of his voice to a small corner in Ed's mind. A semblance of his body was hunched there, protected at his back but vulnerable from the front. Something shadowy crouched beside him, amorphous, moving but contained, like smoke in a bottle. But the shadow had eyes. They were watching me with intelligence and intent. The Darkness Ed was talking about. An invader in Ed's brain, in his mind, with him. Possessing him.

The Flayer of Mithrans. In Ed's mind.

The thing in Ed's mind spoke. *Greetings to She Who Walks in the Skin of Animals. I will drink you down,* the smoke said, with Ed's mental voice. Inside the shadow I caught a glimpse of bloody human teeth and a blade and a sensation of terror. A fast vision opened in the air between us. Ropes and utter agony and the feel of bloody wood beneath my body. It was more memory than dream or threat. In it, the bloody teeth bit down and crunched through small fingers, ripping them off. A scream echoed, high-pitched and shrill. Pain clawed through me as if it were my own. Then in an instant, it was gone. The smoke shape broke and swirled in two different directions, like a tornado inside a tornado, closing over the images.

The Darkness shot toward me. Its mouth opened. Fangs. Dozens of fangs.

With a thrust of power, like blue electricity and the

smell of burning anise, Ed threw me out. The vision ended.

I was back in the circle, lying on the rug, shaking. My tongue was twisted up and around in my mouth as if it was trying to swallow backward, as if it was trying to crawl down my throat. I forced it into place and started coughing. Which jarred the thing in my middle. Pain went through me like a mudslide, darkening and covering everything. I rolled to my side and held myself, shuddering. My throat and tongue ached and when I could let go of my belly, I massaged my throat with one hand. I was cold. Too cold. Throat and hands and feet ached. But the circle was still active. I hadn't broken it.

It took me two tries to speak, and when I did, every syllable hurt. "They're starving him. Hurting him. Twenty-four/seven. The Flayer of Mithrans is inside Ed's brain, trying to take him over." I rubbed my throat and swallowed, my tongue feeling weird. My throat muscles ached. "I had access to a memory or a vision, as if Ed was fighting back, pilfering things from the Flayer's memory."

"How sure are you that Ed's fighting back?" Evan asked.

"Pretty sure? Nothing else makes any sense."

"What's the Son of Deception looking for?" Evan asked, choosing a title that sounded more insulting than the others.

"I don't know. I'd guess that it's trying to break into the memories of Leo and me. Maybe take Ed over completely and use him to come after me. Ed's resisting and counterattacking, but he's . . . he's in bad shape."

"Why do you sometimes refer to Shimon as it?" Bruiser asked from behind me. I turned my head and saw him. He was a hairsbreadth beyond the edge of the circle, ready to break the circle to save me. Which would hurt him. A lot.

I breathed out a laugh, which hurt *me* a lot, and waved him away. "Shimon is more than a vamp. I think . . ." I thought about the shadow, the teeth, the movement of it, and I whispered past the pain in my throat, "I think he can do a sort of psychic possession and control. And while I know that no vamp is human, he feels even weirder than any others I've met."

"He hasn't been human in two millennia," Bruiser said. "He's the oldest vampire undead. It's likely that he's also quite insane."

I described the vision-memory for them. "It felt real. It had texture and temperature and the smell of fresh-cut wood. The stink of a dead body, the cold of blood loss. The sensation of biting off fingers—" I stopped. "There was this awful scream." I rubbed my upper arms, my skin feeling pebbled and cold. "I think . . . I think it was the memory of the black magic used to bring their father back to life. But it was all mixed-up and confused." I remembered the smoke thing. The timbre and flex of the mental words. The twisting, swirling power of tornadoes, so different from anything I'd felt before. The Flayer of Mithrans was . . . other. I gripped my own throat, feeling my pulse, the beating of my heart.

"You're pale as a vampire. You should quit now," Bruiser advised.

"No. I need to call Gee again. He hasn't answered the last fifty texts or calls, but with the signal boost of the witch circle, he might hear me, wherever he is. Just a feeling, but . . . I need him here with me."

"Please, Jane. Don't overdo it." Bruiser shifted a hard gaze, sharp as a knife, to the two witches. "Don't let her kill herself." It was a threat. And it was so cute I wanted to cry, but I hurt too much to cry.

I managed to sit up and was tickled pink that my blood in the shot glass wasn't totally dried out, and that I hadn't spilled it. I folded my legs and took a breath, my eyes on the shot—chalice. *Crap. Shot-chalice.* I liked. Molly would hate it. "Girrard DiMercy. You swore loyalty to me as my personal Enforcer before I was the Dark Queen, before I even had a clan. By my blood and your word, I call you," I said. Molly said a heat-*wyrd* and the blood in the silver shot-chalice boiled in a fast simmer and dried to a crust on the bottom.

In seconds, I felt Gee, feathers fluffing against the cold. He was in his Anzu form and the connection was clear and sharp. I was seeing through his eyes and the world was bright despite the night, like owl eyes. I knew. I'd been in Anzu shape once and owl more than once. Seeing with a night-hunting raptor's vision was always weird. In Gee's sight it wasn't really dark, the ground was snow-free, and the air felt damp and somehow warm, though the distant trees were leafless. At the far-off tree line, I saw bison, a small herd standing in chest-deep snow, their breath blowing, ice crusted around their nostrils.

Gee was perched in a dead tree over a small pool of steaming water. Steam rose from the hot spring in globes of mist and fell in drops, a mimic of the action of the water bubbling, a luscious warmth. It almost looked like Hot Springs, not so far away, but the landscape was bigger, mountains on the horizon taller. Gee was in Yellowstone Park or someplace like it.

"If you fall in, we could make chicken and dumplings," I said, aloud and in my mind.

"My mistress is amusing. How might I serve?" There was something snide in both the observation and the question. I decided to ignore it.

"I'm dying and the Flayer of Mithrans, Shimon, has Ed. I need you to heal me if you can, and help me save Edmund."

"You should have asked much sooner. You are dying and your body is beyond my gifts."

My heart fell. With everything else not working, I had placed all my healing hopes on Gee.

He fluffed his wings and made a sound that might have been pain. "I am not refusing assistance out of pique or stubbornness. I cannot fly. I am healing from battle, little goddess. In addition to all that, I owe you an answer to one question, not a boon, thus I will not come to you now. I will bide here until I am well enough to fly, and then I shall come, as a *favor* to my mistress, whom I serve. A favor to evaluate her death throes and determine if some help is yet available. I am not optimistic about your chances for continued life on this plane."

He was still snide, but I could live with it. He was also

splitting hairs, like in vamp parley, but he was making important distinctions.

"I accept that," I said.

"For now, take up the blue feather and hold it when you are in pain. It will help."

Being pain-free was enough for now. "Blue feather, no pain," I said. "Got it. Who are you fighting? Are you in Yellowstone?"

"Not all of my battles are the battles of the little goddess. Fewer are for my mistress. Even fewer than that are your concern."

Which told me to mind my own business. *Gotcha.*

He lifted a wing and shut off communication. But not before I saw the bright blue blood on the feathers of his chest. And the sliver of steel sticking from the wound. Gee was lethally allergic to anything made of iron.

I was back in the circle. I whispered, "Well, that sucked." And I passed out.

I woke up outside of the circle, on the recliner in the TV room. The chair was warm. I felt oddly pain-free, and raised a hand, touching my middle, fiercely hopeful that the thing inside me might be gone. Nope. Still there. But my fingers closed on something. A feather. That had to mean I had been talking in my . . . trance? Whatever. Aloud.

I opened my eyes to see Bruiser standing guard over me, a fierce expression on his face, the beard making him look like a knight from some olden times. Alex was at his screens. The outside cameras showed the whiteout of blizzard snow. Eli was at the fireplace, guarding the grounds and house and everyone inside it, armed to the teeth and wearing his newest possession—lightweight military armor—over his clothing. His head and eyes moved from windows to doors to useless screens. Molly and Big Evan weren't in the room. Everyone remaining seemed way too tense.

To Bruiser, I asked, "Y'all didn't kill my bestie when I fainted, did you?" My voice was ragged and raw.

"No," Eli answered for him, sounding unamused, "but it was a close thing."

"Okeydoke," I said. "First things first. Thanks for the feather."

Bruiser nodded. "It was in the plastic bin in your closet."

"It helps," I said, surprised. "Like, a lot." Feeling hopeful for the first time in months, I said, "So. What do we do about Shiloh?"

Bruiser said, "I updated Clan Shaddock. Lincoln is sending us two Mithrans and blood-servants capable of running an inn. Or the Official Winter Court of the Dark Queen of the Mithrans."

I let that settle through me for a moment. Two unknown vamps here, at my home. With the kiddos. *No way.* They would be housed in the cottages. In fact, that was where Shiloh would go as soon as help arrived. If Shiloh hadn't needed vamp blood to heal I would refuse the help, but I couldn't do that either. Rock, meet hard place.

To occupy my hands so they didn't betray my shock, I tucked the feather into my waistband, under my shirt and resting against my skin. The pain, now at a safe distance, felt almost like a remembered wound, an old bruise. "These vamps—"

"Vetted. Old, powerful, and not witch haters," Bruiser said.

"Okay. But . . . Official Winter Court of the Dark Queen." I looked up at him. "I'd prefer Yellowrock Appalachia, but I'm not going to able to avoid that DQ stuff, am I? All the pomp and circumstance and bloodletting."

Bruiser's brown eyes bored into mine, as if he was trying to find a way to keep my blood and body and soul all together by force of will. He took a breath so deep it was as if he drew it from his toes, as if he hadn't taken one in hours. "I would protect you from it if I could." A smile formed in his eyes and drew up his lips. "However, it has been my experience that you tend to rush toward any firefight, not away. I do not think you will try to avoid the fury of the storm that is any Mithran."

"I *have* been known to step in where angels fear to tread." Hayyel, specifically. Tentatively, I swung my feet to the floor and sat up. "Not bad. Gee gets points for this." I pointed to the feather under my shirt. To Alex, I said, "Update."

"All kinds of news," Alex said. "I was able to get the four-star Regal Imperial Hotel in Asheville for the visiting fangheads, though after the last vamp stay, the general manager put up a fuss." The last time fangheads had rented out the hotel, they pretty much trashed the place and I had killed a demon out front, an event that went viral, even if most people didn't believe what they saw. "Money talked," Alex added. "It was pricey. And even more pricey to give all their people time off. We paid vacation time for thirty-five full-time employees to keep them safe from the Flayer."

"Good thinking. How pricey?" I asked.

"You don't want to know, but not to worry. Rather than draining Clan Yellowrock's funds, I used the Dark Queen's accounts."

"The DQ has accounts?" I asked.

"Yeah." Alex laughed, the sound more like pain than amusement. "The DQ is loaded."

"Good for her," I said. "What else you got?"

"Shaddock looped in Sheriff Grizzard and the Asheville chief of police," Alex said. "None are happy about the situation, not that they could do anything about it except call in PsyLED, ICE, and the state police. But the snowstorm's going to inhibit and slow any official response. The bad guys will be here before the bureaucracies can decide what to do."

"Before you begin to feel guilty, love," Bruiser said, "there would have been problems no matter where Bar-Judas chose to approach you. He is here illegally. He will kill any human he chooses. You made the best decision you could."

"They could evacuate the city," I suggested.

"Impractical in this storm."

"Put out an alert?"

"Likely to stir panic."

"Surround the hotel?"

"Possible. But their choice, not ours. They have been informed of potential problems."

Alex broke into Bruiser's and my dialogue. "I confirmed which of our supposed allies in France sold Ed out. Clan Roquefort agreed to parley. Clan Fonteneau, one of Grégoire's longtime allies, set Ed up at one of their houses about twenty miles from the agreed-upon parley site. Roquefort found out where they were staying and attacked that location. Looks like Roquefort, Shimon Bar-Judas, his people, and two other clans—Clan Andre and Clan Leclerc—were in on it. Clan Fonteneau fought back, defending the farmhouse, and they may well be extinct, dead to the last scion. Grégoire and his court are finding our people and making sure they have flights back to the U.S. or are safe in situ. He's also taking names, tracking enemy combatants, and finding their lairs. I'm getting into their finances and forwarding him all the intel."

Alex tilted his head down and around and met my eyes. "As of an hour past, Grégoire has announced an open call to arms for his new allies and an open blood feud against your enemies. His primos sent a note to the DQ and the empress of Europe with his intent to kill her enemies to the last drop of blood."

Clan Roquefort and I had a history. They had sent vamps to swear to Leo and marry his heir. And betray the MOC. I had prevented that, and the traitors sent from the clan were dead. Leo had done nothing to the clan in retribution for the original betrayal or the subsequent ones. No, that was all on me. Clan Roquefort was a problem I needed to handle. "Let Blondie know everything we know. Keep him in the loop. Tell him the EuroVamp traitors are to be . . ." I stopped, thinking over my words before I spoke them. Making sure I was really willing to say them aloud. Thinking over the repercussions if I did say them. The repercussions if I said something else or remained silent. Seeing the possible futures and the altered pasts in raindrops had taught me some things. Think, at least a little, before speaking.

I turned to Bruiser but spoke to Alex. Softer, with all the formality I had learned and all the ceremonial words in my vocabulary, I said, "Tell Grégoire, 'So speaks the Dark Queen. My dear old friend Grégoire of Arceneau. We are honored at the loyalty you have displayed. We would award your devotion and appoint you Warlord of the Dark Queen.'"

CHAPTER 5

I Had to Apologize to a Werewolf

Bruiser blinked, his eyes taking on a sheen of memory, as if he searched his past for references and could find none. A faint smiled turned up his lips and he gave me a nod of surprised approval.

I went on. "Our enemies will be made an example. Mithran traitors and betrayers, Naturaleza, killers of humans, and murderers of my people are to be given no quarter. The clan homes of our enemies are to become scorched earth. Any who do not swear to you in my name, any enemy clan Blood Masters and all their master Mithrans, no matter their status, will die. The only quarter given will be to the youngest scions still in chains, the prisoners of our enemies, and the human blood-servants and blood-slaves, provided that they agree to be bled, read, and bound. Those are yours to judge." I closed my eyes, knowing I had just sentenced dozens and dozens of vamps to death. No wonder Blondie hated to rule. This sucked. "These are the words of the Empress of Europe and the Dark Queen. If you accept, proclamations will go out . . . posthaste."

Bruiser's eyes were intensely sad and deeply focused on mine. "As the Dark Queen commands." He glanced at Alex. "Send the electronic message to Grégoire of Clan Arceneau and associated titles. If he agrees, you'll need to draw up the papers and have them approved by the Robere brothers."

The Roberes were both Onorios and one was a lawyer, making them dispassionate judges of vamp protocol. They were also Grégoire's people. It was a good safety measure. I nodded to Bruiser.

"The proclamations will then need to be transcribed to vellum, signed, and go out by messenger as soon as a courier can get through. And this time," Bruiser said to us all, "there will be no doubt. Multiple copies will be sent to every Blood Master and MOC in the Americas, Europe, and Asia."

Alex muttered, "It sounds like war."

His voice so soft I could hear the crackle of flames from the fireplace over his words, Bruiser said, "It is war. Jane's proclamation may decrease the numbers of casualties, and it gives those currently nonaligned a political and diplomatic pathway to peace with the Dark Queen." He lifted my hand and brushed his lips over my knuckles. "It's brilliant, my love."

"This sucks," Alex said. "Not the paperwork. War in general."

I glanced at the small clock on the mantel. It was far past midnight. "I'm going to shift to Beast," I said, "but I'd like to sleep inside."

Bruiser smiled wider, and it was like the sun breaking through the clouds. "I'll pull the queen's doggy bed onto the mattress."

Alex made a snorting sound at the doggy-bed comment. I ignored it. "Alex, please wake me when Shaddock's people turn into the drive. I'd like to—" *receive them properly.* I was still thinking and talking like the DQ. "I'd like to have feet instead of paws when they get here."

"Got it. Night, Janie."

In our bedroom, I folded my comfy clothes and shifted

to Beast. Strength and energy flooded through us. Because
my human form was skinny, my Beast form was skinny too,
all muscle and no body fat, no reservoirs for between meals
or between shifts. I was ravenous. After a meal of raw bison liver and bison loin provided by Bruiser, I/we sprang
to the bed, which sported an extra layer of memory foam
on my side, one with a washable cover. Beast yawned and
stretched, upward-facing cat, downward-facing cat (not
dog; never dog), and lay down, jaw on Bruiser's hand. He
scratched under our chin.

Beast thought, *Mate. Good mate. Brought dead bison
and grooms Beast.*

Yeah, I thought back. *He's coolio.*

*Onorio body is hot like Beast body. Do not understand
coolio.*

I smiled and didn't contradict her. We fell asleep knowing we were safe and loved.

I slept until the smell of pancake batter and cooking bacon woke Beast and we slipped from the bed, leaving
Bruiser sleeping. It was well before dawn and he was tired
and sad and the circles beneath his eyes said he needed
more sleep than he'd been getting.

We padded down the stairs, into the kitchen, where
Beast proved that she could open the refrigerator when
she really wanted. Ignoring Eli's comments about her paw
dexterity and the cost of cow when she could hunt deer,
Beast sank her fangs into a five-pound roast, wrapped in
plastic on a disposable tray, and carried it out the front
door, into the dark of predawn and the new, snow-covered
world. I stepped back from Beast's control, thinking
thoughts of war, and let Beast have full range of her body
to eat, play, hunt, or whatever.

Took in world through eyes and nose and ears. Air was
still. Wind had blown far away. Without wind to knock
drifts off, snow stood more than five inches high on every
branch, stem, and twig, rested on top of trellis and fence
posts in nearby vineyard. Snow was brilliant, heavy white

blanket, soft and sparkling in meager light. Snow had fallen many inches overnight. Many-more-than-five inches.

Beast tossed cow meat, jumped from covered front porch into deep fluff of snow, and rolled to back, looking at sky. It was still cloudy, but thinning haze said there would be no snow for a few hours. Turkey smell came on wind. Sound of hawk calling meant rabbits were out in snow, feeding. Was good time to be Beast. Rolled over and found roast. Tore through plastic and gripped cow meat with claws. Bit dead cow meat with killing teeth and ripped through flesh. Ate. Was good cow meat. Beast was happy.

Went into trees on south side of property to do morning business, spraying, leaving scat. Smelled Brute. Dog stink. Curled nose and chuffed. *My place.* Left scat on top of Brute scat. Was Beast hunting ground, not Brute hunting ground, and Brute scat and scent were everywhere under trees. Beast took much time to mark every place and to scratch into bark on many more than five trees, sharpening claws and claiming territory.

Then Beast raced around big space, throwing snow with paws. Rolled and scrunched and shoved and scooted in snow, grooming privates. Lay again in snow fluff, paws up, belly up and unprotected. Looked at gray sky. Wolf smell came on wind. Brute snuffled into snow next to Beast. Dropped heavy body and rolled. Lay in snow near Beast, panting, stupid dog tongue hanging out of mouth to side like dead thing. Wanted to bat at tongue with claws, but Brute was more than dog. Brute might be making trap, to catch Beast paw in wolf teeth. Beast was smart ambush hunter. Did not fall for stupid dog trick. Rolled to paws, shaking fluff away. Coat moved on skinny, muscular body, loose and warm.

Brute stood too, panting. Made downward dog to play. Beast leaped over Brute. Swiped at Brute tail and raced to porch. Brute followed. Beast raced through cat door and into house, to kitchen where bacon was cooking and Eli stood in front of stove. Eli was dressed as hunter, as warrior, with armor, killing claws, and white-man weapons. Was dressed in black with a white cloth called apron tied around waist.

Beast brushed by Eli. Eli said, "Hey. I saw you steal that roast. Out of the kitchen. Git!"

Beast ran to big, empty room like cave with tall ceiling, at door to front of house. Brute hip-butted Beast. Both tumbled and fell on slick floor. Wolf gave fake growl and batted Beast. *Battle! Battle with Brute!* Paws swatted. Fangs grazed through pelt. Grindylow jumped into play fight, steel claws hidden. Beast claws hidden. Brute claws not sharp, but dull and blunt. Grindy biting at snouts and chittering. Played and batted and growled and tumbled across floor as more bacon sizzled and eggs cooked and air smelled of best food ever.

Deep in mind, felt something. Felt . . . Edmund. Edmund pain rushed through Beast body. Heard panting. Smell of blood in mind. *Pain, pain, pain*, like pain of shift, filled Beast. Saw Edmund in corner. Saw through Edmund eyes. Saw thing with many teeth. Shadow thing. Creature thing with teeth.

Thing in Ed mind turned to see Beast. Was dangerous. *Predator.*

Ed? Jane shouted inside. *Edmund?* Panic like prey must feel in Jane heart. Panic like prey in Beast heart. Creature thing lunged at Beast.

Beast leaped away. Creature scored Beast-rump with claws. Beast swiped with claws and raced into dark.

Beast woke. Was standing four-paw-straddled, head down, shoulders raised, pelt standing on end. Was growling.

Stopped growling. Was safe. Creature thing was not here. Mock fight had stopped.

Kitchen had fallen silent. Was confused. *Jane? What was predator?*

Furious, I took over Beast's body and turned for the stairs, catching sight of Brute. I skidded to a stop. His white jaw was bloody in the spacing of the points matching Beast's claws. Eli was racing to clean up the were-tainted blood and apply pressure to Brute's jaw. Pea was snarling. At me. Her steel claws out and shining in the kitchen lights. *Crap.*

But the thoughts I had found . . .

It was dawn. I had to shift to human form now or be stuck as Beast all day. I raced for the stairs. For once Beast agreed.

Shift. Now! Beast demanded. *No more inside Beast head.*

I felt Beast open the Gray Between as I raced for the stairs. I didn't make it.

I woke stretched out on the stairs, the treads pressing into my ribs and thighs. I was shaking, sick, and naked, and Bruiser was there beside me, folding me in an afghan, one I recognized from the house in New Orleans. It was soft and fuzzy and familiar as it covered me and wrapped around me. He lifted me from the stairs. Carried me to our room. Closed the door behind us. He placed me on the bed and raised the head of the bed upright. It was the fanciest bed I'd ever slept in. Bruiser had picked it out for us, a special cooling memory-foam mattress, the bed itself with all the bells and whistles. I pulled the sheets and blankets over me, making a cocoon for myself, and Bruiser found and turned on an electric blanket, instant warmth pulsing into the weave of the afghan.

He sat beside me. "Eli is bringing you a high-protein hot chocolate."

I didn't reply, the shock of the encounter a steady tremor within me. Because it had been an encounter, not a vision or a memory. It had been real. My connection to Edmund was severed. But Beast's . . . Beast's might be partially intact, like a frayed wire that sometimes still carried a current.

"Do you want to talk about it?" Bruiser asked.

I couldn't bring myself to look at him, staring at the far corner of the room. I asked, "What did you see?"

"I was going to the kitchen and saw you playing with Brute and the grindy in the main room. Then you clawed him. He didn't bite you, by the way, so you're safe from were-taint." There was no censure in his voice. He was self-contained and composed, a rock I could lean on. Which was peculiar. To think of leaning on someone. To need someone.

And other people needed me. Like Molly. Like Eli and Alex. Like my godchildren. Like Brute and Bruiser . . . *Dang.* Bruiser needed me too.

"Yeah. I need to apologize." How bizarre was my life now, that I had to apologize to a werewolf and thank him for not biting me? I focused away from the shadowy corner of the room to Bruiser's face. Reached up and rubbed my knuckles over his scruff. "I really like the beard."

He caught my hand and kissed my knuckles. "This is the definition of diversion."

"More like prevarication."

"Why did you—or Beast?—lose control?"

"Ummm. Waiting for Eli?"

"What do you—"

A knock came at the door. I nodded to Bruiser's unspoken question and he called for Eli to come in. My partner stopped and eyeballed us, suspicious at whatever he saw on my face. "What?"

"You need to hear this too." I patted the mattress on my other side.

"No way am I getting into bed with you and George. Too kinky for me."

I raised my brows at him, thinking of all the things I could have teased him with. And didn't.

"I'll pull up a chair." He gave Bruiser the tall mug of chocolate, lifted the tufted, fringed, upholstered barrel chair, and set it near me. Sat. Crossed one ankle over his knee. Rested his arms out to the sides across the curved back. The former ranger made even the delicate chair look manly. His natural machismo made his entire world look masculine.

As he got situated, I drank down a good portion of the supersweet treat. I needed the calories to replace what I always used when I shifted. "Okay," I said when we were all ready. "I've always known that Beast keeps things from me, but this was a surprise because Beast didn't know it either. My tie with Ed was ripped away when the

SOD Two took him and bled him empty. But Beast's connection is still active off and on. Or was reattached when I was in the witch circle. Or something. Maybe."

"Interesting," Bruiser said softly. He scratched his beard slowly, a new gesture since he'd stopped shaving, one that indicated deep thought. Or an itchy face. Or both.

"While Beast played with Brute, her mind was open and I—we—saw Ed. He was being tortured by the shadow I saw before, but I got a better look at the torturer. It was a creature with shark teeth and huge eyes."

Eli said, "Drink your cocoa."

I did as ordered and drained the last of the drink, the sugar hitting my system with an instant high. Eli exchanged the mug for the blue Anzu feather, and the pain that had become so much a part of me that I tended to overlook it vanished when I shoved the feather against my belly and took a deep breath. "Thanks." I watched my business partner and best friend in the world, all relaxed and comfy in his pretty chair, and knew he was lying by body language to me. He was too slender, too hard, and too twitchy under the skin, evidenced by the tightness of the flesh around his eyes and the utter stillness with which he held himself. Eli needed to go do something with that energy. He needed a job, a battle to fight, a cause to fight for, and he needed it *now*, right this second. It was too hard, sitting in a pretty chair, waiting for the vamp infestation to show up and give him the chance to do battle.

Eli needs to hunt, Beast thought.

Yeah. He does, I thought back.

He needed me too. How very weird. To be needed.

"There was a lot of confusing stuff in the vision/experience/memory/whatever it was," I said.

The men said nothing.

"But it was definitely not human."

They looked at each other. Something communicated between them, something I didn't catch. Something important. "What?" I demanded.

"That is interesting," Bruiser said.

"Right interesting." Eli stood and walked away.

"You're not telling me something," I said, my tone accusing. Because: "I'm not stupid."

"No, you aren't," Bruiser said. And then he got up and left too, closing the door behind him.

"Not fair," I shouted. Neither of them responded. "Dang it."

I dressed and checked on Shiloh in the bathroom. The paralyzed, almost-true-dead vamp still lay in the tub, covered in dried blood, her throat a gaping wound. I needed to fix my life. I needed to find out what was going on. No. I needed to be well so they'd stop treating me like I was sick.

Jane is *sick,* Beast said.

"Shut up. No one asked you."

Beast snorted.

I left the bathroom to find Bruiser back, standing at the bedroom window, staring out at the snow. I scuffed my feet to let him know I was coming and wrapped my arms around his waist from behind. I could hear his heart beating, slow and measured, and remembered the feeling I had gotten a few times recently. I debated bringing up the vision or talking about feelings. My natural inclination was to avoid feelings, so I started there. Because I'm contrary even to myself. "You're depressed," I said. "I hadn't noticed and when I did notice I didn't do anything about it."

"You've been busy dying," he said, heartache and amusement lacing his words. "Besides, my depression is more grief than true melancholy, and either way it isn't your responsibility. It belongs to me and is mine to deal with."

"Uh-huh. I didn't save Leo. Leo's in a coffin because of me."

Bruiser didn't reply. His heart rate didn't alter. But his scent? Yeah. I smelled his grief.

I gave myself a chance to think it all through, and then, when I had it all in place, I said part of what I had put together. "Being Onorio doesn't mean you no longer need vamp blood; it just means you need less. Are you in withdrawal?"

Bruiser turned, sliding through my embrace in surprise.

"What?" I said. "You forgot about drinking? You're an idiot, you know that, right?"

"I never even thought about it. I've been . . . off . . . not myself, for months." His arms went around me and his forehead creased as some other thought occurred to him, but he didn't share.

"We have a few vamps coming. You should mix a little visiting-vamp blood with your wine tonight."

He forehead was still furrowed. "How did you think of that? I didn't, and I'm the blood addict."

"Did you ever think to ask the B-twins about blood addiction in Onorios and what the symptoms of withdrawal might be?"

A frown drew his face down. "No."

Men. They never asked for help or info. Not even my honeybunch. I figured testosterone resulted in brain damage. "Molly was addicted to vamp blood, but it was short-term, not for a hundred years, like you. Her withdrawal was probably a lot faster than yours has been, even with your Onorio physiology at work, and she went cold turkey, with nothing to offset the symptoms. I bet Evan can make some music to ease it for you like he did her. But he can't fix grief. And now we're back to the 'Jane didn't save Leo' part of this convo. And your grief. Which you try to hide because you don't want me to feel guilty."

"I don't blame you, Jane. I never did. Leo made the decisions he thought best and some of them were hard on me, on a friendship we had for most of my very long life. Onorios don't need much Mithran blood, but he didn't feed me for weeks prior to the Sangre Duello. So I have been in the Onorio version of *fame vexatum* for a long time. Months. I should have fed. I have been thoughtless and foolish."

All that was interesting, and an insight into my lovey-dovey's brain. Leo had mesmerized and bled and fed and used Bruiser for decades, yet he still called Leo his friend. *Fame vexatum* was the dietary style practiced by Mithrans—the vamps who didn't drain and kill humans in return for physical prowess, but who starved themselves in return for mental and mesmeric abilities. But that wasn't the important part of his words.

"Why did he stop feeding you?"

Bruiser laughed, the sound almost like pain coming through his chest, and drew me closer. "Grégoire didn't feed Brandon or Brian either. Leo wanted us all free of blood scent. We Onorios were supposed to stay out of the fighting, were supposed to scent as outclan, in case Leo lost and you died, so that we could, possibly, working together, drain Titus unto true-death."

A quiver of shock zinged through me. Leo had laid in contingency plans, a massive cheat, so that if he lost and I was dead, his people could still be free. And now we were facing the most powerful Son of Darkness. The last SOD was coming to Asheville, and we had one Onorio, not three.

More important, Shimon had Edmund. And one Onorio would not be enough to drain such an ancient bloodsucker.

"And there's only one of me here," Bruiser said, speaking my own thoughts, "which limits the Onorio manner of killing him true-dead."

"Yeah. And with the snowstorm and the canceled flights there's no way to get Brandon and Brian Robere—the B-twins—here." But we had Molly. I didn't say that. "About that grief—"

"Sometimes you have to let go of things, Jane. Let go of people, because they die. Even let go of time you no longer have." With a long, elegant finger, he tilted up my chin and smiled down at me. "I gave up Leo and the friendship of a century. It was easier than expected because he had used me, controlled me, and worst of all, forced me to hurt you." He inhaled deeply, a single, restorative breath. "Remembering that, more than anything, has made my grief easier. But I will not give up *you*, not to Leo, not to cancer. I will fight. Will you fight with me?"

I remembered all the people who needed me. Remembered the danger they were all in if I really did give up. "Dang skippy," I said.

My lovebug laughed, the reverberation bouncing high in the ceilings and through his chest and into my arms. "Let's see if your clan mob and the kids left us eggs and bacon."

"And biscuits?" I shouted at Eli, whom I could smell in the hallway. "I'm pretty sure I saw Eli sliding a tray of biscuits into the oven."

"Two. Two trays," my partner shouted back.

One biscuit, two eggs, and another hot chocolate later, I curled into the recliner, hurting, but as happy as I could remember being. The snow continued to fall outside. The sound of children screaming with laughter echoed through the tall ceilings. The smell of bacon and coffee and family and baby were heavy on the air, a satisfying scent.

Molly walked in and dropped Cassy on my chest. "She needs burping," Molly said. And walked out. Carefully, I sat up and adjusted the infant on my shoulder. Began patting Cassy's back.

Kitssss, Beast thought.

"Yeah," I murmured. And that warmth I had felt when Cassy looked at me began to spread. I was maybe, sorta, beginning to come back to life.

The blow caught me in the side. Another high on the outer thigh, safe places to hit someone if you didn't want to maim them. But Eli shouldn't have been able to hit me, not when he was holding back like he was. It sucked being sick. The pain was gone, thanks to the Anzu feather, but I wasn't well. My speed and stamina hadn't returned. I wasn't cured. *Yet,* I added mentally. I wasn't cured *yet*.

I circled my sparring partner, my toes gripping the mat. Trying to breathe deeply enough to fight without gasping or gagging.

Beast is better than puma or Jane. She sent me an image of me in half-form.

Half—I stopped and held up a hand to pause the match, trying to follow the glimmer of hope that—"My half-form may not be sick," I whispered.

Eli danced back, his weight on the balls of his feet, his body carrying that bounce common among boxers. A little to the left, a little to the right, with each low jump. "Not many weapons you can fire with half-form fingers." He wasn't even breathing hard, his brain working as fast as his body.

"But I can totally do the shock-and-awe thing." I grinned, showing teeth, a mean smile. "I'll greet Shimon in half-form."

Eli gave me his almost-there warrior smile, a little evil, a lot hard. "Your brother doesn't know how to half-form. Old bloodsucker like Shimon, never been to this continent? Killed all the weres he ever saw, at first sight? Bet he's never seen a Cherokee skinwalker in half-form. In fact . . ." He danced some more, thinking. "No one had until you figured it out. Yeah. Throw the bloodsucker off his game. So do it. Right now. Half-shift. Let's see how fast you can make it." He stood still and pulled his phone, started a timer. "Go."

Beast?

My Beast moved through our shared mind. She pulled up the Gray Between, silver and gray mist like a sparkling cloud. And she ripped through it. The pain was instant and acute, as if she was slashing through my guts with her claws. I dropped to my knees. Bones cracked. Joints swelled. Fangs shoved up through my mandibles and down from my maxillas. Big honking fangs. My skull cracked like someone hit me with a handful of marbles. My shoulders shattered. My feet felt like grenades exploded inside them. I forgot how to breathe.

I came to on the sparring mat, lying facedown in a little pool of drool. "Well, that sucked," I managed. It came out "Weeee 'at'shhhhu'ed."

Showing no mercy, which made me delirious with delight, Eli bent over me and said, "Took too long." His tone was casual, as if my pain was no biggie. I wanted to hit him, but I hurt too much to move just yet. "If you tried that in a fight he'd be tossing your head around like a bouncy ball."

"Bouncy baw!" a child's voice shouted. "I wanna pay baw!" I got my head turned to the sound and saw Little Evan standing in the doorway of the room, his fists clenched, his bare toes cute and stubby from this angle. He was the spitting image of his daddy, all bright-eyed and fiery-haired. His speech wasn't quite perfect yet, the *L*s there and gone. EJ rushed into the room as if to jump on me and came to a dead stop ten feet away, frozen at the sight of my face. His eyes went wide.

"It's Aunt Jane," I said, the words fang-mangled.

EJ took a slow step back. Froze again. Took another step back. He frowned mightily. Unballed his fists and pointed his fingers at me. Magic trembled in the air, a scalding/glacier tingle that shivered over my skin like—

"No the heck you don't." Eli swept EJ up into his arms and tossed him into the air. The magic vanished and EJ squealed in delight as Eli caught him and tossed him high again.

I rolled over and shoved my hair aside, analyzing what I'd just felt. The kid was already using magic, not something he should be able to do until he hit puberty. Raw, electric magic. To kill me? To see what I was? Or something else? I watched Eli toss the little boy again and then gather him, cradled in the crook of one elbow.

"That's Aunt Jane in a Halloween costume," he said. "No magic allowed."

"But—"

"No buts. What's your daddy say about using magic?"

EJ scrunched up his face and poked out his lower lip. "He hurting me if I use magic."

Eli went still as a sniper and studied the toddler's face. Quietly, he asked, "Hurting you?"

"Daddy making me cry. Fussin' at me. Te'yow me I have a stop. Stoppin' *hurts* little boweys. Right here." EJ touched his middle, over his solar plexus.

"I see. Well. Did you know that there are ways to make that hurting go away?"

EJ scrunched up his face in thought, still pouting. "No."

Eli waited. Patient. EJ scrunched his face up tighter. I drooled a little more.

The scrunched pout turned into curiosity. "How?" Little Evan demanded.

"It's called martial arts. Your aunt Jane was hurting and so she was practicing martial arts."

"In a How'oween costume?" He bent over Eli's arm and stared hard at me. "Dat's a reawy good costume, Ant Jane."

"Uh-huh." Molly was gonna kill me for ruining her kid. I shoved up to my hands and knees and stopped to catch my breath. My pants were about to fall off. I'd lost a lot of weight. Stretching out the hem of my tee, I smeared the spit off the mat. "Show EJ a few moves, Ranger man. I need to see how much stamina I have in this form."

"Hope it's more than you have in human form, Janie, because right now you're dead meat."

"Dead meat! Dead meat! Dead meat!" EJ shouted.

Eli snickered, a sound he tried to hide and somehow didn't manage. "So," my partner said to my godson, "let's talk about balance . . ."

I gripped my pants at my navel and made it to my feet and out the door toward the elevator. "Being sick sucks," I muttered.

"Sick suck! Sick suck!" EJ's voice trailed away as I entered the elevator and the doors closed.

I fell against the elevator wall. Silent, thoughtful, I examined my body as the elevator took me upstairs. I pushed on my middle. No tumor. No pain. *Holy crap.* The tumor was gone. Well, gone in this form. *Meet and greet the biggest, baddest vamp still alive and fight him too. Why not? It's how I killed the emperor.* I made a fist. I wondered if I could put on weight and muscle in this form. Wondered if I could reliably shift from Beast to half-form. Wondered

if I'd shift to human form if I fell asleep or was knocked
out while in this form or if I could hold this shape. "Yeah,"
I whispered. "Stuff to learn. This might do."

I had expected a visit from my new Cherokee Elder at
dawn, but she hadn't made it through the snow. We hadn't
heard from Shimon Bar-Judas. I had time to work on
things.

CHAPTER 6

Beat Ya Butt! Beat Ya Butt!

I changed into clothes that fit my new body shape better—wider at the shoulders and more narrow at the waist and upper hips. I felt good. Better than good. *You knew I'd feel okay in this form, didn't you?* I asked Beast. She didn't answer. *Any reason you didn't tell me?* Again with the no answer. Beast had wanted to come home to the mountains and live and hunt and be a mountain lion for a while. Or forever. Beast had ulterior motives. I felt her move deeper into my mind at that thought, as if seeking protection in the back of a den. *That's it, isn't it? You kept me from thinking about this shape.*

Beast chuffed, deep inside. *Did not know that Jane was not sick in half-form. Was not fact. Have been thinking about fact. Fact is life. Fact is . . . ex-per-'ence. Did not know being half-Beast with no sickness was fact.*

Uh-huh. But I hadn't thought about the possibility either, which was dang stupid.

I studied myself in the mirror and liked what I saw: tall, muscular, maybe a little mean, and totally badass.

I considered pulling on the battle boots, not because

I'd be fighting anyone, but because they had expandable panels at the sides to fit my paw-feet and had room for the claws that used to be toenails. But I decided to go bare-pawed. And wondered what the hard, thick nails would look like painted. Bloodred and sparkly, maybe. Or gold and sparkly to match my eyes. I held out my knobby-knuckled hands and figured it would take a whole bottle of polish to cover all twenty nails. *Worth it. Totally worth it.* I dug in a drawer for polish and found the sparkly red. "Oh yeah. So perfect."

Want kits, Beast thought at me, her tone fierce. *Cannot have kits if Jane is Jane. Can only have kits if Beast is Beast.*

Shaking the polish, I headed toward the kitchen and calories and protein as Beast's truth moved through me, slow and powerful, like a mudslide. "Okay," I said aloud, taking the stairs slowly. "You're right. I guess . . . I've been selfish for a long time."

Now Jane has mate. Jane will never let Beast have kits. Jane will stay Jane for mate.

Ummm. Not necessarily?

Beast's mental ears perked high.

I needed to talk to Bruiser about this. Because Beast was right. I had made no plans to let her live her life until I got sick. *Let's take care of the SOD and then we can plan for you. We might have to go out west or to Canada to find you territory close to a possible mate.*

Beast perked up. *Kits?*

Sure. Why not.

Want strong, big mate. Want fast mate. Want mate with—

Yeah. I got it.

If Bruiser was puma, would want Bruiser as mate.

I chuckled softly. It came out a lot deeper than I expected.

Eli lifted his eyes from the bar where he had a number of handguns in pieces. The place stank of lubricants and suddenly felt more like home. He glanced to one side where Little Evan was eating Cheerios, dry from the bowl, sitting beside him, watching every little movement. Eli had a fan. The former Army Ranger looked out the windows, scanning, his fingers touching the loaded weapon still holstered beneath one arm. On guard. Protecting. Always.

The little boy looked up. "Hey, Ant Jane," EJ said. "That's a really good costume. I learned to breafe . . . bre*athe* . . . and to baw'ance—balance—on two feet."

"Yeah? That's good. Breathing is important." I covered his head with a paw-hand, surprised when the whole thing fit into my longer fingers. Children were so small and fragile.

Kits . . ., Beast thought, the word filled with longing.

I scrubbed Little Evan's head, mussing his hair, and said to Eli, "Thank you." I opened the fridge and asked, "Got anything to build muscles in this form?"

"Babe." Which meant it was a stupid question. Wiping his hands, keeping an eye on his workbench, Eli said to EJ, "Don't touch. Remember?"

"I 'member." EJ crunched down on cereal, his eyes mischievous. "I'm a good lil boy."

Eli sighed as if he knew better than to believe the assertion, stepped up beside me, and pointed. "Roast. Steak. Eggs. Name it."

I had eaten eggs at breakfast, able to keep two down. "Steak. Let's start with a couple pounds and move on from there."

Eli chuckled. "And then we spar for a while. That last attempt was pitiful." Eli turned on the stove grill and pulled a steak from the fridge.

"Mmmm. Beat your butt this time, I betcha," I growled in my deeper voice.

"Beat ya butt! Beat ya butt!"

"Molly's gonna kill you, you know," Eli added casually, turning the gas up high to sear the steaks.

"Yeah. Shoot me now."

EJ giggled and slammed his fists down, scattering Cheerios on the floor. "Soot me! Soot me! Soot me!"

Eli managed not to laugh at me and picked up my godson, placing him on the floor. EJ squealed and took off running in the general direction of his parents' suite. Eli slapped the steak on the stove grill and made the kitchen smell wonderful. Within minutes, he gave me a mostly raw steak cut into bite-sized pieces so I could pretend to have good manners. If Molly was gonna kill me, at least I'd go out with a full belly. In that odd comfortable silence of family, I watched Eli finish the weapon maintenance and clean the bar while I scarfed down several pounds of meat.

As I was wiping delicious beef grease off my lips, Alex walked in and plopped a sheaf of papers onto the bar top. "Your appointment of Grégoire to the Dark Queen's Warlord, thoroughly vetted and approved by Bruiser and the Robere Onorios. Read and sign." He clicked a pen open and held it out to me. I didn't bother to read the papers, but I knew that what I was doing would change the way vamps lived in Europe for . . . maybe forever. I signed with a flourish. Grégoire was going to love being Warlord. And I had managed to avoid having to go to war in Europe. Go, me!

I signed a couple dozen siggies and handed the papers to Eli. Feeling much better about things, I sat back against the barstool and opened the nail polish.

"Can I paint them?" Angie asked from behind me.

"Ummm." I had a mental image of my nails after my goddaughter painted them. It wouldn't be any worse than my own job. "Sure. Why not?"

Angie Baby climbed onto the barstool near me and took the bottle of polish. EJ clambered up on the weapon-free bar top and crawled over to watch, lying with his belly on the cold stone, seemingly without discomfort. Angie patted the seat between her legs and I carefully placed my oversized paw-foot on the barstool and wiggled my toe pads. She giggled and pulled the brush from the bottle, the acetone stench ruining the leftover steak scent. She caught her tongue between her teeth and began painting my nails, her brush strokes slow and smooth. The scarlet was the perfect color.

"It's pretty," she said. When I didn't respond, she asked, softer, "I can't feel my Edmund in my head anymore. Is he gonna be okay, Ant Jane? Am I gonna have my knight back?"

Edmund had sworn fealty to Angie and her entire family, to be their protector, and somehow the two had formed an unexpected mental bond. In the same way that he had been ripped from me, he had been ripped from Angie, and then he had, in the manner of vamps, locked his mental shields down so we didn't suffer while he suffered. But I had no way of knowing if the mental bond could or would be restored and had no way to explain all this to Angie.

"Yes," I said, sounding utterly positive, "Edmund is going to be okay. And he will always be your knight, whether we feel him in our heads or not."

She nodded, her strawberry blonde curls sliding forward as she painted the hard-to-reach little claw. "I miss him," she whispered.

And I was right. It took most of the bottle.

It was long after sundown, a light snow again falling, when Alex shouted that he had a text claiming visitors were arriving. On the way to the front door I glanced at the screen, spotting a gaggle of snowmobiles pulling into the long drive. In half-form, I walked to the door, turned on the welcoming lights, and stepped outside. The roar of the snowmobiles blasted the silence from the property as the first two vehicles accelerated, dashing up the long driveway, creating ruts in the blanket of snow. Lincoln Shaddock's people were here.

The first two vehicles were shiny black. They slowed, then stopped, and two vamps stepped off the snowmobiles at the same moment, each moving as if dismounting from a warhorse. The riders hadn't bothered with coats, because some vamps don't care if it's cold or if they look human, and these two were that sort: African, tall, with chiseled bodies and features, carrying themselves with an assured arrogance that demonstrated their power. They were putting on a show of strength. They succeeded. The snow falling on their dark skin and black clothing wasn't melting, and though I knew vamps were cold-blooded, it was always disconcerting to see the proof. These two were powerful; they would be formidable opponents if I had to prove myself to them. I could smell the vamp scents of ginger, fresh-cut grass, and faintly of jasmine. One was male and one was female and I didn't know them.

Beast peered out through our eyes and snarled with my mouth. A challenge.

Hearing the sound, the two vamps paused, taking in my pelt, my bipedal stance, my nonhuman body shape, my brightly glowing yellow-gold eyes, and the man with guns standing at my side.

Eli nodded to them, a single jut of his head. "The Dark Queen welcomes you," he called out. I just watched. The two didn't relax. But they didn't run or attack. Good so far.

Behind the vamps, six more snowmobiles emerged from the uphill curve of the drive, moving at slower speeds into the open land of the front entrance, toward the parking area. The vehicles were each painted in dazzling shades, from red to mustard yellow to a vibrant blue with flames painted on the sides, and they carried heavily clad humans, riding double. All six snowmobiles pulled sleds with hard covers, likely full of supplies and luggage.

Eli stepped in front of me and leveled his toy at them. He didn't know the two vamps in front and so he carried an Uzi capable of taking them all down in a hail of bullets. If it didn't jam and misfire. Miniguns were apt to jam at the worst possible moment, but Eli carried plenty of weapons if that happened. He was clearly worried about what we couldn't see on the sleds. "The sealed trailer with windows is a Cat Cutter," he murmured. "Cutters are sleds that carry people. Could be an ambush from Shaddock or factions from his people."

Twelve humans. Enough for four vamps. They had two vamps and a cutter. We had Shiloh, so who was the fourth vamp?

Blowing a miasma of exhaust, the vehicles stopped in a ring around the front entrance and the engines went dead; a waiting silence fell on the property. One of the sleds creaked, the sound sharp after the roar. The two vamps turned and faced the sleds, standing at military parade rest, their positions managing to keep Eli and me in their vision.

On the biggest sled, the one I assumed was the cutter, a bird-wing-type hatch rose into the air. Eli didn't tense, so much as flow, toward the movement. The two unknown vamps flowed too, and drew weapons, pointed at us.

Ambush, Beast thought.

From the cutter, long legs moved like spider legs, feet sinking into the deep snow. Lincoln Shaddock himself emerged. Before anyone started bleeding, I called out, "The Dark Queen welcomes Lincoln Shaddock, Master of the City of Asheville. We didn't know you were coming, my friend."

Eli didn't relax, indicating that he wasn't convinced Shaddock's appearance was a good thing.

"Jane Yellowrock," Shaddock called back. His voice was rough and soothing at once, just as I remembered it. "Or should I say, my Dark Queen." He bowed deeply before he took the front steps two at a time, leaving his human bodyguards and the new vamps behind.

I caught his scent and put out a hand to welcome him.

"Let me see you, girl," he said. He took my hand and turned me around in an unexpected dance twirl, scrutinizing me. "I assumed they were joshing me about you being half-cat, but darned if they weren't speaking the truth. I wouldn't have recognized you without them yaller eyes," he said in his hill-country vernacular. "I like the look."

The vamps and Eli stood down at the dance move, their weapons smoothly disappearing. Even if I had never seen a vampire before I'd have known what they were. More important, both wore silver studs in their ears. Vamps were allergic to silver. The silver was a calling card that said the two were very, *very* powerful and a lot older than I had thought. They might not have a city of their own right now, but they were masters. *Strangers.*

Dangerous, Beast thought. "You brought food," I said.

"I can tell by the smoked-meat scent on the air. With this crowd, we'll need it." Shaddock owned and was the chief chef in his own BBQ joint in downtown Asheville. Best smoked food *ever.* I gestured to the door and continued politely. "The forecast suggests we'll have a few days before the snow starts again, but getting to the store will be difficult."

Shaddock gave me another bow, very slight, something that might have been common in his human time, and stepped to the side. I entered the inn and he followed. "You've learned Mithran manners," he said more softly. "Can't say it makes me happy, but if they avert another war, it'll be worth hearing you talk like one of us. And yes. We have a whole cow, half of it ready to serve. The other half is raw for any weres or skinwalker beasts—" He stopped and stared at my teeth as his people began to bring in supplies and his vamp security pair filed in behind and began to scope out the place. "You eat cooked or raw in that form? And how the blue blazes do you talk with fangs?"

"Cooked. And the same way you do when *your* fangs snap down, you old fanghead," I grumbled.

"There's the Jane Yellowrock I know," he said with a human-style grin. "Rude, crude, and delightfully socially unacceptable. Makes me feel right at home." He turned and called, "Kojo. Thema. Come and greet your queen."

The two dark-skinned vampires flowed across the open area and stopped in the foyer, in front of Lincoln. I took them in as they moved, and tensed. "We do not bow to *you*," the man said to Shaddock in liquid syllables.

Kojo's accent was vaguely foreign: not Cajun, Spanish, Latin, or Leo's old-fashioned French cadence, not the more modern version of the language. This was something flowing and ancient with swift and clear vowel sounds, curling like wavelets capping on a lake, brushed by an approaching summer storm. Maybe an African intonation. His tone slipped into something sarcastic and insulting as he looked me over. "Therefore, why should we bow to *her*?"

In an instant, Shaddock moved, a strange popping

sound of speed and displaced air. Kojo was flat on the floor, a stake in his belly, paralyzing him.

Ooookay.

I didn't react. Eli did. The sound of multiple weapons *schnicking* echoed in the space. The entire front area went dead silent. Eli was aiming two weapons, one at Kojo, one at Thema. *Battle wariness.*

Shaddock had taken Kojo down. Thema was still standing, but she slid slowly to the floor. Shaddock had thrown a stake and hit the female vamp in the belly at the same time he took down Kojo. He had been expecting trouble. And *dang*, the MOC was fast. Shaddock also had excellent control. His fangs were fully extended, yet his eyes weren't vamped out.

"Kojo and Thema." Shaddock's fangs *schnicked* back into the roof of his mouth. He indicated the man and woman in turn. "They were *ton-tigi* in Mali. Lost their hunting grounds and their clan around 1350. They've been traveling for the last few centuries, seeing the world."

With my half-formed ears, I heard keys clicking and knew Alex was searching for *ton-tigi*. "Mali?" I asked as my partner holstered one weapon, pulled the stake from Thema's belly, and aimed the remaining semiautomatic weapon at her head. Her fingers formed a fist, but she lay still. To Shaddock I said, "If they're working for you, they don't seem very reliable."

"We have sworn to kill the Makers," Thema said. "Anyone who fights our enemy is our ally. But you are weak and the smell of sickness is on the air."

"The Dark Queen," Eli said quietly, "killed Joseph Santana, also known as Joses Bar-Judas and Yosace Bar-Ioudas, the elder of the Sons of Darkness, and fed his body to the white werewolf."

The woman, splayed on the floor, braced her arms and sat up. She turned slowly to me, her eyes wide. "This is true? You killed one of the Makers?"

Makers. Probably an ancient name for the Sons of Darkness. Gotcha. Snow had melted on her from the warmth of the room, her hair wet and glistening, her clothes spotted and drenched with damp. "Pretty much."

"He is dead? Forever? Never to rise?"

Except for that pesky heart. I really needed to deal with that last body part, which was in the hands of Jodi and the NOLA witches. Didn't say any of that. I said, "Unless he can resurrect himself from Brute's crap, no. He isn't coming back."

Thema reacted to that, a flash of some unnamable, almost-human emotion that seemed to be composed of humor and joy and grief all at once. She managed to get to her knees, one hand over her belly wound, the tang of unfamiliar vamp blood on the air. "And the young Son of Darkness is here? The Son of Shadows is *here*," she emphasized, "*in this place*? This is true?"

The Son of Shadows. Yeah. That fit with the whole "shadow thing" in Edmund's mind.

She drew a knife that gleamed wicked bright in the lights. Eli went all tense/still/dangerous, his weapon in a two-hand grip, aimed at her head.

"He'll be in Asheville tomorrow," I said, my eyes flashing between them, Shaddock's security all scary vampy and Shaddock slouched against Kojo, watching the rest of us.

There was something new and powerful about Shaddock, a leashed, contained capacity for violence, the way a bomb looks before it devastates the landscape. Casually, the MOC removed the stake in Kojo's abdomen. He licked the blood off the wood in a gesture that was nonchalant, oddly amused, and all vamp.

I finished, "The Flayer of Mithrans will *not* be progressing to the inn. He has a place in town."

"There is no place at the inn," Shaddock said, laughter in his tone, oddly quoting the Bible as he pulled away from Kojo.

"We will destroy the Flayer of Mithrans," Kojo said. He sat up in measured movements, reaching for a matte gray case big enough to hold a rocket launcher. "And all he holds dear. We will wipe the lives of his loyal ones from the face of the Earth." He flipped up large thumb locks. *Holy crap.* It held some kind of rocket launcher. Shaddock's new vamp said, "We will scorch the land where he stands and none will escape us."

Two of Eli's weapons were out again, one aimed at the kneeling Thema, the other aimed directly at Kojo. "Touch that and die," my partner said softly.

Everything went still and silent, the way it did with any threat. I could hear Shaddock's humans breathe, short and shallow, the breath of prey when they caught sight of a predator.

Eli said, "This is the Official Winter Court of the Dark Queen of the Mithrans. You do not draw weapons in her presence. You fight with her, at her command, or you leave her territory. This is not up for discussion."

Kojo swiveled his head toward Shaddock, that inhuman move vamps could make, more bird than mammal. He started to vamp out, his pupils dilating and his sclera becoming a bloody scarlet. Shaddock ignored him, amused, watching me. He tipped an imaginary hat at me. This was a test of the DQ. He'd set me up. *Dang fanghead.*

But . . . I had not taken up the mantle of power Leo had given me nor the power of the Dark Queen. Some of the people I loved had been captured or gone missing because I hadn't done my job. Others may have died.

I hadn't done my job because I was sick and it was too hard. *Woe is me.* Except I wasn't sick right now. It was time I fixed things. And with vamps, might meant right. And that meant over Shaddock too.

"Kojo," I growled. The vamp twisted his head to me like an owl, too far, too smooth. "This is the hunting territory of the Master of the City of Asheville. But it is the political territory of the Dark Queen. You fight with me and at my command, or you die. In the moment. And Master of the City Shaddock dies with you, for the insult to my position and power. Choose."

Shaddock tensed.

Yeah, I thought. *You want to play vampire games? Try me.* "You brought them into my territory and home," I said to him, all vamp-formal. "It is my right to drink down all of you."

"You aren't a vamp," Shaddock said.

Softly I whispered, "Try me." He said nothing, his body tense and hard, but his expression uncertain. "I've stayed silent and out of action too long," I said, hoping he understood my words and the meaning beneath them. "People in Europe have died. That is *not* happening here."

Kojo said, "You would take from me the realization of a goal that is seven hundred years in the making, *woman*?"

"Pretty much. First of all, you don't get to blow up my enemies long-distance. I will not allow collateral damage of the humans in my territory. Second, our enemy has my primo. He's using Edmund to communicate and I want Ed back. I'm not giving up my people. Third, my Onorio needs blood, but I can suck it off the floor and feed him if necessary." I figured that last part was insulting enough to prove I was the bigger predator.

Kojo's lip curled and he stood, a willowy, sinuous movement that would do a big-cat proud. Shaddock allowed the movement, stepping back. "You will understand this. I have been used as Translator by the Flayer of Mithrans." The title Translator was imbued with pain and hatred and fear. "I will destroy the entire world before I allow him near my soul again."

"Yeah, well, let's hope it doesn't come to annihilation," I said, "but *I* intend to rescue Ed from the Flayer, and I'll kill *you* before I let you harm my primo. Just so we're clear."

"Can he get inside your head easily?" Eli asked Kojo, moving silently around us, taking in everything, and simultaneously getting a better shot angle. "If so," he continued, his voice so soft it was its own kind of threat, "that makes you a liability."

"No," Kojo said, the single word hard. "Not without him taking my blood once again," he said, his accent growing stronger. "Before, when he stole my blood to claim me, I was his prisoner. He made use of my wife, against her will. Even now, if he tries to drink of me, tries to take over my mind with his spirit of darkness, I will die true-dead first."

"As will I," Thema said. And she was suddenly holding a small subgun, a different configuration, make, and model from one of Eli's, but no less dangerous. Eli moved almost vamp-fast, keeping them both in line of sight, his fingers at the triggers. This was going bad fast.

Thema went on, "We parley with the Dark Queen."

"Okay," I said. "The Dark Queen hears."

"We will feed your Onorio. We will leave no *chevalier vampire* in the hands of the Maker. We will save your servant-knight. We will fight at your command. We will put away our weapons. But we will not give them up."

"Chevalier vampire?" I asked.

"Knight of the Dark Queen," Shaddock said, then clarified: "Edmund." He sounded amused, his eyes moving between us as if we were an entertainment just for his enjoyment.

"Edmund is not just a knight. He's the Master of the City of New Orleans," Eli said, not moving his lethal muzzles away from them, "and the emperor of the European Mithrans, should the empress fall."

Kojo tilted his head, disdain on his face. "The heir of all Europe allowed himself to be captured? How is such a *raeb*, one powerful enough to inherit the emperorship, taken and used by the Flayer of Mithrans?"

I had no idea what *raeb* was, but I understood the question. There was a lot of crap going on here and it needed to be brought to an end, fast. "Betrayal," I said simply.

"I have heard whispers, my heart," Thema said to Kojo. "Those loyal to the Flayer, with territory in the French countryside, helped with some treachery." She added to me, "These same treacherous ones welcomed the Nazis with open arms and gave those of us with darker skin to be tested and used. We fought and killed many, and my heart and I were not taken, though we lost many friends. There is no shame in being bested by betrayal. But vengeance is demanded."

Yeah. Vengeance. That was exactly want I wanted. I put a hint of command in my tone and shifted on my paw-pad feet to better display my scarlet-painted claws. "Put down your weapon, Thema. Stand down, Kojo. Once they stand down, put away your weapons, Eli."

"Copy."

Copy meant he'd heard, not that he would put away the weapons. I sighed. "Pretty please?" I asked. "With sugar on top?"

Eli snorted. Thema hesitated and then dropped her head in obeisance, placing her weapon on the floor. She was really limber. When she stood upright, Eli lowered his little killer guns. The stench of violence began to fade from the air.

I glanced at Eli. "You'll make sure everything that needs to be done is done?"

"Yes, my queen."

My queen? Oooookaaay. Someone was making a point. I said, "And that the meat is put in the kitchen?"

Eli chuckled. "Roger that."

Alex said from the shadows, "If you're interested, I know where the Flayer has been for the last few months." I nodded and he entered the main room, holding a tiny laptop on one arm, the screen balanced open in front of him. "The Flayer of Mithrans has been staying in Chambord Castle, Loir-et-Cher"—he mangled the words—"in France."

"I know this place," Thema said, her voice going tighter, her body drawing up into a fighter's stance.

"The largest French Renaissance castle in the Loire Valley." Alex glanced up at me and I nodded again. Things seemed to be ratcheting down. Dang vamp politics and all the mumbo jumbo that went along with it. Alex visibly relaxed and went on. "The castle was built by Francis the First in 1519 as a hunting lodge for the royal court, but it was rarely lived in. One hundred rooms out of four hundred forty are open to the public. The remaining three hundred plus are private. Lots of places to hide and hunt."

Thema moved to Kojo. He stood and she laid her head on his shoulder. He wrapped one arm around her and pulled her to his side, but they each had one arm free, and the bulges beneath their snow-damp clothing were proof of more hidden weapons.

Thema said, "The Flayer of Mithrans would have taken over what empty rooms he wanted and his scions would hunt in the park and nature preserve that surrounds it, as well as the nearby countryside, taking humans to feed upon. That they are close to so many humans, and yet there are no reported deaths or large numbers of missing humans, implies they are not drinking as Naturaleza. Or were not. If they are truly coming here, and if they truly intend battle, they will need to drink freely."

"They are," I said.

She looked at me, sloe eyes tilted and deceptively sleepy. "Many humans will die, if you allow him free feeding in your territory. His scions will capture you. They will lock you in a cage and drink you down. They will own you. The Flayer will try to take your mind, for you are a strange creature and he desires to possess strange creatures."

"Not a chance in heaven," I said, thinking about Edmund. Then thinking about Hayyel, I lifted my jaw in a Cherokee gesture, pride and certainty in my stance and tone. "I have an angel on my side."

She shrugged, a bony shoulder moving beneath her thin T-shirt. "Angels have little interest in taking the side of humans or strange creatures. If you fight on the side of an angel, he will use you and then discard you."

I'd think about that later. I said, "There's a cottage for you on the grounds. Unit number three." I glanced at Shaddock, who was no longer testing me, but standing with his hands in his jeans pockets, watching us. His face wore a hawkish, speculative expression, his eyes hooded by powerful brows. I wasn't sure if the glare meant he was willing to help and follow me into battle or he was thinking about taking my head and mounting it on a pole. "Unit two is for you," I said.

Shaddock interrupted me. "This place ain't what you might call well defensible. A small army of European fighters is headed this way, along with any local recruits they might find. You gonna parley in town?"

"We have defenses and plans," I said. "Talk to my partner, Eli Younger."

Shaddock nodded to Eli. "Pleasure, sir."

"At your service, sir," Eli responded.

"Unit one belongs to Edmund," I said, getting back to the immediate.

"A Mithran who will be my emperor," Shaddock said. "If he can best me."

"Yup. Once the Flayer is dead and everyone is healed, you can challenge him. He'll love owning Asheville."

Lincoln Shaddock barked a laugh. So did I.

Molly stuck her head around the corner. "You people finished playing fanghead games yet? I need to get in the kitchen."

Smiling a purely human smile, Lincoln said, "Miz Everhart-Trueblood. It's a pleasure, ma'am." He gave her a small bow and stepped aside.

CHAPTER 7

If My Hands Had Worked, I'd Have Flipped Him Off

The Winter Court of the Dark Queen of the Mithrans had a new, traditional sweathouse above the tumbling creek out back. Well after midnight, in the freezing air, I stood in half-form at the sweathouse's open door, smelling sawdust, the glue of the marine-grade plywood, and the pine two-by-fours from the construction. The interior was lightless. My Beast-eyes took their time adjusting to the dark after the snow-bright night outside, but things began to resolve and my brain made patterns of them.

Eli had built the sweathouse according to instructions given to him by Aggie One Feather, my mentor and Cherokee Elder back in NOLA. He had done compass measurements so the sweathouse was aligned to the rising sun on the equinoxes and the summer and winter solstices. There were little doors high in the gables on the eastern side to let in the rising sun on each of these days. A small table near the door held folded cloth, and there were empty hooks on the wall above it.

There was a stone-lined fire pit in the center, in a circular, clay-lined depression. There was an aged oak log, sawn in half and shellacked, the two halves at north and south. There was what could have been a shallow dough bowl, a pitcher and ladle, split wood and kindling, in stacks according to the wood type, each bundle bound by white cord. I smelled oak, walnut, hickory, and cedar. Near the pitcher and ladle was a drum. I walked in and picked it up, studying it in Beast's night vision. It had an ancient clay pot–style base, the opening covered by a new tanned hide, maybe raccoon skin. There were tiny copper bells all around the top, and when I tapped the skin, they jingled.

A memory flashed like lightning through my brain, searing everything in the here and now, taking me back. *A fire in a longhouse. The scent of smoke and man sweat and bear fat strong on the air. Burning herbs, different from the herbs used in women's rituals. Different from the sweathouse. These were harsh and acerbic and stung my nose.*

The longhouse was dark, lit only by a large fire. Men were moving around the fire, each with their left arm out to the flames. Dancing. It was a war dance. My father was in the circle, long legs bare, a breechclout covering his middle. His body was painted with white chalk and ocher and black ashes. His hair was braided in a complicated pattern and there were feathers in his headband, oddly, all hanging down. His bone-and-teeth necklace popped up and down with each step, his toes spread wide. He wore bone anklets and they clattered with each step.

A drum was in the hands of an old man, face lined and eyes whitened by age, his body wrapped in woven robes and a bearskin, the fur turned inward for warmth. The old man was sitting at north, tapping on the drum, a complicated six-beat rhythm, and tiny shells and hollow wood reeds rang with each beat. Rain pattered on the roof overhead. Smoke swirled on the slow air.

I was sitting with Uni lisi, *her smell that of cat and owl and strong woman. Beside her was the outclan priestess of the vampires. Sabina.*

Another shock of electricity zinged through me. I was back in my sweathouse. I tapped the raccoon skin top. The single thrum was sharp. The bells tinkled. Just like my memory. I was holding a war drum of the *Tsalagi*. I had no idea where it had come from. Or when the memory had been except that I was very young. Three? Four? Sabina had been there. With my grandmother, who smelled like an owl. I shivered and the bells shrilled with my motion. A memory of Sabina in my own distant past was alarming. Why had Sabina been allowed to be present at a war dance? Why had I? The war dance was only for the men and the beloved women—the war women.

Sabina was Mediterranean. Had her olive skin and prominent nose been enough like The People for her to be considered one of them? Had she mesmerized them? Drank them down? Left them blood-drunk?

"Crap," I whispered.

I shook the drum. It rang, shrill and strident. New sweathouse. War drum. New memory and a weird one at that.

Maybe the memory came because I'd be breaking in a new elder soon, whenever she managed to get here, out in the boonies. Had the new elder sent a war drum to me? My new Cherokee Elder, found for me by Aggie One Feather, was from Long Hair Clan. Not my clan. Not a skinwalker. But still—an Elder of The People. I wondered what would happen if I showed up in half-form and scared the heck out of her. I might get my knuckles rapped or something.

The sweathouse door closed behind me with a bang and I jumped. War drum bells rang. Outside, a gust of wind hit the sweathouse. Feeling silly, I set down the drum and crossed my arms over my narrow waist, gripping my elbows; boney, knobby joints like river stones. And wondered how my soul home would look, with another elder leading me to healing. I figured I was going to hate it.

It was now intensely dark inside. The sweathouse was small, able to hold six people at most. I hadn't noticed the icy air outside but somehow, in the sweathouse, with no flames in the firepit, no fire-heated rocks, no smell of smoke and ash and herbs that I was used to, the air felt colder. Sterile. Waiting. Did sweathouses need to be smudged? Probably.

I closed my eyes and thought about my soul home. The dark. The hollow echo of water dripping. My mind dropped into the place where my life force resided. The awareness of the air changed, warmed slightly.

I opened my eyes and raised them. Studied the open area of the cave-like place. Like the sweathouse, there was no fire. No flicker of flames, no warmth. No movement of air. It was as if my soul home had stopped breathing and gone cold. It felt empty. Lonely.

The wide space had a smooth floor and walls, stalactites and stalagmites hanging and rising, a few meeting in the middle in bizarre-shaped columns. No sign of Beast. A medicine bag hung on my chest. My father's medicine bag. Here, it was no longer tattered and faded, the deer hide still smelling of tannins and dyes. I was wearing pants and a long shirt wrapped and tied with a cloth belt, dressed the way my father had dressed. I was in half-form and carried a knife at my waist, one with a deer antler handle.

The domed ceiling rose over me, pale gray and feathered.

Hayyel's wings were draped on the roof and down the depth of my soul. He was watching over me. Or just watching me. "What do you want?" I asked him, the words ringing. "Is it to kill the last son of Judas Iscariot? Do you want the blood of the Son of Shadows on my blade? Do you wish me to destroy the maker of vampires? Will you be done with me then?"

Something stirred in the air behind me. I turned but no one was there. A familiar voice spoke into the silence, melodic and lyrical; unlike the dripping water in the distance, it didn't echo. "Walk into the dark of your soul home. Walk into the passage."

I peered into the tunnel in the far part of the cavern, a long curving hallway. I had made my way into the dark here before. There had been a waterfall in the distance,

but I didn't hear the roar of the water now. I stepped into
the gloom, following the snaking tube-like tunnel, darkness all around me, my feet sure in the perpetual night,
Beast's eyes glowing, the world appearing in deep shades
of greens and charcoal and black, my paw-feet-pads steady
on the cold floor.

Within a few yards, the roar of water came to me faintly.
I rounded a curve and the air grew wetter, the rumble a
vibration beneath my paw-pads. The tunnel narrowed and
twisted. It opened out into a bigger room, the floor littered
with cracked and broken stone. A stalagmite had fallen
and shattered and now blocked my path. An underground
stream gushed from a hole in the rock wall just ahead and
to my left. The cascade sent plumes of mist and water droplets into the air. Each was pristine and perfectly round.

I stepped over the broken stone and stopped at the
edge of the underground river, the water a good ten-foot
drop below me. Downstream, I saw the presence of future
time in the water droplets. I saw war among the arcenciels, war with lightning, storms, eruptions of volcanoes,
earthquakes. There was fighting in the heavens like angels
and demons in battle. Human jets and bombers circled
among them, firing weapons that did nothing to the rainbow dragons, passed through the demons without effect.
Nuclear bombs detonated in the atmosphere. The droplets grew crimson and vanished. Instead of battle in the
droplets, I now saw a dry and barren world. A war-ravaged
world with craters and rents deep into the Earth's crust.
The crimson tint obscured the timeline. In its place, I saw
droplets depicting a wet and dripping world covered with
mold and slimes and colonies of bacteria the size of dinner
plates. In the next spray human bones were piled high in
desolate and broken cities, as if thousands of bodies had
been shoved out of the way, to rot. In other droplets and
sprays, I saw emptiness, no living humans, no mammals,
no birds, no reptiles, no insects. Not anywhere. I understood that every single droplet vision was a variant of
the world after arcenciel war. After human war. After destruction on a scale I never dreamed even in nightmares.
I closed my eyes and forced the visions away.

When I opened them again, my gaze traced the passage of water from upstream, between the rocks, where the water roared from the chasm, above the waterfall, high into the past. My childhood came alive in the droplets. *Edoda*, my father, teaching me to throw an ax. His body, on the floor of our cabin. The sensation of cold as I painted my face in my father's blood. My five-year-old hand clenching the knife that killed my first man, *Edoda*'s murderer.

I followed the trail of my life in the droplets back along the flow of the underground river, downstream into my own future. Seeing death and war, seeing hope and love. Seeing my future evil as I killed and ate humans, then my death as a liver-eater at the hand of an elderly Eli. His rage and sorrow and determination as I tried to kill him and Alex and three small children.

My entire life was death and destruction. And each droplet of my future was a world of even more horrors if I didn't fix what was happening here and now. Or if I allowed the arcenciels to go back in time and destroy the vamps at conception. Or if I allowed the war in the heavens to start. But I didn't know how to stop any of that.

I studied each potential world, each possibility as it rose and fell into the fast-moving river, upstream and down. A series of them showed torture. Disease. Destruction. War. Another series showed the vamps and the trail of bodies as they attacked and killed entire villages. Others displayed vamps hanging in storage lockers, their blood harvested. Most droplets of the underground stream were filled with fear and pain. The very few that led to peace and living humans and a healthy world were a narrow spray that started with me. But there was nothing that showed what I did to avert a war. Nothing that showed me how to get through to the narrow possibility of goodness.

A sound like a silver bell echoed in the chamber.

I turned around. The beautiful man stood in the tunnel behind me, no wings, no halo, but so beautiful that Michelangelo would have killed to carve his likeness.

Hayyel smiled at me, an expression so sweet it broke my heart. "As your Alex might say, hatred is fear on illegal drugs, a passion that would defeat love. And so there is always war."

"Hate is fear on steroids," I corrected.

He tilted his head and walked closer to me in my vision. His smile faded. "More arcenciels work to find a way to go back two thousand years in the past. Soon there will be enough of them in agreement to make the leap."

"To destroy the Sons of Darkness." I hadn't known it took a lot of them to time-jump so far, but it made sense. The vamps I knew who had been collecting them all seemed to want more than one. "You want to use me to stop them. I'm a pawn on a chessboard to you, just like I was to Leo Pellissier."

He frowned slightly and I felt my insides quiver in dismay. I didn't want him unhappy.

I realized he was manipulating my emotions. "Stop it," I said. "Do that again and I'll walk away."

He lifted his chin, scowling as if I had pointed out a flaw in his perfection. And maybe I had. Humans were supposed to have free will—but I wasn't human. He could manipulate me any way he wanted. I wondered if his boss knew he was trying to alter the current reality on earth. And then I wondered, not for the first time, if he was one of the fallen. Had I been played by an angel of the dark posing as one of the good guys?

"I am not among the fallen," he said, throwing back an arm as if sweeping back a wing in disgust. "I do my duty. No more."

"No more? Uh-huh." *Liar, liar, pants burning in the fires of hell.* There was more here than I was being told.

"You, however, have not done your duty. More than once you have held a trapped arcenciel in your hands and have not ridden it to correct the evils you have seen. I gave you *power*." He pointed to my middle. "You did not use it. Instead you play this game as half of a beast, hiding from the magic that is yours to use."

I touched my belly, confused. He had to know. But . . .

"All the magic, all the timewalking, gave me cancer. I'm dying in my human form."

And I coulda sworn Hayyel was . . . surprised. "The power makes you stronger."

"It tore my DNA into shreds. Last time I looked, it was four strands instead of two. I told God I was sick. I prayed. I shifted. I'm still sick. Timewalking and the weird magics in my middle are killing me."

The door in the sweathouse opened. The vision dropped away. Frigid air swooshed in. The smell of vamp churned around me.

I whirled. Saw everything, backlit by the dim night against the snow. Two vampires stood in the open doorway. Strangers. Male and female. Vamped out. Armed to the teeth.

They went for weapons.

Beast shoved power into me. Speed. Tearing the blade from my belt, I attacked. Leaped. Dove into the snowy world, blade out to one side, claws out on the other. Whatever they expected, I wasn't it. They didn't move fast enough. The vamp-killer cut through the body of the one on the right, midline, at the waist. My arm and shoulder jerked with the impact. Left claws went higher, taking out the flesh below the collarbone, the left side of the throat, neck, up the back of the jaw and ear. One swipe. I landed off-balance. Tucked and rolled. Smelled Eli. I kept rolling. Three shots rang out. Three more. Three more. Three more. I came up behind a tree, stayed tucked. Located Eli in the dark. Sitting in a tree. Cold-suited. Headset with oculars and mic. Heard the faint clicks of a weapon mag being replaced with a fresh. I inspected the vamps. Both were still down on the snow. I took my first breath.

The vamps smelled strange. Acidic. Like boiling vinegar. I almost expected the snow beneath them to melt and boil, but nothing happened. The vamps stayed down. Eli dropped to the ground, silently moved through the trees and up to the bodies, his weapon out.

"Any more of them?" I asked.

Eli said softly, into a mic, "Activity?" To me, he said,

"No. Alex found these two working their way in from the main road, through the trees. They startled a deer and it ran into the path of a laser monitor or we might have missed them. I'll be installing more cameras in the morning."

"Get Evan to help. He might be able to set some kind of far-ranging magical warning thingy in place."

"I'll be sure to ask for a magical warning thingy." He sounded amused. I grinned at him in the dark, showing lots of fang and teeth. He snorted softly. "They skirted the house and the cottages, taking photos, then came here, as if they had notification you were inside."

"Or someone told them about the sweathouse. Construction crew? Delivery help? How trustworthy are Kojo and Thema?"

"Shaddock says they've been bled and read and he knows the recesses of their minds."

"But?"

"Kojo and Thema are centuries older than Lincoln Shaddock," Eli said. "Not sure I'd trust the MOC on this." He tapped his mic. "Copy," he said into it. To me he added, "Kojo and Thema are on the way to carry the two back and interrogate them. Don't attack the friendlies."

I grunted and walked around the bodies, looking them over, checking pockets—empty—and clothing labels. Expensive Parisian clothing. Expensive Italian shoes. They carried a good dozen blades and two handguns each. I confiscated everything and started to close the sweathouse door. There was blood splattered on the wood in a swoosh I recognized, thrown from my claws. I had wondered if the house needed to be smudged before it could be used. Now it needed to be purified, ritually cleansed. *Crap.* I walked away, to face the creek farther down the hill.

On the frozen breeze, I smelled ginger, fresh-cut grass, and the trace of jasmine that identified the vamps Kojo and Thema. Didn't turn around. Didn't want to see them carting away our victims, enemies, and whatever else they were. Heard the two pick up the possibly dead vamps and carry them away.

I'd come back at dawn and cleanse the sweathouse, in

case my new spiritual Elder came calling through the snowfall. For now, I followed Eli back to the inn, ate a half gallon
of ice cream and a container of previously cooked pasta,
some of Shaddock's fantastic BBQ ribs, and half a chicken,
cold from the fridge. It was an odd combo, but I needed
calories and the sensation of eating solid food. Satisfied, I
crawled into the bed next to Bruiser and fell instantly
asleep.

The sky was only faintly gray when I stood outside the
sweathouse door again, hesitating, surprised, seeing that
someone—Eli—had washed off the splattered blood. I
touched the wood and looked around, up in the trees and
rock ledges. He wasn't visible, but I caught his scent on
the air. I said, "Thank you."

"Welcome," Eli said, his voice coming from far off,
keeping watch. "Want company for a bit?"

I smiled slightly. "Sure." Knowing I was safe, I went
inside, squatted at the fire pit, and studied the fire-starting
paraphernalia. In the center of the pit, I emptied out a
plastic zipped bag of flammable stuff: well-dried slivers of
beech and sycamore bark, lint, and what could have been
Brute's wolf hair. I untied a double handful of kindling,
slivers of pine and cedar heartwood, and layered that over
the lint with larger splits of well-dried oak. A book of
matches allowed me to light the fire, the sudden illumina-
tion and acrid stench of phosphorus mixing with potassium
chlorate, sulphur, and burned hair.

I sat on the cold ground, babied the flame as the kindling began to burn. Spotted a six-pack of bottled water
and downed two in succession as the flames caught the dry
wood. I sat at the fire and Eli entered, took a place across
from me, his movements silent. He smelled like snow and
a little like protein bars. He squatted so we were on a level
and I could feel his eyes on me.

"Janie, what's up?"

I thought a moment and went with the truth. "The
sweathouse has been complete for, what? Weeks? And I
already got blood on it."

"You're talented."

My half-form laugh sounded like a kitten growl. "Yeah. I'm good at blood. And death. And killing people."

"Janie." He sounded pitying. Which I hated. "You sitting here for a while? I'm going to check on the two fangheads and get some grub."

"Grub." I shook my head, smiling. "You mean a pile of greens and a chunk of steamed fish. Yeah. I'm going to sit here for a bit." I met his eyes in the firelight. "Have you slept at all?"

"Enough." He stood and put his hand on the top of my head for a moment in what felt like a benediction or blessing. He left me to my thoughts and closed the door on the dawn air. I felt, more than heard, him moving away.

I fed the fire. Added an oak log. Opened the herbs in the packages, put a stick of dried rosemary to the edge of the flame, and watched as it flared and smoked and scented the air. Thought about Hayyel and the dream. Vision. Whatever. Time passed. I began to sweat. My pelt darkened and lay flat to my skin. I hadn't known I could sweat in this form. It made me itch. I drank water. Scratched. Added herbs to the flame.

One packet of dried herbs was a white sage smudge stick and I held the tip to the fire, where it blazed up, faded to red hot, then to a smoking black ash. I stood and lifted the smoking smudge stick to the north, east, south, and west, the smoke rising and filling the small building. A peculiar sense of contentment began to fill me, as amorphous as the smudge smoke. I fed the fire and relit the smudge. I carried the smudge stick to the four corners of the room. Held the smoke high and watched it climb to the rafters. I prayed. Sat back down.

After a time, the door opened. The heat that had built up whooshed away. I didn't react in fear or surprise at the sudden interruption. I just sat there, smelling Eli and a woman on the air. He was close by, had brought her to me, which meant she was safe.

The woman stood in the open doorway, lit behind by snow and daybreak before she stepped inside and closed the door. She took off a coat and hung it on a hook by the door. Topped it off with a knitted hat that was crusted with snow. Unlaced snow boots and toed them off. She turned to me and put her hands on her hips, surveying me in the light of the fire. She didn't run screaming at my half-form or rap my knuckles, so I looked her over too.

She was mid- to late sixties, stout, with broad shoulders and a belly. Her arms beneath a pullover shirt and a loose sweater were strong, brawny. Her hips and thighs beneath jeans were muscular. She had jowls and a saggy neck. A complicated steel-gray braid hung over one shoulder to her waist. Her appearance was not the whole of her at all. She was stern, stable, well rooted in herself, a steel blade of a woman. "Aggie said you were a skinwalker but not a liver-eater. A shape-shifter but not a were. You look like a monster."

"I am a monster."

She snorted. "No doubt. You stink. Go jump in the creek. I checked and there's a deep pool just downstream of a log that fell across it. When you get back, strip and put on a tunic. I'll be smudging your sweathouse."

I thought about arguing, about telling her I had already smudged the building, but she likely had her own measures. I stood and moved to the door. She stepped aside. I went out into the cold and the door closed behind me as I looked around in the dull dawn light. I spotted Eli. So much for him taking a break. He was twenty feet high in a leafless tree, the branches a black etching in the grayness. He was securing a camera on the tree to cover the entire area. He paused and sat back on the branch he straddled, one hand on the camera. Wind gusts had died away and the air was so still and so cold it fairly crackled. The smoke from the sweathouse smelled strong and heavy, the air so lifeless that the smoke had fallen back to the ground and made a smoke-fog hanging two feet off the snow. I looked in the direction of the creek and back to Eli.

"The vamps?" My breath blew in a cloud and rested on the air.

"The silver rounds are proving to be a problem. They're too young to recover as fast as I'd like. Maybe I should have shot them a little less."

"Mmmm. Maybe, maybe not." I stuck a thumb at the creek. "I have to jump in the water."

"Better you than me." Eli grinned at me, that rare, fully open grin, showing teeth. "The water's about thirty-eight degrees. You're gonna freeze your ass off."

"Well, crap."

Eli laughed. "Swimming hole is that way." He pointed more downstream.

I walked to the creek, following a trail through the snow broken by the Elder. The bank where she had stood was twelve feet above the water; the far bank was low, sandy, and littered with driftwood and plastic water bottles sticking up above the snow, and raccoon poo that rested atop the frozen white blanket. Deer tracks showed that a herd drank from here, only yards from the house, almost as if they were taunting Beast. I found the log across the water and walked out over it, my paw-feet sure on the iced-over bark. The pool below me was deep and still and green. From upstream came the splashing of a small drop. Farther downstream the water picked up its pace again, louder with whitewater. I stripped and tossed my clothes to the bank. Took a breath. Closed my nose flaps. Stepped off the log. Plunged down. Deep. Blackness closed over me.

My entire body went into spasm at the cold. I forgot how to swim, how to breathe. How to even float. My heart raced. Panic chased through me. My throat closed up entirely. My feet hit bottom and buried to the knees in the muck. Blackness was intense. A waterlogged tree was jammed into the bottom beside me, branches broken. I hadn't thought about that possibility. I could have impaled myself. The only light was up, toward the air, where dawn was brightening the sky. I was growing cold fast. I reached out and pushed against the dead tree, pulling my buried feet from the mud and clay and rotting vegetation, and shoved off toward the surface.

I breached like a dying whale. Gasping in a breath that spasmed through my chest. Forcing my arms to move, I swam to the bank, my limbs already stiff and clumsy. I splashed too much trying to get to the high bank and then I had to figure out how to get up it. I grabbed twisted roots that seemed to come from a sycamore, pulling my weight up the nearly vertical hill. At the top, I staggered, so cold my heart was doing funny things. My pelt was drenched and I shook to get the water off, feeling like a dog as water shot out in a fine spray.

I sat on the snow, landing hard on a hidden root, my breath ragged and coarse. By my left knee, lying on top of the snow, was a brownish feather, eighteen inches long, wide near the shaft, narrowing midway down at the notch. The flight feather of a golden eagle. I looked up, from the feather to the sky, searching for the raptor, but saw nothing, and then down, along the trail the Elder had taken to and from the creek. Twenty feet upstream, her tracks marred the snow next to mine. There was no way she could have thrown this feather unless she tied it to a rock. The feather was resting on top of the snow, leaving no indentation, only the markings of the quill and, more faintly, the barbs, as if it had fallen slowly from the sky.

Carefully, I lifted the feather. Pulled myself to my feet, my knobby hands on a low branch of a tree. I was so cold I had stopped shaking and was feeling almost warm, which was a dangerous sign of hypothermia. That told me my half-form was subject to extreme temperatures. Good to know, if I survived the cold this time. Holding the feather in my right fingers, I pulled my icy but dry clothes on over my damp pelt and trudged to the sweathouse, my bare paw-feet barely lifting from the snow.

My toes caught a root. I tumbled into a drift. Face-planted. And the snow didn't feel cold. *Great. I* was *freezing to death.* I managed to struggle upright, to my feet. Eli was laughing, a hearty chuckle on the morning air. If my hands had worked, I'd have flipped him off. As if he knew what I was thinking, he laughed harder. I held on to the feather and, feeling like a drowned rat, made my way back to the sweathouse. Opened the door. Heat boiled out, steamy and herbal, and I closed the door behind me fast, breaking out into a shiver so violent my fangs clattered.

CHAPTER 8

Pain Is a River . . . and Anger Like a Great Fire

The woman wasn't watching me, so I set down the feather, stripped at the door, hung my damp clothes on an empty hook, and pulled on a shift from the stack on the table. Woven unbleached cotton with little nubs in the weave. I hauled it over my shoulders and tugged it down my wet body, and when I wasn't an embarrassment to myself, I picked up the feather and dropped my body at the fire pit, letting the heat soak into me. "That s-s-s-s-sucked."

"Mmmm. It was supposed to. I am Savannah Walkingstick of Long Hair Clan, an Elder of The People."

"Not my c-c-c-clan," I chattered, "not a skinwalker."

"No. There are no skinwalkers left among the Tsalagi."

Which meant she didn't know about my family. Interesting. "I'm here."

"You are a self-described monster. Skinwalkers were once the men and women who led us into battle. According to my grandfather, the last one was put down like a rabid dog in 1872, in Oklahoma, for eating the liver from the still-living body of a small child."

She was baiting me. Deliberately. Were her words part

of the ceremony? Or was she just mean? Or . . . she was afraid of me and this was a form of defense. Yeah. That.

I let her words sink in as I shivered, remembering the vision of Eli killing me when I turned into a liver-eater. Maybe there was a reason to fear me. I reached back and pulled my messy braid around to drip on the clay floor, my movement releasing the odor of wet cat. I placed the feather on the floor between my bent knees. "Why are you here? Why did Aggie One Feather pick you to lead me through ceremony and not someone like Hayalasti Sixmankiller? We're in the same clan." I leaned in toward the fire, though the heat was intense and my shivering increased.

Savannah sniffed. "That old woman? She may be old enough to be an Elder, but she has no wisdom or healing in her heart or hands. My father was an Elder and his father before him was a Medicine Man. I can lead you to healing of the spirit if such is possible for your kind of monster."

Which told me that Savannah didn't know that Sixmankiller was my grandmother. And she truly had no idea she was a skinwalker. Or how old she was. Interesting and interestinger. "And if my kind can't be led to healing?"

"Then I will help your people take you to the top of the mountain and throw you from the heights to the rocks below."

Well. At least she was honest.

She added shavings of wood to the fire and flame flared. The smell of cedar smoked into the room. Her eyes settled on the feather at my knees. "Where did you get the eagle feather?" she asked, though it was more a demand than a simple question.

"It was on the snow at the creek bank. I figured you put it there."

Savannah frowned at me, her lips and jowls pulling down hard, making vertical tracks in her face. "I would never give you a primary flight feather. Mother Eagle herself gave you that feather." Savannah snorted softly, a familiar, tribal sound, full of emotion. She clearly thought

Mother Eagle had made a bad choice. "Yesterday, an eagle left me a feather. A golden eagle tail feather. That we
both received a feather is a sign that we must work ceremony together." But she didn't sound too happy about it.

She went on. "Aggie One Feather and her mother have
led you through many ceremonies and I am not certain
that you can be healed. It is possible that you have walked
a path into death for so long that you are no longer able
to find a way to life, to healing, to Full Circle. But I will
guide you as well as I am able."

"Thank you, *Lisi*," I said.

She frowned harder. "At least you have learned humil-
ity. We will start with masks." She indicated my pelted
body.

"I am willing, *Lisi*."

She made a strange, ruminative sound. "Today we will
talk about this mask and your totem and your guide." She
blew through her nose again, but not so hard, not so full
of negativity. "You wear a mask, the mask that all others
would see as the face of a monster. Two questions. Why
do you not conform more to human shape? And how do
you see yourself?"

"I'm dying in my human form," I said, touching my
face. It was pelted and slightly numb from the cold. "I was
stupid and that stupidity gave me cancer."

"Stupid or foolish?"

"Probably a lot of both. I've spent my life taking
chances. That resulted in some spectacular wins and
some really bad losses."

Savannah was opening a packet of dried herbs and
said nothing, so I went on.

"My skinwalker magics are my own. My . . . my totem,
what I call my spirit animal, brought magics of her own,"
I said, speaking of Beast without naming her. "She is a
real and tangible presence inside me."

Walkingstick didn't disagree with my words, but I
could tell she disagreed in principle. I thought about telling her that I was two-souled but let it go. If she asked, I'd
tell. Maybe.

I said, "There are things I can't talk about, because

they aren't my secrets to tell, but suffice it to say, I fought a coven of black magic witches, and their magic . . . I guess you could say it pierced me. It left a trace of darkness inside me. It's been there for something like three years. And then, after I met rainbow dragons called arc-enciels, I was given the ability to timewalk by an angel of the light, one called Hayyel."

Savannah paused in pinching out bits of dried herbs and dropping them into a mortar for grinding, her fingers unmoving. "Dragons?" Her voice went up in pitch. "Angel? Timewalk?"

"Yeah. I can stop time. I can move outside of time. But every time I do, every time I did, I ripped my DNA. It's shredded and doubled. When I look at my genetic structure, instead of a double helix, I see four strands. The magics and cancer that are tangled up in my human middle are in the shape of a star—a witch's pentagram. I'm a mess. So yeah. I'm dying in my human form. I just discovered that I'm not dying in my half-form or my Beast form, so I'm staying in them for now."

"The angel . . . You saw this being? In person? Face-to-face?"

"Yes, *Lisi*."

She was silent for a while, adding herbs, but more slowly, and hesitant, as if she had lost her place. I wondered if she was a Christian or a pagan or a . . . whatever. Angels weren't necessarily considered real by all religions. She might now think I was concussed or nutso in addition to being a monster. Not a good combo.

"You can move *back* in time," she clarified. Not as if she didn't believe me, which was odd enough, but in a hopeful tone. Her eyes lifted from her own fingers to my face, hers filled with fear and hope and grief. "You can change things that happened in the past." Her words were laden with import, with dread and apprehension and agitation.

She saw the answer in my face, and her eyes went wider, then unfocused, her breathing shallow and fast. Her fear morphed into something different, and the scent of excitement erupted from her pores. This woman would go back into the past no matter the cost, if she could save someone, a particular loved one, who had suffered an injury or who had died unexpectedly. I nodded slowly. "There's a high price for timewalking. And sometimes you only make things worse."

Savannah dropped her eyes again. Her voice was without emotion when she said, "My daughter was raped by my boyfriend when she was twelve. I killed him. He was white so I went to jail for five years. You . . . You could go back and stop him." It was hopeful and desperate.

Pain is a river in her, Beast thought, *and anger like a great fire.*

"I have the gift," I said, sighing softly, my nose flaps moving. "But it's a curse too. I can see the timelines, the possibilities of each course of action. Changing history, even recent history, has negative results, sometimes really bad outcomes. The farther back you go, changing history, the more drastic are the shifts in the timeline. And, not to be selfish, but timewalking is killing me."

Anger burns her, Beast thought, sounding confused. *Man is dead, yet anger still burns her.*

That's called hate, I thought back. *And hate is never a single cut by a single blade.*

Savannah breathed in and out, the sound hard and full of the tumult Beast sensed. "Aggie said taking you to ceremony would remake me. I didn't believe her." She sat back, and I realized she was wearing a shift like mine, having changed while I was trying to drown and freeze my butt off. Now that my nose was warmer, I smelled the smoke of native tobacco and white sage from where she had purified the sweathouse for ceremony. "If . . ." She stopped, started again. "If you could change the past for my daughter, would you?"

I studied the woman sitting on the floor in front of me. I thought about what I would do to save Angie Baby if she had been the child Savannah described. And then, understanding opened a cold fist in my chest. "If I went back and stopped him, and I told your younger self that you had sent me back to stop him, would you believe that he had tried to hurt her? Or would you get angry and tell me I was crazy and defend him?"

She jerked and whipped back an arm as if she might hit me across the flames of the sacred fire. She stopped, her arm back, her body frozen. Her eyes went wide and then closed. Moisture gathered in her lashes, glistening in the flame light.

"You knew," I said. "You had an intuition and you ignored it. Or your daughter had complained about him and you ignored her."

The flames popped and cracked. Savannah's arm slowly dropped as tears trailed down her cheeks. "Chala hated him. She'd leave the room every time he was around. She was rude to him. And I didn't listen to her. There were warning signs. But I loved him so much that I ignored them. I was *stupid*. I was so . . . *stupid*."

"Been there. Done some stupid," I said.

"I'm a monster," she whispered, quoting me. I said nothing and her face hardened. Savannah's eyes opened. "I should get you another Elder. I'm not ready for this."

"You could," I said. "You probably should. Or"—I picked up the flight feather—"we could do this together. Long as you don't try to hit me again," I amended.

Savannah stuttered a laugh. "So this is a ceremony of healing for me too?" She reached over and pulled out her eagle feather from her pile of herb packets. "*Tail feather*," she said, as if that was a bad thing. "Presumably I'm to be looking into the past while you're meant to fly into the future. *Selu*, the corn mother, is laughing her ass off at me."

Savannah sighed and her body relaxed. She met my eyes. "I can't change the past. Like you, I can go only forward. Will you walk the Full Circle with me?"

"I will."

She nodded tiredly. "Let us talk about the masks we wear, your cat and my . . . pride. And anger. And shame."

Two hours later, we stopped and drank a decoction. It wasn't awful. It was actually pretty good. "Aggie gives me tea that tastes like roots and twigs and silt from the bayou."

"Aggie's clans are from a different persuasion than mine. Aggie's clans are from Eastern Cherokee and from Western Cherokee." She sniffed as if that was a bad thing. "The Western band got mixed up with the Cree, the Choctaw, Seminole, Creek, and Chickasaw. Their Medicine Men and Elders took too much from other tribes, picking a bit of this and a bit of that. Their ways are not always the same as Eastern Cherokee, and their herbs are not the same. Their medicine is not the same. Besides, you seem capable of inward thought without being drugged."

I almost said that she sounded prideful about her racial purity, but that was a mountain I didn't want to climb.

"Tell me about the dragon," she said.

I tossed back the cup of herbal tea. "There was a moment in my own home, when Gee DiMercy and Soul came to . . . visit. Kill me. Whatever. When I had first learned to timewalk."

The memory came to me on the scent of musky soap like something from a brothel. And the smell of Leo Pellissier's blood. It came in jumbled, overlapping, out-of-order images and smells and sensations, as if I was living them again and had just stabbed Leo. He'd had a silver stake in his belly, bleeding out on my floor in NOLA. Bethany, the not-quite-sane outclan priestess, had tugged the stake out of Leo. It made a gross sucking, grinding sound and black blood bubbled out after it, smelling of silver and death. The nutso priestess held her cut wrist over the open wound and blood dripped in, hers so thick it was almost congealed. Leo still looked dead. The smell of Bruiser's blood was on the air too. He was badly injured. There were too many vamps in my home, and the ones I halfway trusted were out of action.

An odd prickling sensation had raced over me. I knew that feeling. I was still holding weapons, which I gripped more firmly, staring at the front door. "We got more company coming. *L'arcenciel.* Coming from thataway." I pointed down the front street.

Eli had flipped the overturned couch over Alex and

Bruiser, just as the light, brilliant as the dawning sun, glared in through the broken front door in stained-glass tints, like fireworks, but silent, no pops or sizzling.

A long alligator snout had entered, full of teeth and widened into a frilled head big as a water buffalo. A massive arcenciel, with a flicking black tongue and giant eyes, orange and bright. Her teeth were pearly and the frill on her head white and red. Soul.

Gee DiMercy sank to his knees, mumbling in a language of consonants and hoarse coughing sounds. "Soul?" I asked. "You want to tell us what's happening?"

Her reply had been like bells ringing in an empty cathedral. "Your magics call to us. We see you in the Grayness Between Worlds. Your magics called the hatchling," she accused. "She followed you, yet you did not protect her. You allowed her to be taken."

"I did what?" I hadn't known there was a hatchling, or that young ones were emotionally unstable, sometimes violent. I hadn't protected the first hatchling on earth in millennia.

"You did not intend her harm?" Soul had asked, reading my face.

I shook my head.

"We old ones did not know there was a hatchling," Soul said. "There have been no young ones in over seven thousand years. Now her magic has vanished."

Gee said, "I will help you to find her and return her to the Waters of Life."

"Come to me, little bird," the arcenciel said. "I smell her scent on you. She bit you, yes?" Soul laughed, not unkindly. "Let's fly together. And you can tell me all you know of the hatchling." The memory broke up, pulling me back into the sweathouse, leaving me with a sense of something vital slipping away.

The hatchling. Not Soul's hatchling. And the hatchling would be *returned to the Waters of Life*. The ocean, I had presumed, at the time. But . . . what if the Waters of Life were the Grayness Between Worlds, as Soul had called them? I needed to talk to Soul.

For now, I told Savannah some of what I knew about

the dragons. Knew, not guessed, not ruminated on. *The facts, ma'am. Just the facts*, a line from an old TV show. I told her nothing about how to trap one or how to ride one. Nothing to bring hope to a woman so guilt-ridden and so needing to alter the past.

The Elder nodded, thoughtful, and changed the subject. "You have been many things in your life. And more than one person. Tell me all the names you have been."

For Tsalagi, names and titles were often one and the same, so that was a lot of things. I stretched back against the oak seat, and my body crinkled with the movement, pulling and burning in each crack and crevice. My pelt was crusted with salt. I didn't think pumas sweated, so this was all human sweat. I took a plastic bottle of water from Savannah and put it to my mouth, squeezed it flat, the water going straight down my throat. "I was given the baby name of *We-sa* at birth. Sometimes *Gvhe*. Then *Dalonige' i Digadoli*, Yellowrock Golden Eyes." I stopped.

"The white man gave you the name of Jane Doe. Later you added Yellowrock, yes?"

I nodded. *Dalonige' i meant gold, the gold dug from the mountains and found in the creeks. The gold the white man wanted so badly that he stole tribal land and sent the tribes west on the Trail of Tears.* The yellow eyes because skinwalker irises were yellowish. Neither were traditional or clan names. "And I've been Janie and Legs and Leo's Enforcer and Killer and Dark Queen."

"If you could rename yourself with any word that best fits who you are now, what would it be?"

Beast is better than Jane alone and puma alone, Beast thought at me. *Beast is more. Beast is us.*

Ahhhh . . . , I thought. "Beast."

"Beast. There is no Tsalagi word with the exact connotation as the English *Beast*. A better name might be *Tlvdatsi*," Savannah suggested, "panther. Since the human part of you is dying."

I had been a panther for far longer than I had ever been Jane, but that name was not quite right. "Beast," I said. "Just Beast."

The Elder tilted her head in acquiescence. "To find

healing," Savannah said softly, "we must accept what we are. For me it is to accept that I failed my child. That all my pride will always be false. That any success will always carry the taint of my failure. Do you accept that you are Beast? For the sake of healing, will you take that name for yourself for a time, as a reminder of personal sacrifice and strength?"

I breathed out a laugh, more whisper than anything else. "I'm not going to try to get that put on my driver's license, but sure. Yes. We are Beast. Not that I know what to do with a name."

I had slipped, but she didn't react to the pronoun *we*. "There is power in self-acceptance," she said. "In ceremony to change names."

"Who are you, then?" I asked.

"I have been, for many years, *Udalvquodi*. Arrogant," she translated for me. "I am now *Unastisgi*. Crazy. I do not know what I will become after I have moved through the liminality between one part of being and the next."

"What?" I asked, a stack of memories suddenly squirming at the back of my mind like worms on a fishhook.

At the expression on my face she went on. "All the worlds line up and down and all around, like the small pockets of a honeycomb." Savannah held up her hands, slightly cupped, and showed how the cups of a honeycomb rest one on the others in a pattern of strength and solidarity. "You, Beast, sit in the liminality between one part of being and the next. You are becoming a new thing. Hence the ceremony name."

"Liminality," I whispered. "That was it."

One of my stacked and squirming memories came clear to me. It was a conversation I had with Rick's cousin, Sarge Walker, a pilot who lived outside of Chauvin, Louisiana, south of Houma. He'd been talking about liminal lines and liminal thresholds. I had said to him, "I've heard of sites and places on Earth where the fabric of reality is thin, where one reality can bleed into another. Places where the coin stack of universes meet and mesh and sometimes things can cross over from one reality to another."

Sarge had replied, "Liminal thresholds are theoretical, the type of conjecture toyed with when physicists have drinking parties and alcohol loosens their tongues."

"I was told that the Earth has three liminal lines. They supposedly curve across the Earth. One starts in south-west Mexico, curves across the Gulf of Mexico to Chauvin, Louisiana, then follows the Appalachians east and north in a curve like the trade winds sometimes make, but more stable, static, bigger, and smoother. Then it curves across the ocean."

The memory faded, leaving behind the beginning of . . . something. Wisdom. A solution. A memory of an arcenciel long before current time.

I had been in Louisiana, and was now, once again, in the Appalachians, two places where one of the biggest liminal lines ran. A place where Beast had once seen a young arcenciel and let the young one eat her dinner. That realization made my salted pelt stand up on end. I had been pulled back and forth between parts of the world touched by liminal lines. Coincidence? Or serendipity? Or the plans of a higher being? *Hayyel. Dang it!*

"Beast. Beast?"

I raised my head to see Savannah. "Sorry. Woolgathering."

Beast wants to gather and eat sheep.

I laughed and the Elder glared at me.

The session broke up moments later, as if Savannah Walkingstick could tell I had been pulled out of the necessary frame of mind to continue. We dressed in our clothes, mine damp, sour, and stinky from creek water.

I walked her through the snow to her car and watched her leave, her four-wheel-drive making fresh tracks in more new-fallen snow.

When I was sure she was gone, I went to the house, to Alex's work area, and asked Alex to pull up a map of the liminal lines and ley lines. And to overlap them. There were way more than three lines of earth power. There were dozens of ley lines just across the U.S. And there were also a series of pentagrams across the U.S., formed by ley lines, perhaps the most clear one in the Southeast. One of the lines passed between southeast Louisiana and close to Asheville. "Well, dang," I whispered. I was right.

I touched my middle and investigated myself with Beast's eyes, eyes that could see magic better than my own eyes could. I might not have cancer in this form, but my own pentagram magics were still clear and potent. "Do me a favor," I said. "Start looking for any ley lines that run through this property, especially if it intersects this liminal line." I pointed.

"Why?" he asked, his voice dropping low, like mine.

I had a possible answer, but I wasn't ready to commit. *Hey, we have a ley line on this land. How's that for coincidence!* Not. Because if we did have a ley line near here, then I had to assume that Hayyel was involved in the happenstance of . . . of everything, making sure I purchased this land and would be here to discover it. Worse, despite his surprise when he realized that I had a magical tumor, it might be possible that Hayyel had participated in my getting sick. I didn't trust the angel. "Not sure yet. But it's worth checking out, to see if something magical or odd is close by."

"Okay fine. But you need to shower. You're"—his face took on an expression of glee, having caught me in a sin once often ascribed to him—"stinky."

"Yeah. I am." I ruffled his curls with my too-big hand and ran out of the room and up the stairs for the shower. Fortunately for my enjoyment, Shiloh was no longer lying in my tub.

CHAPTER 9

You Are the Dark Queen of Holding Grudges

I was trying to eat—my fangs made it hard to chew oatmeal—when a sleepy Alex brought my cell, his laptop, and three other tablets to the kitchen. It was as if he was moving his electronic HQ. He set the cell on the counter near my elbow. "Your brother," he said.

I glanced at the cell and at Eli. "Guess he doesn't mean you."

"Negative. I'm not a timewalker. Can't be here and on the phone to you at the same time. Take the call."

"Mmmm. Do I havta?"

Eli's lips did that twitchy thing that passed for a smile. Or gas. Or cramps.

"Fine. Speaker," I said. Alex tapped on the screen and the speaker came on. "Yellowrock here," I said.

"E-igido. Dalonige' i Digadoli," he said in the speech of The People. "I have received your message." *E-igido. My sister.* "I have also spoken to *Uni Lisi,* our grandmother. She wishes to *Nuwhtohiyada gotlvdi."* *Make peace.*

I thought about the memory of the longhouse and the

old woman and the outclan vampire. I started to reply and stopped. There was so much to learn. To remember. My silence went on too long.

"You cannot avoid family and clan forever, *e-igido*."

"Whatever. I'll just avoid you all as long as you avoided me." I sounded snarky, like a teenager with few social skills and less wisdom. And I didn't care. My gramma might have evil ends in mind. It wasn't like she had ever baked cookies for me. Not by a long shot. I smiled, knowing it wasn't a pretty one. "That means I can ignore you for a few years."

"Perhaps we deserve that. But your anger will eat at you from the inside, *e-igido*. I know this. I have dealt with my own anger. My own loss."

Littermate wishes to teach Jane. Beast was stretched out on a ledge in my mind, in the alcove that was her den in our soul home. Her tail snaked slowly back and forth, the gesture amused and irritated all at once, as only a cat can be. *Jane is Beast. Beast is best hunter. Beast does not need male littermate to teach.*

I upended a liter of Gatorade, crushing the bottle with a crackle of plastic, forcing the liquid down my throat. It was empty in two seconds. I tossed the plastic in the recycle bin, where it rattled. *"Usdiga,"* I said, in Tsalagi, using a term I hadn't known I remembered, one that meant *baby boy*, or *little brother*, a word that could be kind or insulting depending on circumstances and tone. Mine made it a faint insult. "I don't have a lot of time right now. Family reunions will have to wait until I live or die. You got my message so you know the Son of Darkness Number Two, aka the Son of Shadows, aka Shimon Bar-Judas, aka Shimon Bar-Ioudas, aka the Flayer of Mithrans, is on his way to Asheville. You know I'll likely have to fight him."

Ayatas didn't answer right away. Maybe I was on hold. Maybe he fell asleep. I was ready to hang up when he replied, his tone all business, no longer family oriented. "PsyLED is tracking this vampire, as are a number of state and federal agencies and departments. The Flayer of Mithrans will not be a problem to you, my sister."

"Sure. Because they've done such a bang-up job so far, protecting the humans and me from the big bad uglies. I'm betting that with the exception of you, it's a humans-only tracking team after Shimon, and not one single witch or vamp in the group."

"He will not concern you," Ayatas ground out. "Stay out of this."

I rubbed my forehead, feeling a headache coming on. "I'm safe. Everyone is safe. The gov'ment is gonna protect us all. Forgive me if I have little confidence in any of you."

Ayatas sighed through his nose, a Cherokee breath that could mean so many things in different contexts. It brought an unexpected, but short-lived, sense of comfort to me. He said, "You do not have clearance for anything I might know." He hesitated. I waited. "However, I know a great deal about the creature called the Son of Shadows. One of my units has done some digging and we believe a core group—or a splinter group—of his people have been in the States for some time. Several of my people are quietly tracking him."

Onscreen, the footage replayed, two vehicles pulled up in my driveway and the blond vamp ripped out the throat of my scion. They had known where I lived. I shared that insight with Ayatas and added, "You may be right that there are splinter groups here, or antagonistic groups here." They had bled and read Shiloh and she had told them everything because she was weak and unprotected. I had left her weak and unprotected, when she could have been safe with Amy Lynn Brown and Clan Shaddock. She was part of my clan and she had been tortured on my watch. "They know where I am," I said softly.

He was silent, and I wondered if he was multitasking, not really paying attention. He asked, "Is your home defensible?"

"Now, that was a good question, *usdiga*. I'm impressed. It isn't defendable against rocket launchers or tanks, but we aren't sitting ducks." And one group of vamps might think we have two of their people, who might actually both be true-dead from Eli's silver-shot. Didn't say that.

Nope. "Shimon officially arrives in town tonight at dusk for parley. I plan to do all the talking and chitchat at . . ." I stopped. "At an agreed-upon location, one where all the humans have been sent away, so no locals will become collateral. If there's a war, with blood and guts and casualties, it'll take place out here, at the winery, far from the tourists."

"Tell me where he will be. I can help. In my official capacity."

As opposed to his brotherly capacity. He was speaking in the voice of PsyLED, not whatever another option might be. And I knew that if the government was involved, they might just bomb the hotel and to hell with any human casualties. Or Edmund. I nearly whispered, saying, "No. If it comes to a fight, better hope I win, because if I die, he'll become your official problem, *little brother*. And it won't be fun and games, like the Sangre Duello. It'll be war. You might want to have the National Guard on standby with rocket launchers and tanks just in case."

He didn't reply to that one. And it let me know I had been right about the kind of help that was being offered.

"Where is Soul?" I asked.

"You haven't heard from her?"

Which wasn't an answer. I hated it when people played games. It made me want to claw them, maybe draw a little blood, make a point.

Beast is best hunter. Want to hunt with littermate. Track and eat big deer.

I thought you were ticked off with him. And not right now, I thought back at my other half.

"Soul took some vacation time, and she's due back. She hasn't checked in with HQ yet, which is unlike her. The director fears that something has happened to her."

I put his comments together and said, "You think she's been taken by fangheads? Kidnapped?" *Along with Edmund and Tex and Ronald and Derek,* which I didn't say aloud. Ayatas didn't answer. Soul in the clutches of the Flayer would be bad. Very, *very* bad. Soul was the only creature keeping the arcenciels in check from changing the timeline. I remembered the visions of war I had seen in my soul home.

I shifted my gaze to Alex. On his laptop, he was already tracking Soul through credit card use and cell phone. I did not want to know how he had that access.

"I . . . do not know," Ayatas said slowly. Which, again, was not an answer.

"Or she's tracking the Son of Shadows and is too busy to get back to you." Or she's doing arcenciel stuff. My bet was door number two.

"I'll be in touch, or one of my people will." I ended the call without saying goodbye and ate two big spoonfuls of hard-to-chew oatmeal, thinking. The oats tasted strange in this form, and felt odd on my meat-tearing teeth; the sweet taste of sugar was barely there, but the milk was the elixir of the gods. I tilted my head to Eli. "You think I'm holding grudges?"

"Babe." His tone was reproving.

"Janie, you are the Dark Queen of holding grudges," Alex said.

"Grudges and hate make you weak," Eli said.

"Is it justified?"

"Oh yeah. But remember that Ayatas is under orders and can't help freely the way your clan members can. He's constrained by the law, his vow of office, and his own honor. Your Cherokee family is an asset you aren't using, out of pique, when they could probably be helpful. Keep all that in mind." Eli, being all strategy on me, suggesting I use my by-blood family as a tool instead of treating them as people who had hurt me. That was an interesting way of viewing things. Cold and heartless, but interesting.

To Alex I said, "Update me on the liminal lines."

He spun one of his tablets to me, and on it, a map of the world spread out, crisscrossed by lines in reds and blues and yellows. "There's more than three. One liminal line runs from NOLA through Hot Springs, to New York State. Another runs from the Bahamas and through the mountains of NC." He traced blue lines that moved in arcs like trade winds. "They cross ley lines all over the place." The ley lines were red, and they could be straight or curled or could follow riverbeds or other geological features.

"How about interdimensional shift openings?"

"For starters, the Bermuda Triangle. Maybe here." He pointed to a spot in the Atlantic Ocean. "And here"—he pointed to Greece—"is a maybe. Here in the Sangre de Cristo Mountains could be another. And here." He shifted his finger to a place under the waters of the Gulf of Mexico. "It's close to where you were rescued by the arcenciels not so long ago. I'm guessing they were keeping an eye on the spot where they used to travel back and forth." His eyes were sunken and there were dark circles beneath them. "All the rift openings were lost in some tectonic shift."

I wasn't sure what any of that meant, but I knew Alex needed rest. The big bad uglies would be in Asheville at dusk. I patted him on the shoulder. "Get some sleep. That's an order."

It was noon and the house was full of a hundred children all running and screaming through the open space. That was the way it sounded anyway, as I climbed the stairs and fell into bed. I was about to find out what would happen if I went to sleep in half-form. I closed my eyes and fell into slumber.

I woke to the feel of my whiskers being pulled. "Ow. That hurts!" I said, grabbing the little hand.

"Dis isna a How'oween costume," EJ said. "You tolded me a lie."

"How did he get in here?" Bruiser asked from my other side.

"He's got magic," I said.

"Not good magic. Waymon dead. I hadda stick him in the ground. It made me cwy."

I checked to make sure all the private parts were covered or pelted and sat up. "Who's Waymon?"

"Him my tu-tle. Mama said you sick like Waymon. Are you gonna die? Can we bury you in the backyard with Waymon?"

"Um, no. I do not intend to die and you may not bury me."

EJ pouted for all of five seconds. "You wanna see my maaarbal?" He pulled a marble out of his pocket. It was a large white one with a blue cat's-eye swirl in the middle. I was groggy with sleep but something about it hinted that I shouldn't touch the marble. In Beast-vision it was magicked, a small golden sparkle of power against the little boy's hand. It was a version of a *no-see-ums* working. Maybe a *no-touch-ums* working. And beneath that was a *tracking device* working. It was a multilayered charm and it glowed with power.

"Mama says I gotta keep it in my pawket all the time." He put it back in his pocket and patted his jeans. "My sissy gots one too, but hers is purple." He leaned in and kissed my cheek. "Don' die tonight, Ant Jane." He slid off the bed and out the door, his little feet stomping down the hallway.

Bruiser reached out an arm and encircled my waist, pulling me close to him, my butt against his middle. He nuzzled my neck. And started snoring. It made me smile and I closed my eyes as sleep pulled me back under.

I woke screaming. Fighting. Pain like my flesh being flayed from my back.

"Jane! Jane, it's a dream! Jane, stop fighting!" Bruiser's voice, afraid. The smell of his blood on the air.

I went still, chest heaving, unballed my fists. Tried to slow my breathing. Couldn't. "Edmund. They're skinning him alive."

From the doorway, Eli said gently, "We're here, Janie. We'll handle it." A weapon made clicking noises as he safetied it.

We'll handle it. Because I couldn't. "He's in a bedroom. In the Regal. There was a parley there once. I recognized the room Grégoire, or maybe it was Leo, stayed in." I looked at Bruiser. "You're bleeding."

He gave me that devil-may-care grin he had worn when I first met him. "My fiancée packs a punch."

From the open door, I heard screaming. *Angie Baby.* The electric sensation of her magic swept through the inn. I threw back the covers and raced from the room, pulling on Beast's strength and speed. The house was the dusky dark of heavy clouds and densely falling snow, lamps lit and tiny stairway bulbs glowing. Took the staircase in a single leap. Landed three-pawed and sped across the central magic area into the far wing and the panicked screams and the smell of magic. I caught myself on the doorjambs and swung to a stop in the open door. Angie was on the floor, a coloring book open and crayons scattered everywhere, but she wasn't coloring. She was on her back, her fingers stretched up, screaming. Her magic writhed and twisted, rising, tightening, trying to form a tornado of pure, raw energy.

Big Evan stood over her, playing his wooden flute. Molly stood at his side, feet braced, arms to the sides, hands pointed downward, drawing power from the earth. She was sweating. On the bed, the baby had started to cry, a thin, demanding wail. Eli slipped in, sprinted to Cassy, rolled across the bed, gathering her up, his momentum rotating them both to safety. Little Evan was sitting on the bed, watching, a finger in his mouth.

There was no circle. Nothing to contain the magics Molly and Evan were working with and fighting. I'd seen them trying to contain their daughter's raw power before. That time she had ripped the roof off the house.

Bruiser placed the Glob in my hand and *le breloque* on my head. The crown sealed itself to me. Freaky as always. I studied the Everhart-Trueblood magics.

There was no circle. Nothing I would disrupt. I walked toward the three. Molly's eyes snapped to mine. Her face was strained and desperate, and I could almost feel the death magics pushing against her control. Her mouth formed one silent word: *Help.*

I circled to the side, so Evan could see me too. His eyes were tight, the skin at the corners wrinkled, face pale against his red beard. He worked to maintain a steady breath and soothing notes, watching me. I knelt by Angie and . . . stopped. *Flying. Crap.* It was okay to fly without knowing the rules if it was just me who got hurt. But—

"Hurry," Molly said, her voice hoarse.

Eli disappeared from the room, the baby and EJ each

over a shoulder, taking them to safety. I gripped the Glob so it didn't touch anything but my hand. And placed my fist on Angie's chest.

Nothing happened.

All in or nothing. I thought, *Okay, you feathered flying angel. She calls you* her *angel. Save her!* I touched the Glob to Angie's chest.

And the magic storm that was my godchild stopped. Just stopped.

The stone and iron and wood splinter and Blood Diamond and whatever parts of my own body had gone into making the Glob heated. The Blood Diamond had been used to steal children's magics, but in the past, the children had to die first. This time the Glob sucked up the excess magics, Angie's and Molly's and Evan's too, ripping them out of the air.

Angie sighed and fell asleep. Molly fell onto the bed. Big Evan dropped like a rock, falling toward me and his daughter. I grabbed Angie up and somersaulted across the room. Banged my head and elbow on the wall and an end table. Big Evan landed and the floor shook.

I came up to my feet.

I was holding child and Glob, the magical talisman out to the side. A vamp stood in the doorway. In daylight. Storm light. Whatever. It wasn't natural, except for the dark of the storm and the age of the vamp. Thema carried a sword and a ten-mil.

"Son a wish ona swish," Molly said, the consonants mostly missing, the vowels drunken.

"'M unna uke," Big Evan said.

"You puke, you clean," Eli said, reappearing. He stepped around the vamp standing in the doorway and added, to her this time, "She needs a bottle. There's breast milk in the freezer and a card with microwave instructions."

"I am not a nurse for human children," Thema said. "I am not a blood-servant to stoop to such duties." Eli plopped Cassy into her arms. Thema's eyes went wide. The baby, hungry, stopped wailing, rolled her head, and nuzzled at Thema's chest. "Ahhh. Ahhh . . . ," Thema said, holding the baby away from her like she might a wriggling skunk.

Big Evan gagged and vomited all over the rug.

I stood, holding a sleeping witch child. "Where's EJ?"

"In the workout room with Alex."

"Gimme," Molly said, pushing up to a sit, one arm out at me. I placed Angie on her lap. "What the hell was all that?" she asked as she drew a trickle of power from the earth and the surrounding woods and magically inspected her infant and eldest daughter. Milk stained the front of her clothing, her body reacting to the need and terror of her children.

"I still have a connection to Ed. He's using it to let me know he's close to breaking. When he let down his shields, some of his pain must have filtered through his link with Angie." I had no idea how much the child had absorbed or would remember, but even a microsecond of Ed's torture couldn't be good for her. I turned my head to Eli. "Pack up. It's early, but we're heading to that parley."

"I'm coming," Molly said. "Lemme shower off the milk and fear sweat and then nurse Cassy. No need to make the fangheads salivate."

"I'm comin' too," Big Evan said, pushing his bulk to his knees and then to his feet, grunting. Before Eli could say anything: "I know, I know. After I clean my mess off your fancy rug and shower off the stink. We'll be ready in fifteen."

"Who will take care of our children?" Molly demanded.

"Shiloh?" I asked. "If she's healed enough?" Shiloh was their niece and a witch-vamp too.

"I do not know how to work a microwave," Thema said from the door, a hint of panic in her tone. "I do not know what to do with this child. I will fight all of the warriors of the Flayer of Mithrans myself alone, if someone will take this *bébé*."

Cassy began to scream. It was a high-pitched, demanding, furious wail. Thema looked as if she might faint. Or drop the infant. Or toss her like a basketball on fire.

"I'll take her," a soft voice said from the side. It was one of Lincoln's servants, Barbara, or maybe Bridget.

Something with a *B*. She gave a soft smile as Thema all but flung the child at her. "I'm an empty nester for over thirty years, but some things you don't forget, like how to take care of a little one. Hey there, sweetums. Let's get your tumtum some mama's milk, yes, that's a good baby."

"Tumtum?" Thema said, before adding what might have been a prayer or a curse word in that liquid African language.

"I've called Lincoln to let him know we need Shiloh and to gear up to meet the visitors," B said as she wended her way to the kitchens, bouncing the baby in her arms.

I shook my head at the utter composure of some blood-servants. Squalling babies, kids out cold, vamps in panic mode, witches on the floor, me in half-form, and ... tumtum. "Shaddock trains his scions and chooses his clan members well," I said. "I'll be ready. How are we getting to Asheville? Shaddock's snowmobiles will take hours."

"Weather is holding," Eli said. "No reason we can't take Grégoire's helo."

I stopped and turned back to my partner. "You still got the helo up here?"

"It never left Asheville Regional Airport. Pilot will set down on the front lawn inside of thirty."

That would be dusk for real. Probably true-dark and zero visibility in this weather. "Good work, Ranger man. You"—I pointed at Thema—"gear up. You said you'd fight the warriors of the Flayer of Mithrans? Well, you might get your wish. The Dark Queen commands your presence." I almost said *Look alive*, but that might have been taken as snark by the undead woman.

I raced up the stairs and stripped, shoved aside the new armor Eli had ordered for me, and pulled on the older, scarlet fighting leathers and my double gorgets. I tucked my father's fragile medicine bag inside my own, mostly empty, much more modern one. Eli had made it for me, telling me it was time to live my life as the Cherokee did, by Full Circle and harmony. I had done nothing with the bag, putting it off because I was dying. I sealed the bags into a pocket in the lining of my beat-up red leather jacket, thinking that I should have done what Eli said and tried to find some harmony sooner. I sorta kinda needed some harmony right now.

I considered the sword I'd practiced with but never mastered and put it aside. Instead I sheathed the vamp-killer I'd used when I was fighting Titus, the former European emperor. I'd taken his head with the steel-edged, long-bladed, silver-plated knife, one created especially for beheading vampires. I added the curved Mughal ceremonial blade, arranging it across my middle in its scarlet scabbard. These were the same blades I had used when I took the head of the Son of Darkness too. My lucky blades. I snorted with amusement.

No guns. Eli would have enough weaponry to take down a T. rex. No holy water, because it was old and the blessing wore off after time. I shoved seven silver stakes into the sheaths on my left outer thigh and seven ash wood ones into the sheaths on the right. Added all my throwing knives, which included the one I had thrown at the SOD to shut his sorry yapper up, long before I killed him. Three lucky blades. *Coolio.*

I combed out my hair, yanking on the tangles, and left it loose, like a taunt, an insult. *You're such a poor fighter I didn't even bother to braid my hair out of the way.* That kind of taunt. I rearranged *le breloque* on my head and studied myself in the bathroom mirror. The scarlet nails were the perfect complement to the red leathers. Thought about putting red lipstick on my cat lips. I raised my lips, showing my fangs.

Beast chuffed. *Would look like kill. As if Jane ate enemy as prey.*

"In that case I should paint Brute's mouth."

"I beg your pardon?" Bruiser asked from the bedroom doorway.

I chuckled, liking the vicious sound of my Beast-voice, feeling strong and in control. "Nothing. You look spiffy."

He was dressed in deep charcoal armor, nearly black, from head to toe. Military-style stuff, except tight, to show off muscle and weapons, and solid-color matte, no camo. He stood beside me, one arm slipping around me, pulling me tight to him, not the gentle caress he gave my human shape, but a firm, almost demanding pressure. In combat boots he stood five and a half inches taller than me in my bare paws. I reached up and scruffed my knuckles across his beard. "Don't get killed."

"Don't get killed," he echoed.

Outside, I heard the sound of the helo. "Who's guarding the inn?"

"Shaddock's humans are guarding the children and Alex, who is well trained with firearms, thanks to his sessions on the range. Stop worrying." He indicated the front lawn. "After you, my Dark Queen."

This was the helo's third trip into Asheville, which was possible only because the refurbished Bell Huey had new deicer systems on the rotors, couplings, windows, and pretty much every other part. A storm system slid along the mountain range, which always made the weather unpredictable, but Eli had kept a bored former military pilot on retainer to fly at a moment's notice. The first two runs had brought in equipment and the support team. I had watched them take off from the parking lot at the inn, two of the heavily dressed bodies carrying long cases and gear bags that clanked, probably long-distance rifles or maybe that rocket launcher I had thought about, as well as equipment for accessing empty buildings and getting to the roofs. B and E stuff. I didn't want to know. Even with the extra seats removed and multiple trips, the refurbished Vietnam-era Bell Huey could only carry a few people, so it wasn't like we had many fighters on our side.

Kojo, Thema, Shaddock, Eli, and several of Shaddock's humans with combat experience were already in place—people risking their lives and their undeaths trying to save my friend. For this trip, the seats had been put back in and the passengers were Molly, Big Evan, and me strapped into chairs, with Bruiser crouched down in the cargo section behind the seats. I had forgotten how horrible the vibration was. No ear protectors worked on my not-human-shaped head and the sound was deafening. Beast growled and complained the whole way. I ignored her.

The Huey jostled hard on landing. The empty parking

lot on Hendersonville Road chosen by the pilot as landing site hadn't been scraped and was still carpeted in
many inches of white, the asphalt beneath deceptively
lower. Fortunately or otherwise there were so many of us
in the helo that we didn't slam against anything hard
enough to injure, though my teeth did clack together. We
disembarked from both sides and sped away from the helicopter, through clouds of prop-dusted snow, good cover
as we raced into the protection offered by a brick wall. Eli
appeared out of the night, shouting over his comms systems. He asked how we were, filed away the answers,
filled us in on who was where, and passed out headgear
with mics and earbuds.

Mine didn't fit. We had never tested for my higher-
than-human cattish ears. Beast chuffed in amusement as
Eli made a fix that included a part of a plastic spoon, some
duct tape, and an extra shoelace. The shoestring tied
under my chin, hidden in my pelt. It might have been a
pretty cool idea except that the spoon was red and the
duct tape was some special-order pink stuff. Not badass at
all. But it worked and that would have to do. As he
worked, the snow stopped and the city lights flickered,
throwing us into snow-bright darkness. The earbud crackled. I adjusted the mouthpiece.

"Yellowrock, you copy?" Alex asked into the earbud.

"I copy." The helo rotored out of sight. The city lights
came back on, a dull yellow that slowly brightened.

"Listen up," Eli said. "Everyone maintain prearranged
positions unless fired upon. Thema at my ten. Kojo at six."
That made Kojo the best shot, and me the one who was
being protected. A well-armed human woman appeared
out of the weather and took her place at Kojo's side.

My partner moved into point in a crouched run, in the
glow of streetlights reflecting from the snow. The Regal's
entrance was ahead on the corner. Eli was dressed in his
cold clothes but I could see him in Beast's vision, weaponed up like a black-ops mercenary on a limitless budget.
Which he was, I realized. Money for this situation was
almost unlimited, the constraints on our equipment
solely a product of time and the weather. With more time

and opportunity, every bell and whistle known to the military could have been ours. And would be soon, I figured.

I spotted others in the dark. Half the people with us had headsets with multiple oculars or single multifunction oculars: low-light, IR. One guy had a virtual-reality-style headset but with only one ocular, for reasons I didn't understand until I saw the drone in his hands. He scraped the snow off a patch of blacktop, placed the device with its four rotors and multidirectional cameras in the center and the explosive device mounted underneath, and the drone took off, almost silent in the constant low hum of the distant snow movers.

The air felt warmer than it had, but that thought must have jinxed us because the sky opened up and sleet began to whisper down, then to patter down, then to flood. This was going to make egress slippery. Ten seconds later, the drone came down in a clattering heap of broken rotors and shattered high-impact-plastic body. The pilot acted as if he'd lost his best friend.

Eli glanced to me across the night and I nodded, indicating that I was going ahead with the mission to rescue Edmund. Into comms, he said, "DQ and Shaddock in the center, behind Dumas. Everhart behind the DQ, Trueblood behind her. Kojo at the rear. Kojo, I don't see you. Kojo you copy?"

"I *copy*. I am here." The words were terse and irritated. Kojo seemed like the type to want to be at the front of the squad, leading the attack, not at the back protecting us all. I glanced around and spotted the warrior, partially concealed behind a snow-blanketed car in the adjacent parking area.

Our current pattern was like a diamond, the center group tightly positioned, the outer, diamond-shaped ring flaring to the side and in front, with shooters at high points on nearby roofs, providing cover.

"Alex," I asked over the mic. "Does our guest know we've arrived for parley?" I'd been convinced not to walk into a hail of weapons fire by surprising a vamp in his lair.

"He's expecting you."

"Move out," Eli said. The sleet began to beat down

hard, strafing into my pelt and burrowing in deep where it would either melt and trickle or clump up like small snowballs and chill me.

Hate sleet, Beast thought.

Following Bruiser, I focused on my footing, on getting around the piles of snow left by snowplows, concentrated on the scents in the air: roasted meat, salmon, human blood, the mingled stink of unfamiliar vamps, and the stench of something dead riding high on the air, possibly on top of the hotel. Beast's puma paws were designed to keep snow from packing in between the toe and center pads. Our half-form paw-feet were more human-shaped, and snow and sleet packed under our toenails with every step.

We entered beneath the arch on the corner, Eli and Thema slipping into the shadows and inside. Bruiser and Shaddock conferred, something about shock value and entertainment value getting us what we wanted. I shook snow out of my pelt. Molly and Evan held hands, Molly's eyes closed, her lips moving. She was speaking a working, her magics clear and lively, not the dark night of her death magics. Evan was humming, his music a focal no one else might notice. No one, meaning the vamps and their servants inside. Evan was once again putting his witch-in-hiding status on the line, this time for a man he knew only because of me. They should have taken the kids and gone home.

I had to get Ed. Now. Fast. And get my people out.

The main doors opened. I stood straight and tall. Strode into the building and past the reception area. No one was behind the counter. No one alive anyway. Bloody boots stuck out from behind.

We pushed through to the interior. The heat was like a furnace, dry and slightly smoky. "The Dark Queen," Bruiser announced, his voice echoing as I passed into the main room, "and the Master of the City, Lincoln Shaddock."

The furniture that was usually placed in the receiving room was pushed back against the walls, leaving the space open. The fireplace was massive, four-sided, centered between four pillars, and everything in the room was arranged around it, meaning the vamps standing in a semicircle.

My eyes adjusted to the lights quickly and I slowed as the room opened out, giving me time to take in the tableau, because no way was this unstaged. The humans were sitting on the floor at the feet of the vamps, some bleeding and in chains, others giving the impression of pets with pretty collars around their necks. There were dozens of humans and twelve vamps. Twelve powerful vamps, the entire group except for three wearing pure white. Something moved in the background, a fast blur of darkness with a flash of crimson, behind the vamps and humans. It was gone before I could tell what it was.

Set to the side of the enormous fireplace was a gold throne. A gold-plated throne, rather. It had been constructed of what looked like femur bones and human skulls coated with heavy layers of gold. Shimon was literally sitting on the bones of his enemies.

Just inside the main room, I stopped. The people with me stopped and spread out, Lincoln at my left shoulder, the witches just behind him. The humans with us spread out into the fringes, acquiring firing positions sufficient to avoid hitting us. Our few to Shimon's bunches.

Ed was lying at the base of the throne, at the feet of his torturer. Ed had been skinned, from his buttocks, up across his scalp, to his forehead. From his hips, up his stomach and chest, to his chin.

I didn't scream. I didn't wail. I didn't attack. I showed my fangs. I extruded my scarlet claws and gripped the Mughal hilt near my waist. I forced a snarl of a smile instead of giving in to the scream that was riding at its heels. Shimon had tortured my heir. *My friend.* He hadn't done that by accident, but I didn't know what the Flayer's goal was, so I waited, though all I wanted was to attack Shimon and save my primo.

Edmund's head raised. "The tribal woman comes to call," he said, sounding unlike himself. Understanding came fast. My primo was still speaking the thoughts of his captor. The vamp was in his head. Shimon was posed, lounging back on the gold, his long black hair flowing over his chest, a chest that was covered in a chitinous armor, shining and hard. I had seen this before, in Natchez, Mississippi. It was an exoskeleton like that grown by the vamps there, who had undergone mutation and become partially insectile in reaction to too much . . . too much time magic. *Oh crap.* I had focused in so intently on the arcenciel time magic and my own timewalking that I had forgotten about witch time circle magic. This magic took multiple witches and a nonstop working circle and large quantities of the iron spike of Golgotha. The witches forced into the time circle had no choice, no way to get free, no way to stop the working. The working killed them, one after another.

Shimon was watching me and must have seen my understanding because he suddenly relaxed, smiling. "Yes. You see what is possible for the Sons of Darkness." His lips didn't move with the words, but there was no doubt who was speaking to me through Edmund's tortured lips. "The magic of time," he said, in case I misunderstood.

Somewhere he had put witches into a time circle and forced them to work it, and they were dying. They were tools, nothing more. Like his possession and control and torture of Edmund. I'd kill the Flayer of Mithrans for Ed alone.

Hayyel would be tickled pink.

Before I could speak, Lincoln stepped around me. "It is my belief that both of the Sons of Darkness could read. Yet, here you are, in my city, without presenting yourself to me, in di-*rect* contradiction of the original Vampira Carta, and the Vampira Carta of the Americas. You owe me fealty, you foul creature."

"Kill the Dark Queen, give unto me her magical items, and I will depart your shores."

"Ain't happenin'," he said, sounding more mountain man than Blood Master. "I reckon you and me'll have to battle, then. Once my queen's done thrashing your butt, expect to meet me on the field of battle at dusk. Of course, that's assumin' there's enough of you left to fight."

While Shaddock spoke, I had let my snarl fade away into disdainful neutrality. "You will release my primo to me," I said, sounding bored.

"You will release my brother to me," Shimon said, sounding bored-er.

I laughed, managing to sound entirely unperturbed. From my peripheral vision, I watched as Eli and Thema maneuvered around the room for the best firing positions. The unchained humans on the floor watched too, their hands hidden. Yeah. Too many against our few. Bruiser was to my left. Molly shuffled to my right. Big Evan moved behind her, humming so low it vanished into nothingness. Magic rose on the air. Shimon didn't seem to notice. He had no witches with him and either he had changed himself too much to use his own witch magic, or his control of Edmund kept him from seeing and hearing the magic I felt rising in the air.

When my laughter trailed off, I sighed, stealing a ploy from Leo's playbook, shaking my head. "Ah, *mon ami.* I bring you a sad tiding. Joses is . . ." I tapped one claw, one time, on the jade hilt, as if looking for a better word. Tapped again, the sound ringing in the sudden silence. ". . . dead."

"Foolish female," Ed's lips said. "The Sons of Darkness cannot be killed. We are truly immortal."

"Not so. Dead. Headless, heartless, chopped up into small pieces." I let my smile widen, showing my fangs. "For starters."

The last hints of the languid pose vanished as Shimon sat up. "Where is my brother? What have you done with the pieces of his body?"

"Give me my primo."

Edmund began to scream. The wail was unlike anything I had ever heard, a note so painful it hurt my ears like fingernails on a blackboard, like rats being roasted alive over a fire, like piano strings made from the guts of a human prisoner, but ten times louder than any of these sounds. The hair on the back of my neck stood on end, my ear tabs folded over in reaction, and my eardrums vibrated stridently. He was killing Edmund with just the power of his mind. I caught sight of the thing in the background again, but it was gone too fast to register as more than a charcoal-bright blur. It moved fast enough to be a vamp, but it didn't look human-shaped.

Moving slowly, so the gathered would know that I wasn't attacking, I pulled the Mughal blade and the vamp-killer. I had never properly cleaned the blades. They were still coated with the blood of Joses and Titus. I grinned, showing all my teeth, all my viciousness. "I killed your brother with these knives. And I'm going to kill you."

CHAPTER 10

After I Chopped Him into Kibble, I Fed Him to the Wolf

The screaming note went silent. The stillness ached with its absence, and Shimon sniffed the air. His black-on-black eyes widened as he recognized his brother's blood scent in the rancid stench of decay, even over the stench of the assembled vamps and the herbal scent of Ed's fresh blood. Edmund took a breath. "Impossible," Shimon said with Ed's lips.

"Problem," Kojo said across the public channel, in my earbud. "Do you see? Shall I let it pass?"

"Affirmative," Alex said into the comms system.

I smelled him before I saw him and I started to laugh for real. Brute appeared, jostling Evan aside, shoving between Lincoln and me, his head at my hip, all three hundred plus pounds of him. The white werewolf was growling, the sound like boulders grinding, like grizzlies fighting. He had missed the helo ride, but an angel-touched werewolf who could timewalk didn't exactly need a helo. There was no grindylow with him, which was odd in a room full of humans, but that was a problem for another time.

So softly that the Flayer of Mithrans had to lean in to

hear, I said, "On the contrary, you bucket of crap. After I chopped him into kibble, I fed him to the wolf." Brute growled again. More Leo-like, I repeated, "Let my primo go. Abase yourself to your betters. Or suffer the evil that will follow."

"My brother is not dead. I would know this. Therefore you lie."

I remembered the heart in New Orleans, kept by Jodi and the witches, safe from this thing. But I didn't let that show on my face. Maybe he really could tell there was a scrap of his brother left alive. What did I know? "Give me Edmund Hartley."

Into my earbud Alex said, "The woman in purple, standing against the fireplace pillar. Her name is Monique Giovanni. She's Onorio from Italy."

"Copy that," Bruiser murmured. He focused on the woman, who had brown hair and skin the color of hazelnuts. Monique was wearing a shade of purple that reminded me of black grapes. Her eyes shot to Bruiser and she went pale. The sensation of magic kicked up a notch, peppery and electric on my pelt tips. She had been about to drain one of our vampires. Now she was too engaged in a mental Onorio battle to hurt my people.

In Shimon's syntax, Edmund said, "Perhaps we might effect a trade. Offer me something I would want. Or someone." I didn't know which of my people he thought he could trade for, but that wasn't happening. His fingers fanned out, casually, "It is said that you have found the iron spike of Golgotha, and that it is yours. I have an appreciation for antiquities. I will trade your primo for this artifact."

Leo had once said, *"The Europeans' greatest desire is for the remaining iron from the spike of Golgotha."* Because the iron could control vamps and witches and time itself. The iron and its magic were the most powerful metal on Earth. Shimon had to have a small piece at least, in order to create a time circle and to chitinize his own body. I had a few pieces, but not a full spike, not that I'd tell him that. Beside me, Bruiser began to breathe harder. I smelled his sweat. "No," I said. "Give me Edmund Hartley."

The sensation of magic in the room went even higher. I thought my ear tabs might burn from the power. "You will give unto me this spike," he said, his tone laced with mesmerism, directed straight at me.

My knees went weak. My stomach went sour and sick, and my skinwalker magics began to race. I wanted to throw up, pass out, run with my tail between my legs. The Flayer could create fear, paralyzing terror. I couldn't even breathe.

Beast growled deep inside, pierced my brain with her claws. The pain was needle sharp, and I settled. I managed a breath. I didn't spew. "I will give you nothing," I said, sounding almost like myself. "You will give me Edmund Hartley."

The Flayer laughed, the sound like velvet and brandy and the stink of human ashes. Leo had never laughed so powerfully, so full of might. Beast sent steel into our knees or they might have buckled. "No," he said. "I have claimed him. You have lost him. The thing you call Edmund is mine by right of might."

Impasse. I stepped to the side, seeing Eli. He was in firing position, halfway concealed in a niche behind an open door. My fingers twitched toward my throwing knives.

To the side of the insectoid Shimon, two of his vampires fell, dropping as if dead. My first thought was Bruiser. But he was busy. So . . . Molly and death magics. As the vamps landed and bounced slightly, she inhaled, nostrils fluttering, excited, satisfied, yet wanting more. Her eyes closed in ecstasy. It was like sex and desire and power all mixed in together.

Shimon flinched. Just a little. His eyes flicked to my side, to Molly's face. He said something with his own mouth, words Ed had never heard or couldn't interpret, a curse for certain. Recognition, rage, a hint of something else in Shimon's eyes. *Avarice.* He wanted Molly or wanted her dead. *He knew what she was.*

Edmund was bleeding from his eyes, watery, bloody tears. He was lying on his side, draped over the feet of the last Son of Darkness. Two more vamps dropped. Ed's mouth fell open; his eyes rolled back in his head. Shimon was killing him. I forgot to breathe. Molly chuckled, an evil witch cackle of pleasure and absolute strength.

Evan hummed a note so high his voice nearly broke. Stress drained his face to a pasty white. Wild hunger lit Molly's. Bruiser, on my other side, was gasping, his magics erratic, rapidly depleting as he fought his first Onorio.

Evan took Molly's hand and altered the note he hummed. They were working together to control the death magics and point them at the enemy, at Shimon, but he didn't fall, didn't react at all. Molly was close to losing control and frying everyone in the room. Everyone *except* Shimon.

The Flayer's eyes fell on the big witch, knowing Evan for a sorcerer. Greed brightened his eyes. He wanted them both. He lifted a hand as if he was about to throw a stone.

Magic. Danger! Beast thought.

I didn't have time to plan. I flicked the throwing knife at Shimon. It missed the seam in the carapace at his neck and bounced off his chest. *Oh crap.*

The vamps in the semicircle all stepped forward, in unison, under the control of one mind. No wonder Shimon hadn't felt Evan's and Molly's magic. He was fully engaged, using his own.

His vamps each pulled handguns. Fast. Aimed them at our tight group.

We were outnumbered, outgunned.

We were screwed.

Unless I could pull off a bluff.

I managed not to throw up and in my best Dark Queen royal hauteur, I said, "Let Edmund go or we will kill all of your people and go on with our business. And Brute"—I placed a hand on his furry head—"will eat the evidence. Are you hungry, Brute?" The werewolf chuffed, tongue dangling, white fangs showing in a doggy smile. The weapons instantly re-aimed. All of them at Brute and me. *Oh goody. Yeah, that helped.*

Time slid sideways, that battlefield slowdown where I saw, felt, heard, knew, everything, in layers of tactics and potential outcomes. Everything happened in slow motion.

In a flash of sapphire light, Gee appeared in front of me.

"Hold!" Gee shouted, throwing his blue-on-blue magics into the air. Shimon's head rocked back against the gold-plated skull of an enemy with a *thonk*, like the sound of a war drum struck by an enemy's skeletal fingers. In a single instant, he bounded to his feet. His jaw ratcheting wide. Six-inch fangs snapped down. The elongated teeth were black as night, the color of obsidian. The tips of his fangs touched his carapace.

The vamps around him readied their weapons for firing, multiple *schnicks*, bright and dangerous. Eli murmured, "Aim high, vamps only, upper chest. No collateral damage. The humans may not be acting of their own volition."

Evan whistled a single note. A *hedge of thorns* snapped up around us, the magical shield glittering and visible, but not strong. It might slow the rounds as they fired. But . . . Shimon didn't know how weak the *hedge* was.

"Hold!" Gee shouted again. He looked healed, whole, but Gee DiMercy was magic wrapped in spells and tied up with glamour. He could be missing limbs and I wasn't sure we'd see that. His magic swirled into the room, a vibrant blue.

Time still in battle phase, two more vamps fell, their weapons clattering to the floor. Molly was laughing softly, whispering, "Yes, yes, *yes.*"

On Gee's shoulder stood a lizard, striped and swirled in shades of red and blue and vibrant green. I knew that lizard. Gee had taken him from a vamp I killed. Now it had scarlet wings, had morphed into a miniature lizard-dragon. It leaped. The lizard dove at the woman in purple and took a bite from her ear lobe. Monique jerked, pulled from the fight for a microsecond. Bruiser managed a shaky breath and firmed his stance, but the woman snarled at him and leaned into the battle as blood trickled down her neck.

The lizard whipped around the room and flew back to

Gee. It hovered over Gee's head, scarlet wings moving so fast they were a red smudge in the air. The SOD Two leaned forward. Silent. Watching the lizard and the Onorio battle. He coveted everything he saw. Until another vamp fell. This one landed across Shimon's arm and slid to the floor.

Shimon said, "Why should I listen to you, Misericord? You and your kind killed my young and stole my Mercy Blade from me."

"Your long-chained were never coming back. They had raved for a thousand years and it was long past their time." Gee leaned in, looking taller and more muscular than normal. His skin darker, hair in dozens of braids. "You caged your Mercy Blade and stabbed at her mind." His voice dropped down into a lower register. "Misericords do *not* sing for your pleasure." He pointed at Edmund. "Give him to my queen or suffer another attack by my kind."

The Flayer snarled, fingers tapping on a femur.

Edmund rolled over and stood. He lifted one foot and took a step toward us. Another. Another.

"Moll, stop," I said softly. "Please."

"Yes. Okay. Stopping," she said, staccato. But I could hear her need, her craving for death's power in her voice.

Ed stumbled and Gee raced forward. Caught him, the small man leaning into the bloody muscle of Edmund's abdomen and picking him up. Speaking fast, Gee said, "We are grateful for the act of bounty bestowed upon us by the Flayer of Mithrans."

A woman dressed in white, standing near Shimon, turned to him and slid her weapon into her clothes. "We are magnanimous. This once," she said, in the strange intonation Ed had used. I figured she was now interpreting.

Gee turned with his burden and glanced at the *hedge*, his eyes saying, *Let it down. Let's go.* Aloud, the words urgent, he said, "My *Queen*."

The *hedge* didn't fall. Bruiser was wavering on his feet. Monique Giovanni was equally exhausted, her purple dress sweat-stained, but she was clearly older, more

experienced and more powerful. She was going to win.
The vamps still standing still had guns. The lizard flew in
a flashing, stuttering circle around the room, Shimon's
eyes following. Another vamp fell, this one bleeding from
her mouth. The Flayer turned his eyes to his people and,
oddly, he looked uncertain, as though he hadn't realized
that his people were falling.

Bug creature has not seen his children fall, Beast
thought. *Has not seen lizard fly. Has not seen half-form of
Beast. Bug creature is confused. Is not used to being confused.*

Ahhh, I thought. "Put down your weapons and we'll
leave in peace," I said, urging his momentary indecision.
Shoot us and we're all dead. Didn't say that.

The woman at the Flayer's side began to bleed in a
scarlet stripe down her left side. I realized that the flaying
of the vamp's flesh was the result of the Flayer of Mithrans using her brain. He took his title from the act of
using his magic. *What a peach.*

Beast pawed to the front of our minds and peered out
at her. *Is not fruit. Woman vampire smells ugly. Like
smell of sick flashlight. Same as vampires killed in snow
at sweathouse.*

*Bad batteries. Acidic. Yeah. Though I'm not sure what
it means or if we can use that.*

Shimon, his eyes locked onto Molly's face, waved a neg-
ligent hand. His vampires' weapons disappeared. Their
hands reappeared in front of them and clasped together,
like some bizarre synchronized dance of parade rest.

Edmund's hands twitched too. I wondered if Shimon
had left a listening/control bug in Edmund's brain. *Crap.*

The Trueblood *hedge* fell in a showy shower of red
sparks. The lizard flashed through the air to Gee's shoulder and curled his striped tail around the Mercy Blade's
neck. Bruiser staggered.

"Have your people call my people," I said, somehow
pulling off the ironic, mocking tone I was going for.
"We'll do dinner. Parley. Talk politics. Religion. Killing
people. The usual."

Shimon and the bleeding woman laughed together, sounding eerily exact.

Gee carrying Ed, Evan steadying Bruiser with a hand on his arm, Molly breathing hard and fast, we backed out the door and into a blowing, black night, storming with sleet. The city power grid went off, leaving us in total darkness for too many heartbeats. It flickered on and off a few times, and steadied in the on position. Lightning lanced across the sky. The wind and ice cut through my pelt like frozen knives.

Shaddock eased up to my honeybunch and offered his sliced wrist to the drained Onorio. Bruiser took the wrist in shaking hands, pulled the MOC's wrist to his mouth, and drank. I turned my attention to my partner and listened in.

"Say again," Eli said into his mic. He cursed, soft, succinct, savage. To me, he said, "Our transport is in a ditch. We're on our own."

"How does a transport vehicle end up in a ditch?" I asked, because I knew Eli and Shaddock had planned for all eventualities.

"Apparently the driver had a snort of liquid warmth and drove off the road. His backup is—was—a pair of four-by-fours and they're buried beneath a ton of plowed snow, for which we can thank the city of Asheville's snowplows."

Do not like sleet! Beast thought.

In the distance I heard the sound of snowplows, brining trucks, and the fainter sound of a police siren. Then more sirens, closer to us, and I feared for a moment that the vamps in the Regal had called the cops. Even in North Carolina it would probably result in days of paperwork to have so many weapons on hand and dead bodies in the hotel, but the units turned away.

Eli said, "Follow me," and ducked into the driving storm. We trailed him. Eli tapped his mic and went onto a private channel for a discussion with someone, likely the Huey pilot, and oddly, he left me out of the loop. As we raced across the street into the protection of a covered doorway, I thought about being left out for a good dozen steaming, ragged breaths, my small clouds swept away by the icy wind. I'd been sick for months. Eli had, in the way of command structure, moved on. I was proud and sad and jealous and angry all at once, so I kept my mouth closed on any of the things I might have said. We huddled in the doorway, the sickly smell of Ed's blood making my insides crawl. My primo was asleep, and hopefully not suffering. Bruiser leaned against a wall, looking like a broken doll, his eyes closed, his face pale, even after sipping on vamp blood. He seemed to be having trouble catching his breath.

Brute eased up beside Bruiser and sat, pressing his shoulder and his wolf-warmth against the Onorio.

Shaddock leaned in to him and said, "You'll feed from my wrist every evening as long as I'm here. No argument, young'un." I could have kissed the MOC. Bruiser murmured his thanks.

Eli said, "Master of the City. Can you offer us safe haven?"

"Can't do much about the weather or the lack of power, but I can call my people and get us to the restaurant. I can start a wood fire and feed you reheated barbeque," Shaddock said with a very human grin, "and bed you down on the floor in the kitchen, but there's no power, and it's on the other side of town. Gimme a little time and I'll roll or bribe a tow-truck driver to get us there, but it'll take a while.

Eli tapped the mic back to the public channel and then off. To Shaddock and me, he said, "Rock meet hard place. All the hotels are filled. All the B and Bs within walking distance are filled. There's no vacancy anywhere. No readily accessible, defensible, empty buildings to take over and hunker down in. The city shelters are unprotected against fanghead attack and are too far off site to reach them on foot in the storm." He swept his eyes over the buildings and up and down the street.

Shaddock said to me, "I can commandeer a snowplow or steal a car. You just say the word, but again, that takes time and the storm is getting worse by the second, Jane."

"Sitrep," Eli said, and I gave a chin jut to show I was listening. "Anyone not evac'd out will bivouac in a hostile environment. Freezing to death or being attacked by enemy vamps is no better than the possibility of crashing in the helo. It's *possible* for the Huey to take off into a sleet storm, but that will mean the choice of either flying through the sleet and risk icing up, or flying above the storm in the warmer inversion layer to get out of the bad weather, and that risks the weather change at each altitude transition.

"He hasn't made a decision on whether he's willing to risk it, but if he decides to make a run, he'll carry a maximum of seven passengers. In the event he does decide to transport you, his flight plan and altitude will depend on a lot of factors, like the position of the storm, wind speed, the altitude of the inversion layer compared to our current altitude, and the altitude of the inn. And he might have to alter everything at any moment."

"So it's wait out the storm here together or split up and it's gonna suck on board. Got it. Where did the storm come from?" I asked.

Eli gave his barely there twitch of a smile, knowing what I was asking. "Not magic. We've been keeping an eye on two weather fronts. We're currently right on the edge of both, giving us this," he pointed up.

He turned his attention to Moll and Evan. "The helo's upgraded deicing systems are the same currently in use on Marine Hueys. The pilot will go through a deicing process before taking off, and the helo has ice meters that tell him how much ice is building up on the frame of the helicopter while in flight. But any ice accumulation on the rotors doesn't just mean they'll be heavy; it means they warp, in which case he lands fast or you crash. I've seen the bodies of people who crashed. It isn't pretty and there's no walking away from it."

Molly shivered and exchanged that silent communication common between old married couples. She nodded and frowned, thinking. Evan studied the sky. Eli scanned the streets again and back to us. Lightning ripped across the sky and thunder boomed like distant cannon.

"No matter how bad it gets here," Eli said, "I'd rather you stick it out on the ground. It's safer."

"No. We have to get back to the inn," Molly said, with the resolute tone of a mama bear. "Our children are there."

Eli nodded and turned away, talking to the pilot again.

Angie Baby. Alone. A ticking time bomb with no finesse. Shiloh the only witch on the premises to keep her in check, a Shiloh who was still healing from having her throat ripped out.

EJ, all power and no training.

Only Shiloh . . .

"We have to go back," I said. "Bruiser?"

He shook his head, eyes closed, his lips barely moving, saying, "Too sick. I'll wait it out here."

"He needs to feed again," Shaddock said, "now and often." He sliced his wrist with a tiny black blade and again offered it to Bruiser, who drank a few more sips before pushing the meal away.

"It's been a while since I had blood. Can't take more. I'll be okay until nightfall, as long as I don't use my magic again until then." Bruiser opened his eyes and managed a sickly smile, directed at me. "Promise."

I wanted him with me, but there wasn't a lot I could do about it. Silently I slid my eyes from Eli to Bruiser and back, asking Eli to take care of him.

My partner tilted his head. "You know I will."

I took a breath, thinking. *Seven of us.* "Ed, of course." I almost said Gee could fly on his own, but I saw the Mercy Blade's blue healing magics spreading over Edmund's body and Ed was still out cold. Gee was using his Anzu magics to keep Ed unconscious and out of pain. "Gee and Shaddock, with me, if you're willing?" Gee and Shaddock nodded agreement. I steeled my heart and said, "One of the Everhart-Truebloods because if we crash, they'll have one parent left."

Molly paled, her red hair blowing and sparkling with sleet. Evan, the air witch, whistled under his breath, his gaze far away, thinking, evaluating the storm.

I said, "That's five, so two others, whoever we need most. No gear. No weapons. Light load. We can send in four-wheelers or the snowmobiles and the sleds to bring back anyone who stays, but it will be midmorning at the soonest. Decide quick, people." It felt good to make demands. Real good.

"I'd be mighty appreciative if Kojo and Thema could go. If the storm shifts, they might not survive a sunny day without proper cover."

Eli tapped his mic, again talking to the pilot: "One lift, seven passengers. How does it look?" He listened and talked, his face grim. "Copy. Extraction point? Copy. Thank you, Captain. You make it, and there's a bonus. Yeah, in addition to living to see the dawn," he said with humor, his eyes glancing at me, "we'll make sure you have a bunk for tonight."

I nodded. The pilot would be unable to get back to Asheville. We'd put him up.

Eli finished, "I owe you. Out." To the rest of us, he said, "Okay. We have a hike to the extraction point. Who's on the Huey?"

"I am," Molly said.

"Moll—" Evan started.

"No. You have a chance to keep that storm front to the west. To help adjust the inversion layer higher or lower, where the pilot needs it. You can't do that in the air; you need a circle, on the ground."

"You can do that?" Eli asked.

Big Evan sighed, the sound gusting from his barrel chest, audible even over the storm. "I can help. My magic isn't geared for weather, but I know the methods and I have my pipes." He patted his coat, where I assume he kept his flutes, which were his weapons of war. "But I don't like it, Moll."

Molly slid her arm through her husband's. "I know. But it's best. Besides, I'm so cold I'd never survive out here. My milk would freeze."

I wanted to laugh, pretty sure that was a joke. But not totally. Could a mother's milk freeze in her boobs? Before I could decide how to ask that, Eli led the way into the blowing snow and sleet.

Lincoln stepped into place beside me where I trudged at the back of the group, trying to shake the compacted

ice balls from under my toenails with each step. It wasn't
working and Lincoln's eyes were sparkling with laughter
at my leg shaking and foot waggling. He said, "There's
lizards that do that dance step." Before I could respond
he said, "I'll summon Kojo and Thema. We'll keep the
humans and the witch lady alive in the event of a crash."
He looked me over with a critical eye. "You can shift and
live, right?"

"Theoretically." My Beast *might* survive a leap out of
a slowly falling helicopter.

Big Evan said to Eli, "The Cathedral of All Souls is
that way." He pointed off to our right. "An Episcopal
church. I know one of the lay ministers or whatever they're
called. I've sent a text, hoping I can get us permission to
use the premises."

"Good thought," Eli said. "We won't have barbeque,
but a church is the safest place we can hole up. Let's get
your wife on board the Huey."

The sound of rotors cut through the air.

The ride through the storm was cold and miserable, once
again deafening without the ear protectors. The turbulence slammed us around until we hit the inversion layer,
where the wind whipped in the other direction and rain
beat against the windshield and windows all around, and
the Huey tried to turn upside down, just for funzies.

Beast growled through my mouth and complained the
whole way about being in the belly of a metal bird. Halfway there, Molly threw up from the turbulence. The smell
of vomit and Ed's torn flesh and old blood and soured
breast milk were not a good combination. We were all . . .
Wretched was a good word. Completely wretched.

My stomach wasn't happy and the stench meant that
Beast was having kittens about it all, bouncing off the
walls of my/our brain. It was funny and annoying and I
knew she would get me back for making her fly again. I'd
probably wake up human, lying in mud two feet deep, or
perched naked on a billboard. Beast chuffed in amusement and settled at that thought, planning evil against me
as only cats can. Go, me, for giving her the idea.

For a while, in the inversion layer, we leveled out, but that part of the trip was short and the passage back into the storm, with winds in the opposite direction as we descended to land, was horrible. The landing was more a controlled crash, and I heard metal things popping and twanging and snapping. The Dark Queen would have to repair her Warlord's Huey. My teeth snapped together on a final bump. The skids settled.

"Ladies and gentlemen, thank you for choosing Bell Huey Airlines," the pilot said. "Watch your step as you disembark. And I thank you for the bunk on the layover."

The rotors began their slowdown whine as Molly ducked and raced for the house. Lincoln, Kojo, Thema, and Gee, carrying Edmund, climbed out of the Huey and traipsed around to the back of the property. I glanced at the pilot, realizing I didn't know his name, and decided he was busy. "Thank you," I shouted to him. He didn't look up, but he did give me thumbs-up. I stepped to the ice-slicked, crunchy ground, following the vamps and Edmund (who looked like a slab of raw meat slung over Gee's shoulder) around the house to the finished cottages. The little Anzu was a lot stronger than he looked.

Lincoln opened the door to cottage one, the unit set aside for Edmund, and the inside lights came on. The cottage was set up like a four-star hotel suite, the décor in whites and grays, with a king bed, two pullout couches, an Oriental rug, a small kitchenette with quartz cabinet tops, and a bath that could have been designed right out of an HGTV makeover.

Gee carried Edmund to the bath and put a knee on the edge of the tub. Kojo came up behind him and together they lowered him to the bottom, Gee holding Ed's head to keep it from bouncing on the porcelain. Gee stood up and backed away, as Lincoln stepped into the bathroom doorway behind me, pulling off his T-shirt.

It was not what I was expecting, all that expanse of flesh and ripping, rippling, striated muscle pressing beneath skin. Hairy bare chest and nipples and—

I jerked my eyes away but not before Thema noticed me looking. At my side, she said softly, "He is indeed a fine-looking piece of man flesh. Though his bum is lacking, I fear."

Before I could figure out how to respond or how to stop the shock that flushed beneath my pelt, Edmund's head raised. Fangs clicked down, the sound barely registering in time for my eyes to snap back. Before I could shout a warning, Lincoln Shaddock *moved*. Popped into the small space beside me. Caught Edmund's head. Directed Ed's desperate, insane dash for lifesaving blood to his own neck. Edmund savaged the flesh, biting, biting, sucking in the blood. Lincoln slid his arms around Ed, his voice hoarse from the fangs so near his larynx, saying, "I gotcha, bub. I gotcha."

Tears filled my eyes and I said to the Master of the City of Asheville, "Thank you."

"No problem, Queenie. It's my job." As master of a city, it truly was, and I inclined my head. Shaddock added, "Invading vamps in my city. Injuring a Mithran without my leave. Didn't even bother to present themselves to me? I got me lotsa cogitating to do on just how to react to this'un, and how I'll take his head," he said.

Ed gulped and gulped, sucking down blood like a starving man. There was no sanity in his eyes. I had seen Leo blood-starved. Leo had tortured me after he was drained. I fought down the memory-fear and the old horror. The effect on vampires' brains wasn't pretty, and sometimes vamps didn't come back from that precipice. Neither did their victims. I steadied my breathing before the nearby vamps caught the scent of yesterday's fear.

"He has been deeply traumatized," Gee said, his eyes fastened to the two in the tub. The Mercy Blade was perched on the closed toilet seat, his posture much like that of a big bird, his arms tucked up and his knees beneath his chin. In the white tub, Lincoln was smeared with thin blood and Edmund was breathing in and out, an almost inaudible whine with each breath.

From beside the tub, Kojo said softly, "The Son of Shadows is a dark cloud. His mind eats at the brain and the heart with fangs unlike any other. His magics slice the skin from our bones. I still carry his scars on my soul." He shook his head, his scalp beneath his short-cropped hair catching the light. "I cannot feed one who has been a vessel for the shadow."

"Why?" I asked, just as softly.

"For fear the darkness will find its way to me again through my blood." That sounded like black magic and demon possession all at once. I knew blood demons existed, but my understanding was limited. Maybe demons could pass through shared blood as well as familial bloodlines.

Thema called for Shaddock's human blood-meals on her cell. She asked for six. That meant the rest of the vamps would be more hungry than usual. When her call was over, I asked, "Is there a chance that Edmund's brain is tied to Shimon's? That the SOD can hear everything we say?"

Kojo shrugged, an odd, disconnected movement of his shoulders, as if those muscles were out of sync with the others. "Your Edmund is very powerful. But there is nothing upon the face of the Earth like the Flayer of Mithrans and his shadow when one is possessed. Anything is possible."

That was an unconventional way of phrasing it. The smell of Edmund's blood on the air was so strong that I only realized Molly was walking up behind me when she spoke. "Edmund swore loyalty to me," she said, "and to Angie and to my family." She let a small breath go, shifted her position closer to my side. She was nursing, rotating slightly, swaying slowly side to side, Cassy in a sling. The scent of baby, mother's milk, and the purity of earth magic was intense. Her darker power was back under lock and magical key, and Molly's relief at being with her children seeped through her pores, strong and clean. "It's an Everhart responsibility to protect him. I have some shielding workings I can try, to protect his mind and to guarantee that we have privacy."

Kits. Keep kits safe, Beast thought at me.

"Are you sure?" I asked, seeing the small head at the crease of her upper arm, barely visible beneath a cloth diaper she had placed over herself to nurse. Smart, considering that some vamps were evil dark creatures and I didn't know where Lincoln's newest stood on the sanctity of children. Then I remembered the death magics Molly had used at the Regal, and the vamps falling. Moll was not in danger.

She looked up at me as if hearing my thoughts and led the way back into the living area of the cottage. "They weren't dead. They're drained. The vamps back at the hotel," she clarified softly. "And yes, I'm sure. It's what a Glinda does."

I chuckled at the name. She was talking about Glinda the Good Witch, from *The Wizard of Oz*. I peeked back into the bathroom and saw Shaddock tap on the tub, three times, like a TV wrestler asking for backup. Thema took his place, guiding Ed's fangs out of Lincoln and to her throat.

Molly dug into her pocket, held out her hand, and dropped a small, carved amulet into mine. Everything went silent and my eyes shot open wide. She took it back and placed it on the coffee table at the foot of the sofa, restoring the ambient sound. "It's a monkey ear charm. You know, like the monkey with his ears covered? Put it on Ed. He won't be able to hear us strategize."

"In case the big bad ugly is still in his brain. Gotcha." I lifted the wooden round and carried it to Ed, where I tucked it under his armpit. His flesh was icy. Dead. I removed my hand perhaps a little too fast.

Molly chuckled, the sound wry and darkly amused. I could almost hear her say, "Big bad vamp hunter can't stand the touch of a harmless vamp."

"Gee," I said. "Talk to us about arceniels. About the problem or war or whatever is going on in their world or their relationship with each other." When he didn't reply, I said, "Soul isn't calling anyone back. So far as I know, she's never gone dark before."

Gee tightened his arms and legs, as if trying to preserve body heat or as if trying not to be noticed by a predator, shrinking small. The tiny striped snout stuck out of his collar, the winged lizard, curious. "There is a war," he

said, "between Soul and the other arcenciels on this
plane. Since you killed Joses Santana, the elder Son of
Darkness, the younglings have fallen away from guidance
and counsel and wisdom. Soul has battled this past
week to bring them back to the true path. The pres-
sures of leadership have driven her into lack of control,
into foolish acts. Her mistakes have cost the goddesses
greatly."

"Why would me killing the Flayer of Mithrans cause a
war between the arcenciels?"

"I do not know." Which was ominous.

Molly's cell rang and I saw the name on the speaker
face. Amelia, her sister. "Hey, sis," Molly said, "what's—
Wait. Let me put this on speaker." One-handed, she
shifted the cell and pressed the SPEAKER button on the
face. "Say that again so everyone can hear."

"We're under attack," Amelia said. "Regan and I were
working late at the Seven and got stuck here by the storm.
We were on cots with lanterns lit when fangheads attacked. We initiated the building's defenses and we're
armed, but the bad guys are not going away."

Amelia and Regan were Molly's human sisters. The
Seven was Seven Sassy Sisters, the family restaurant. The
defenses were probably some form of *hedge of thorns*
around the building, one that could be released by a simple command or a touch to an amulet, by a human. Last
time I checked in with them, the human sisters carried
concealed and were always armed, which was smart for
anyone working late in an isolated location, and doubly
smart for a member of a witch family anywhere. Amelia
kept a twelve-gauge behind the counter. Regan carried
two very different semiautomatics with matte black
grips—an H&K with silver-laced nine-mils for vamps, and
an S&W loaded with hollow points for humans and rob-
bers. The Everhart family was not rich. They'd be out of
vamp-killing ammo fast.

"Hold tight," Shaddock said. "I got a few scions laired
not too far from there. Providing they can get the snowmobiles running, reinforcements will be there in ten.

Maybe fifteen with the storm." He pressed his own cell against his ear and turned away to talk.

"Who was that?" Amelia asked. I heard breaking glass. Someone had gotten through the outer defenses. Gunfire followed, punctuated by the piercing ululation of a vamp dying. "Again. Who was that?" she demanded, shouting.

"Lincoln Shaddock," I said, loud enough to be heard in her gunfire-damaged hearing. "The Master of the City of Asheville. He's sending reinforcements. Don't shoot the rescuers."

Amelia said some very unladylike curse words. Molly laughed and patted her baby's back, burping Cassy.

Beast was deeply interested in the infant on Molly's shoulder, her entire body language protective and covetous. Mentally, I stroked the head of my other half and she thought at me, *Kit in danger from injured vampire Edmund?*

I thought back, *Molly is a death witch who just drained but didn't kill some vamps. I think she's got it in hand.* Aloud I said, "You got stakes? Holy water?"

"Stakes, if it comes to that," Regan said from farther away. "I'm boiling water. A good scalding hurts no matter if the flesh is dead or not."

"Undead. Not dead," Thema said from her position feeding Edmund.

"Yeah? We can arm-wrestle over that distinction if I live through this," Regan said. Then she challenged, "Whoever you are."

"I am Thema. I am a Mithran. We will arm-wrestle. If you win," Thema said, readjusting Ed's head against her throat, much like Moll readjusted the baby's head against her breast, "I will part with a small gold statue of the Buddha that I stole from a temple over two hundred years ago. What will I gain should I win over your puny human arms?"

It hit me that Thema was distracting the humans until help could arrive. It made me want to kiss the vampire, but I figured she needed blood badly right now and I might get bitten for my trouble.

"If you win, I'll give you an amulet made by my sisters. It lets you see witch magic three different times," Regan said. "That's worth more than gold."

"I will not argue with this," Thema said. "Done."

The outer door opened and humans filed into the cottage, slamming the door after, shutting out the storm. I knelt at the fireplace in the main room and coaxed the wood to light. Shaddock, now wearing a shirt, directed his humans to feed my Edmund, who had become calm and controlled enough to not attack and kill. The MOC checked his watch. Made another call. There were more gunshots over the cell connected to the store. Then the boom of the shotgun. No vamps screamed this time. I could hear the human sisters breathing hard, ragged.

I realized what I had just thought. *My Edmund.* I was thinking and feeling about Ed as if he belonged to me, just the way Leo had said, *"My Jane,"* claiming me. That started an itch under my collar, but before I could deal with that, Molly called out, "Jane. Call Carmen. She's trying to get through and I'm betting my nursing blanket that she's under attack too."

I dialed Carmen Miranda Everhart Newton, one of Molly's witch sisters. "Jane," she answered. "Are you with Moll?"

I put her on speaker. "Yes. She's safe. So are the children."

"I'm at Mama's, spending the night through the storm, and we've got four dead vamps outside the house. What the hell am I supposed to do with them?"

"Dead-dead or some other kind of dead?" I asked.

"Burned to a crisp. Mama has some a-maz-ing wards," Carmen said.

Lincoln paused in what he was saying into the phone and looked my way, interested. "Burned?"

"Mama's good," Molly said, pride in the two words, and maybe a smidge of warning for any future plans the MOC might have to harm local witches or to seek vengeance for the death of the attacking vamps.

Lincoln raised one hand in peace and smiled, showing no fangs, but listening in without shame. "My territory has been invaded," he said. "I owe the attackers no fealty. If they attack my cattle, and my cattle kill them, I got no problem with that."

"Not your cattle, Shaddock," a different voice said over my cell.

"An alliance with me would give you protection," Shaddock said, his voice sliding into warmer tones.

Over the connection, Bedelia chuckled, a knowing laugh not far removed from a TV evil witch cackle. Bedelia used to be the Everhart coven leader. She had kept multiple witches alive through puberty. She was powerful and canny. "That would be a mighty unfair alliance, Lincoln, darlin'. You need magic. I got no need of fanghead blood."

"The offer remains open, leader of the Everhart clan of witches, as always."

My eyebrows went up. So did Molly's. Bedelia and Lincoln Shaddock knew each other? The local witches and vamps had clearly made arrangements in case of paranormal problems, and had done so without me having to issue a direct order. Why couldn't more Blood Masters make nice-nice with the other paras in their territory? Then I remembered the fact that before I killed her for summoning a demon, Evil Evie Everhart had attacked Lincoln and had mucked up the talks between Leo and the Asheville vamps. Maybe Lincoln and Bedelia had good reasons to make political agreements.

"Back to the bodies. They're in the open," Carmen said. "When the sun rises, what's left will be ashes."

"The witches of Asheville may not be aligned with my clan, but they are under my protection," Shaddock said, his tone letting us know he was still talking to Bedelia, "part a my territory and land. Let my enemies burn with the sun."

Bedelia laughed again, less cackle and more knowing. *Yeah.* These two had a history I wanted to know about. She asked, "Molly, have you heard from the twins? Are your sisters safe?"

Boadacia and Elizabeth, aka Cia and Liz, were the

youngest witches, the most adventurous of the Everhart clan, and I was suddenly worried. "No. I'll call. But we need to maintain an open line of communication. Okay if I give Shaddock your number?"

"I've got Bedelia's number," Lincoln said, "I'll call."

The local MOC had the number of the Everhart Clan mother? I so needed to hear this story. Once my friends were done being attacked. "Lincoln Shaddock will call and keep the lines open." I pressed END and called Cia's number. She answered.

"It better be good, Yellowrock," she said, crabby.

I chuckled sourly and said, "Does a vamp attack at Seven Sassy Sisters and a vamp attack at your mom's sound good enough?"

"Son of a witch on a switch," Cia said. "Calling Liz on the laptop line and checking the perimeters." A moment later Cia said, "My place is safe so far, but on the security cams at Seven, I count two vamps, dead, or nearly so, and three more still active on low-light. And I see two humans sneaking up in back. Liz, your wards up? Because I see two vamps on your back deck."

Over the connection, I heard Liz say, "I see 'em. Take that, you thrice-damned bloodsucker."

"Oh. Nice work, sis," Cia said. To us she added, "She just tossed a magical frag and singed two vamps so bad they aren't getting up."

"Magical frag? Singed?" I asked.

"A magic bomb we've been working on. And *singed* as in burned them to charcoal."

Shaddock chuckled softly and muttered, "I do love the Everhart women."

"Ah hell," Cia said. "Tell Molly her place is getting dinged."

"I felt it," Moll said. "No fanghead is getting through our wards. Not to worry."

Cassy burped, a soft, sweet sound, and Thema's eyes landed on the diaper-covered baby in Molly's arms. For half a second or so, a faint human smile appeared on her face; then her expression returned to vamp-scornful. If I had blinked, I'd have missed it. As if she were patting a baby, she patted Ed's head. "All is well, young one. You are safe," she said, though I wasn't sure if she was speaking to the baby or to my primo. Or both. "There are humans here now, Edmund Hartley. Feed." She stepped away from the tub and a human woman pulled off her shirt and climbed in. She was wearing a halter top under the shirt, giving him access to a broad expanse of human flesh.

"My people are approaching the restaurant," Lincoln said. "They'll take down the human attackers first and then the Mithrans. Try not to shoot my people," he added wryly. The information was passed along. Then everything went silent. Minutes crawled by.

Lincoln's cell dinged. "Yes?" he answered. Smile wrinkles creased his face. "Good work, Holly, Gerald. See about making the building secure from the storm. Then if the women want to go home, you will provide escort. Or keep watch there. Whichever the ladies decide to do." He stopped and listened. "Of a certainty. I'll make sure that Molly knows you are present."

Before he could hang up, Molly called out, "Holly! Gerald! Thank you! And tell my sisters about the teapot. They'll know who you are then."

"Teapot?" I asked.

No one answered. All the callers had signed off. I inspected Edmund, whose flesh was showing signs of regenerating, a pale white membrane covering muscle and tendons.

Molly, whose baby had clearly done a stinky in her diaper, patted Cassy's back and said, "I'm heading back to the main house. This cottage is too small for all the humans and paras."

I was about to assign her an escort, when Alex buzzed through the cottage's modern-day version of an intercom. "Janie," he said. "Trouble in New Orleans. Get in here."

"Well, dang," I muttered. I had to go back into the storm and I had just gotten the snowballs under my toenail pads thawed. I glanced down. At some point I had chipped my pretty toe-claw polish.

"The responsibilities of leadership," Lincoln said. "I sympathize." But his tone said he didn't, at all.

I trudged from the relative warmth of the cottage, Molly at my side, to the back door and mudroom of the inn. I kept a hand under her elbow and wondered what the baby thought when she looked up at me. Would the nebulous memory of my Beast-face stick in her deep unconscious brain somewhere, to come back as nightmares in her future?

"What's that?" Molly asked, pointing to the west. I followed her finger and spotted the colors and light show of a magic working. I remembered the earthquake and bright lights Beast had thought were *white-man lights*.

Something tugged at the back of my mind, like a fish on a line, vital, as if I knew it was important. The lights looked like a bright witch circle. Then I remembered the exoskeleton on the SOD. *Ah. Yeah.* "Moll, could there be a time circle there?"

"Not out in the open. Time circles need to be underground, in a cave or a windowless basement, someplace where the sun and moon can't interfere."

Beast thought at me, *There was earthquake and brighter lights there, after.*

Yeah. Lights were there before the earthquake, but dimmer. "Molly, is there a ley line near Evangelina's old house in Hot Springs?" Evangelina was Moll's sister, the opposite of Glinda the Good Witch. More like the Wicked Witch of *Oz* fame.

"Yes. Not a big one. But a line leading to a stronger one we can draw through. And not too far away is a liminal line, but we don't usually draw power from that. It's in the Nantahala National Forest, on land claimed by the Cherokee tribe, up near Robbinsville. Everharts are polite about borrowing earth power."

"Do liminal lines lead to thresholds?" Liminal thresholds were locations where the borders between worlds were thin, where things could crawl or cross through. I wasn't in the mood to fight some big bad ugly from another realm.

Molly yawned, her jaw cracking. "Sometimes. But there isn't one near here."

"Okay. So nothing magical over there." I pointed.

Molly cast a *seeing* working with mumbled *wyrd*. "Probably a showy circle to impress human customers. A small clan of weak-as-well-water witches moved in over that way. The Shookers. They take human customers, put on a show with lots of lights. We checked them out. There are no indications of dark magic or blood rites on them or on their property."

Molly knew her business, but I made a mental note to get someone to check on the Shookers come morning.

Walking into the heat of the inn/house was like being smothered by a heated blanket. Brute, who had not made the flight back with us, raced in between our legs, nearly toppling the two bipeds. I caught Moll and offered to pull her boots off. Baby at her shoulder, she sat on the small bench near the door and lifted a foot. I pulled off her boots and placed them to drip-dry on the rack.

"Thanks, Big-Cat," Molly said, levering herself up before I could help. "I'm going to change a diaper, put all my babies into the bed with me, and get some shut-eye."

"You sure you're okay?" I meant with death magics, and she nodded. "Thank you," I said. "I doubt we'd have made it without you. I like having a Glinda on my team."

"Of course you do." The rest of her words filtered back as she padded for the elevator. "Glinda had horrible fashion sense and awful hair, but she had good timing, and that 'click your heels three times' thing is legendary."

With a claw, I dug the snow and sleet out of my toenail pads and out from my foot fur, dried my pads, and pawed my way to the office. I needed to get out of the red armor, but I could stand it for a few more minutes. "What's so almighty freaking bad in NOLA?"

"This," Alex said. He hit a key. "Footage of Sabina."

Sabina was the only outclan priestess in North America. She had been with *Uni Lisi* in my toddler memory of a war dance.

"I am badly damaged," she croaked. On the recording, her throat made a horrible noise that might have been a cough as she tried to breathe. "Near true-death. The larger fragments of the Blood Cross are destroyed." She coughed as if she was breathing blood. "My mausoleum is on fire. I dig through the earth . . . with the last sliver of the cross in the Americas."

The audio cut off.

CHAPTER 11

Is That a Royal Decree?

"I lost the call," Alex said. "Haven't been able to get it back. I'm thinking Sabina's underground. Or true-dead. And we have this." He punched a key on the keyboard and three video feeds came up on his oversized monitor, but I had no idea what I was looking at. As I puzzled out the video, Alex went on, "Isn't her mausoleum inside a church? And made of stone?"

"Yeah," I said. "What am I seeing?"

"The vamp graveyard. It's on fire. Everything is on fire. Every single thing. All the stone."

"All." I leaned to the screen, picking out the crypt where Leo was buried. It was in flames, fire licking up and down the stone, eating through the door. Tears gathered in my eyes. "Don't let Bruiser see this when he gets back," I said softly.

"Copy that," Alex said. "I got Wrassler on cell. HQ was under attack too, but they're handling it. The big problem is at NOLA PD, Eighth District. Bloodsuckers have attacked there too."

It took a moment for me to figure out what he meant

and even then I didn't believe it. "Vamps attacked NOPD? The human police?" A sinking feeling rose from my toe pads to the top of my head, making it hard to think. Vamps did *not* attack human law enforcement. It wasn't done. Ever. Except that there was a war among vamps in Europe and they were attacking humans there. And now here. I watched the screen as multiple recorded events played out on it. Everything was changing. "Who are the attackers?"

"They didn't leave calling cards," he snapped. "The witnesses and the security footage indicate they're speaking some language I don't recognize. I'm trying to ID them with facial-rec software, but that'll take forever if I can't narrow it down to country of origin."

"Do you think they're working with the fangheads here?"

"No. They didn't seem to know you were no longer in New Orleans. They were trying to draw out the Dark Queen," Alex said. "Wrassler sent a pic of a message they left at the front door of NOLA HQ. It specifically demanded that your head be tossed out to them, no longer attached to your body. Clan Bouvier provided armed assistance to the police until they had things under control again."

"Good." The last thing NOLA vamps needed was problems with the local cops. "Play Sabina's message again." I watched the stone of the graveyard and the marble of her mausoleum burn as I listened to the priestess's message.

"I am badly damaged." That horrible cough sounded as if she was hacking up a lung. "Near true-death. The larger fragments of the Blood Cross are destroyed." Cough. "My mausoleum is on fire." Long silence. "I dig through the earth . . . with the last sliver of the cross in the Americas."

My cell dinged and I answered, "Wrassler? You okay?"

"We're fine, Leg—" He stopped just as he was about to call me Legs. His voice changed into the formal tones he once used for Leo. "Empress. But there are police in the front entrance. "What are your orders, my queen?"

My queen. Bruiser was in a sleet storm. Ed was skinned like a deer for butchering. Eli was taking care of business in a bivouac in freezing conditions in an unheated church—the best possible place for humans seeking shelter from vamps. The Asheville MOC knew nothing about NOLA. I was on my own.

I said something that my housemothers at the Christian children's home where I grew up would have washed out my mouth for. With lye soap and a spanking too, most likely. Alex found it all highly amusing, blowing a teenaged snortle through his nose.

I said, "First order of business, I will not be referred to as queen. Got that?"

Alex asked, "Is that a royal decree?"

I swatted the back of his head.

Alex rubbed the spot as if I'd hurt him, but he was grinning. "You want Gee and Shaddock in here?"

I showed my fangs at him in what might be called a smile, in some universe, and nodded. "Please."

Laughter and his normal New Orleans accent in his voice, Wrassler said, "I miss you people." Without giving us time to respond, he went on, "Alex, see if they might be speaking Romansh."

"Romansh?" he asked.

"It's spoken in some EU countries," Wrassler said. "There's some of the former Atlanta vamps on the video too, five who took off rather than submit to Katie when she took over as Master of the City there, and three I recognized on the video footage as having fled when Rosanne Romanello defeated the New York City MOC. They were all with the fangheads who attacked us, so it's a mixed bag, maybe a new alliance."

He was describing a batch of masterless rogues, the kind I used to track, stake, and leave true-dead. "I want to see the vid," I said.

The younger Younger nodded.

Wrassler said, "Yes, ma'am," like a good Southern gentleman of a recent but bygone era. "And some good news. Derek showed up on the HQ steps. He's been beaten to a pulp and bled nearly dry, but he has a heartbeat. Vamps are feeding him and will turn him if needed. He signed the papers."

Derek had signed papers permitting himself to be turned if he died? "Oookaaay. Tell him if he grows fangs, we'll get Amy Lynn Brown down there to get him through the devoveo as fast as possible. And make sure his mother has someone to continue her treatments." Derek's mom had cancer and Derek was working as the full-time NOLA Enforcer to keep her fed and healing. Last I heard she was holding her own. And then it hit me that Amy was here in Asheville. In danger.

I cursed again, this time under my breath. One step at a time, my old life and responsibilities in New Orleans were descending on me. I could run away again. I could turn human and die. Or I could stay in half-form and deal with treachery. Save my friends.

Gee and Shaddock entered the back door. I could smell their magic and mixed scents on the air. "Gee, Lincoln, get in here," I called. "I need advice."

"I attend my queen," Shaddock called back. I had a feeling he was picking on me and when I saw his face, I was sure of it.

Brushing sleet off his shoulders, Gee said, "The little goddess has my attention."

I would deal with the goddess stupidity later. I didn't know if Gee called me that because I could timewalk, or because of the power I had over *le breloque*, or if it was because of the curse of the Anzu that kept his kind from truly shifting shape. Or just to be annoying. And I didn't have time to figure it out now.

"First, is Amy safe?" I asked Lincoln.

"Yes. The little girl, my scion, is safe," he said, his expression going grim.

Relief eased the unexpected tightness in my joints, but a tension headache was starting behind my eyes. I used to have a lot of those in NOLA.

I nudged Alex. "Explain it to them all so we're all up to speed. Wrassler, you're on speaker. It's Alex, Gee, and Shaddock. Everyone else is stuck in Asheville in a snow-storm."

"Huh. It's spring here. We got green tomatoes in the garden. I'm putting you on speaker here so the security team can listen in. The cops are banging on the door, but they can wait."

Alex talked. Wrassler talked. It didn't take long to get everyone properly debriefed, except Eli and Bruiser, who weren't here to advise me. Wrassler said, "We got a warning from a loyalist in Spain who says Shimon is in the U.S. for several things: he wants *le breloque*, new territory, and Amy Lynn."

"Everyone wants Amy. Okay. Go talk to the cops," I said. "If they don't have warrants, don't let them in. If they do have warrants, stall. Remind them that the HQ is actually a sort of ambassadorial location and get the State Department involved to slow them down. If they are there to ask for vamp backup at NOPD, call the local clans and get some experienced fighters there to help law enforcement. Call . . ." I stopped, a stutter of surprise at what was coming out of my mouth. "Koun. Did he accept the position as Acting Enforcer of Clan Yellowrock until Derek is found and can resume his duties?" I asked.

"Yes," Wrassler said. "He said he's yours to command."

I'd be testing those bonds of loyalty. "Tell him I said to organize the Mithran resistance."

"Yes, my queen," Wrassler said.

"Call the Robere twins in Europe and get them to talk to the cops if needed." I paused, thinking through the list of things I needed to do, like acquire new legal counsel. I needed a high-profile, high-powered legal team. "We need a legal office on retainer in NOLA, someone with experience in international law and finances. Is that something you can handle?"

"I can make some calls. I'm thinking ABC—Aurieux, Boutté and Cuvert De Boisblanc. They've got thirty-five lawyers on retainer and can help with everything from family law to customs problems. If they don't deal with it, they'll find someone who will."

"Call them. In fact, call them before you go to the door. Send them an electronic retainer. And keep me in the loop."

"Will do, Queenie." Wrassler disconnected.

"Queenie," Alex mocked.

I let him. Being teased was a spot of normalcy in my life.

Lincoln said, "You gonna tell me why you're still in half-cat form? And why you're hiding out here instead of being in charge of all this mess in New Orleans?"

"Sure. My human body is dying of magic cancer. This one is healthy. And stronger, faster, and more agile than my human shape. Plus, between you and me, I quit. I sent a letter to Edmund resigning the job of Dark Queen and empress and leaving it all to him. Either he never got the letter or he decided he didn't want the job and is winging it until something else happens."

Shaddock sat on the ottoman in front of the sofa and laced his big hands between his knees. "Shimon didn't seem to know that. Therefore, I agree. If Ed got the letter, then he kept that information from the Flayer of Mithrans even under duress, with the younger Son of Darkness in his mind."

Which would make Ed way more powerful than he appeared. I grinned again. "Correct." To Alex, I said, "Make sure our people can get back here at first light. Whatever it takes. Eli and I need to go scouting to the west. Oh. And see if you can find Legolas." Alex looked confused. "The blond vamp who tore out Shiloh's throat. He wasn't at the Regal. He's mine. Personal combat."

"On the contrary, Queenie," Lincoln said, making it a permanent nickname. "He insulted my empress by harming her primo on my territory. Technically, according to the Vampira Carta one and two, he's mine. Personal combat, to the death," he said to Alex. "You find him, you let me know."

Alex tilted his head to me, his long curls bobbing, eyes flashing amusement. "Protecting our Queenie is not gonna be easy. She likes to fight her own battles."

"Which she can do. But if we end up fighting through layers of pissant, lower-echelon-level bullyboys, that's not her fight. It's mine." Shaddock glanced at me. "We clear on that?"

"Crystal. I'm heading for bed. Alex needs shut-eye

too, if one of your people can man the screens and the security system. Later."

I went up to Bruiser's and my room and crashed, my nose on his pillow so I could surround myself with his scent.

I slept until ten, when the mattress moved and I smelled Angie and EJ. Both kids climbed up on the bed, Angie on one side, EJ on the other. I grunted, my face buried in a pillow and covered by a veil of my long hair. "I'm still wearing my costume," I said.

"Dat not a costume," EJ said. "Dat's Ant Jane Big-Cat. Mama said so."

"Even though I'm ugly?" I asked. "Scary? And have big teeth?"

"The be'er to eat you with," EJ said, and giggled.

"Ant Jane isn't a wolf. She's a big-cat," Angie said.

"Like the one we saw outside the window? Except her not spawtted."

I reached back and pulled my hair out of the way, rolling over slowly. I sat up on the bed, glad to see that I'd fallen into the sheets fully clothed. "Spotted? What spotted cat?" I asked softly, remembering the scat on the edge of my hunting territory. "And how big was it?"

"It was big," EJ said. "Big as a lion!" His eyes went wide and his arms spread out.

Angie was watching me too carefully, her strawberry blond curls tied back in a tail. "Mama said it was prob'y a house cat, but it was too big. It was a big-cat, Ant Jane. Bigger than your big-cat."

"Did it make a noise? A sound? Did it roar?"

"It did this," EJ said. He made three coughing noises and then he opened his mouth and tapped on his cheeks, making a hollow noise. "And then it did this." He snarled and made a roaring sound. Almost like an African lion. Almost.

It seemed the cat from the small creek on my hunting territory had decided to come closer. I rolled out of the bed to my feet. "Show me."

EJ reached up with both hands, a demand to be picked

up. I swung him up in my arms and, when we were in the hallway, up to my shoulders to ride.

Angie took my hand, a big girl, though the desire to be carried through the house on the shoulders of a Beast-form Aunt Jane was evident in her eyes. She led me to the kids' room, past the bed and the sleeping Cassy, and up to the window, where she pointed at the tree line. "See the pine tree?" she asked. "Right there. Under the branches."

EJ squealed as I swung him down from his perch to the floor. "Okay. You two stand here and watch for me. I'm going out there and I need you to let me know when I'm in the exact spot, okay?"

Angie nodded, all grown up and serious. "I'll do like this." She waved both arms over her head.

"Good."

EJ just turned and raced from the room. "Toddler help" had its own parameters.

I left the room and the house at a trot, sprinted through the icy air, across two inches of solid sleet, to the tree line and the only evergreen. It was a wild spruce, not a pine, but close enough. The stink of male cat came to me, strong, the cat spray of a territory marking. It had followed me back here, whatever it was, based on the spray and scat that Beast had left on the territory boundary. I looked back at the window where Angie stood, silhouetted in the overhead light. She waved her arms enthusiastically.

I bent and crawled beneath the cedar fronds and saw what I was looking for and had hoped not to find. Paw prints. Not a dog or a wolf, which would have left claw marks at the tip of each toe, but a clawless print, four-toed, like a large mountain lion. But the center pad was too big for a mountain lion, the toes too close to the back pad. Not a bobcat, not even an exceptionally large one. This was indeed a big-cat print. Large spotted cat could mean that PsyLED was watching me. Unit Eighteen, in Knoxville, had a spotted African leopard on its team, and surely all of PsyLED knew by now that vamps had invaded Asheville.

Cat is not Africa cat, Beast thought. *Is not werecat. Is other cat. Is cat from Beast's hunting territory. Do not know this cat.*

Okay. I was going to have to go cat hunting. Soon. But I had things to do first.

Back at the house, I threw a steak on the hot grill à la Eli, liberally sprinkled it with salt and pepper, and let it sizzle for a few minutes. I flipped it, gave that side the same treatment, turned off the flame, and picked up the two-pounder with a BBQ fork. The fat spat and spit as it dripped on the hot grill.

I spotted EJ, peeking around the corner. Holding the steak over the stove grill, I spoke over my shoulder, saying, "Aunt Jane can't use good manners like I'm supposed to. My teeth are too big."

"The be'er to eat me with, Ant Jane. Can I watch?"

I thought about that. I could say, *Yes, but don't tell your mama.* Which was unfair to Moll and Big Evan. Or I could say, *Go away,* which hurt my heart. I said, "Grown-ups eat with a fork and knife and not with their fingers. I'm gonna be eating with my fingers. It's embarrassing."

"Oh," EJ said. A few moments later he added, "I'm gonna go find sissy."

"Thank you, EJ."

"You we'come, Ant Jane."

I heard him patter away and tore into the half-raw steak, swallowing big chunks. *So good.*

A soft noise made me whirl, and I saw Angie Baby peeking around the corner, one eye visible, one eye hidden. EJ peeked around too, his head lower. So going to find Sissy meant bringing her back here. I wiped my mouth and grinned, showing my fangs. EJ giggled. Angie said, "Can I braid your hair, Ant Jane?"

I went very still, meat in one hand, halfway to my mouth. For the Cherokee, the braiding of hair was ceremony. The placing of one's entire self, one's physical and one's spirit self, into the hands of another. There had been a time when I let anyone braid my hair, not knowing the significance of the act. "Do you know how to braid hair?" I asked her.

She nodded, her strawberry curls bobbing. "Mama taught me."

"Okay." I put the meat into the fridge, washed my hands, and said again, "Okay." I lifted both kids to sit on the bar, feet dangling off. "You fall and I'll be mad."

"I won't faw, Ant Jane," EJ said.

Angie just pushed me around and gathered my hair into her hands. She stroked her fingers through it, from my nape to my hips, long brushing motions. She began to braid my hair, her fingers slow and a little clumsy. Warmth rose from the floor, from the soles of my feet, along my spine, and up to the top of my head. I breathed out, tension leaving my body. For the first time in a very long time, I relaxed.

Molly and her kids had taken a nap, and the children were still sleeping when Moll joined us in the TV room/office. Her hair looked like a half-inflated helium balloon, puffy on one side, flat on the other. The baby was over one shoulder and Moll was doing that rocking, swaying, bouncing thing that seemed common to human mothers.

Beast watched Molly as if she was prey but sent me an image of a mountain lion nursing kittens. The mama cat was flat on her back, front and back legs outstretched and milk-engorged teats facing up. On four of the teats were young kits. *Kits of Beast kit. Beast brought meat to kit and helped teach young to hunt. Kit and kits left Beast's territory for place of setting sun. Beast never saw kits again.*

I'm sorry.

Molly took a seat on the sofa and began patting the baby's back. Moll was making tiny humming noises in the back of her throat, like half singing, none of the notes in any particular key, but the sound was soothing nonetheless.

Beast is sad. Beast loves kits.

I sent my other half an image of two cats hugging, and when she didn't respond, I turned my attention to real life in the TV room/office and updates that I knew had to be waiting.

Alex was watching replays. On the big screen, divided into two larger screens, were the spectacles of the fire at the NOLA vamp cemetery, and the encounter with the SOD in the Regal. In NOLA, I watched as the rock itself burned and melted into puddles of lavalike molten stone. I dropped into the heated recliner, threw my feet up, and watched as the chapel whooshed up in flames and swirled into a fire devil, high in the air. In the Regal Imperial Hotel, I watched as vamp pairs fell and Ed bled. On the hotel footage Alex had hacked into, I stood there as if I hadn't a care in the world, my half-form full of false moxie. False. But I walked away with all my people. I couldn't help the smile that pulled back my lips and exposed my fangs.

On the security cams recording from inside the Regal, I watched as my party walked away. And the SOD drank two humans down as if they were bottles of cheap wine and tore out the throats of two fangheads. No one died true-dead, as scions rushed in to save everyone. But the SOD was a bloody little bastard. I was going to enjoy putting the rabid dog down.

"Janie," Alex said. "I got word about the Shookers, that witch family you mentioned. They answered their phone and seem to be fine. The circle you spotted was theirs. They said they'd put up stronger wards. They also checked in with the other witches in the area and all are okay. They'll notify us if anything changes."

The rest of the morning dragged by. Molly and Shaddock's human Enforcer—who went by the nickname Bunny, for reasons no one thought to share with me—and Gee DiMercy were discussing options and plans without including me. When I requested, politely, I thought, to be part of the discussions, Gee made a little fluttering motion with his hands, like a bird fluffing his wings. "My mistress, your primo was torn from your mind and from your binding. Has that state been remedied?"

I scowled at them, which was a fearsome sight; I'd seen my half-form scowl. But Bunny laughed, a silly little titter. She stood all of five feet and maybe a hundred pounds fully clothed. I could break her in two with my half-form fingers, but she wasn't scared of me. Weird. "No," I said. "Ed isn't back inside my head."

"Then we will discuss all our plans with you once they are finalized, my queen."

I'd been dismissed. I had discovered that my half-form didn't need much sleep. It was full of energy too, a constant low hum of the need to run, to fight, to do something. I was so tense my shoulders ached, nerves close to fraying. Anything. So I paced like a cat in a cage, my braid whipping around like a snake on a string. A Medusa cat. Which might have been funny under other circumstances.

Through the windows, I caught a glimpse of the two human Everhart sisters, Regan and Amelia, wandering around in the snow, heavily weaponed, chatting, heads together, pointing and gesturing as they walked all around the inn and cottages. I must have missed something while I slept. Last I'd heard, they were in Asheville. I asked and was told that they had been escorted in, by Lincoln Shaddock's scions Holly and Gerald, at great personal danger, through the storm. I watched as the two human girls— young women—built a fort and started a snowball fight with Shaddock's humans.

When I couldn't take it anymore, I left word with Alex and raced into the icy world. Snow crunched under me, my back half-paws breaking through the top crusty layer. The cold felt wonderful, and inside me, Beast rose and stared through my eyes. *Hunt and eat deer in half-Beast form?*

Gack. No. No way. But a hard run, and checking out the grounds. Our nose is pretty good in this form. Let's see if we can find where the spotted big-cat came onto the property.

Beast is not nose-to-ground hunter, she chuffed. *Jane should hold on to tree.*

Why? I asked as I gripped the narrow trunk of a young tree.

In an instant, she opened the ancient neurological pathway, the parts of my brain she had augmented with the stolen sensory ability of the bloodhound we had been several times. Its olfactory system was intense and shocking and I stumbled against the small tree.

Beast chuffed again, amused. *Jane is silly puppy falling in snow.* She sent me an image of a clumsy pup face-planting in fluffy powder.

Ha-ha. I don't remember it being this intense, I thought at her. Slowly I caught my balance and breathed in through my open mouth, over the scent sacs that were all Beast's, letting the myriad scent patterns settle inside me. Pine and oak and maple and rocks and ice and snow and intense smell of the inn, with vamps and humans and witches, each with his and her own individual pattern.

Vamps smelled of herbs, funeral flowers, green peppers, blood, sex, and barbeque.

My people smelled of . . . clan. Of home. Of littermates.

Big Evan scented of testosterone and ham and magic. EJ of urine and mischief, which I had no idea had a scent until now. Angie reeked of magic so strong it hid any scent of her own from this distance. Molly was the smell of milk and motherhood and anger and death. I/we parsed her scent, able to deduce by scent that she was fighting for control every moment that she lived. She was locked down so tight her scent aura practically squeaked with the nervousness and pressure.

We don't have KitKit, I thought. *She can't possibly control her death magics for long, not as upset as she is.*

Beast can care for Molly, she thought at me. *Hayyel made Beast better cat than little mouser KitKit. Beast is better everything than KitKit.*

She sounded certain, almost offhand, as if she really could help to control Molly's magics. And if the angel who haunted my life had given her something, some power . . . *You want to explain?*

Beast ignored me.

Fine. Though it wasn't. I hated it when Beast hid secrets from me. I drew in air and located the spotted-cat scent. Racing through the cold, Beast and I hunted the big-cat. We trailed him for two miles, through the snow, until his scent disappeared at a plowed road. And we lost him. I knew who it was, who it had to be, by the time I lost the scent. And I was all kinds of stupid for not knowing who it was the first time Beast smelled the cat scent. I was an idiot.

It was a long jaunt back to the inn, and I did a lot of thinking on the way.

By noon, my nerves settled by the hours outdoors, we were joined by the two witch sisters, Cia, a moon witch, and Liz, a stone witch, riding on yet more brightly painted snowmobiles through the newly falling snow. Carmen wasn't with them, nor was Bedelia, the two witches not willing to take Carmen's child into the weather—which was unpredictable at best—but this was more Everhart sisters than I'd seen in one place since I killed their older sister Evangelina. Shaddock had arranged the transport for them and for our people still stranded in the city, a dozen snowmobiles roaring up and depositing riders and passengers.

I felt the weight of worry fall off my shoulders as Eli trudged into the house, taking in the new inhabitants. He mumbled something about Janie's bizarro battalions and needing a shower and a power nap. He lifted a thumb to me in passing and went to his suite.

My honeybunch dismounted, followed Eli in, and slid in behind me at the window, wrapping me in his arms. He kissed the top of my head, his Onorio scent heated and his hands steady, no longer shaking with weakness. At his touch, all my tormenting energies melted away and I realized I had been worried, edgy, until all my people were back. "You get some vampire blood?" I asked, sighing, resting back against him.

"Those sips from Shaddock last night, love, had a delayed reaction. I began to feel better within an hour and I'm well enough for now. We found inflatable mattresses in the church and slept quite well until we were rescued." He nuzzled my hair. "I've been offered the blood of Thema or Kojo when they rise at dusk. I'll be fine until I can drink from them. What *are* they doing?" he asked of the people in the snow.

"I have no idea. Apparently I am not to be told war plans until after the fact."

"Ah." His lips smiled against my hair. "The onerous job of the queen. Waiting."

I grunted.

The Everhart sisters and some of Shaddock's humans had finally started work with a set of trenching shovels and snowmobiles, racing around the inn and the cottages, tracing and digging a narrow trench around the property, the engines loud enough to wake the undead, and their voices complaining loudly that the humans always got the hard-labor jobs while the witches and vamps always got the sexy jobs. By listening silently, standing in the shadows, we learned that the trench was part of the Everhart-Trueblood defense of the inn. It was going to be the biggest *hedge of thorns* they had ever made. Bigger than I had ever heard was even possible. In spite of their grumbles, the workers were energetic and laughing.

"I rested well for a few hours, but I think I'll take a nap," Bruiser said. "Tonight may be long and miserable."

"Or the snow might get worse and nothing might happen."

He kissed the top of my head again. "We can always hope." Bruiser left me at the window and trudged up the stairs, like Eli, looking for a power nap before nightfall.

CHAPTER 12

Something with Fins. Or Wings.

"Are you sure about this, Janie?" Eli asked through the windshield.

I/we nodded. Eli had put chains on the tires of an SUV, loaded in enough weapons to take over Asheville, and gassed up at one of the few places that had electricity this soon after the snow and sleet, and this far out of town. We had headed west, toward the area where Beast and I had seen the bright lights, not talking, but listening to Cia's boyfriend on his latest album. Cia was dating country singer Ray Conyers, who had a voice so smooth and perfect and full of sexual passion that it had to come from the devil. Seductive and able to slide into roughness that felt sexual and intense. Made me want to cry in my beer with him, except for the whole "doesn't have a beer" thing.

When we ran out of scraped roads and new songs and only fresh snow lay before us, piled up in drifts on what might still be a road (but there were doubts), Eli pulled over. I said, "I'm not sure what I'm looking for."

Eli gave a soft *hmmm* of sound and checked over

one of his new toys. It was a high-tech bow that was all angles and strings and round doohickeys.

"I'm not sure what I'll do when I find it, whatever it is." Eli gave that soft sound again, unconcerned, letting me talk. "I had to get out of the house or I'd end up fighting Brute to control my anxiety and hyper state. And my people are making plans behind my back."

"Which is their job, Janie," he said, setting aside the bow and picking up something that looked like an over-sized target pistol. "Let 'em do it."

"I hate it when you're so calm, when I'm so not."

Eli made a small hint of a mocking smile. "Sucks to be you sometimes . . ."

"Not helpful."

Which only made his taunting grin spread.

I climbed out of the vehicle and crunched across the snow to hunch behind a boulder heaped with snow and ice. I stripped, folded my clothes, shivering and miserable, and shifted to Beast.

Slinking slowly from drift to drift, Beast carried Jane folded clothes back to SUV. Dropped clothes at tire. Crouched. Gathered body tight. Leaped. Landed on warm hood. Shoved our face at windshield. Showing teeth. Snarling. Eli didn't look up. He just gave tiny lip quirk that passed for human smile. Began speed-loading magazines for white-man gun. Beast dropped belly to top of warm SUV engine, thinking. Was still thinking when Jane woke in Beast mind.

What are we doing?

There is no prey to chase at inn, Beast thought. *Want to chase wild turkey.*

You know they can fly, right?

Chase bison in Edmund car.

Not happening.

Window came down. "Com'ere," Eli said.

We leaped to ground and raised up, putting front paws on SUV, shoving head inside where warm air scented of Eli and home. He reached out and secured gobag around our neck. "I got food, a gallon thermos of coffee, new reading material, and a few new weapons. I'll put out laser monitors and cameras on the bumpers once you're out of the area. I have a signal"—he waggled his cell at me—"and if you start wavering in and out of range, I'll send you a ping on your cell."

I/we lifted a paw to gobag next to gold-nugget-and-cougar-tooth necklace we never took off, and peered at seat beside him. Fanned out on it were slippery papers called magazines.

Jane read: *Guns & Ammo, Handguns, RifleShooter,* and one titled *Garden & Gun. That's for the highbrow, überwealthy, übersnooty, übershooty types.*

On top of papers was Eli newest toy, called tech bow.

I/we chuffed at it and Eli said, "PSE Archery Carbon Air ECS 32 Compound Bow, in black. Fifteen hundred dollars. Modified to fire handmade arrows constructed of carbon fiber reinforced with ash wood and plastic with silver tips." He patted deadly toy. "I'll be here. Take as long as you need."

I/we leaned in and swiped at his neck and ear with tongue. He tasted of Eli. We snorted into his ear.

"Stop that," he said, laughter hidden in tone. "Go do whatever it is you need to do."

I/we dropped to ground and trotted into snow, leaping and dodging rocks and fallen trees. It was midafternoon.

Jane thought, *I'll give us three hours or until the snow starts again, whichever comes first. The storm front isn't stuck over us, but it's a narrow band, several thousand miles long, and it originated in the north pole. It's riding along the ridges of the Appalachians. We'll have more snow or sleet or freezing rain soon.*

Hate sleet.

Beast jumped into the nearest tree and clawed her way up. We paused there and she sniffed for male big-cat. She got no hint of cat, but did smell bear and squirrel and owl and maybe a hint of magic, though it vanished as fast as it came. She leaped to the next tree. And then the next. Covering ground fast. I let her run, chasing whatever she wanted, while I thought.

Molly and I once had a conversation about my soul home. The gist was that Molly wanted to know if it was a real place. I was pretty sure it was. At the time I had believed the limestone cave was located near the white quartz boulder where I found my Beast shape, near Horseshoe Mountain. But now I had other thoughts. Now I thought it might be located near the Nantahala River gorge, near the spot where my father had told me I was expected to care for my baby brother. In the memory, I had looked down at my feet, and they had been small next to my father's. My mother had been pregnant. I must have been just past my first shift. The gorge was a sacred place for The People. So all that made sense. But I was more than a hundred miles from the Nante—the Nantahala River—and nearly that from Horseshoe Mountain, via rough terrain on foot. I had to make time to go search for the cave, in case Moll had been right about the importance of the physical cave itself to my well-being. Soon. As soon as I killed some more fangheads.

Beast came to a stop. We were perched over a narrow cleft of gorge. From deep below came the shushing of fast-moving water, falling through boulders. *Beast remembers cave,* she thought at me. *Door? Opening to cave?*

The entrance? I thought back. *Like a dark place in the face of the earth?*

Tsalagi covered it, like Puma concolor *covers kits to keep them safe?* She sent me a vision of a tiny black space at the base of a small ravine. Water plunged down not far away. The woods smelled deep and green and alive in her memory, so it was before the hunger times. Or long after. *Was good hunting. But door was too small for Beast to enter. Beast will take Jane there when Jane kills enemies and kit killers and bloodsucker vampires.*

Holy crap. You know where my soul home is.

Beast did not leave scat at cave. Did not mark territory.

That's not what holy cr—Never mind. *Can you find it again?*

Beast does not know if opening was cave of Jane's memories. But sound of faraway falling water was like this. Smell of forest in winter was like this. Sun was over ridge from place of setting. Tall mountain was to place of sun rising.

Beast brought up the smell/sound/taste/look/directional sense of the memory. The all-in-one sensation made me vaguely nauseous.

Jane in We-sa *form hunted with* Edoda. *There was much small prey there, rabbits, fun to chase.* Beast looked up at the cloudy sky, found the sun in the west. *Was not here. But Beast can find place of small door into blackness.*

Soon, I thought at my other half.

Soon. Will hunt rabbits near cave where Edoda *taught* We-sa *to hunt?*

Yeah. I'd like that. Next time we go searching new stuff. Meantime, I have no idea where we are. Are we heading in the general direction of the lights you saw when you landed in the stream?

Beast snorted, insulted. *Jane likes to play at being cat. Beast always knows where Beast is. Jane is human. Jane is always lost.*

No argument. The sun's setting soon. Let's get on it.

The sun nestled on the tree line when I/we saw a sliver of bright magic. If we had been in my human form we might have missed it, but in Beast sight, the magic was a coruscating, scintillating prism of power. We had trotted many miles and ended up over a narrow, very deep crevice. *You sure about this?* I asked my Beast, staring down into the rock-strewn, tree-clogged dark rent. It looked as if the earth had cracked open eons ago, and a mad, dark fae had taken over. Snow clung to the rock faces for the first twenty feet down; then it stopped, where the temps changed. There, the snow down the sides of the cliffs had melted, refreezing in a glistening crystalline shell. And below that, the stone faces had held the temps above freezing. Bracken grew from cracks in the rock face. Moss draped the stones, swathed the trunks of trees that clung to the smallest fracture, and carpeted every inch of exposed stone and earth as the rocks fell away into the earth. At the bottom was green, green, green, every shade of green life. Moist air, a mist like a thin fog, rose in the chasm, wet and warmer, to freeze on the glistening surfaces or hit the cold and drip back as rain. The chasm had its own microclimate, an amazing little place in the deeps, and I wanted to explore.

Beast can leap there and there and there. She looked from place to place as she thought at me. *Then stop. Pick places to leap after.*

Yeah. *You can't see the bottom,* I reminded her. *And you need to be back up before nightfall. Climbing this wall of rock after dark will be impossible. Dangerous. The "you fall, we die" kinda dangerous.*

Beast does not *fall. See magics at bottom.*

Uh-huh. I hate when you do this.

Beast chuffed and leaped. The forest floor seemed to push back against our back paws. Air swept up under and around us. Beast's tail whipped and snapped. Beast pushed off on a root that angled away from the wall, letting the three-inch-thick wood carry her weight long enough to change trajectory. A rock ledge, almost an inch wide, offered a second toe-pad hold. A narrow tree trunk, growing at an angle, was the third. But Beast didn't stop. She caught all her weight on her front paws, twisted, and thrust off it. Down and down again. A controlled fall that had me fighting to keep from screaming.

Beast was still chuffing. *Fun. Fun. Many more than five fun!*

Holy crap. Crapcrapcrap.

We dropped down and down and leaped ahead a dozen times, gaining as much as twenty feet forward with each leap. Down a crevice that had to be five hundred feet straight down. The ravine narrowed and then widened, and finally Beast stopped, her four paws smashing down, gripping a fallen tree, her weight slamming down behind. Still. Unmoving except for her breath. Twin billows in the darkness that was the artificial night.

Ahead, the ravine opened into a wider place, dark and snow sprinkled, with colossal ancient trees like out of a fairy tale. It was like a miniature old-growth forest, an oval of maybe three acres, deep with bracken and jagged fallen limbs and one ancient fir that had fallen and lay rotting. The air was warmer here, heavy with mist, a primordial place. It smelled of water, water on the trees, on the ground, hanging in the air, dripping, yet I had a feeling that rain seldom fell here. It was too isolated, cliff walls rising on every side. Water dripped, a constant patter. In the distance, an owl hooted, a plaintive sound. Magic glistened and danced on the steamy, still air.

Beast leaped and leaped from branch to branch, landing carefully on the mossy, wet bark. We were fifty feet from the forest floor and it was too dark to tell what was buried beneath the leaves and the rotting detritus of . . . centuries? The magic grew closer.

The tree branch beneath Beast's claws changed, suddenly distinctly dissimilar. *What?* I thought.

Tree is not winter dead, not sleeping. Tree is true-dead. Air smells sick.

I took a sniff. And caught a whiff of sulfur. *Brimstone? Be careful!*

Is not same smell as Evangelina's demon. Is different.

Crap. Be careful!

Beast is always careful.

So says the puma who just dropped several hundred feet into a crevasse.

She trotted along one limb, dropped to another, and peered around the trunk of the dead tree. Beneath us was a small blue pool of steaming water. Deep in the center of the pool was a rent, like a black crack in the skin of the earth, pointed on two ends, wider in the middle. In the center of the pool it looked strangely, menacingly, like a snake's vertical pupil in a blue iris. It was a hot spring with a deep opening into the earth.

Steam rose from the hot spring in globes of mist that coated the trees and then fell in drops. The water bubbled, a delicious warmth if not for the faint stink of sulfur. Chemicals that were killing the trees all around.

The spring was heated and magical, and though it was beautiful, it was deadly. The hot spring was clearly part of the geology that created the microclimate, but the minerals in the water—maybe the water itself—had changed recently.

The trees were freshly dead, not rotted. The heated pool had left only a narrow ring of minerals around the edges instead of the thick crust I'd have expected. There was power in the spring, visible in Beast's sight, power glowing through the water. Magic ascended with the hot spring, a rosy, vibrant energy visible in Beast-vision. This was . . . this was a magic heated pool.

In the deep iris of the pool something bright flashed by. Something with fins.

Or wings.

It flashed by again.

Arcenciel. That's an arcenciel, I thought. *Oh crap. This place . . .* I looked around, remembering Molly's explanation of liminal lines and ley lines. *This is one of those rare places where multiple ley lines and maybe a liminal line cross over. This is a liminal opening. A rift. Holy crap. I found a rift.*

Light blasted from the pupil.

Blinding.

Fast as the light, Beast whipped her body. Leaped. Flew back behind the tree trunk. At least twenty feet, into cover.

An arcenciel flashed up. Mouth open, teeth glistening. Throwing steaming water and magic. The scent was mineral and blue, if blue was a scent. The smell of arcenciel was unlike that of another creature. The smell of silk, of blue swallowtail butterflies, their wings still damp from the pupae, the scent of burned bamboo. And like the scent of nothing at all.

I/we peeked out and watched as the young one hovered in midair like a gigantic hummingbird, flinging water from her wings and tail, her entire snakelike body vibrating. She alighted on a boulder, skimmed open her diaphanous wings, like panes of purple, lavender, and black crystal set in deep gray leading. Her body was the charcoal of darkly tinted glass, her frills and horns in the purples of her wings. Her tongue was a black leathery thing, split in two at the tip, and she flicked sulfur water from herself. Ten feet long, she was fully dragon formed, and her gigantic eyes were the color of bluest labradorite.

I had never seen her before. She was . . . new.

There was something that suggested that she was not only young, but powerful, and used to going her own way. And maybe she was hungry.

Beast is not prey.

Beast is not at the top of the food chain right now, I thought.

Beast is best hunter.

Yeah. Beast best be quiet as the night.

There had been discord in the arceniel world, with most of the species wanting to kill Leo Pellissier and others wanting to try to go back in time to wipe out all the vampires. Soul had walked protection around the island where Leo had fought his Sangre Duello to keep him safe, but it hadn't been enough. Leo had died. And I had to wonder if Leo's death was the one thing Soul had been forced to give up to keep the arceniels from going back in time, to keep the arceniel war from happening. Leo's death. And the death of Titus, the emperor. And . . . crap. The death of the Son of Darkness, Joses Bar-Judas.

I had given her all three.

One way or another, I had killed them all.

I still didn't know what the rainbow dragons needed to be able go back in time far enough to kill both of the SODs, and what that might do to the timeline of human history. Hayyel had shown me many timelines.

One had been war among the arceniels.

I tensed. If this young one was here to join or instigate a war between Soul and others of her species, should I try to kill her?

I had ridden on Soul's back. I still had a scale from the arceniel Opal. I wondered if I could shape-shift into an arceniel using the scale. And if so, what would that do to me? Would it be the same kind of black magic that turned my kind into *u'tlun'ta*—liver-eater? Would it be the same kind of evil that shifting into the living form of a human was? Or would shifting into an arceniel heal me?

Could I . . . Should I try to stop the war? Which action

was the most moral, which the most immoral? How horrible to allow my worst nightmares to live because I knew that even worse things would happen if I killed off the known and existing horror.

Even thinking about such a thing was a slippery slope.

The arcenciel snapped her wings closed, tilted back her head, and opened her long mouth. And she began to sing.

If magic was notes, it would be this. This sound that was the taste and scent and sight of light, like honey and buttercups and daffodils and the scarlet of sunset. It was the sound of light, like lightning and the *shoosh* of a crimson leaf settling to the ground. It was the texture of pearls and the chill of cut sapphires. It was the sound of silver bells ringing in an ancient temple. The vision of the rubies glittering. All that magic shivered through Beast's pelt. The song called and cajoled and promised the answer to mysteries and the offer of the peace of death.

Midnote, the arcenciel snapped open her wings and jumped high, flying straight up. Singing. Calling. And she was gone. Cats don't cry, but Beast blinked away tears. Her entire body was quivering like a violin string beneath the bow.

Go back. Go back to littermate. Do not like it here, she thought at me.

Yeah, yeah. Okay.

Her paws on a narrow branch, she rotated and raced away from the rock walls, around the fae garden, and up a more gradual slope, climbing trees and leaping from stone to stone, not resting, not slowing. We raced through the glowering dark and up the crevasse walls, leaping. Too fast for the lack of light and the ice buildup on the protrusions. I withdrew from the front of her mind, letting Beast have her body back.

Her front paws slipped. Beast tumbled. Thick tail rotating. Above us, a grinding rumble sounded and stone broke lose. Plummeting. Bouncing off, stone on stone. Crashing echoes. Beast caught her balance on a dead tree, branches wedged in stone. A branch cracked and the tree slipped. She pushed off and landed on a ledge so tiny her paws barely fit, lined up in a row, her body pressed to the wall. The broken boulders landed below, crashing and shattering.

Fun! Beast thought.

No. Not fun. Holy crap!

She leaped again and raced upward, until we were at the top of the ravine, some quarter of a mile away from where we had gone down. I didn't ask if she knew her way back. My mind was filled with too many questions and not enough answers. And with visions of falling, our cat body crushed by boulders. Beast sped back to the SUV. Leaping from branch to branch, over rocks, and scattering icy clumps of snow. She was panting hard, her paws hot on the snow. We had come a long way, and if it hadn't been so cold, Beast would have been overheated long before we saw Eli's headlights in the dark.

Stop! I thought.

She halted. So fast she nearly toppled forward. Only cat balance, dropping to her haunches, prevented her fall. *Eli would never leave the lights on, advertising his location,* I thought.

She raised her head and scented, drawing in air over her tongue and the scent sacks in the roof of her mouth. She made the faintest *scree* of sound. *Smell vampires,* Beast thought back. *Smell strange vampires.*

Oh crap.

Beast moved slowly through the darkness, back paws into front paw prints, *pawpawpaw*, overlapping, steps silent. *Silent.* She leaped into the branches. Approaching the lights and the stealthy sounds, her puma ears picked up.

Scent vampires. More than one. Not more than five.

No way anyone could have found us. They had to track us. Crap. Eli had stopped two vamps at the sweathouse. I bet they evaded the sensors and monitors and put devices on the vehicles. Crap, crap, crap.

Do not smell Eli blood. Littermate is uninjured. Or strangled.

Strang— That's a big freaking help.

Jane is welcome. Beast sometimes kills prey by holding

neck until deer falls asleep. Then Beast kills. Sometimes prey dies from holding bite.

From thirty feet high, Beast approached the SUV. SUVs. There were two of the vehicles now, ours and a red Range Rover. Lipstick red. Like the one that delivered Shiloh to us. The red vehicle had its lights on.

Four vampires stood in a wedge on the snowy road, facing into the bare trees. Three of them wore jeans, dress shirts, and dark ties. One of them wore a fancy wool coat. Lego, his blond hair whiter than his pale skin. Eli was nowhere in sight. Hidden in the dark. Lego hadn't been at the Regal with the Flayer of Mithrans. I studied the others and decided they hadn't been there either. So it was possible, likely even, that we had two groups of vamps in town, both of them threats. *Well, isn't that just ducky.*

Is not ducks, Beast thought. *Is vampires.*

Yeah. And I don't have time to shift.

Jane is dying. Beast is best hunter.

"You will give us the crystal," Lego said, speaking into the trees. "The dragon that Joseph Santana wore is mine to ride."

Joseph—Joses—the elder Son of Darkness, had owned a crystal with an arcenciel trapped in it. The dragon made it possible for Joses to navigate through time, at least to a limited degree. Until a fight took place and the crystal broke, freeing the dragon, and Joses got bitten. Arcenciel bites made vamps nutso-bonkers-crazy, so crazy Joses had hung on a wall in the lowest basement in vamp central in NOLA for a hundred years, raving, his powerful blood Leo's to drink. These guys wanted *that* crystal. They had inside info, but it was outdated. I had given a spell to the arcenciels that would free them from any crystal, and I had fed Joses to Brute. So far as I knew, the big meal didn't even cause the werewolf heartburn.

Seconds had passed as all that ran through my mind, with an undercurrent thought and sensory pattern by Beast. She took in the trees, the branches, the tops of the SUVs, the headlights, the position of the vamps, and the likely position of Eli, based on where the vamps were facing.

Eli is in tree, there, Beast looked to our right, about twenty feet off the ground. In Beast's night vision, I could make out the silver green of my partner. He was wearing his cold suit, probably invisible to the vamps, but they could likely smell him and pick up his heartbeat. Beast gathered herself tight, claws partially protracted, touching the cold bark.

"Oh. Well, you see, Bubbah, there's a small problem with that," Eli said, his tone laconic, his voice filling the emptiness of the small clearing. "The crystals are all broken and the dragons are all free. And Joseph Santana, aka Joses Bar-Judas, aka the elder Son of Darkness, aka asshole of the paranormal world, is true-dead." He chuckled, his battlefield mirth, more death than amusement. "And by the way, as long as we're on the subject of dragons, the arcenciels are pissed at the vamps for the slavery-in-a-crystal thing. They're thinking about war."

As he spoke, the three other vamps spread out, moving into the dark. Beast gathered herself. There was a soft *sssss*, followed by a prolonged thump, as if a vamp had dropped into the snow and banged his head. The smell of vamp blood spread on the air.

Another *sssss*, and a second thump, this one a tumble. We placed the sound and Beast gave a cat grin, all teeth and viciousness. *Flying claws,* she thought. Eli was playing with his new toy and he got off two shots with the bow before the vamps figured out what was happening and moved. I heard a *pop* of vamp movement, displaced air, fangheads faster than the human eye can follow. Yet, Beast's eyes tracked both by sound, movement of air, smell.

Beast is best hunter. Before I could react, she leaped. Front legs stretching, claws out, back legs shoving hard.

She fell fast in a horizontal-distance-to-fall ratio that spanned the vehicles, the entire clearing, and hid her in night shadows on the other side. I never saw the branch she landed on, just felt gravity jar through our body as she half landed, half shoved off and vectored at a sharp angle that stole nothing from her momentum. She fell again. Fast.

Beast rammed into a softer body. Claws ripping. Grabbing. Teeth sinking in. The crunch of bone and tear of tendons. The taste of acid, hot peppers, and cold blood. *My vampire prey. My meat. My blood.*

She rode the vampire down. Slinging her head back and forth, dislocating the vertebrae. Cold blood splattered. We bounced on his back. Beast continued working the spine, back and forth. Until she ripped out a chunk of vertebra.

Holy crapoley, I thought.

My meat.

I got that. But you might need to eat later.

In the trees, the sound of gunfire was sharp and nearly painful. Protectively, we tucked our ear tabs. Sniffed. Smelled the stench of guns and blood on the still air. Human blood.

Eli blood? Littermate? Beast thought, raising her head, tracing the sound and the scents. Her tongue slicked her jaw and nose clean of the strange vamp blood. Tasted bad.

Snow started to fall, large, saucer-sized things too big to be called flakes. Heavy and wet, they made a noise when they landed, like tiny *plumffs* in the silence.

Beast has vampire one. Two vampire, with flying claw in body, is there. She glanced toward something in the snow. I didn't have time to focus through her eyes. She turned her head. *There is three vampire with flying claw in body.* She looked up and into the darkness. An enormous snow-pancake landed on her snout. Another between her shoulders. *Eli is there. Smell Eli blood.* Beast jumped straight up, sank her bloody claws into the trunk, raced high. Into the tree branches. Stretched into a sprint across the limbs toward the blood scent.

Drew up hard. Stopped. At the base of a neighboring tree was Legolas look-alike, dark blood on the icy white carpet. Heavy white snow landed on his fancy coat and white face. A shaft protruded from his chest, directly over his heart. We smelled the acrid stink of vamp blood and silver. Lego was a goner unless we got a master vamp to bleed and read and revive him. Blood splattered over his body.

Above him, facedown on a branch, was Eli. Arms and legs had been holding him in place. Now all four dangled. Blood ran off the fingers of his right hand, stained his cold-coat sleeve. He wasn't moving. Beast made a single long bound, hard and high, landed, claws sinking into the bark, beside him. Claws on her left arm retracted. She swatted his face. Again. Sorrowful, anguished, she thought, *Much blood. Too much blood.*

Eli shifted slightly. He began to slide. He might not survive the landing.

No! I/we screamed. *Puma concolor* scream. Pain blasted through my arm. Fingers with retracted claws grabbed him. A humanish hand. Holding littermate. Pain ratcheted through my hand bones and up my arm.

Other claws sank into bark and wood. Opened mouth. Bit into back of coat. Knocked things on top of Lego.

Medical supplies, I thought. *He was trying to treat himself.*

Littermate heart is stopping, Beast thought, grief racking through us both. *Littermate is becoming meat.*

No. I need two hands.

Beast thought for a moment. *Cannot stand on two paws on tree.*

Okay. We need to let him down. Not drop him. He'd break a bone and then he'd be dead fast.

Is better than being dead slow.

No. We still have three paws. Can we hold him in one hand and teeth and climb down the tree?

Am not jaguar or leopard. Jaguar or leopard can walk down tree with dead prey better than Beast. Puma concolor *can climb with dead prey. Can drop dead prey. Cannot walk to ground with dead prey. Call new/old littermate?*

I remembered the smell of big-cat in the snow. I hadn't wanted to accept it, but I had known the truth of what Beast was saying now. Ayatas FireWind had been on the vineyard grounds. He might still be here, somewhere. Maybe close enough to hear if I screamed for help. He would know the call of a puma. He would know it was me. But the chances that he was close by were small. I hadn't smelled him, not anywhere on my trek.

To save Eli, I was going to have to shift into half-form, on this branch, without falling, without dropping Eli, and toss him over my naked shoulder and carry him to the ground. Yeah. That worked. I backed slowly, *pawpaw-paw*, pulling Eli into place on the branch. Precarious but stable for now. His heart was racing, too fast. Stuttering.

Beast, I thought. *Half-form. With retractable claws on all four paw-feet and a full puma face. And fast.*

Beast thought a moment. *Jane will hurt.*

Kinda figured that. Hurry.

Jane will hurt like prey in fangs of sabertooth lion.

I reached around the branch and sank my claws in. *Go.* And she was right. It was bad.

CHAPTER 13

My Blood to Your Blood.
Your Heart to My Heart.

When the pain eased and the shift was over, my snout was fully mountain lion. My arms were some funky form of puma/human and fully pelted. I still had my fangs in Eli's jacket and was holding on with both hands under his arms. There was a lot of blood and he stank of near death. If he hadn't had access to vamp blood in New Orleans, he'd be dead now already. I gripped the bark with my retractable back claws, let go his jacket. Pulled him up over my shoulder as I sat up. Straddled the branch, getting snow and bark in places I'd be sorry for later.

With Eli over my shoulder and his blood dripping down my spine and through my pelt, I scooted to the trunk of the tree. Sinking my claws in, I pulled myself to a standing position. I was breathing heavily by the time I managed it. We were twenty feet up. At least. I gripped the tree, four-footed support, arms around it, bare boobs scraping on the bark. And I began the torturous descent. I was cursing steadily through Beast lips by the time I reached the ground. Relief swept through me like boiling oil, and I broke out in a sweat. I stumbled drunkenly through the snow, overbalanced by my partner, bark rash up my belly to my neck and all along the inside of my thighs. I opened the back hatch of his SUV and lay him gently on the floor space, shoving weapons and Eli stuff out of the way.

Over the sound of my own breathing I heard a heart-beat. It was fast and irregular.

I raced back to the tree and gathered up the medical supplies and slung the bow over my shoulder. I evaluated Legolas as I raced past. He had two arrows in him, the silver points buried in his chest. Silver was a deadly poison in vamp blood unless he was überpowerful or his master was handy. Not him. I sprinted on to Vampire Two and found him with a carbon fiber and ash wood arrow lower down, in his belly, the silver tip all the way through and out the back, the wound paralyzing but no longer poisoning, keeping him in a type of stasis the same way a stake would. "You'll do." I shoved the arrow deeper and grabbed his left arm. I ducked and drew him over my shoulder, into the same position recently vacated by my partner, and jogged back to the SUV. "I don't know if you can feel while paralyzed by ash wood, but I hope this hurts like a mother," I said. Vamp Two didn't reply.

I dumped him into the hatch area with my partner and ripped open Eli's shirt, revealing gunshot wounds. Two chest wounds, one below his right shoulder, in and out, that had to have clipped the artery that fed his arm, and probably nicked a lung. The other was on his lower left chest; that probably took out a rib and his spleen and maybe a kidney. Its exit wound larger. Much larger.

I tore open four of the next-generation XStat syringes and shoved them each into a wound, depressing the plungers almost simultaneously. The specially coated, biode-gradable sponges shot into his body cavity and stopped the bleeding within seconds. But he was cold and his breath rate was too fast. Eli was in shock.

Eli was already dying.

He needed a trauma team and multiple transfusions and surgeries.

Or vamp blood.

Pulling one of my partner's blades, I sliced Two's shirt off and raked his inner arm with my claws. His blood smelled horrible. I hesitated and then licked a claw. The taste was even worse, burning my tongue.

I spat it out, remembering the first time a sane-ish vampire caught my scent. The first time I smelled their blood, like sulfur and nitric acid, something caustic. Awful. And then Bethany healed me. Everything changed when I was healed by Bethany. Why?

Beast likes blood. All vampire blood is strong. But not for littermate.

There had to be a . . . a "come to Jesus moment" between paranormal predators before scent and blood taste were acceptable. Leo had accepted me and that made my scent acceptable to his people. I let Bethany heal me with her blood.

I was the Dark Queen. That supposedly gave me power and gifts, probably accompanied by lots of things I should be able to do, unknown gifts. I was the freaking, dang Dark Queen of the fangheads. That had to mean that I could, theoretically, claim bloodsuckers. I'd done it once. With Edmund.

I didn't want another vampire servant.

Eli's heart skipped a beat. It stuttered fast. Skipped.

I tore my wrist with my fangs, deliberately missing nerve and artery, and held the welling wound over the vamp's mouth. I reached for the Gray Between.

Skinwalker energies burst from my chest and rose around me. I reached for the magics that were mine and the magics that were other—witch and vamp—and gripped them together in my mental hands. Power strummed through me, heated against my palms. I pulled the magics away from the star pattern of my middle. They gave a soft twang and realigned into two figure eights, one in each mental hand. One blue-gray, one scarlet, both pulsing in time with my heartbeat. Okay. That was new.

I studied the energies of life around me. Eli was the stagnant stink and dark reddish brown of death, with only flickers of living blue and purple. His life force had almost bled away. The vamp's energies were darker, deep rose in tone, and smelled of ginger. Despite the ash wood in his belly, he was still undead. I touched one finger of my free physical hand to the vamp's chest and tapped the vampire energies. They rang with a note like a fingernail striking a crystal glass.

The first drops of my blood dripped into his mouth. A version of words that I vaguely recalled from Leo came to my mind. I snarled as best I could with my Beast-mouth, "My blood to your blood. Your heart to my heart. Your loyalty, I demand. *Now.*" And I reached for his mind. His heart.

His soul . . .

I ripped out the ash wood arrow. The vamp swallowed.

His brain was a kaleidoscope of shadows and light, pinks and purples and a burst of what looked like glitter in black light. His name was Klaus. He was sixty-two years old, born in East Germany. He was weak. A lower-level vamp.

I remembered the silver chain that once bound Leo, king of the U.S. vamps. I fashioned a silver chain of the Gray Between and wrapped it around Klaus's energies. Tied it to myself, in my soul home. I realized that wouldn't help Eli. I reached for Eli's energies and braided a second tiny strand of my skinwalker magic to Eli's will to live. "Just a minute or two," I whispered. "I'll break it as soon as you're stable. I promise."

I held Klaus's wrist so that blood dripped into Eli's mouth. "Drink," I pleaded. "Please drink."

The blood dripped in. I feared I'd choke him to death. A cold breeze swirled through the SUV, stealing what warmth there was. Ten drops into Eli's mouth. Twenty. Finally Eli swallowed. He managed five small mouthfuls without coughing.

I dripped vamp blood into Eli's torn flesh at each of the wounds, watching as they closed. I sliced a cut along the vamp's other wrist and went back to Eli's mouth, feeding him. After three swallows, he turned his head away, grinding out the words, "God-awful. Worse 'an greasy grimy gopher guts."

A small gulping sound left my throat. "Gastronomically

gruesome," I agreed, the boil of relief simmering through me again. The vamp groaned and I shoved the arrow back into Klaus's belly, rolled the vamp against the sidewall, and dressed Eli's wounds by placing layers of gauze over the top of each. I secured them in place with stretchy wrap.

"Sick," he muttered. I rolled Eli so he could vomit, and my partner's stomach emptied. The stench was blood and stomach acids. The vamp blood looked clotted and slimy.

I wiped Eli's mouth with his cold coat. It wasn't very absorbent. "I'm getting you home. Hang in there."

"Silver shackles in the . . . metal chest," he managed.

"No time. I'm getting you home." There were blankets and a down quilt and even an electric heating pad that ran on the car battery in the sidewall compartments, and I wrapped my partner in the folds and turned on the pad to combat the shock, which killed people faster than simple blood loss. Tucked his feet and his body between the crates and chests and loose gear, his feet higher than this heart.

"Babe." He stopped and exhaled slowly. I thought he had passed out. Then he finished. "Get clothes. You got . . . hairy boobs."

"If you're looking at boobs you aren't going to die." Chuckling, I broke Klaus's neck with a vicious twist, slammed the hatch, and raced to the front, where I turned on the SUV and set the heater to max. Then I negotiated a six-point turn and eased up even with the red Rover. I stopped and got out, opened the other driver's door. Found a key fob in the console and tossed it in Eli's SUV. With my partner's knife, I sliced through the sidewall of the driver's-side tires. Then I pulled through the dark and headed to the inn, calling Alex on the way.

I felt the SUV cross a magical warning system when I turned into the snow-blanketed drive. The *hedge of thorns* was a half mile ahead and it dropped as I made the last curve to the inn. It was huge, the biggest *hedge* I could have imagined. The moment we crossed it, Lincoln Shaddock himself raced from the front porch and into the snow. He nearly tore the hatch off its hinges getting it open, and his wrist was already bleeding. He held it to Eli's mouth. Thema, who had followed him into the snow, lifted Eli like a baby, side by side with Lincoln, carrying my partner inside. I had dressed as I drove, so I wasn't an embarrassment to myself or anyone else. And when Bruiser opened my car door and stepped close, I turned and lay my head against his belly. And burst into tears.

My honeybunch stroked my head and massaged my neck, which was unexpectedly pelted, and brushed behind my ears, all the while murmuring soothing sweet nothings. After too long a time for a badass woman with fangs and claws, I pushed away. He let me go.

"I passed the outgoing team. Did you find them?" I asked.

"Our team hasn't arrived, and they haven't passed a red Range Rover with two bad tires, but Kojo says there are fresh tracks in the snow that match that sort of damage. He thinks we missed them and expects to find them gone. The snowmobiles are trying to follow the tracks, but it isn't likely that the attackers will stick to back roads when the county has kept the main roads plowed."

"Eli wanted me to take the time to silver cuff them."

"In which case they would still be there, or their backup would have rescued them already and Eli would possibly be dead. Don't second-guess yourself in battle-field situations."

That sounded like Eli more than Bruiser, but I nodded and breathed in his scent, warm and citrusy and Onorio spicy. "There's a vamp in the back. He's temporarily bound to Eli. Eli shot him with an ash wood arrow in his belly and I broke his neck. He can be healed and bled and read."

"Good thinking." He paused, his hand unmoving on an ear tab. "Temporarily bound to Eli?"

"Yeah. Apparently as Dark Queen, I can do things with paranormal energies." I gave him a brief description of what I had done.

"That is very much like the way I bind with Onorio energies."

Which meant that I could, possibly, drain a vamp the

way an Onorio could. Interesting. "Could you bind me?
Could I bind you?"

Bruiser frowned, thinking. "Doubtful. Leo wasn't successful binding you, and I am not as powerful as Leo.
Anamchara mutual binding might be possible."

"No, thanks." I chuffed a breath and stood. "Love you,
but I don't need a third person in my brain."

Bruiser's eyes moved down my body. "You're injured?"

I looked down and the tree rash had seeped through
the sweatshirt in pinkish, bloody smears. "Nothing a shift
to some other form won't help." I explained about the
strange shift and the tree burn.

Although his concerned expression didn't alter, I
could have sworn that Bruiser smelled amused.

Inside, I ate a half-raw steak and trudged up the stairs to
shower and shift and make plans. On the way home I had
told Alex everything about the two groups of vamps in
town, more to keep him occupied and not in a panic
about his brother, and to give him something to do, than
out of urgent necessity. He had called in online help in
the form of Bodat, his gamer friend, to do research into
Legolas. I was sure he'd have something soon.

The shower water was hot and painful on the tree rash,
but I let the pain center me and hold me to the *now* so I
didn't look at the water droplets of time. Droplets that
might show me a way to keep my partner from getting
shot. I kept my eyes shut and grieved and soaped and
rinsed and let myself suffer. It was the very least I deserved.

When I was clean, I gave myself to Beast and let her
choose the form I'd take. I took that pain too, as my due,
and ended up a Jane-faced, unfanged, hairless half human with hard, fixed claws and long black hair. I dragged
myself back upright from the shower floor and turned off
the water. Dried my more familiar, healed body and
pulled on athletic undies and black Lycra yoga pants
along with a tight tee that covered my skin but left no
doubt that I was ready for battle. I looked pale so I put on

lipstick, red, the color of the Range Rovers and the color of Eli's blood. So I wouldn't forget that Legolas was mine. Added my double shoulder holster with the matching crimson grips—battle ready. The holster chafed my skin through the thin material, but I didn't care. I changed out the ammo for silver. Hair down, barefoot, I opened the door to the hallway.

Ed stood in the hallway, waiting. He said nothing. I waited. He still said nothing. My tone noncommittal and uninflected, I said, "Ed."

The silence stretched. I waited some more. Finally, he said, "I fear that in getting me free, you have shown Shimon all your cards. He cannot be beaten. He will attack this house and kill us all." His voice was broken, hoarse.

"Follow me." I turned and took the stairs at a springy fast pace that forced Ed to use his vamp powers to keep up. When I entered the central area I shouted, "Molly? Got a minute?"

"I got a minute, Big-Cat," she whispered, sticking her head around the wall from the baking kitchen, "but if you wake up my babies I'll skin you alive."

"Understood. Edmund seems to think that we've showed the big bad ugly all our cards and that Shimon will win. What's your professional witch opinion?"

Molly laughed, her red curls bouncing, body language looking innocent and prey-like, though her expression was definitely not prey. Her face was set in dangerous lines. "Not happening, Eddie. Not now, not ever." She stared at my primo. Her scent was ripe and intense, the musk of an apex predator. She had been practicing her death magics and I wondered how many trees in the forest out back she had killed. "You look like you've been tortured, healed, and tortured again, my fanghead friend."

"I'll live."

"Not really. Undead isn't alive."

"I'll take what I can get until my mistress and my sworn family are safe."

"Yeah?" She stepped around the wall, her hands fisted and a sprig of rosemary in her left. "You've been the prisoner of a mad vamp, possessed by his madder witch spirit.

I'm guessing he left a little something-something inside your head. You gonna let me take a look?"

"I'll die true-dead before I give up the sanctity of my mind again. No. You'll have to trust me."

"Trust?" She chortled as if he had said something witty. "Again. Not happening, Eddie. Not now, not until the Flayer is dead and eaten, though if we find a few days free, I could maybe create a *detection* working that might give us warning if you get a brain visitor."

"Yes. Thank you. Should you find time," Edmund said.

That shut Molly up. I could tell she hadn't expected him to agree.

Deep inside, Beast purred. She liked Ed's scent and Molly's scent and the words they volleyed back and forth like gunfire. I walked backward into the TV lounge, studying my primo as I went. Ed was silent, his footsteps following me, his eyes on Molly.

Ed was wearing black from head to toe, the clothes not fitting well, the sleeves and pants legs rolled up. I recognized Eli's wardrobe. Someone had given my heir and primo some of Eli's clothes to wear. He did look like crap, his hair lank, his neck a patchwork of scars that looked like a burn victim's. Edmund moved without that sliding grace of the Mithran as he stopped in front of the TV, his hollow, empty eyes on the screen that was replaying the scene at the Regal.

Before we reached the TV room, Molly said from the kitchen, "Witches don't need your help. You know that, right? My magics are the certainty of that."

Gently, Ed said, "If you use *all* your magics, Witch of Death, you may well kill everyone, human or para, in a twenty-five-mile radius."

I glanced back. Molly looked as if someone had slapped her, face pale and shocked, bright spots on each cheek. Witch of Death sounded like a very nasty title in my primo's world. Shimon had been in Ed's mind when the SOD Two recognized what Molly was. Witch of Death. *Dang.* I led Ed into the office.

Evan and Molly followed us both and the big guy

stood behind his wife, in the doorway. They moved together, like magnets attracting. Evan asked, "How do you know?"

Edmund said, "Any Mithran would know your power, Witch of Death. Even if I had not known before, I felt death at your call in the hotel main room." He pointed at the screen where the event played over and over. "There and then. When the first two Naturaleza fell as if truedead. It was not a *spell* calculated to bring down the Mithrans, but pure, raw death magics."

"Do you think the FOM knew what they were?" I asked, sitting on my recliner.

"Once I would say yes, absolutely. But he has changed. He has developed a . . ." Ed chuckled, the sound not real laughter, but not fear and death either. ". . . a thick skin." Ed was talking about the exoskeleton. He was making a joke, even so soon after rescue. "He is darkness and shadow, and nothing but a close-in detonation of a large-scale bomb or being burned in a cremation chamber may take him into true-death now." Ed slid a glance my way. "Or being eaten by an angel-touched white werewolf. The only good thing about this change and the magics he is now using is that the Flayer of Mithrans has lost the ability to detect some other forms of magic." His eyes moved to the Everhart-Truebloods on the sofa. "Except for death magics, it seems. I do not know why."

Before the two witches decided to test out their secret-not-so-secret weapon on Ed, I said, "Why didn't you take over as emperor? Why didn't you announce my resignation to the vamp world?"

Ed looked back at the screen, where the two videos were showing in loops. "Grégoire and I discussed it. We called a meeting of the Mithrans who received word of your resignation. We watched all the video footage of the Sangre Duello. We decided that you would make a grand figurehead. That we should both, Grégoire and I, seize territory in your name and hold it, until such time as the Soul of Night, the Son of the Screaming Darkness, the Son of Shadows, the Flayer of Mithrans, should rise from his recent rest and announce he was coming for you. We knew it would not take long for his hubris and narcissism to send him after you."

"So I was bait." *Again,* I thought. *And always.*

Ed shrugged, not a human movement, but as if his shoulders writhed like snakes. "Shimon was always one to speak loudly, to make grand gestures. When he did so, our plan was to strike, kill him, and bring his body to you to dispose of as you did his brother. Once he was dead, accepting the crown of emperor would be a simple thing for you or for me, should you still wish to retire. But Shimon did not announce. He attacked first. An unexpected new ploy for the eldest among us. I was not prepared for him to act out of character, in opposition to millennia of recorded and witnessed actions and reactions. I was caught unaware."

Something flashed through my back brain, half-remembered and then gone. Trying to tease it back, I said slowly, "In Shimon's time, names had meaning. I understand why he'd be called Soul of Night, Flayer of Mithrans, and even Son of the Screaming Darkness. But why Son of Shadows on top of Soul of Night?" I sat a buttock on the table edge. "I mean, he's old enough to be a daywalker, but there's no evidence he pops from shadow to shadow or anything."

I thought about the vision I'd had of the shadow that had been trying to infect Ed's mind. Of the way Ed's hands had moved when Shimon had controlled the minds of his scions and humans. "The shadow inside your vision? Did it . . . possess you totally?"

"Control of my mouth was not true possession, my mistress. True possession is when there is no longer resistance."

I wasn't sure I agreed with that answer. I wasn't sure it was a statement of truth either.

Ed opened his mouth as if to speak again. Closed it. Carefully, he turned to Evan and Molly and said, "I pledged my honor to your family." He swung his eyes to me. "Sabina told me that my life is bound with theirs and with yours. When you accidently claimed me"—he smiled slightly and breathed out like a human, releasing tension—"you put a protection over my soul. The shadow of the Flayer of Mithrans was not able to penetrate that shielding."

I still didn't know what the names really meant, but I had a feeling that they were all important. That they all told me something about the creature we fought, if I could only figure out what. I gave a truncated nod. Because what if the FOM told him to say that?

"Sabina told me that there would come a time when warriors would gather against warriors," he said. "And that I should tell you to remember the *Bubo bubo*."

I didn't tense, but it was a near thing. Conundrums upon enigmas upon dilemmas. Sabina in the longhouse with the warriors and my grandmother. Sabina smelling of owls. Sabina seeing my owl form once and speaking Mithran prophecy.

"Your hair needs braiding." His fingers twitched as if to reach for me, but he halted, unsure, as if reading my almost-distrust.

I felt like a traitor to suspect him, but . . . "Ummm. I'm good right now," I said.

His eyes moving back to the witch couple, Edmund said, "Shimon recognized the power of Molly and her husband, Evan. Like his brother, he wants to kill or possess all witches. Your friends, the family to whom I swore fealty, are in grave danger. Keep them close to your breast and beneath your wing." Which seemed an un-Eddie-like thing to say.

"Go to bed with a few blood-servants and drink," I said. "We'll have a plan in place soon." *But we might not tell you what it is.*

He turned and left the room. For the first three steps, it was like watching a reptile walk, not Edmund. Then he slid into Ed's smooth gait. Over his shoulder, he said, "I will bleed and read and partially heal your Mithran prisoner, and turn his loyalty to me. We will know all he knows."

I hadn't noted that my detainee was lying in the front entrance where someone had dropped him like the undead body he was. "His name is Klaus," I said.

"I do not care." Which, again, was a very non-Ed thing to say, and made me wonder how much of the Flayer's mind was still part of Ed's. "Alex," Edmund said, his voice compulsion and request all at once. "Would you put on 'Evil Mama' by Bonamassa." Alex told Merlin to play the song, and the strains instantly filled the speaker system in the entire main level, a song about knifing a man in the back. I wondered if Edmund felt I had done that to him, or if he was trying to warn me that the Flayer still resided in part of his mind.

My primo picked up Klaus's arm and dragged him through the house and out the back door, the hard-driving guitar and accusing lyrics hanging between us.

Klaus left a trail of melted snow tinged with blood. His shoes came off, resting a few yards apart in a bloody patch.

The blood reminded me that Ed was a vampire in every way. A hunter. A predator. A killer.

However. Edmund swore fealty to Molly and to Angie Baby. No matter what else, I knew he would protect them all.

Molly, however, wasn't so sanguine. She and Evan stepped over the trail and headed to their rooms. Her narrowed eyes followed Ed as he went through the house and out the mudroom door, Klaus's body banging over the threshold and down the steps. The door closed behind them. Silent, without looking at me, they went to their rooms.

I checked in on my clan. Bruiser was busy with the high-level vamps in Shaddock's cottage, talking about the immediate future battling Shimon, and the more distant future when the Flayer of Mithrans was dead. It was a formal parley, the kind of meetings that Leo Pellissier had reveled in and the kind of meetings that I slept through. In his room, Eli was sleeping off a near-death experience with Thema curled around him. They were both naked and I didn't want to know what had happened between them. Molly and Evan and the kids were in their rooms with the door shut. Moll's sisters were closeted with them. Alex wasn't talking to me, bingeing on energy drinks. I was on my own.

I pulled on a sweatshirt over my comfy clothing, found the arceneil scale, the eagle feather, and my father's medicine bag. And my own. I took three throwing knives and a vamp-killer, just in case more vamps found a way onto the property, and walked through the now-swirling snow to the sweathouse.

There was no music here accusing an "Evil Mama" of doing bad things. It was silent and cold, even the ashes. I closed the door on the ice and started a fire using matches, a bag of Fritos, and a tiny bottle of vodka I had swiped off the wet-bar shelf. It wasn't traditional. I didn't care. The combo of greasy corn and alcohol lit the curls of bark and dry splinters, and the fire spread quickly to the larger pieces. When I had a good blaze going I used the long pole I found in the corner to open the small door in the dormer that would both let out smoke and let in light, so I'd know when it was dawn.

I sat by the fire and took the weapons, pushing them behind the nearest half-log seat. I dug the snowball crystals from the fur between my toes and flicked the melting ice into the dark.

Carefully, I spread my treasures on the dirt floor in front of my bent knee, all but my gold nugget and mountain lion tooth, which I wore around my neck. I had the eagle feather. The arceneil scale. The medicine bags. The Glob. The crown of my Dark Queen office.

My own medicine bag was dyed a dark green on one side. I opened it and found it wasn't as empty as I had believed. There were two bits of waxed paper, folded over. Inside one was a pinch of raw native tobacco. In the other waxed envelope was what smelled like white sage. The bag was too small for the golden eagle flight feather, but its contents were a good start on a real medicine bag, which should contain the things the earth gave, the symbols of a life well lived. Eli had chosen well.

My father's medicine bag was old and faded, the edges soft and powdery. I hadn't noticed until now, but once there had been something sewn on the bottom. Maybe a beaded fringe. Maybe a bit of woven fabric. The ancient medicine bag was full. I had never gone through it, never searched the contents. It had seemed disrespectful, until now.

Carefully, I opened my father's bag. It was so old there was only the hint of scent. Rotting deer hide. Tannins. Inside was a small length of jawbone, the teeth attached, a child's teeth. Mine, if the memory and my brother were right. I didn't remember and he hadn't been alive when I was hit by a white man hard enough to break my jaw, to knock the bone chip from my face. Five-year-old me had tried to kill him for raping a Cherokee woman. He had tried to kill me right back and nearly succeeded.

I shivered, my spine frozen, my face and chest and hands warming at the fire. One-handed, I rearranged the rocks ringing the fire. One rock was actually a rounded-out bowl, shaped and smooth. Another rock was long with a rectangular cleft, like a tunnel down the middle. Ceremonial objects. Still one-handed, I set them to the side.

My bone and teeth felt alien and oddly menacing in my other palm.

Slowly the sweathouse warmed and my shivers decreased. Time passed. I sweated. I woke once to find myself lying by the fire and added logs to it.

I dreamed and, in the dreams, I hunted as Beast. Deer, turkey, catfish, alligator, were all my prey. Blood and fury flashed through me as I tore out the throat of a man who was cutting down the trees of the forest and denuding the mountains. I mated with a strong male, the pain intense and tearing, followed by the contentment of knowing I carried kits. I raced along high ridges and leaped down cliffs onto small ledges to climb into a tiny den. I suckled a litter, hungry, and knowing there was nothing to eat, not anywhere.

Scents changed. I smelled the warmth of spring and fresh blood and the glory of the hunt. I smelled the memory of my first shift, the excitement and the fear sweat. I chased my first rabbit as *We-sa*. I tasted my first fear-soaked blood and ripped the steaming meat from the carcass.

I dreamed the memory of fighting *tlvdatsi*. And stealing Beast's body and her soul.

I heard the door of the sweathouse open and I sat up. Grit from the floor was crushed into my face, along with the teeth of my childhood. My brother stood in the opening. He entered and closed the door on the icy night. The firelight illuminated him. Tall, dressed in jeans, snow boots, a down vest, and a peacoat. The clothing was deeply wrinkled, as if it had been balled up and put away for months. He peeled out of the coat and removed his boots and socks.

I brushed the grit from my face, gripping the teeth and bone in my palm. The dream was lucid, intense, rich with texture, scent, sound, vision. I could even feel the irritation of the sweaty grit beneath my fingers.

Barefooted, Ayatas FireWind, my brother, came to the fire and bowed his head to me. He said, *"Nuwhtohiyada gotlvdi."*

I tried to swallow but my throat tissues were too dry. I croaked softly, "You asked that once before. I said no. Why ask again?"

"I came to you with an impure heart. I came to you *udalvquodi* and with *kanalvisdi*—arrogant and in secret anger. I came with the jealousy of a foolish boy. I deserved no gift of peace from you. No welcome. I carry the shame of my weakness and I beg forgiveness of the elder sister, the beloved woman of my clan."

Beloved woman. A Cherokee phrase for *war woman*. I gave him a tribal shrug and a soft grunt. It communicated that I was listening, and that, while I wasn't accepting all he came to say, I was hearing his words, allowing his presence, and I wasn't going to try to kill him. Yet.

"May I sit at your fire? I have brought *nodatsi aditasdi*. It is the recipe made by our mother. It will quench your thirst."

Nodatsi aditasdi. Spicewood tea. One made strong, of sarsaparilla and other herbs, with notes of vanilla, caramel, wintergreen, and licorice. I remembered. My mouth wanted to water and would have if I hadn't been sweating for hours. I inclined my head. Ayatas sat across the fire from me and stretched an arm up, removing a pack that had been slung around him on a single short strap, hanging at his back. The bag smelled of leather and steel and herbs and gunpowder. And oddly of jungle cat and the ocean. He pulled out a liter of spring water and reached around the fire to the equipment left by my Cherokee Elder. His hand paused, as if startled, as it passed over the war drum. But he took the mortar and pestle from the center of the pile. Removed a zipped plastic bag from his near-empty gobag and poured some dried herbs into the stone mortar. The intense scent of sassafras filled my nose and I dreamed a dream within a dream, of my mother, sitting on a low stool before the fire, pouring tea for me to drink. *Nodatsi aditasdi*. Mama's spicewood tea. This time my mouth did produce a little moisture.

My brother ground the spices and poured them into the bowl I had placed in the fire. The stone was hot and the herbs made little popping sounds as he added water, a little at a time. As he worked, his yellow eyes lifted to me several times. "You came to sweat with no water. Was that intentional?" He added another log. Sparks and smoke rose on the air.

I gave the Tsalagi grunt again. My braid slid over my shoulder. It was gritty and crusted with sweat salt. A messy braid with several duplicated twists and hanging strands. The braid of a Cherokee was an indication of spiritual status and mystical strength. The hair was rebraided only by someone completely trusted. Ayatas's braid was perfect, a complicated weaving of maybe a half dozen strands. It was neat and economical and beautiful. Angie had braided mine hours ago, and from a style standpoint it was awful. But it was braided with love and that counted for more than style.

I couldn't decide if I cared.

Ayatas stirred his tea with a long splinter of wood from the fire, adding a smoky, ashy flavor. "*Adawehi* has folded his wings over you, *e-igido*."

Adawehi. Cherokee for *angel*. My voice sounded as rough as broken stone when I said, "His name is Hayyel. He's totally untrustworthy. Treacherous. Devious. He claims to be the hand of God, and while he did help us fight a demon, I'd never let him braid my hair."

Ayatas looked at my messy braid before returning to the preparation of the tea. I got the feeling that time had passed when he lifted the bowl with both hands and poured the tea into two wood cups. He replaced the bowl in the hot ashes and lifted the cups in his hands. This was an odd dream.

"*Ugalogv*, my sister. Drink."

Ugalogv. Tea. I took the cup and waited until he lifted his cup to his lips before I sipped. Then drained the cup and wished for more. There was still water in the one-liter bottle. But Ayatas handed me a fresh bottle instead. I wrapped my lips around it and crushed it with one knobby hand as I drank it down.

He was right. I hadn't brought water. Hadn't thought about replacing the water bottles I had used during my last sweat. I set the empty aside and accepted the salt tablet Ayatas offered. The door to outside opened. Icy air swept into the room. The fire blazed up high. Faster than I could follow, my brother was holding a semiautomatic, centered on the doorway.

Edmund stood there, outlined by darkness. He looked at my brother, took in the weapon, ignored it, and transferred his gaze to me. "Thema was watching the security cameras. She saw a spotted big-cat race onto the property and shift into a naked man. He disappeared. I came to see that you are safe. Are you well, my mistress, my Dark Queen?"

"I'm just ducky," I said, my voice sounding more human and less croaky. "Update. Why was Thema watching the screens?" Old vamps were seldom tech-savvy.

"She is capable. Alex is sleeping, exuding the stench of poison energy drinks. Eli is healing. Lincoln Shaddock is working with the witches to secure the grounds, yet this one"—he pointed at Aya—"got through the defenses."

"How?"

"He reads as skinwalker. Like you. They are adjusting the *hedge of thorns* for were-creatures, and the white werewolf is feeling unwelcome. The wolf is most insistent upon being with you." Ed stepped aside and Brute pushed through, into the sweathouse. The smell of wet wolf was strong on the air.

Ayatas turned the gun on my werewolf. Brute snorted with amusement. Edmund said, "Brute ate the Son of Darkness. I doubt you could kill him with anything less than an atomic bomb. If you harm my mistress, I will hunt you down and flay the skin from your body. Then I will tan the flesh and make a horsewhip from it."

Ayatas sighed and put the weapon away with a soft click of Kydex. The wolf plopped down beside me and dropped his enormous head in my lap. That was when I realized that I wasn't dreaming and hadn't been for some time. I was awake. My brother and my primo were both really here, and the wolf was asking for scritches. My life was . . . not my own anymore. Hadn't been for a very long time. I put a hand on the wolf's head and massaged his ears. He sighed and closed his eyes.

"My mistress acquires the strangest pets." Ed backed out and closed the door.

"Why do I have the feeling," Ayatas said wryly, "that I am included under the designation of pets?" I didn't answer. He asked, "Why do you trust that werewolf?"

"He was part of a werewolf motorcycle gang. Then he was trapped in a *hedge* with a demon that was eating him alive. Then Hayyel appeared and saved him." I shrugged slightly. "Approved by one who claims to be an angel. Who am I to disagree?"

Brute yawned hugely, his fangs dangerously near my hand. His breath was awful. "Holy crap, wolf, what have you been eating? Rotten meat and raw onions?" Brute didn't answer.

Ayatas had gone immobile during my truncated story. "Motorcycle gang. I had a run-in with a werewolf gang on bikes long before they were out of the closet. Outside of Billings, Montana. In 1974."

Brute turned his head and chuffed again, his icy blue eyes on my brother, narrowed with laughter.

"I barely got away with my life."

A chill raced over me. I hated it when synchronicity

and serendipity combined into something that was too coincidental to really be only that. And I wondered how long Hayyel had been hovering over my life, whether I was in human or Beast form, watching over my family, pulling strings, setting things in motion. I scowled at the wolf head in my lap.

"There was no white werewolf in the pack," Ayatas said.

"Brute wasn't white until after the encounter with Hayyel. Before that he was red and big as a fire truck."

My brother swore under his breath, recognizing the wolf from the description.

"You and Brute have a history. Interesting, that."

Brute yawned, showing killing teeth. He closed his eyes again and made a sound that might be a fake snore.

"Will you talk to our grandmother?"

Abrupt change of subject. "Sure. After the invading vamps are dead or neutralized. I'm too busy right now for a family reunion." Though there was that pesky memory of the longhouse and the woman who hadn't belonged. "Later," I said, to Aya and to myself. "Later."

"I'll hold you to it." He stopped.

I knew what else he wanted but I wasn't going to make it easy on him. I gave him my best Beastly toothy grin.

His scent changed but his voice was smooth and unperturbed when he asked, "Are you ever going to show me how to achieve the half-form you wear?"

"Who knows. It could happen. And it might not." Which was a lot more positive a response than the last time he asked.

He stood without using his arms or hands, twisting and pushing upright with his legs until he stood straight and tall over me. "I hope this is the beginning of peace between us, *e-igido.*"

I thought about peace, and how alliances were built on many things—DNA, shared history, cultural similarities, shared resources, mutual protection, change of circumstances, mutual need. I already shared some of those with Ayatas, but not all. "Are you going to help us against the Flayer of Mithrans?"

"It's complicated. At the moment I have to say any help would be . . . unofficial. Someone in PsyLED Unit Eighteen found video of a torture scene from inside a local hotel."

He had to mean the hacker on his Knoxville team. I waited.

Ayatas's face was set in stone, showing no emotion as he said, "When the FBI saw the level of violence and the compulsion the Flayer of Mithrans was using, controlling all those Mithrans and humans, the interagency directors decided that PsyLED would no longer have lead on this, for fear that we would be more easily controlled and infiltrated by paranormals. I might as well have been told to stand down."

I raised my eyes, realizing what it meant that he was wearing civilian clothing, no badge, no official dark jacket with *PsyLED* on it in big white letters. He had entered my land in cat form and changed shape and dressed. He'd worn his pack the way Beast did, full of clothing and supplies. I said, "That's stupid. Humans are much easier targets for fangheads." Ayatas didn't reply. "If you're here, then PsyLED, ICE, ATF, DOD, the National Guard, and every yahoo redneck cop from here to Memphis knows about the vamps. Who's going to show?"

"ICE took lead. They were planning a military raid on the Regal Imperial. They were driving in from Charlotte, arriving in force, with plans to work with Asheville PD, Buncombe Sheriff, and NC State HPD." It didn't escape my notice that he didn't mention PsyLED. "But the ICE contingent was trapped by a massive rock- and snowslide on Highway 26 and the National Guard isn't keen to go it alone, not without bigger weapons and more people." He chuckled shortly. "The up-line brass are barely controlling their hysteria. Interagency command wants tanks. Rocket launchers. Local politicians want no property damage or collateral damage. It's become a bureaucratic nightmare. ICE is trying to regroup and take back roads to I-40, but the weather isn't cooperating. And since the quarry is trapped in Asheville, and they haven't attacked the population en masse, I think they'll wait until the sleet abates to try again. For now, as they try to get their people in, and in place, you're on your own."

"Big surprise."

"You can ask for help."

Help? From whom? I asked you and you said no. And then I let his original words flow through my memory. He had said he couldn't help officially. "So how can you help us?"

"Information. Things your IT people may not be able to discover. Things you need to know."

"Like?"

"Your enemy is no longer at the Regal Imperial Hotel. I received word just after I arrived at your estate that there had been no recent movement in the hotel. The local LEOs sent in a mobile recon robot and saw nothing alive or undead. The Flayer of Mithrans, his scions, and any blood servants he left alive have moved elsewhere. There were four bodies stacked inside the front entrance and a trail of blood that led to the central fireplace. No one else will share that with you."

He didn't add the obvious—that the fangheads had left behind a crime scene that would take days to work up. Did Alex know? Did he have access to the police robot video? "Do you know where they've gone?"

"No. There was a citywide blackout that lasted four hours. There was also a fire that spread to several houses and took the attention of the first responders. We think they moved then."

I thought about that as he waited. After it all settled deep inside me, and I realized how difficult all that would make any strategy we attempted, I said, "I'll think about it, Ayatas. For now, stop marking territory on my hunting grounds or I'll make you wish you had."

Ayatas chuckled softly, and I realized he thought he had made headway in creating a relationship with me. Maybe he had. I didn't know. "So now you know my cat scent. It is a step toward reconciliation, my sister." Carrying his gobag and extra clothes, he left through the door, shutting it softly. He had left me a liter bottle of water, which I drank down. Somehow, it felt like a peace offering.

Keeping one hand clasped on the teeth and jawbone that had once been mine, I tossed the bottle into the recycle pile and scratched the wolf's ears. He closed his eyes and blew out a breath that fluffed his lips in a *bbbbbb* sound. Softly I said to the werewolf, "You helped your crazy-ass werewolf bitch to torture Rick LaFleur."

Brute's eyes opened and he rolled them up at me.

"Yeah, I remember. In return, you were tortured by a demon and rescued by an angel, who then cursed you to stay in wolf form forever. You and your angel helped set all this in motion, all of my long-term involvement with the vamps. All my acquisition of magics that are killing me. How much of my reactions to Rick are the result of angelic interference, hmmm? How much of what I've felt all these months is real and how much has been forced on me?"

The stinky wolf chuffed and rolled over, exposing his belly, his crystal eyes on mine.

It was a submissive gesture and I had no idea what it meant. "You're no help at all."

He chuffed again and blew out a dog breath of contentment.

Together, we fell asleep.

CHAPTER 14

A Hunk-a-Hunk-a-Hot-Man

Just before dawn I woke again, Brute bouncing on my chest as if he were doing CPR on me. Chuffing that awful stench into my face. It was more effective than smelling salts at waking me up. "Gah! Get offa me, you stinky dog."

He chuffed with laughter but backed away and sat. He weighed around three hundred pounds and I felt as if my chest had caved in. Trying to get my elbows under me sent shocks of pain around my ribs. "You'd make a sucky service dog," I grumbled.

Brute was blocking the door with his body and teeth and big doggy grin, watching me struggle. I was hurting and I needed to pee. The fire was mostly coals; I was freezing and needed a coat and gloves. Didn't look like the werewolf was going to help me with any of my needs.

"What?" I demanded, creaking into a sitting position, hoping my bones weren't broken. "Owowowowow. I think you left bruises."

Brute lay down and scooted on his belly toward me, pushing something with his front paws. It was the arcenciel scale. The scale was both clear and iridescent, the firelight bringing out shades of red and orange and yellow in the midst of the blues and greens. "You—correction—Hayyel wants me to do something with the scale, doesn't he?"

Brute nodded, his big head moving down and up once.

I turned the scale over in my hands, feeling the pliable strength, tracing the ragged edge where the scale had been torn off. "Arcenciels can timewalk. It doesn't even do anything to their DNA. Not that they actually have DNA as I know it, since they aren't from Earth. There's no way to know if their DNA might help me." I pressed my own clawed fingernails against the scale. They didn't penetrate. "Unless I look inside."

Brute chuffed.

If I tried to become another sentient being, that would lead to madness, the kind of madness that made my kind into serial killers. But just to look inside the snake in the heart of things? That had never caused trouble before. It should be safe enough. Maybe. A small voice deep inside whispered that I was skirting the edge of the abyss again, but I decided to ignore it.

I crossed my legs yogi style, held the arcenciel scale in one hand, and dropped into the Gray Between. The scale sparked and grew hot as the silver energies rose around me and melded with the energies in my belly. I hesitated, watching as the rotating pentagram-energies inside me siphoned off motes of silver power from the Gray Between and added them to the pentagram. Was the new pattern a way to accumulate and store energy, or was it a toxic form of magical energy? I still didn't know for sure, but I was betting on toxic. The pattern inside me grew brighter, the red and gray and silver motes shining like tiny stars. The scale mirrored the shape, a diffuse reflection of my own energies.

Which was when I noticed the braid of skinwalker energies and the two threads that portioned off. I had forgotten to remove the threads that tied Eli and Klaus to me. With the mental equivalent of scissors, I snipped each one. I couldn't tell a difference, but it made me feel better to set them totally free.

Satisfied that I had rectified a potential problem, I concentrated on my energies and dropped deep inside myself. My DNA was in its new shape, four strands instead of two, tangled and twisted and knotted in places. Threads of broken DNA fluttered, looking tattered and frayed. I identified bits of my human body. Bits of Beast. And . . . bits of bloodhound. Bits of *Bubo bubo.* Bits of male sabertooth lion. Things I hadn't looked for before, things that shouldn't be here inside me.

Beast? Are you here?

I heard a soft padding, growing fainter as my Beast retreated. She wasn't going to answer. I figured that meant she had something to hide. And it hit me. *You,* I thought, snarling. *You brought all the extra DNA in. You kept the twisted DNA from the half-form. You . . . You dang cat!*

She didn't answer. I had to wonder how much of this extra DNA had been gathered upon orders of Hayyel and how much had been the result of Beast wanting to be bigger, better, faster. And how much she wanted to have kits. If I couldn't find a way to give her kits, would she be willing to kill me to get total control of her life again? I was a naturally suspicious and distrustful being and I felt a smidge of guilt for the untrusting thought, but then, Beast had often acted behind my back.

See scale, she thought at me.

I blinked and saw the reflection of my DNA buried in the pentagram energies in the arcenciel scale. My heart thumped unevenly, a hard, backward rhythm. My energies sped up. Unexpectedly, I fell inside the reflection of myself. Tumbled into the image of my energies in the scale. Rolled and hit hard against something I couldn't see, some barrier that stopped my movement and left my soul bruised.

It was a backward, mirrored image, though not an exact copy. The reflection I saw was subtly different. Less frayed. Less broken. Less knotted. As I watched, a single strand changed position as if pushed by an errant wind. I considered what had happened, and I realized that the arcenciel scale was displaying a vision of my broken self.

And maybe a map to fix things. A map of how to fix . . . me. Maybe that was the true power of the original shape-shifters. To shift directly from within. I sank deeper into the pattern, the image of myself in the scale.

I drew up the image of myself, as my DNA really was. I sank, deeper, darker. Into the seat of my skinwalker power. The ambient noise changed, echoing slightly, as if my breath and heart beat against stone walls. I opened my eyes to see my soul home. I imagined the two images and set them on the walls of my sacred place. Side by side. I found the errant strand that was, in reality, still broken inside me.

I glanced at the dome overhead. Hayyel's wings were there, feathered and protective, but no way was I going to talk to the angel I distrusted. I thought about God, the creator God worshipped by the Tsalagi and by me, though I had lived a life of violence rather than the meekness I had been taught as a child. *Okay, God. Fine. You say you'll lead if I'll follow. Let's see whatchu got.*

Gently I pushed the single frayed and flying strand of real DNA into place, matching the reflection that wasn't. The small strand slid home with a certainty that spoke of belonging. If sound existed here, it would have clicked, like one of Eli's guns into its holster. I pulled my hand back, almost shaking with excitement.

Arcenciels lived forever. They could walk through time, changing it as they saw fit. They could change *themselves* as they saw fit. They were true skinwalkers, able to shift shape without following the genetic pattern in bone or teeth or flesh, able to acquire and throw off mass, able to do all that and . . . and . . . walk through time, back as far as time went. *At will. Oh . . .*

I looked up at the feathered wings overhead. Hayyel might have had an agenda of his own, but he was also a messenger. I looked back at the two images on the wall of my soul. I realized I had waked with one hand still clasped. I looked down and opened my fist. Even in the vision of my soul home, I still held my own DNA. The perfect DNA from my childhood. *That* was the healed vision in the reflection.

I had stumbled into it. This was . . . I had no words. This was important. Vital. Maybe my way out of dying.

But. I hadn't stumbled into it. *Brute* had shoved the arcenciel scale at me.

Hayyel had done this.

I saw my hand, my teeth in my palm. It was my human hand. Jane's hand. Not knobby-knuckled and weirdly furred, but golden-skinned, slender, and strong.

But I wasn't just Jane anymore. I was Beast too. If I chose the perfect DNA reflected from the teeth onto the wall, if I accepted healing, I might lose all I had become. I might lose Beast.

"If I heal the DNA, I might go back to what I was. I don't want to be what I was. I've gained something over the years that I don't want to lose."

Jane gained Beast. Beast is stronger than Jane or Puma concolor. *Stronger than screamer cat and skinwalker together.*

"Greater than the sum of our parts."

Beast thought about that, and I realized she was standing by my leg, not touching, but studying the pictures on the stone wall. *Beast does not want to die. Beast does not want Jane to die, not even to have kits. Mountain lion and Jane are two. Beast is more than two. Beast is more than five.*

Tears gathered in my eyes at the truth of her words. Five was the highest number Beast understood. More than five was incomprehensible to her.

Beast is big. Bigger than big. Beast is . . . Beast is like hand of Jane's God.

"We are *not* an angel."

No. Beast is not angel. Can hunt and kill. Jane is war woman. Can hunt and kill. Can heal. Can love. Can . . . Can teach and learn. Can choose.

I considered what she meant. "Angels don't have free will."

Together we looked at the mangled DNA map. *Beast wants to stay. Beast wants to live.*

"Okay. So healing isn't going to be fast or easy, but it's possible. I don't have to die right away. That makes it easier to keep going. Maybe I can heal a little at a time without losing you. Eventually. For now, I choose to never be completely Jane again, even if it means never being completely healed." In my dreaming state, I reached down and scratched Beast's ears, the way I had scratched Brute's.

When I woke again, I was in Jane's form. Human. Dawn was graying the sky, sending meager pale light through the small door I had opened in the gable. The fire was out, the ashes barely warm. Brute was stretched out beside me, his werewolf warmth enough to keep me from freezing to death. I stirred and Brute sat up. "I'm brushing your teeth when we get back inside."

Brute chuffed and gave me a doggy grin, tongue lolling, as if to say, *You wanna play? Bring it.*

I touched my middle. The pain wasn't so bad. The star-shaped tumor was . . . It was smaller. My breath hitched. It was smaller. I stood and stretched slowly and discovered that I could move without pain. I wasn't well, but I felt better, even in human shape. As if I had a little more time. As if I could stay human-shaped for a while longer, maybe take fewer meds.

I gathered up my weapons and toys and tore open the door. Raced through the sleet, into the house, and up the stairs to our bedroom. Silently, I placed all my magical toys and blades on the dresser and used the bathroom as fast as possible. The relief was an intense pleasure. I showered off the salt and the stench of an all-night sweat and did all the girl things. Dried off.

I raced out of the bathroom and threw myself on our bed. On top of Bruiser.

He wasn't totally asleep, and he came fully awake fast, recognizing me, my scent, my laughter. "Jane."

"Hey, sweetcheeks."

"Are you objectifying my bum?"

"Totally. Love me?"

"With all my heart."

I kissed him, hard, scrubbing my human face against his scruffy bearded face, wrapping my arms around him.

"Prove it," I growled, pulling away so I could see him, so he could see me. "Love me." He hesitated, questions racing through his eyes, clear as if I was inside his brain. "I'm not healed but I'm a little better. Well enough for this. Well enough for us."

We hadn't been together since I got sick. He had been so damn considerate, kind, gentle. I didn't want any of that. I wanted wild and raucous and I wanted it *now*. I raked my human nails down his naked side, not breaking the skin but demanding.

Bruiser didn't hesitate again. He rolled me over and under the warm blankets with him. He kissed me, gently, then slanted his face over mine, his mouth over mine, his tongue into mine. Something exploded within him. Onorio scent burst out. And he loved me. He *loved* me.

Dawn had arrived and moved into midmorning when we managed to get our legs working and stumble to the shower. The smell of Bruiser's citrusy soap and sex and sweat rinsed away. Twice. Perhaps overly clean, we dried off, and I rubbed CBD oil and hemp oil into my skin. Bruiser helped. Twice. Which resulted in a third shower. Weak in the knees, we dressed, and, holding hands, walked down the stairs to the long bar that separated the two kitchens.

Thank God for the barstools. I barely had the energy to drape myself over the bar. The entire main level smelled of yeast bread and bacon and eggs and pancakes.

Molly had turned on the lights in the baker's kitchen and fired up one of the commercial ovens. Sweating, her red hair in bouncy curls, she slid bread tins into the oven. She was liberally dusted with flour. Eli and Liz, Molly's witch sister, were standing side by side at the big, six-burner stove in the commercial kitchen, Liz flipping pancakes, Eli moving a lot slower than usual, turning bacon and scrambling eggs with a spatula. But they looked cozy together. Maybe a little flirty. Eli had a type and Liz was fearless and powerful and maybe a little dangerous. Yeah. He'd like Liz.

Molly's sister had been out of the dating scene for a

long time. And she was cozied up to a hunk-a-hunk-a-hot-man. She was flushed and I didn't think it was because of the stove top.

The baker's oven closed and the scents of yeast bread and oatmeal and eggs and pancakes floated through the air. And bacon. I had missed bacon. My human self was hungry. Starving. As if he heard that thought, Eli turned and found me sitting at the bar, his eyes dark and intense. He placed the spatula handle in Liz's hand and walked slowly around to me. His feet were encased in wool socks and he wore jeans and a heavy, loose sweatshirt. He stopped just outside of my personal space, holding my gaze. Bruiser glided off the barstool beside me and stepped into the kitchen, toward the commercial coffeemaker, giving us privacy.

"You look better," he said.

"You look alive. I was worried there for a while."

"Janie," he said, reproof in his tone.

I chuckled and held out my arms. Eli stepped closer and we hugged. It was a bro hug, all back patting and awkwardness. And it made me want to cry with happiness.

He stepped away before it could get too girly and said, "Want pancakes?"

"And bacon. Lots and lots of bacon. *Pounds* of it."

"Let's start with four pieces and move up from there," he suggested. "Not interested in cleaning up bacon puke. You'll have to trust me on this one."

"Spoilsport."

After the best breakfast in ages, I dropped on the sofa in the TV room/office. I called Soul, expecting to get voice mail, prepared to leave a snarky message. Instead, Soul answered. "Assistant Director, PsyLED."

"Oh. Ummm. You're back. Not missing. Not kidnapped." *Out of touch for days and taking three weeks of leave and now suddenly back on the job? Like that wasn't weird?*

"Why would I be—Never mind. Spit it out, Yellowrock. I'm on a crime scene."

"Since when does the ass director do fieldwork?"

"You think I haven't heard that one? Try harder. And I'm here because an arcenciel was spotted in Knoxville killing a local farmer's beef cattle."

"Oh. Ummm. We got a problem in Asheville. A nasty foreign vampire—"

"Is in town and ICE is handling it," she interrupted. "ICE and PsyLED do not play well together, and when things got contentious, a meeting was called. It wasn't pretty and it pitted my boss and the director of ICE against each other in front of the secretary of defense. She sided with ICE. They kicked us out of the meeting. I have nothing to offer you, Yellowrock."

"Info exchange?"

"You first."

"The vamp is the Flayer of Mithrans. The other Son of Darkness. In the recent past he had, or currently he has, witches in a time circle somewhere nearby. He's wearing, well, growing, an exoskeleton."

Soul whispered a curse and I heard a car door close. The ambient noise on her side went soft, and I figured she had gotten in a car. "We have dealt with this in Natchez. I'll see that my people refresh their memories on the reports. As I recall, exoskeletons are the result of genetic changes that force vampires into insectoid forms. It happens when a vamp is trying to alter or bend time with witch magic. Correct?"

"Yeah. ICE can't handle this." The only thing that might—assuming they could find Shimon—was extreme force. Rocket launchers. Guided missiles. "They have to have a time circle somewhere."

"Any idea where the circle is?"

It was likely that Soul was going to give me nothing. But I took a chance. "No. But I did find a rift, down deep in a cleft of stone. And an arcenciel flew out of it. Juvie, maybe ten feet long. Lavender and purple wings and charcoal body."

Soul was silent for a little too long for my comfort level and I was afraid she was going to hang up. She was breathing too fast, her voice strained, when she said, "You know where a rift is? A *new* rift? And *active* rift?"

"Yes."

"In return for its location, you want help, under your command."

Relief made me sag against the sofa. "Anything you can swing my way. I also want to know everything you have on liminal lines and liminal thresholds." No one knew much about how they worked or even what they were. No one except arcenciels and maybe the Anzu.

"Most of what I know is what your kind refers to as theoretical physics. However, my kind came through a rift. We were worshipped as gods for eons by the primitive humans. We taught them mathematics, the positions of the stars, geometry, farming, and how to build with wattle and daub and then with mud bricks. Later with rough stone. How to use hydrodynamics for farming, plumbing. How to build canals. The art of stonemasonry and lapidary."

"The People of the Straight Ways," I said. "Canal builders, long before the pyramids were even conceived of."

"Yes. Then the climate changed very suddenly and floods were massive, accompanied by earthquakes and the loss of human civilizations all over this world."

"I got that part. The indigenous people who survived said the bones were piled so high that when the wind blew, it was the sound of bones dancing."

"The portals between worlds were lost in the tectonic shifts. We need access to a new rift."

I said nothing, waiting, enjoying my new talent of forcing people to talk while ticking them off, all at once.

Soul ground out, "My people are trapped here. Jane. Don't play stupid games that could get people killed, yours or mine. You know where a rift is?"

"Yes. There's a new rift. Or it looks new. And it's definitely an interdimensional opening."

Soul hesitated. I had learned to bargain and she had figured that out. As if saying the words hurt her, she asked, "If I try to get you military help, you'll take me there?"

"No. Not just try. I need guaranteed help fighting the

Flayer and help finding the witch time circle so we can shut it down. This is to be under the command, or with shared command, of the Dark Queen. Quid pro quo. And I also want clarification and info."

I could almost feel Soul grinding her teeth. Her dragon-of-rainbows teeth—big pearly fangs. The tension on the cell connection ached with potential violence. "Clarification on what?" she nearly whispered, as if to keep from shouting. And I knew I had won.

"Back last fall, I freed an arenciel and destroyed the geode she was trapped in. In return, you and the other arenciels pledged to help Leo and the city against the Europeans." I stopped. Soul said nothing. "In the Sangre Duello, your people waited to help until Leo was dead. Even after I gave you a spell to keep your people from slavery, forever." Carefully, I added, "I want to know why the arenciels didn't help keep Leo alive."

Soul laughed, bitter humor. Arenciel laughter was usually like bells and gongs and woodwinds playing, but not this time. Now there was nothing but discordant notes. "I'll play your little game. I fought my own people to keep the vampires alive, you stupid cat. I'm still fighting them to keep them from going back and destroying the Sons of Darkness before any vampires were ever made. It's battle in the skies, three of us and the little bird against all the others."

I remembered the arenciel war I had glimpsed in the water droplets in my soul home, and fought to keep goose bumps from rising along my neck. Was I on the cusp of everything deadly I had seen in the future? "Because the human timeline would alter drastically if the first vampires are destroyed before they can achieve undeath," I stated, seeking the clarification I needed.

"Yes. I fought them into stalemate. In return for them allowing *you* the *time* to destroy the Sons of Darkness, I had to let Leo die. I had no choice. I did the best I could to honor both commitments."

She had changed history just enough for Leo's head to not fly off into the distance, as I had seen in one timeline, but to be still attached by a remnant of flesh in the current timeline. Dead, in a mausoleum in the fanghead cemetery. I had hoped that thread of flesh was also a thread of hope, but Leo hadn't risen. He never would. I had gone to the graveyard and caught the stench of rot from his tomb.

Carefully, I said, "Your best? No. You were foresworn. Foresworn to the Dark Queen of the Mithrans." I had just accused Soul of breaking an oath brokered in an interspecies parley, a deadly insult if she disagreed.

"Son of a bitch," she spat. "I'll see what I can do to get you help and information." She ended the call.

I set my cell on the table beside me, beginning to feel the tiredness in my muscles and my gut. I'd been human too long. But Soul still owed me. I wondered when she would figure that out.

Alex stumbled into the TV room, where I sat, alone, staring out at the snowy world. He carried a tall, canned energy drink and took his seat at his empty desk chair. He smelled horrible and he looked worse. "Too many energy drinks?" I asked.

"Go away, Janie." He looked my way and did a double take. "You're human-shaped."

I chortled. "Yeah. For a little while. I found a way to slow the progression of the cancer. Temporarily."

"Everything in life is temporary. Even life itself."

"That sounds very fatalistic."

He said something under his breath and punched keys. Opened a laser-light keyboard on the desk. Tapped the desk there too. He was using multiple keyboards at once. Screens came to life everywhere.

I moved up behind him, my eyes taking in the screens. Nothing looked out of place. Nothing looked unexpected. No invaders. No big-cats. "Alex?" I asked softly. "What's wrong?"

He stopped, his fingers clenching under the laser light. "My brother nearly died. Again. It's hard."

Softly I said, "If you can get him to sign the proper papers, and if he dies, and if I can get him to a fanghead in time, I'll make them turn him."

"Lot of *ifs* in there. What if it's an enemy fanghead?"

I laughed, and it was a nasty, awful sound. I remembered Klaus, the vampire I had claimed and bled to save Eli in the snow. Claiming was evil. Was a type of slavery. I had set him free, but it had been an afterthought, not something I planned, but I'd do it again in a heartbeat. "I'll force any fanghead I can find to turn him. And then, if necessary, I'll kill the vamp to keep him from claiming Eli. And I'll bargain with my own life to get Amy Lynn Brown to feed him, exclusively, for a year."

Amy Lynn had special blood that helped vamps through the devoveo—the ten years of madness after being turned—in record time. Her blood, exclusively, would mean a clean, fast, sane transition. Hopefully. And as the DQ, I could make it happen. "And that goes for you too, now that you signed the papers. We're family."

"Promise?"

"Pinky swear." I held out my pinky finger. He reached back without looking and stuck his pinky finger in the air. I hooked mine through his and we squeezed. Pact made.

"Ant Jane! Ant Jane! Ant Jane!" EJ hurtled from the kitchen into the TV room. "You gots Jane face!"

I lifted him up into the air and tossed him high. When he landed in my hands, a twinge of pain slanted through me. I'd already been Jane too long. "Not for long, though. I'm about to put on my Beast face."

"The better to eat you with," Angie Baby said from the doorway opening. Her face was set in disapproving lines. Or—

"Jane?" Alex said. "We got problems."

I had wandered toward Angie and I returned to Alex, EJ over my shoulder, me leaning over Alex's shoulder, looking at the screen that held his attention. Instantly I whirled back to the doorway and picked up Angie Baby. I shielded her from the view of the screen and carried her back to Molly. Angie was shouting, "No fair, no fair, no fair, no fair!" as I carried her and her brother back to the kitchen.

My BFF took one look at my face and shushed her child. "You need doors on the office," was all she said.

"Yeah. I'll put it on the list." Back in the office, I gestured for Alex to put the camera feed on the main screen.

"It's the feed from inside . . . maybe a church or a fancy spa," he said, "and it's being sent to me. I can't track it. Not yet." There was a lot of wood and stone and the vision of a trickle of water falling softly, like an ornamental fountain in the corner of the screen.

Center screen, the Flayer of Mithrans was killing his interpreter. There was no sound. Only the awful footage. The female vampire was clothed only in blood. There was no flesh left on her arms, hands, calves, feet, neck, or face. She was a limp and empty vision of dripping crimson, held upright, clasped close to the chest of Shimon Bar-Judas, one arm around her waist. Her eyes were open, staring, blank, human, human as she likely hadn't been in . . . decades? Centuries? I had no idea of her hair color. Her head was scalped. She was a broken, skinned doll. And the Flayer was facing her at the camera, chatting to it through her mouth as if there was volume.

"What's he saying?" I managed, sounding calmish.

Alex's fingers flew over his keyboards. "I'm sending the feed to a deaf chick I know for a lipreading interpretation, but with the fangs I doubt she can tell me anything. I'm trying to find a cell I can hack—Hang on. Got something."

I studied the face of Shimon. He was vamped out and so was his mouthpiece. She had upper and lower fangs, top and bottom. I had no idea what she might be saying until the audio suddenly came through Alex's speakers.

Then the woman's voice came over the sound system. "—kill every human for ten miles. Claim every Natureleza and every Mithran for twenty miles. Tribal woman and her pitiful followers, you will be mine or you will be true-dead. I am king. I am the god of the blood-drinkers. I am all there is for life and death and for any future that defeats the dragons. You will kneel to me. I will drink your blood and eat your flesh. Your witches will enter my circle and give me *time*. All time. I will rule from the beginning to the end, the alpha and the omega . . ."

I made a slashing motion to Alex and he cut the volume. "He knew we would find him and hear this."

"He spent a lot of time in Ed's head," Alex said. "He may know us better than we want him to."

"Oh goody." I sighed. "I get the megalomania," I said. "I get the belief that, because he's lived so long, he thinks he deserves something. Even worship. But something feels off." I walked closer to the screen with the fanghead and the bleeding woman. Her fingers were working, twisting and bending and—"Alex. Get your deaf friend to read the fingers. She's using the . . . whatchu call it . . . the deaf alphabet."

Alex cursed under his breath. "American Sign Language hand alphabet. Yeah. Got it. I have a feeling that whatever she's signing, it isn't what the fanghead wants her to say."

We fell silent. In the background I heard Angie and EJ screaming in laughter. I also heard Big Evan's woodwind pipes and felt distant magic glance across my skin. Cia and Liz were at work in the parking lot. Something about their magic felt odd, felt shadowy and smoky, as if the world had burned from within their workings. It was a trace of dark magic or demon taint, and either one terrified me, but there was nothing I could do about that. Not now.

"Humans in danger," Alex said. "Cantrell, my deaf friend, says the bloody woman is saying that over and over. 'Humans in danger. Send DQ. Help.'"

DQ. Dark Queen. Asking me for help. An act of compassion or a trap?

"I don't believe that one of the Flayer's vamps would care about humans," Alex said, echoing my thoughts.

I said nothing, but my entire body tightened. Silently I walked away, up the stairs, and changed into my half-form shape. Lying on the floor, panting, in pain, I thought about the message. It was probably a trap. Fangheads were good ambush hunters. But . . . I was the Dark Queen. This was my job, or would be once I figured out where my enemy was. I weaponed up. Thinking about my clan, my people who would be on the firing line with me and in danger if I failed. I hadn't heard back from Soul about help. Ayatas was useless. Rick LaFleur was not answering. The LEOs were trapped in an avalanche.

My people and I were alone. I needed to be ready when the opportunity came.

My mind on autopilot, I dressed and braided my hair, repainted my claws with the last of the scarlet polish. I looked in the full-length mirror. My hair was in a fighting queue, with multiple silver stakes in it like a crown. Six throwing knives. I didn't put on boots, but I did secure a tactical pocketknife in the deep boot sheath and a tactical fixed blade over it. Someone searched me once I put on the boots? They'd find the fixed blade easy peasy, but chances were good that they wouldn't stick their fingers into the space below and find the folded knife. My dual shoulder holster and matching nine-mils. I slid my lucky vamp-killer into its sheath. This blade had been made for me by Evan to replace the one lost when I killed Molly's sister for calling a demon. The vamp-killer had taken many enemies since then. It was mostly superstition, but I felt safer with it on me.

I heard Molly's fast steps up the stairs. My half-form ears were better than my human ears. She was calling out before she reached my doorway. "Someone's coming up the road. I can feel it through the *hedge* and Alex says two monitoring devices indicate something passed through." She swung in the doorway, arms holding the doorjamb to either side, bouncing on her toes.

I gave a slight smile. "You could have texted."

"I need the exercise. I need to get away from the kids. You coming or you just gonna stand there looking all bad-ass?"

My cell dinged and I tapped on the speaker. Alex said, "You and Molly get back here. The car's now being chased at five miles an hour through the snow, by two more cars. Eli and Bruiser are on the way there but it's slow going in the drifts. Witches are in place. Need you here."

Molly turned and raced back downstairs. She was wearing running shoes, doing cardio. "Move it, Big-Cat!"

I followed and entered the office, where Alex had the main TV screen partitioned off into twelve screens, each with a different view, none of them showing dying bloody vamps. The kids were putting a puzzle together on a big coffee table that hadn't been there earlier, juice boxes with tiny straws and a bowl of grapes between them. They were under a personal *hedge*, big enough to cover the kids and the table. Neither child looked up when I entered, seemingly focused on the shaped pieces before them. *Uh-huh. Sure.* But, Molly's problem, not mine.

"With one of the outer-perimeter cameras, I spotted Soul inside the lead car. She's being chased by the other cars, driven by blood-servants of the Flayer," Alex said. "But an arcenciel doesn't have to let herself be chased."

"Right," I muttered, taking in the different screens. I had seen Soul shift to her rainbow dragon form. And to a tiger. She could be anything she wanted. So why stay human-shaped, trapped in a slow-moving car, one that was having trouble staying on the narrow drive, swerving and sliding across the ice? The car revolved slowly left and began a slow spin as it approached a raised curve, the road higher than the woods around it. The car behind her was wearing chains. It revved up, throwing snow from all tires. Its bumper nudged Soul's car. Just hard enough.

Soul's vehicle left the driveway, made a circle half on the verge, and tilted. Almost leisurely, its front end slanted down and slid off the raised drive, down into the trees. It hit two small trees that should have stopped it, but lack of friction and momentum sent it sideways, into more trees, crumpling the passenger door and sending showers of ice and snow from branches to cover the windshield and roof.

The car wasn't stopped; it twisted and spun farther, down into the denser trees, wedging itself in, finally coming to rest facing back up the driveway, the headlights brightening the gray day. On the screen to the left, I could make out Eli following Bruiser through the snowfall. Bruiser moved like a vamp, fast and graceful. Even with a body full of vamp blood, Eli was less nimble than usual and a lot slower, falling behind in the half-mile sprint. Brute was nowhere to be seen.

Alex put something in my hand and I pulled on a communication unit by muscle memory. This one fitted my cat-situated and shaped ears. Eli had been making me custom-fitted headgear, in his copious spare time. My eyes got teary at the thought, but I never took them from his slow, jerky lope through the snow-crusted trees. I could hear both men breathing deeply, but they communicated by hand signals, not speech. Bruiser moved right and down. Eli moved left and to higher ground. They disappeared from the screen, Alex working to find them again.

The two chasing cars came to a stop on the driveway. Headlights illuminated the falling snow. Two females leaped from the first car. Two men from the second car. They were wearing winter gear, holding weapons. Agile and fast. Well-fed blood-servants.

The women reached the undented car doors and wrenched them open. I expected Soul to leap away as an arenciel. To attack as a tiger. Or even an African lion. Nothing happened. The bigger blood-servant reached into the car, holding something in her hand. Clear and iridescent.

She had a scale from a rainbow dragon. There was a smear on it. Blood? If so, *whose*?

Over the headset, I heard weapons fire and saw the two male blood-servants drop behind their opened car doors. Like that ever helped in real life. *Not*. Eli, however, was behind the trunk of a decent-sized tree, protected. Firing. Pinning the men down. Alex had found his brother's vest camera and pinned it to the screen.

On the other side of the screen Bruiser appeared. He practically flew along the low-lying ridge. Firing.

The woman without the scale slid and fell. It didn't look clumsy. It looked dead. The woman with the scale turned, her weapon tracking for the threat.

Bruiser leaped, weapon out front. Firing high. *Cover fire.* The woman didn't fall or duck. She lifted the weapon to Bruiser. Still in the air, Bruiser fired. Collided with the woman. They rammed into the roof and side supports of the car.

Fell into the snow.

On the screen showing the chasing cars, the men ducked into their vehicle and backed down the driveway. Eli didn't pursue them, but he did place three centered shots where the driver's head should be and three more where the passenger's head should be. The car kept moving away.

Eli eased from behind the tree and across snowdrifts

to Bruiser. Together they zip-tied the hands of the two women with extrawide ties, which meant the woman I thought had been killed hadn't been. Soul, wearing jeans and a sweater, and not her usual flowing garb, left the safety of her car but didn't shift, even now. She looked cold. Miserable. Pale. Her silver hair was tangled. Something was wrong, but that would have to wait. We had prisoners. That meant we had info.

I left the TV room, the sotto voce argument between Big Evan and Molly, the louder discussion by the Everhart witch sisters about anchoring the *hedge of thorns*, and the puzzle the kids were playing. Walking around the last cottage toward the creek where Soul waited, I could make out the soft drone of voices and made a cone of my hands on the window to see inside the unfinished, unheated space.

The inner walls were two-by-fours and the outer walls were uninsulated, but it kept the wind out, which seemed good enough for Eli and Bruiser. They were talking to one prisoner, *talking* being a euphemism for a combo of military interrogation techniques and mind bending. My business partner/brother was asking the questions; Bruiser was standing behind the human woman with his hands on her head, whispering, pushing with his magic. Onorio energies had a scent and a texture—hot and burning and prickly. There was no mistaking it. The only other time I'd been around when he did this, the stink of burning things had been so strong I hadn't noticed the sensory components of his magic. His mind bending. That was my word for Bruiser's reordering of her thoughts, brainwashing her the hard-fast way, to force her to become his. He hated it; I could see that from the tension in his shoulders, the stress on his face and tears in his eyes. But . . .

The same old excuse military commanders had used for eons still held true here. Lives were at stake and she was our enemy. She would have killed us or Soul in an instant. She had value only because of what she might give us. Which sucked.

The woman was talking. Baring her heart and soul. I

had known my honeybunch could twist vamps to love him. That was the Onorio superpower. But I hadn't known he could twist humans. From his body language, I was pretty sure he hadn't known he could either. The smell was distantly familiar enough to make me wonder if the other Onorios I had known had tried that with me. I remembered a fight in a workout room once, where the scents had been vaguely similar to this. And right after that I had claimed I was Leo's Enforcer. *Dang, dang, dang.* Had the other Onorios tried to tie me to Leo? Or worse, to Grégoire? Was this ability why Leo had been so mad at Bruiser, because he refused to use this talent on me? *Crap.* I hated to be so suspicious.

Eli caught my eye and nodded to Bruiser, hand gestures saying he'd be right back. He left the cottage, silent, officially my second, which meant half bodyguard, half champion. My friend and chosen brother. He was pulling on a cold coat when he closed the door, leaving Bruiser inside with his prey, alone.

"Is Bruiser okay without you?" I asked.

"Yeah. He's good, in control. He doesn't like what he is or what he can do, but he understands it's necessary. Bruiser has access to Alex via comms. If something goes wrong, it will likely be magical in nature and nothing I can help with. But." Eli looked to the tree line rather than at me. "George's acting in opposition to his basic nature. He's doing things by choice that he was forced to do when he was under Leo's thrall. Things he did to you. Once again he's doing things he isn't proud of. He's not going to be a happy man for a while after this."

It was odd hearing Bruiser referred to by his real name, and I gave a belated truncated nod. "I didn't ask him to. Or make him."

"Course not. And that might be even worse. He's doing it out of necessity, not under compulsion."

"Yeah. I get that. I just don't know what to do about it."

"Be human for him a little more often." Eli barked with quiet laughter. "Give him some of that sweet, sweet lovin'."

"You're an idiot."

"But a good-looking, hunky, amazeballs idiot, right?"
I laughed, which he had surely intended.

"On the other hand," he said, "there's Shaddock."

"What about him?"

"That guy has power, Janie, way more than was apparent before you promoted him. He claimed the vamps who attacked the sweathouse, and they were all at least fifty years old. It took all of an hour each."

"That's fast. But then . . ." I grimaced. "Shaddock has access to Amy Lynn Brown and . . . he actually made Amy Lynn. Maybe there's something extra about him, something Leo missed? Something we all missed?"

"We'll keep an eye out." Eli looked grim and I wondered if there had been a good reason Leo refused to promote Lincoln Shaddock to MOC. Something I hadn't known about when I gave him the city.

"Yeah. Thanks." I turned away, stopped, and turned back. "I'm glad you're in my life."

Eli gave me a battle-worthy smile, which is to say, not much of anything. "Somebody's got to keep you alive."

Together we tramped through the snow, me barefoot, more ice balls working their way up under my toe pads and toenails. The snow-sleet frozen mixture was now crusty and about fourteen inches thick. I held up a paw-foot and shook it. I said, "It'll be a bugger to get the ice out of the hairs on my feet."

"Bet that's not something you ever expected to say." I showed my fangs to him and he chuckled before he continued. "You going to talk to Soul?"

"Try to. You know why she wanted to jump in icy water instead of coming inside?"

"No idea. I'll stay out of the way." He faded into the trees. Softly, from the snow-covered forest, he added, "Hey, babe. Try to not get killed."

CHAPTER 15

Not Cat and Mouse, Beast thought. Beast and Boar.

I heard Soul before I saw her, and from the way the splashes slowed and stopped, she knew I was near. The faint breeze carried my scent to her even before I approached the high bank and looked down. In the icy pool made by the mountain stream, she was swimming, unexpectedly naked. I wasn't rude enough to stare, and couldn't be sure, but I thought she might have fins instead of hands and feet. Her silver hair was swirling on the surface, caught in a current I didn't see or moving all by itself. Her eyes were silvery too. We watched each other, silent, two predators at the watering hole. Soul cracked first.

"I smell disease leaking from your pores. Do you understand why you are sick?"

It was an odd form of the question. Not "Do you *know* why you are sick," but "Do you *understand* . . ." "Skin-walkers aren't meant to walk through time," I said. "Time-walking and absorbing all the magics I came across ruined my DNA. I have a tooth with healthy DNA and can heal myself, but I might have a five-year-old body and have to grow up again." *And I might lose Beast,* I thought. *Not willing to do either.*

Puma concolor *and Jane are Beast. Best hunter.*

Dang skippy, I thought at my Beast.

Soul tilted her head to the sky, her eyes still on me, and said, "You have a scale from an arcenciel. Take the scale and go to the interdimensional opening. You can use the scale to see your damage, and to heal yourself. Or you can swim through the rift and you will be healed."

Yeah. Sounds so easy. I didn't believe the shape-shifting creature in the water and neither did Beast. Soul wasn't quite human right now and I had no idea how that might affect her brain, her instincts, her mores, or her personality.

"There will be a price," she said, "no matter which method you choose. And danger. There always is. But there are ways and methods that make either path less dangerous. Take me with you and I will show you the safest way in."

People who wanted something had a way of bending the truth to suit them, and Soul had just made this a bargaining session. We had made a number of deals in the past. Sometimes she held up her end. Sometimes an agreement with her meant nothing. I didn't have long to negotiate. After dark, Soul would be able to see the magic of the rift through the trees anyway. Of course, she didn't know that yet. I hated politics and the half lies that came with political maneuvering, but I'd clearly learned a lot from Leo—and from Beast—because I knew what steps to take. A game of cat and mouse.

Not cat and mouse, Beast thought. *Beast and boar.*

None of my swift thoughts showed on my face as I asked a question I already knew the answer to. "Are the local PsyLED agencies going to help me destroy the Flayer of Mithrans?"

She frowned and the winter-cold water swirled as if fish swam with her. "I was not able to obtain their agreement. If those hunting the Flayer of Mithrans locate him, they will target him with missiles. They will claim a gas

leak or a terrorist attack. But they will make certain that
he is no more."

Which was exactly what I had figured. Still, hearing it
spoken in Soul's not-quite-human tones was a shock. Fear
crawled up my spine on tiny clawed feet. "So no bargain.
Tell you what," I said, thoughtfully. "I'll take you to the
rift, but not until the Flayer of Mithrans is dead."

"I cannot command the others. I am not their empress."

Something about that pinged on my subconscious, but
nothing swam to the surface. So I went on the offensive,
just a little. "You and the arcenciels owe me. No matter
what you say, your kind are foresworn. And so are you
personally. You gave your word. You may have done the
best you could, but your best . . ." Not *sucked*. That was
too emotionally charged. The right word eluded me for a
moment. "Your best was *insufficient* to repay the boon
you owe me personally and the contract agreed upon—
that the arcenciels would help Leo in the Sangre Duello."

The pool was no longer icy. In the moments I'd been
negotiating, the small pool had begun to churn and
steam. To bubble. To simmer. Soul was either mad or excited. Maybe both. Her emotional state was heating the
water.

Soul said, "I, perhaps, can get Opal, Cerulean, and
Pearl to assist. The others are unlikely to fight for you."

*Four dragons. If she followed through, that might be
enough.* And then other possibilities popped into my
brain. "The arcenciels you named already owe me personally," I said, not adding that I'd have to find the rainbow dragons first. "You're bringing nothing to the table."
I leaned closer to the water. "This is what I want in return
for taking you to the rift. I want eight dragons, you and
seven others, to stand with me and to fight the Flayer of
Mithrans and his vampires and allies. To find and free the
witches caught in the *wheel of time* spell. And I want *all*
the arcenciels to agree to give me the *time* to kill him. In
addition, I want all arcenciels to agree to leave the vampire timelines untouched. To leave the vampires alive and

in place from conception through history. To leave the bloodline intact and in place from Adam and Eve, or his and her equivalent, through now. To leave all the paranormal bloodlines in place, untouched, alive." That was pretty broad and very narrow at the same time. I hoped I had made it tortuous enough.

"I cannot promise eight of my kind."

I raised my eyebrows, wishing for the ability to lift only one in that snide, slightly insulting manner that Leo'd had. "I'm listening."

"The four. *Perhaps.* And if the Flayer of Mithrans dies before actual battle?" she asked.

"If the Flayer dies without them fighting and with his bloodline, timeline, and historical line untouched, then all debts will be paid."

"I can agree in theory."

"Not good enough."

Soul splashed the steaming water. Fins and silver hair caught the cloud-gray light. Steam made little balloons of pale mist, puffing high into the air and hovering over the water. "There is one problem to all you ask. I can no longer access my dragon form." She laughed sadly at whatever she saw on my face. "I have been punished for changing the timelines when Leo was at Sangre Duello and his head flew from his body. I am stuck in human and mer-form and cannot shift into my dragon. I can bargain back for my true form if I have access to a rift. Which you are hiding from us, the dragons of rainbows and air, who own all rifts."

"Your kind doesn't own the rifts," I said, my brain trying to find the point that was still eluding me. "You didn't make them. The rifts simply are."

"I am under attack for not letting my sisters go back in time to destroy all vampires," she hissed, fury rising, the water simmering harder, steam rising from the pool in heavy clouds. "Only the Mercy Blades, eleven in all the world, have kept their word to the Mithrans, have backed me against my own kind."

"And if you get access to a rift?" It came to me. "You'll jump through and be gone, and our bargain will be trashed."

Soul narrowed her eyes at me like a ticked-off mermaid. "Yes. It means I may be pulled through to another world and leave you alone to finish the fight with the Flayer of Mithrans. Rifts are dangerous," she repeated.

"And if you fall through, the other arcenciels will go back in time and kill the SODs before they're even born."

"Killing the Sons of Darkness before they are born has been a potentiality since you were crowned with *le breloque*." Her tone was sour, bitter as wormwood.

Empress, Beast thought at me. *Soul is not the empress of the arcenciels. Jane has crown.*

It hit me, like being slapped with the fin of a bathing dragon. Beast was right. I had *le breloque*. I was empress of the vamps and, with the corona, I was also the Dark Queen. The arcenciels wanted the crown. They wanted a lot from me and I held the royal flush—the corona. Before I had time to reconsider, I took a big honking chance and said, "You help me with the Flayer of Mithrans or you get nothing from me. The holder of *le breloque*, the Dark Queen of the Mithrans, no longer negotiates with the people of the rainbow dragons. The beings worshipped as gods by the People of the Straight Ways have been foresworn too many times." I lifted my jaw into the air. "I've told you what I want. Take it or leave it."

Soul spread her mouth wide. Her predator teeth flashed at me. She lunged from the heated pool, mouth open wide. I ducked and slipped on the icy ground. Rolled to my backside hard, back to my knees, through the snow. Not fast enough.

Her teeth tore through my shoulder, ripping my clothes and taking off a layer of flesh and muscle. Blood pulsed into the air, scarlet and shocking against the sea of white and grays and blacks of snowfall. Soul reared back, a cobra position, flared and violent.

She took two rounds to her torso, kill shots had she been human. The shots echoed in the trees as she flipped in midair and arced back into the water with a gigantic splash. The water churned white and red and the bloody pink of diluted blood, changing quickly to blue, to black, and back to the murky brownish green of the creek. She vanished beneath the surface. I fell to my knees, ears deaf.

Stunned, I slapped my pawed hand over my wound and said, "What the . . . She bit me!"

"Jane!"

"I'm okay," I whispered, lying, as pain blasted through me. A chunk of flesh was actually missing, the wound so wide and deep I couldn't cover it with my good hand to apply pressure. The teeth had torn through arteries, nerves, bitten muscle away. My blood was pumping fast, saturating my clothing, drenching the snow around me. The pain grew, a gnawing electric agony. I couldn't breathe. Couldn't move my fingers or hand. Arcenciel bites were poisonous. And psychoactive. And it looked as if regicide was commonplace in arcenciel circles. "I have to shift."

"Yeah. Fast." Eli raced through the trees as blood pulsed through my grip. "Why did she bite you?" he asked as he reached me.

"I made the mistake of acknowledging I was her queen. I don't think I was supposed to know that and I think it pissed her off."

"That looks painful," a woman's voice said.

Eli targeted the woman faster than I could focus. Liz Everhart stood in the trees, dressed in blue snow-ski gear, cross-country skis on her feet, her scarlet hair partially hidden under a hat the same blue color. "Easy there, big boy. I'd hate to bury you. Again."

Big boy? Again?

Eli scowled at her, but my half-cat nose picked up a scent from Eli's skin, strong even over the smell of my blood. He set his weapon down and pulled medical gear from his pockets.

Eli wants witch woman, Beast thought at me. *Mate for Eli?*

Hey. I'm dying here, I thought at her, just as I fell forward and my head bounced on the snow.

Eli caught me, too late, demanding, "Shift. Shift now."

"At least I'm not wearing boots," I said. Or tried to. The world telescoped down to pinpoints of light. And Beast tore through me.

*   *   *

Beast sat while Eli pulled Jane clothes off. Flicked ear tabs as Eli and witchy Liz talked. "I've never seen a skin-walker shift. That was pretty amazing."

Eli grunted, eyes alert, searching sky and trees like prey, his white-man gun in his hand. One-handed, he peeled Jane bra off Beast front legs. Was much blood in Jane clothes.

Liz witch slid through snow on flat boards. Looked like play. Wondered if Jane could play on flat boards. Wondered if Liz witch would let Beast chase her on flat boards. Wondered what Liz witch tasted like. Then saw shield around Liz witch. Beast could not get through shield, even with killing teeth.

"What bit her? I saw what looked like a shark, but I'm pretty sure we're a little far inland for a shark."

Eli paused. "I assume, since you saw that thing, and you're still here, that you're under a *hedge*."

"I'm not stupid, Ranger man."

Ranger man was Jane name for Eli. Was strange to hear witch say it.

Eli grunted again and scratched Beast ears. Beast leaned into Eli fingers.

"Are you still pissed because I dumped snow on you? Because if you're nice, I might offer to share my shield. I'm sweet that way."

Eli pushed Beast head away and rolled up Jane clothes. Beast stepped to side and watched Eli and witch. Wanted meat. Remembered deer tracks on other side of pool of water. But pool of water had teeth-fish-Soul in it. Was kit mistake to jump across pool of water to other side and be ambush attacked from below water. Beast sat back down. Chuffed at Eli.

"Hungry?" he asked Beast.

"Starving. There's a good barbeque joint or three in town. Are you asking me on a date?" Liz smelled of laughter and happiness and mating interest. Beast again curled thick tail around paws for warmth, and watched.

"No. There will be no dating."

Eli lied. Beast did not like lie. Lie was confusing, to say one thing when another thing was true. Eli wanted to eat meat with Liz. Eating meat was part of *Puma concolor* mating. Was part of human mating too.

Liz laughed. "Liar. You like me. Admit it."

Eli smelled of laugh but frowned hard instead.

"Your brother said you have a type. A little dangerous and a lot self-sufficient. I have a type too. I like honest men who like to laugh and who aren't scared of me. When you decide you're ready to stop lying, stop scowling, and pull up your big-boy panties instead of cowering in fear of witchy me, give me a call."

Beast chuffed softly. Liked Liz witch. Witch gripped poles and slid through snow.

"Wait," Eli said. Liz stopped. Tilted head like cat, curious.

Beast sniffed air. Was mating on air. Human mating was better than food.

"The thing in the water was Soul. I might have just killed the assistant director of PsyLED."

"That would suck," Liz said, her tones saying she was laughing and speaking lie. Beast did not understand why Liz witch would laugh and lie.

Eli made sound of amusement that was . . . cat-snide. Like cat laughter when cat pushed dog off rocks into mud. "And beside that whole 'might spend my life in jail for killing the assistant director of PsyLED' thing, I just got out of a good relationship with someone I liked. A lot."

"Got out? You broke up with her? Why?"

"She'd get something in her head and she'd keep pushing. And pushing." Eli stood and touched Beast head. Beast rubbed head into Eli hand.

"What was she pushing for?"

"For me to go on a cruise with her. I hate boats."

Beast rubbed head back into Eli hand. Ears itched. Witch said nothing. Just watched Beast and Eli and scratching ears.

"I hate being on the ocean," Eli said.

"Hmmm. Scared?"

"Seasick."

Word was hissing like snake.

Liz witch laughed. Laugh was low, like purr, and Eli body reacted again. Beast looked from Eli to witch. "You ever tell her that?" she asked.

"She never asked. But she wanted to live on a boat when she retired from the force. Kept pushing that too. Communication is a two-way street and she didn't care enough to ask, so I never volunteered."

"Passive-aggressive. Childish."

"No argument. I was."

Liz witch spun stick in snow, making it seem to dance. "So what do you want, if not to live on a boat after retirement?"

"A family. Kids. A home. White-picket-fence kinda thing. A woman who likes guns. A woman who's independent. "

"Having babies was a little faster than I intended to go, but since we're there already . . . Guns don't bother me but I don't like 'em much. They're unreliable. They jam. They can be stolen and used against me or against others. Guns need ammo to work. I prefer magic. I'm a stone witch. We don't do well around salt water so cruises are out. I like mountains, but I'm fine with flat land as long as I can bring rocks with me. I like kids well enough but I don't intend to raise 'em alone. I want a man who does diapers and dishes. And the house has to be stone-clad, not brick or that vinyl stuff. Don't need a picket fence because my wards are better than any ol' fence. Oh. And while I don't like making love in the dunes, I do like piña coladas and getting caught in the rain."

Eli didn't answer but fingers stopped scratching. Felt tension course through Eli body like chasing rabbits.

"Song lyrics from the eighties," witch said, eyes on Eli.

"Nineteen seventy-nine. Not the eighties."

"Whatever. Before I was born. Make you a deal. You don't like something I do, you tell me. I don't like something you do, I'll tell you. In between you make me steak and a salad and we'll talk."

"Jane's facing a war. I don't have time to chase women."

Witch laughed again. "Chicken." Her feet made shush-ing noises on boards as she moved toward inn. Over shoulder, witch said, "Watch out for snowdrifts over your head, big boy." Witch moved back to house.

Eli said mating word. Beast did not understand. Eli wanted to mate. Talked of mating. Yet did not chase mate. Humans were silly kits. Beast stepped away and *pawpawpawed* to stream bank. Dropped belly to ground and belly-crawled to look over pool of water, belly in snow. Water was no longer making steam. Was no longer bloody. Soul was sitting on tree over pool. Was wearing thin human clothes. Was not wet. Soul wore strange jew-elry on leg. Dragon looked at Beast and covered jewelry with dress. Said nothing.

Eli moved up to Beast and nodded to Soul. "I see you survived the shots."

Soul looked away. Nodded.

"You want to tell me why you bit Jane? If you had been in your dragon form, you'd have killed her."

Soul looked frustrated, like a juvenile kit that tried to take large prey and failed. "I'm not always the same per-son when I shift shape. My brain works different, I think different, I feel different, I perceive enemies differently." She shook her head, face in a snarl. Looked at Beast. "I beg forgiveness."

Beast does not forgive. Beast kills enemies. Beast snarled at her, showing killing teeth.

"I'll be up to the house when Jane shifts back," she said.

"To talk to the holder of *le breloque*?" he asked. "The one you just tried to kill to get the crown? I don't think so. If I knew how to kill you, you'd be dead."

Soul laughed, sound angry and dull and wrong. "I am well aware of your desire to kill me, Eli Younger, but I am now in control of my former murderous tendencies. That said, I'd kill every human and para for twenty miles if it meant averting a war."

"War?"

Soul did not answer. Asked instead, "Are you going to talk to the pretty witch?"

Eli did not answer, but body smelled frustrated. Angry.

Beast did not understand "not answer." Was confused.

Soul sighed. Smelled fishy and bloody and not human. "I won't try to take the crown again. But you let that witch get away and you're dumber than you look."

Beast wondered if water drops in soul home showed what would happen if Eli did not mate with witch. Wondered if Soul was pushing Eli to one place in future.

Eli blew air through nose. "Stay away from my partner. Come on, Janie. Let's get you a steak."

Am Beast. Not Jane. But followed Eli to eat dead cow.

I shifted back to Jane in the shower and woke lying on the chilly tile, thinking over Beast's thoughts and concerns, and worried about Soul's attack. It was out of character and it didn't make sense in any way. I wasn't sure how to address the attack or if I should even try. I had a hard time letting things ride, but this seemed like one of those times when I needed more info and intel before I jumped in trying to fix it all. Soul had some seriously big teeth and I had a feeling that I might not survive being bitten again. My scarlet leather jacket was ruined. Fortunately I still had a box of new military-style armor Eli had ordered.

After I rubbed the CBD oil over my belly and dressed, I went looking for Bruiser. Merlin had changed the music on the sound system; Chris Stapleton was crooning "Tennessee Whiskey" through the speakers. It was soothing music, not martial enough to plan a war.

Bruiser was sitting at the bar, a cut-crystal glass half-filled with amber liquid in one hand. He smelled of tension and frustration and shame. He had just bound a human to himself with his Onorio magic and he hated it. Likely hated himself. I slipped up behind him and slid my arms around him. Rested my head on his shoulders. "I'm sorry. I'm sorry you did that for me. I'm sorry I've made our lives so difficult."

"Leo. Leo set all this in motion. Not you. You're keeping us alive and free."

I said nothing. We were alone in the kitchen, dim lights under the cabinets giving a faint light.

"I learned things from her," he said. "Not enough to pay the price of my soul for what I did. But I learned things. You told Shimon that the white werewolf ate his brother, but he already knew that some part of Joses/Joseph was still alive. He knows Joses's heart is in New Orleans, and I don't know how he learned its location except from Edmund's mind, gleaned during the final minutes of his possession. Shimon wants the heart and wants Brute dead. And wants you dead for feeding Joses to the wolf."

I drew in a breath, slow, steady. "Is Jodi in danger?" Jodi worked for NOPD and was from a witch family. And she had Joses's heart.

CHAPTER 16

Once We Finish with the Mustache Twirler

"I've called Jodi in New Orleans and told her to check on the heart and make sure it's in a safe place. Jodi says she'll put it in a null room and get back to me."

I said nothing. Just hugged tighter. Silence was a powerful tool for giving someone space to talk. Or not. As they wanted.

"I was blood-drunk for nearly a hundred years. When I came out of it I was angry. Angry for all the things Leo had me do, things that seemed right, at the time, because I was bound so tightly to him, but that were wrong. Evil, sometimes."

He took a breath that shuddered through his chest. "I'm Onorio. I have . . . gifts. Yet I didn't try to save Leo. Because of the way he used me, for so long, when the sword was striking, I hesitated. I could have reacted; might have saved him. But I didn't move." He sipped the amber liquid, scotch, I thought. Nasty stuff. "Leo made a weapon out of me. Made me a killer. And with Onorio magics, I was able to move as fast as a Mithran. Faster. And I let Leo die. I let my friend die out of pique and childish anger."

"You were sworn not to interfere. The outclan priestess would have killed you instantly if you had tried to change the outcome of the duel."

"Who's life was the more valuable? Leo's or mine?" Bruiser may have laughed, but the sound was too broken to be certain. "I thought I was doing the right things when I was blood-drunk. I thought it was the right thing when I used Onorio bindings on Nicolle, who is now pining for me, banished to Rosanne Romanello's Sedona clan home. I thought it was the right thing to let Leo die. Just as I think it was the right thing to mind-bind that woman. But . . . my reason is so faulty, so defective, that I don't know *what* is morally right and proper anymore."

I squeezed his shoulders. Nicolle was a vamp Bruiser took from Grégoire's home after she tortured some of the vampire's people. That was the place I first smelled the scent and texture of Onorio magics, mostly hidden beneath the onslaught of other, more potent smells at the time. Softly, my breath featherlight on his skin, I said, "My grandmother did the same thing to me. I've often wondered if I would have been my grandmother's willing assassin had I stayed with the tribe and not been thrust into the blizzard on the Trail of Tears. And I think I would have. I think the violence she bred into me when I was a child was addictive. I would have become more and more like her, until, or if, I finally saw the truth, like you have."

"And what is that truth, my love?"

"That we are killers. Morally malfunctioning. But with the ways, means, abilities, power, and in the position to do the right thing in the end."

"The end does not justify the means," he said.

"We all have the potential to do awful things when our minds are not our own. Yours was not your own when Leo had you."

A sudden thought came to me, and with it came the scent of shame. Rick's mind hadn't been his own when Paka spelled him and stole him away. Even though I caught the scent of magic, I let him leave with her instead of trying to find out what was wrong. I let him go because

I was hurt and shocked and embarrassed at a public humiliation. That was something I needed to deal with.

"Now you have your eyes open," I said. "You can go forward into the future with who you are now."

"Meaning stop dwelling on the past and do the job that needs doing now."

I shrugged against his back. He sipped again. I had the feeling this wasn't his first scotch of the evening.

"Do you think the blood of the SOD made everything happen the way it did?" I asked as the liquor went down his throat with a soft sound. "I mean, Joses had been bitten by an arcenciel. They make vampires crazy. Leo's uncle and then Leo himself drank from Joses, when he was raving insane, hanging on the basement wall. They imbibed dragon poison through the blood that they stole. That changed the way they thought, the plans they made, the alliances they made. Maybe even made them worse people than they would have been otherwise." I felt surprise quiver through Bruiser. "And then you drank Leo's blood as part of the primo binding. Not much, but maybe enough to make you think and be different from what you would have been otherwise."

"I don't know. Every time I close my eyes, I see another victim," he said. "Remorse and regret and repentance. Onorio powers are to bind and kill. Even you."

"What about me?"

"Leo used his magic on you, against you, trying to turn you to his own ends from the moment he met you. Leo's compulsion magic was powerful. And Leo's magic through me made it more so. Leo knew I was deeply attracted to you. He used that attraction to control and compel both of us. And that, my dear love, is the biggest regret of all, that Leo had access to you through me."

I had known all that. Had even figured that Leo had used Rick's betrayal and my reaction to it to draw me closer to his side and closer to Bruiser. To say that Leo had been Machiavellian didn't even scratch the surface of his hopes, strategies, schemes, and plots, layer upon layer for centuries. But I had been attracted to Bruiser, and when Rick left, I fell into Bruiser's arms just like Leo had expected. What he hadn't expected was for that attraction to dilute his vampire control over both of us. I said, "Until you fought him for control of your own life and mind."

"I fought him for you, Janie. If not for you, I might have remained under Leo's control forever. That alone makes me less than honorable."

He had also been a teenager when Leo took him and claimed him and started feeding him blood. Stockholm syndrome times two. But I didn't think he'd listen to reason or forgiveness, not in his current mood. "Maudlin," I drawled out.

"What?" Bruiser sounded affronted.

"Isn't that term for what you're feeling?"

"Maudlin means oversentimental, overemotional, tearful, and lachrymose. I am none of those things."

"Coulda fooled me. We were all his tools and weapons and targets. Even though he couldn't blood-bind me, he still made me his servant. He knew I'd fight to keep the witches safe."

Tentative, Bruiser asked, "Who will I be if I'm not someone's servant?" And that cut right to the heart of the matter, drawing blood with a savage twist.

I remembered the words of the redheaded witch in the snow and said, "I don't want a servant. I want a man with a mind of his own, wants of his own, and a life of his own."

"I've had none of that. Ever. I'm not sure who I am. Not anymore."

"I'm a war woman. I have to save my friends."

Bruiser said, "You are a servant to your destiny."

I scowled at that, wanting to disagree.

"And you may want a man with a mind of his own, but I've never had that. I'm a servant." He made a huffing breath of surprise. "How . . . odd. That I didn't realize that until now. I'm a servant, born and bred and twisted into shape by Leo for decades. To be a servant. And now to be *your* servant." He seemed shocked and sad about that. His back straightened. He twirled the glass on the counter. "I'm yours to command."

I didn't want a servant but I wanted Bruiser. I had no idea how to merge the two desires. "And after all our enemies are dead and our friends are safe? Who will you be then?"

"Our chances of surviving the Flayer of Mithrans are little to none." He tossed back the scotch, pushed away from the kitchen bar, and away from me, and left the room.

Flayer of Mithrans, a terrible, wholly deserved title. I took Bruiser's seat and prayed. Because there was nothing else I could do. Nothing at all.

It was after dusk and the snow/sleet/frozen rain mix had started and stopped a half dozen times. Two weather systems were vying for power over the Appalachians, one Gulf warm and the other arctic cold.

Soul hadn't made an appearance at the inn. Bruiser was still overemotional. Eli was still single and snarly. Alex was still hunting Shimon Bar-Judas in every spa, hotel, and big private home he could find. Alex had also managed to get access to all the Regal's stored security feed and was keeping an eye on every current thing at the hotel, the macabre hotel camera feed up on secondary screens the kids couldn't see. PsyLED CSI, including my birth brother, ICE, and the FBI, had finally made it to town. They had begun carting bodies out of the hotel. The feebs were all ticked off to have missed the culprits, their body language furious and worried.

The witch adults were in the winery's front yard, inspecting the *hedge of thorns* ward and discussing ways to make it more impervious to attack. They were less worried and more . . . having fun? Like a family reunion combined with bloodthirsty dangerous vamps on the prowl.

The local vamps and their humans were in and out of the inn and the cottages. I spotted my victim, Klaus, cheerfully following Shaddock or one of the other vamps around like a puppy. He didn't even need a leash to be compliant to his current minder. Which made me a little sick.

The other prisoners were out like lights, under a *sleep* working, well secured with steel and silver.

The kids were watching a Disney flick and eating popcorn. Cassy was napping. She seemed to sleep a lot.

Sabina, in New Orleans, had disappeared. She had been hurt, burned, in the attack on the fanghead cemetery. She hadn't been seen since her cell phone call to Alex.

HQ in New Orleans were not answering the phone or text or e-mail or anything. Alex couldn't raise them at all. Alex couldn't access the cameras in the old building. Alex—and thus we—were blind, though Eli had called in a favor, and so we knew the building at least was still standing and seemed to be occupied.

Jodi's cell phone went to voice mail. The WooWoo room rang without an auto response.

And Brute had shown up again. He had dragged his big mattress into the TV room and was snoring like a freight train, Pea lying on his shoulders, the stink of wet dog filling the room. EJ was curled up against Brute's smelly, hairy side, sound asleep, a bowl of popcorn in the curve of his little knees, spilling over. The cute nearly melted my heart.

Except for the kiddos, the tension in the TV room could have been cut with the blade of a sword. I didn't know where the invading fangheads were. Alex hadn't found the Flayer. Eli was running out of weapons to prep. It was the vamping hour . . . *Crap*.

I went to my suite and pulled out all my fighting gear and lined it all up on the bed. There was a lot of stuff. Of the fighting leathers provided by Leo, none had survived the many duels and battles and . . . Dang. The holes in the white leathers and the black leathers were significant and bloody and they stank, even after Eli had cleaned the leather.

I tossed the ruined, holey whites and blacks into the corner and pulled out the big box containing the armor Eli had ordered. The smell when I opened the box wasn't leather; it was vaguely chemical, sharp and bitter. The set on top wasn't the camo I expected, but was scarlet. Not as flamboyant as Leo's but made with military armor, Kevlar, Dyneema, and a layer of anti-magic.

The scarlet armor could be adjusted to fit the broad shoulders and narrow hips of my half-form perfectly. My old boots were still perfect on my paw-feet—not because the cold bothered me, but because I was tired of digging ice balls out from under my claws.

To go with the scarlet armor, I laid out the two gorgets to protect my throat: one gorget made of titanium overlaid with silver, and the more decorative, repaired, gold gorget set with citrines. I laid out the gold arm cuffs shaped like snakes, which had once belonged to a redheaded vamp who just would not die. When she finally was beheaded, and stayed dead, and Bethany died, I had ended up with the bracelets. The cuffs would be loose on my wrists, having been made for a woman's upper arms, and they no longer contained magic of any kind, but they *looked* magical. I had thirteen wood stakes, thirteen silver stakes, and three glass vials of expired holy water—not that any vamp would know it was old. I had a boot box full of magazines loaded with lead-silver rounds and regular rounds. I had the double shoulder holster, a hip rig with a nine-mil and sheaths for the stakes. I had a sword sheath with a double-bladed flat sword for blood duels. I laid out three throwing knives. There was the Mughal blade in its red velvet sheath, my sword of office, a blade that came with a long history and a prophecy that the wearer would not die in battle, or some such nonsense. The Mughal blade was a gift from Bruiser.

I had *le breloque*. It glimmered a soft gold against the gray coverlet.

The Glob, with the Blood Diamond and the sliver of the Blood Cross, the iron of spikes of Golgotha, witch magics, and my own flesh cooked into it by lightning. It was an ugly, fist-sized weapon. I had used it to protect others and myself, but I had no idea if that was all that I could do with it.

I laid out all of Molly's trinkets, witchy amulets given to me over the years. There was a tiny *hedge of thorns* captured in a small amulet. There were witchy locks that usually went on my bastardized Harley. There were other, less powerful things I had used over the years. And there was the bone earring carved like a coyote, the earring that had appeared in my stash after a night of really bad dreams. Molly hadn't made it. It just . . . appeared. Presto. Like magic. Good magic. Safe magic. I smiled at the thought. Bruiser, still quiet, had been sitting in the small chair in the corner, watching me lay out my toys, his eyes hooded with grief. He lost Leo. He expected to lose me because I was still dying, albeit more slowly. And his grief and malaise were like a cheese grater on my nerves. I wanted to kick him, but that seemed really unkind and unproductive.

I set the armor and amulets on the bed and said, "Dude. I think all that advice about pulling yourself up by your bootstraps and just getting over pain or guilt or abandonment is hogwash. But wallowing in the filth of your own past isn't helpful either. The things you went through don't own you. You own them. What you do with them, how you survive, whether you survive what was done, is up to you. I love you, but you have to make a decision. Give up or fight."

"Leo's fight?"

"Leo's gone. It's our fight now. Who cares who started the battle as long as we finish it?"

Bruiser's eyes went narrow in thought. I left the gear strewn across the big bed and returned to the TV room. On the way down in the elevator, I received a text from Jodi Richoux, the cop in NOLA who had the heart of the elder Son of Darkness. Attached was a photo of the heart. There was some sort of mass on the side and things were sticking out of the heart itself, like arteries and veins. It wasn't showing any signs of rot—not at all. It was still gross. Below the photo were the words *Is safe in a Null Room. Shape and color suggests lung and blood vessels are growing. No sign of decomposition. Lachish Dutillet is in null room next door. She says to burn it. Witch council is considering.*

I studied the heart. If it could regrow the entire body, which had been posited, it would have all the power but none of the memories, none of the learning or training. It would be a mindless vessel for the FOM to use as he wanted, until the body and brain developed new memories and personal will to go with the new physical life.

I detoured to the back of the house, following my Beast-nose, and found Brute, who was now curled up on a bed with EJ and Angie Baby, the infant between them, and a neon green Grindylow resting over the wolf's back. At some point in the last few minutes, the kids had been put down for naps—with a three-hundred-pound werewolf nanny. And Big Evan had to be okay with it. They were on his bed.

The paranormal creatures were alert, watching me in the doorway, so I waggled my fingers at Brute, asking him to come with me. He slowly untangled himself from the small bodies and left them asleep as he gingerly stepped to the floor. Pea, the grindy, held on to his white fur. In the hallway I showed the resident werewolf the photo of the heart. Brute licked his lips and chuffed at me, recognizing the heart.

"Yeah," I said. "Leftovers. It's regrowing. What happens when there's a full-grown body and brain to go with the heart?"

Brute tilted his head to the side in question.

"Could the Flayer of Mithrans use his brother's body and magic to make his own stronger?"

Brute's ruff stood on end and he growled softly. His crystal blue eyes narrowed and he held my gaze in a very nonwolf, nondominant stare.

"That's what I thought." I should never have given the heart away. Brute should have eaten it all and then we wouldn't have this danger. Brute turned and crawled up onto the bed. He curled around Angie, put a paw against the baby's side, and lay his heavy head on EJ's hips. The grindylow crawled around his shoulders and neck and snuffled in close. Brute blew out a breath and closed his eyes. He really was in protect mode. I had no idea what the wolf thought about the baby witches he was protecting, but I figured an angel-blessed wolf wasn't the worst creature to have as a guardian. EJ curled his chubby fists in the white fir and held on in his sleep. Angie Baby snored softly, her breath puffing into the white fur. "You keep them safe," I whispered. "No matter what."

The wolf didn't answer but his ears twitched to show me he had heard.

I turned and found myself nose-to-chest with Big Evan. I looked up. "Umm. Hi?"

Evan grinned at me through his thick red beard. "It's dark. Vampire time. Edmund wants to talk to you," Evan said.

Molly, half-hidden behind his bulk, grabbed my sleeve and tugged me away from the doorway. "We want to talk to you first. About my death magics."

"No."

"No what?" Molly asked her eyes narrowing. People didn't tell the volatile redhead she couldn't do stuff.

"You can't use them to drain the vampires," I said, hearing the stubborn tone in my voice. "You can't guarantee you can stop draining, and you might take some of our people." I thumbed to the bedroom doorway. I didn't bring up Beast's assertion that she could act as familiar for Molly. I didn't know what would happen if we got busy and took our attention off Molly. She could kill everyone around her. I wasn't risking her or the kids. Or my clan. "Or some of your people. Like your kids."

Molly's eyes flared brighter. "We have to—"

"And why are you letting them sleep with a werewolf?" I accused, deflecting her. "Are you nutso?" Yeah. Accuse her of being a bad mother. Get her mind off her death—

Molly punched me. Hard.

"Ow."

"Yeah. Right," she said. "Short, postdelivery mama hurts the big bad vampire hunter. You listen to me," she practically hissed, stalking close, her face only inches from mine. She reeked of power and fury and I barely stopped myself from backing away.

Over her head, Big Evan was slowly shaking his head no. Whatever Molly had planned, he wasn't in agreement with it. But he wanted me to be one to tell her no. *Great. Make my life easy, why don't you.*

"I could kill the Flayer of Mithrans with my death magic, but yes, it's hard to stop. However, I could drain them all a little bit, and then Bruiser could take out the leader. Between an Onorio's magics and mine, we could take them all down."

Evan continued to shake his head. Stopping instantly when Molly looked around. *Coward.*

I asked, "What do you do with the excess undeath/ unlife energy when you pull their magics to yourself?"

"What?"

"You have to put the energy somewhere. Where does it go? Where did it go when you drained the vamps in the Regal?"

"I—I—What do you mean where did it go?" Molly demanded. And then her eyes cleared. "Son of a witch," she swore. Her hands tightened; her eyes went wide and unfocused. She spun around as if looking for the missing magics.

Speaking slowly, I said, "Molly?" She whirled back to me, eyes wild. "That was a direct, face-to-face confrontation." I continued. "Shimon has his own Onorio who nearly killed Bruiser. If they took out Bruiser, they could try—" I stopped. Bruiser had been wallowing in misery and guilt and that was not normal at all. Was my honeybunch spelled? I held on to that thought and returned to the discussion at hand. "If Bruiser was out of the picture, the Onorio could turn her attention to draining Edmund. And Ed might have had his brain rewired by the Flayer when he was being possessed and flayed. Our options are limited."

"Okay. Options. Right," Moll said, her eyes still too wide. "I'm listening."

And she was. Sorta. "Edmund could challenge SOD Number Two to Sangre Duello. Or I could challenge him to the kind of fight I had with Titus and fight him outside of time. Shimon was a witch before he was turned, so magic would be allowed. But that might kill me before I killed him, because if he has timewalking magic, and I think he has some, he might be way better than I am. Or . . . we could just kill him in his sleep. Assuming he sleeps by day. Assuming we could find him. Or maybe the arcenciels can be convinced to attack and bite him all at once. I've negotiated for eight arcenciels to help us, the way they were supposed to in the fight against Titus, but I haven't heard back. If Shimon has an anode nearby, he might be able to capture them. In fact, that might be what he wants. Or worse, maybe the time circle he's had going somewhere is being powered by trapped arcenciels rather than witches. Arcenciels who've been trapped for so long that they don't know about the new spell that frees them. And maybe his plan is to rule over time forever with the arcenciels under his magical thumb. And maybe he knows a counterspell and can keep them trapped. Shimon's been around two thousand years. This might be a brand-new way to use arcenciels, to ride them through time."

"You've been thinking about this."

"Yeah. I have. Thinking is all I've had to do while I was trying to die. Thinking the long game, the way Leo used to, is hard. It's like 3-D chess with four sets of pieces—white, black, red, and green. I suck at it. But I can see part of the boards. And all of them are deadly. And honestly, I can't see how we'll win against him."

"We'll win," Evan said, sounding too confident.

Molly agreed. "In a direct confrontation with fang-heads, with time to prepare, witches always win."

"His brother could walk through time. Probably Shimon can too," I said. "Time always wins when pitted against magic. And I can't promise I'll live through another timewalk long enough to kill him." They still looked unconcerned. "He has witches at his disposal, or maybe even arcenciels. In a time circle."

"And we'll save them once we finish with the mustache twirler."

"The what?" I asked.

"The evil horror," Molly said placidly, "who wears a black hat, twirls his mustache, and says *mwahahahaha*, as he dips the good guy in acid or in a tank filled with hungry alligators."

I frowned. The Son of Shadows *was* like that. Pure evil all the way. The creature had no redeeming qualities at all. Even Hannibal Lecter had been erudite and intelligent. Dexter had only tortured the bad guys. All bad buys had something or someone they loved or something they were passionate about, even if it was only their own bodies and needs. But Shimon was allowing himself to be altered, giving himself an exoskeleton that would likely be awfully ugly, awfully quickly. But . . . names. The names of the Flayer all meant something. I felt a chill, knowing I had missed something. Something important.

"What?" Molly said. "What are you thinking?"

"There was the dark blur with the flash of red in the background at the Regal." I texted Alex to go over the tapes, see if he could spot the dark blur and identify it. I got back one line.

I'm like, 30 feet away, you know.

The kids are sleeping, I texted back.

As I read his reply, Molly got a phone call. And staggered. "Are . . . Are you sure?"

Big Evan tapped the cell onto speaker, mouthing, *Our neighbor.*

"Everything is burning, Molly. I'm so sorry. I called the fire department as soon as I saw the smoke, but . . . your house was mostly gone by the time they got there."

CHAPTER 17

I Don't Eat *Family*

"Shimon burned your house," I murmured. Guilt punched me in the chest and opened a dark pit inside me.

Molly walked away and talked for another five minutes, getting particulars. But none of it really mattered. Shimon Bar-Judas had burned my BFF's home. Molly had lost her orchids. Her big Aga stove. Evan had lost his home studio and all his instruments. The kids had lost all their toys. Molly was crying. Evan looked as if all his blood had pooled in his boots, face too white against the red of hair and beard.

The pit of guilt inside me grew wider and deeper.

As Molly was getting off the call, Evan's cell rang. It was Molly's mom. Frowning, he tapped his cell on too, and answered, "Hey, Bedelia, what's going on—"

"The working got through the wards. The whole place lit up in seconds, a flash fire." Molly's mother was crying. "We're okay. But only because of the old root cellar. We went down and through it and out on the creek side. We're okay," she repeated, whispering, "but the house is in bad shape. Lots of fire and smoke and water damage."

Molly took Evan's phone and tapped off the speaker. Privately, to her mother, she said, "We'll be home as soon as the weather lets up. You, Carmen, the kids, and the animals go stay at Evangelina's, okay? Put up a ward there. Attach it to the ley lines below the house."

Evangelina's house was sitting on ley lines close to a liminal line. Powerful. Very powerful. Any ward opened on that old house should withstand anything. The ley lines were how Moll's sister had captured a demon and set a lot of the mess of my life in motion. Molly's death magics had first appeared there, and to this day, nothing would grow there.

After a lot of magical strategy chitchat, Molly ended the call and leaned against her husband, her red hair against his broad chest. "I have to call the insurance company. Our rates are going to go through the roof. Which we don't have anymore, it seems." She sobbed once, hard. Big Evan pulled her close, tears in his eyes too.

I walked away. They were in danger because of me. They had lost their house because of me. My fault. Guilt, my old frenemy, clawed into my soul. "Jane," Alex called as I moved through the empty inn area. I waved him away and made it to the front door. Yanked it open, the icy air instantly clearing my head.

A *gong* shivered through the air, through the floor, through the walls. *Gong. GONG. GONG!* The *hedge of thorns* around the house wavered and shook in a coruscating wash of light.

I raced outside. Big Evan thundered through the inn after me. Molly was on our heels, moving faster than I ever remembered. I stopped and they passed me. The ward bonged over and over, a steady thrum of dissonant notes, and I pulled on Beast's night vision, placing all our people.

The witch twins were standing back-to-back in the snow. Focals lay at their feet: moonstones as big as my fist at Cia's feet for the moon witch; Liz was a stone witch, and she had a huge, clear orb at her feet, quartz, maybe, and beside it was a two-foot-long multicolored crystal spire of tourmaline, as big around as my arm.

Shiloh raced at vamp speed from the side of the house, a popping smudge of movement. She threw her back to the shoulders of the twins, facing out. Cia made a little *erp* sound. Liz cursed. They hadn't known she was here. I had forgotten to tell them, and it seemed Molly had forgotten as well. Shiloh dropped a strap over her head and shoulder and aimed into the dark with an AR-17. There were extra magazines in her belt, each holding thirty rounds. "Hi," she said to the two witches. "It's been a while, and I'm a little different nowadays, but you're my aunts. I'm Shiloh, and what you can call a combo witch. Earth and a little fire. I'm making myself a conduit and giving you my magic to use while I keep you safe from human weapons."

"But. You're a vampire now," Liz said, intrigue and horror on her face.

"I don't eat *family*," Shiloh said, amused and exasperated. "And being a bloodsucker doesn't stop my magic."

I loved that girl. Shiloh was badass. She looked fully healed from having her throat torn out. Always a plus. The gonging bonging continued, speeding up slightly. The ward over the house and grounds brightened and dimmed with each percussive stroke.

Molly dropped her back to the twins' other shoulders, so they all four stood facing outward. Big Evan scuffed a ten-foot circle in the snow crust and took the north position. "We have air," he said, speaking of himself, "earth-death, stone, moon, and earth-fire. Five of us. My power, my will to your wills."

"My will to your wills," the others repeated. Quickly they fell into that meditative state that synchronized their magics.

It wasn't a perfect circle. They needed a water witch to make it perfect. But it was an Everhart-Trueblood grouping, and that made it powerful, linked by bloodlines and love. Which was the first time I understood that Molly's family knew about her death magics. I was proud of Molly for telling them. It couldn't have been an easy convo.

Big Evan pulled out a multitubed flute, the kind the god Pan always used in stories, and blew a soft, tremulous note. The circle flared up and the witches each took a step to their assigned places.

Edmund moved slowly to stand beside me. He wore a bandolier-style holster with two nine-millimeter semi-automatics and four full magazines of ammo. Double swords hung at his hips. He looked pale and scarred and so very *not* ready for combat. "My queen," he murmured. My lips tightened in frustration.

On the snow-covered lawn, the witches sat and arranged their focals. Evan said a *wyrd* and the circle he had made in the snow blazed once, a soft white light. At each witch the light sparked once, changed color, and a tendril of energy rose to the center, where it met the others. They twined about and sent up a sparkling, rainbow-colored braid that converged on the ward overhead. The ward that was shivering sound and light across the inn's grounds.

Eli joined me and placed a comms system around my neck. I stuffed the earpieces into my upright ears and adjusted the mic for my snout. He handed me my Dyneema, Kevlar, and anti-spelled armored vest, which I Velcroed on. Over it went the shoulder/spine rig that held three weapons, dual shoulder nine-mils and the Benelli M4 in a spine sheath. The hip rig with one nine-mil and vamp-killers with fourteen-inch blades on each hip. When I was weaponed up, he placed the Glob in my hand and extended *le breloque*. I pocketed the Glob but hesitated at the crown. This was one of the things the Flayer of Mithrans was after. I didn't know if I should taunt him with wearing it a second time. But I reached out and took the crown. Placed it on my head. It changed shape and tightened, securing itself to my head.

"Thank you," I said to my partner and my second. Eli was fully kitted out in cold gear and weapons. "You are *not* going out of the ward to reconnoiter," I said.

"Yes, Mama. I'll be good, Mama."

Even I caught the sarcasm, but I decided to ignore it. "What does Alex see?"

"Nothing. Nothing at all."

Which was very bad. That meant the enemy had found

all the security measures on the property and figured out
how to avoid them, or they had mojo—magical or tech—
that we didn't have. I looked along the walls of the house
to see Lincoln directing Thema and Kojo up onto the
roof, each with long-distance rifles and tripods. He sent
his other fangheads around the house into secure locations, spots I was sure he and Eli had chosen in advance.
"The prisoners?" I called to the MOC.

"Secured and unconscious, Queenie. You see anything?"

"No. Not yet."

"Mama!"

"Mamamamamama!!"

I whirled in time to see Lincoln Shaddock, Master of
the City of Asheville and BBQ chef extraordinaire, catch
both witch kids and swing them up in his arms. He carried
the screaming children back inside and shut the door.

The gonging grew in sound, a painful cadence. I caught
Big Evan's eyes. Tapped my ear. He gave a truncated nod
that was mostly just beard bumping on his chest like a half
dozen red squirrels hanging on his jaw, flicking their tails.
Evan changed out the Pan flute for a long, thick reed in-
strument and blew a note I could hear over the noise. The
magic moved across the air, a heavy, cottony texture to it.
The gonging sound decreased.

Into my earbud, Alex said, "I see two approaching
combatants. They . . . Damn. They have an outclan witch
priestess. She's in robes like Sabina. And she's glowing
even on the camera feed. Like she's leaking power."

"Where?" Eli asked.

"Front door is clock heart facing twelve. She's at
twelve, about halfway down the hill. She's under a *hedge
of thorns* that looks like it's made of blood, it's so thick.
The ringing attack on the ward seems to be starting from
near the same place."

His voice strained, Edmund said, "This outclan. White
robes or black?"

"Black."

"Aurelia Flamma Scintilla," Ed breathed. "Not her
given name. Not her surname. But her chosen name."

In my earbud, Alex said, "Diving into the files for intel."

"Copy," I said into my mic. "Ed?"

"Yes, my queen," he said, almost too softly to hear beneath the awful gonging attack on the ward.

"Tell me everything you know about Aurelia."

"What I know is gossip gleaned while I was back on the continent," Edmund said. "She grew up in a tiny village outside of Rome in the late 1800s. She eschewed magic as evil and dedicated herself to the church. She was a cloistered nun until her convent was destroyed one night by a young rogue. Three of her sisters died. She killed the vampire, embraced her magic, and has spent the years since destroying Mithrans."

"How many years?"

"Roughly one hundred and fifty in her quest to kill us all, though she is not a Mithran, not a Naturaleza, and not a blood-servant."

"Then what is she?" Eli asked, checking his weapons. "What is she doing here?"

"Aurelia is a *senza onore*. A dark form of an Onorio, and an outclan priestess," Edmund said. "Flamma Scintilla means *flame spark*, and she has a unique gift. Pyrokinesis. She is a Firestarter, a very dangerous one. I did not know she was in the States. And I find it difficult to believe that she is working for the Flayer. She hates vampires. She has no master, and only drinks from the Mithrans she kills."

"Unless the Flayer has something on her or has someone she loves." I thought about the fire at the NOLA vamp graveyard, the stones themselves burning. "Does Sabina know her?"

"Yes. They hate each other. And Aurelia is a far more powerful worker of magic than Sabina. Or George. Or Grégoire's boys. Perhaps stronger than them all put together. If they hope to drain her, they would have to work together."

"The timeline for the fires in NOLA. Is it possible she started them and still got here?"

"Barely. But yes," Ed said.

The last time we ran into a *senza onore*, Gee had rubbed

the blob into my hand as if that did something mystical. He said we two were the only ones burned by the *senza onore* spells, as we were the only goddess-born present. So did that make me more susceptible to *senza onore* spells? A little more uncertainty in my life was really freaking great. "So why is she here, tonight, with a master vamp?"

Ed's voice was right behind me. "I do not know, my queen. She was not with him while he was . . . flaying me for his use."

I turned to him, his scars visible even in the uncertain light. "Because she was in New Orleans burning the vamp graveyard?"

Thoughts flashed behind Ed's eyes. "Sabina?"

"Don't know. She was trying to get away the last time she contacted us. But if she's burned she'll need to drink and regenerate."

Alex said, "According to cams, there are twenty fangheads surrounding the property, plus the leader, for a total of twenty-one. The outclan. And four humans. That's the ones I can see, and they just suddenly showed up on the screens."

"How did they get so close?" Eli asked.

"Beats me. They avoided the sensors somehow. Sending locations to your tablet."

Eli pulled his tablet and tapped it awake. The small screen was covered with camera feeds, and he swiped one that gave an overview of the sensors that were lighting up the security system. There were twenty-two different spots of light in a rough circle that correlated to the Everhart witch ward. Farther back were four smaller spots. The humans, probably out of the way, waiting to feed any wounded vamps after the battle. "How?" Eli asked again. "They were hidden under movable wards? Without a witch to open and maintain them? They came in over the trees? *How?* We have *motion sensors.* Lasers. Cameras everywhere."

Alex said, "I don't like this."

"*Senza onore,*" Edmund said. "She is strong."

"Then why hasn't she burned us out already?" I growled.

If the ward failed under the onslaught, we'd have twenty vamps and a pyro inside with us. So of course it started to snow again, making vision difficult. The ward was permeable to air, snow, and rain. *Lucky us.* But something wasn't right. I said, "Vamp speed? If they knew where the sensors were, could they speed through and the device think it was a glitch?"

"No," Eli said shortly.

I spotted three of the twenty. Then a fourth. I moved through the snow to the witch ward and the Everharts. The witches' sweat was strong on the night air, drenched in the reek of fear and the stench of anxiety and struggle, as if they fought a battle they had already lost. "If the ward falls," I said to them, "stay put. I'll keep you safe."

"The kids," Molly managed, her face running with sweat. The snow around her had melted down to the muddy earth. Earth magics warring with powerful death magics.

"Lincoln and Brute have them. They're safe."

She nodded, sweat staining her clothes and sticking her hair to her face. All the witches were showing strain.

"Hang on, Molly."

She didn't nod this time but I knew she understood, because tears started at the corners of her eyes. She had been through the wringer in the last bit. Her home had burned. Her mother, sister, and toddler niece were in danger. And . . . If Molly and her family had been at home, they would likely be dead in the pyro's fire. It would have been Molly, her husband, and the children against these creatures. I wouldn't have had time to get to her. And she would have used her death magics.

The gonging increased, harder, faster, pounding louder, even over the protection of Evan's spell music and the circle's casting. It hurt my ears. Lightning shot upward from the ground at the outer ward, to meet in the center with a thunder of sound.

Beast. We're going to have timewalk, I thought.

Jane will die.

I'm gonna timewalk in half-form.

Jane will die.

A single pure *GONG* sounded and the ward shivered.
My hand tightened on the Glob and I drew a vamp-killer,
slightly curved steel blade, the back flat and fuller, all
silver-plated to poison any vamp I cut.

Light and power and the stench of ozone and burning
rubber billowed out from the ward like noxious steam.
Molly was crying, shaking, fighting calling on her death
magics. But if there was any time to use them, now
seemed like it. I opened my mouth to tell her to use her
magics.

A shower of sparks fell from overhead. A burst of
golden light shot through the ward.

And the ward fell.

Six shots rang out. Not one of the enemy vampires
dropped. Not possible for Shiloh, Kojo, and Thema all to
miss at this distance. But they did.

The vampires attacked, sprinting toward the inn. Un-
bloodied. Vamped out. Mouths open in silent battle cries.

I rushed forward, muscle memory taking over. My
half-form swept the vamp-killer back and forward in one
smooth motion. I took the head of the first vampire. Felt
no resistance. The bloodsucker rushed forward, head still
attached. I stopped. Whirled. The vamp was fine. How
had . . . "It's an illusion," I shouted. But how many were
illusion and how many were real? I dashed to another,
slashed my vamp-killer across him. He kept going.

"A *figment* working," Molly called, her voice pained.
"I can't tell how many."

Shiloh, Kojo, and Thema were still firing, but no vampires fell.

I raced to another. And another. None fell. I tore at
the Flayer himself. He stood still, tall and beautiful. Smiling. I barreled into him. Leading with my blade. The
silver-plated steel sliced through him. There was no resistance. Nothing. I fell beyond him, nearly tumbling. And
that was when I realized he wasn't there either. Even he
was an illusion. A human-looking one with no exoskeleton. Created by someone who hadn't seen the Flayer recently.

"Holy crap," I snarled, my paw-feet sliding on the snow. Even if I bubbled time—

From behind the house I heard a scream that was part bell, part raw terror. *Soul.* She was in the creek. Outside the ward that was no more. I pulled on Beast-speed but that wasn't enough. I reached for the Gray Between and the power that let me slide through time.

I hit something. Or it hit me. Vamp-fast. Like slamming into the proverbial brick wall. Head first. Didn't see it coming. Didn't see it disappear. Head spinning, stars like snowflakes on a black background. I tried to catch myself but . . . I was already lying on the ground. In a snowdrift. I sat up too fast. Reeling. Nauseated. I put a hand to my side and my palm came away black in the darkness. Bleeding. The something—whatever it was—had cut me. My blood splashed across the whiteness of snow, two splotches. My vision was wonky, cross-eyed, and I couldn't make it align. My ears came back on and I heard a muffled distant screaming. I made it to my knees and stumbled uphill to the front of the house.

The Everhart witches were gone, the circle a charred, muddy ring. The *hedge of thorns* was gone, a bigger charred, muddy circle around the inn.

Ed and Eli were gone. The scent of their blood rode on the air, carried over the cat-stink of my own blood. There was no one around me. Except a body in the snow. The smell told me it wasn't one of ours. Vamp. Dead. I wouldn't risk touching a booby-trapped corpse and left it there.

I found the front of the dark inn in the night. Not where I thought it would be. I'd somehow been moved. Or thrown, fifty feet, at least. I smelled something burning on the air. I staggered toward the house. The front door was hanging open. The lights were out.

I reeled up the stairs. I had lost my vamp-killer. And a lot of blood. My pants were drenched. But I had enough of my wits to get inside and put my back against the wall beside the door. Hoping my eyes would align, my belly would settle, and I would adjust to the darker, warmer world of the inn. I pulled a nine-millimeter, hoping I wouldn't have to try to aim. Lots of hopes in there.

Molly wailed.

I pointed the weapon at the floor, closed one eye, and followed the sound of her grief and fury to the suites in the right wing of the inn. Molly, now silent, was sitting on the bed holding a screaming baby. Big Evan sat beside her, silent. Completely silent, and very, very still, holding Angie in one arm, the other around his wife.

I looked around for EJ.

He was gone.

That was why Molly had been screaming. Her son had been stolen. Again.

I fell. A slow unchecked arc, to the floor.

"This is why the fangheads came. To get a witch kid. And an arenciel." It was Molly's voice, her tone so full of fury it was vibrating. I tried to open my eyes, but the pain in my middle was too great. My eyes wouldn't open. I was so tired. . . .

"They used a *figment* working," Alex said. "Five of them were real; all the others, including the outclan priestess, were illusions. Really good ones. They mimicked the results I'd expect on infrared and low light. There was no way you could tell the reality from the fakes."

Except for the missing exoskeleton. Shimon had looked human and I had missed the differences until my sword whipped through him.

"Jane is awake." Bruiser. Voice soft. "Thank you, Edmund."

"A little blood is nothing."

"She would have died if not for you. So might Lincoln."

"Would that I could lay down my life for my queen." When Ed spoke again, it was a whisper, horror in his voice. "Would that I had protected your son. I am foresworn."

"No," Big Evan said, his words paced and tight, "not your fault."

"Not your fault, my Edmund," Angie said, her voice thick with tears.

I heard movement, but from my position on the floor I had no idea who was doing what. "How . . ." I stopped. Licked very dry lips. Tasted Ed's vamp blood, salty and tart, which I had missed in the shock of waking. I managed to get my eyes open and tried again. "How did it happen?"

His voice a monotone, so like his brother's voice when upset, Alex said, "Deconstruction of the attack: While we were being distracted in front and all around the perimeter of the ward by illusion vamps, two fangheads— the one you call Legolas and the ginger-haired one—came in by way of the creek and chained Soul in a crystal."

Five vampires had done all this? Gotten in through the wards? Nearly killed so many of us? "They got Soul?" I asked, because that couldn't be true. She could get free. She had a spell that could be targeted from inside, to break a crystal. "Where was Gee during all this?"

"Don't know. And yeah," Eli said. "They got her."

Alex said, "Then they knocked out the power to the house."

"I hadn't had time to move it from a single power source to solar and battery redundancies." Eli sounded cold and quiet and utterly furious.

"The Everhart sisters found what they're calling a magical sonic drum near the north point of the *hedge*," Alex continued, "some kind of a onetime-use device to break a *hedge of thorns*. Wouldn't have worked on a small, tight personal *hedge*, but a bigger one, like the one over the inn, or over the Everhart homes, has weak spots. Even an Everhart *hedge*."

Big Evan looked up at the Everhart witches, his arm still around his daughter, her face buried in his shoulder. "We have to find out how that device works and who's building them. We have to find a way to strengthen our wards against them." He sounded guilty, as if he had failed.

"Not your fault," I said. It was mine. Every last bit of it was my fault.

"Shiloh's a decent sniper. She took down a fanghead out front," Eli said. "Silver-lead rounds. I sent Thema to decapitate him." Eli paused, breathing slowly. "When the *hedge* fell, they came in through the back and cut Lincoln in half. Nearly killed him. If it wasn't for Shiloh and Edmund . . ." More softly he said, "They took the kid."

"Not your fault, either," I managed, feeling for my belly and the deep gash that had been there. I encountered only bloody clothing and smooth flesh. It was still tender and felt like I was brushing ground glass across it when I touched the fresh scar. But I'd live.

"They raced in through the fallen ward," Evan said, "timewalking. They cut Lincoln. Stabbed the werewolf with silver. And took my son."

Alex said, "They didn't move like Janie. They were less timewalking and more time-skipping. Here and then gone and reappearing a moment later in a different spot."

Angie pushed away from her father's arms. She was sweat-soaked and the stench of her anger burned the air. "I'm sorry, Daddy. I tried to save us. But EJ wouldn't wake up. I carried the baby to Unca Lincoln, who was hurt. I opened a ward over them. I was going back to get EJ, but . . ." Tears spilled down her face. "The vampires got there first. I couldn't save my brother."

"No, sweetums. This is not your fault." Big Evan pulled a hankie from his pocket and wiped his daughter's face. "Not your fault. Not at all."

"It is. The vampires put a light on us. I made mine go out, but EJ's chest was glowing like a light."

"A witch finder," Big Evan said softly. Pressing the handkerchief into Angie Baby's hand, he looked up to me. He reached up and removed a leather thong from around his neck. Hanging from it, a marble was encased in a macramé basket, looking remarkably like the one in EJ's pocket. I blinked at it. "Witch finders are devices that draw on an unshielded witch's personal energies and glow so they can be tracked. They were used extensively in the Dark Ages during the fangheads' ethnic cleansing of witches, but we've never seen one here. The moment the *hedge* fell, the vamps knew where my children were." With a finger he spun the marble and said, *"Persequor."* In Beast's sight, I saw a tendril of power flow from the witch into the marble. It glowed brightly and pulled hard to the left. "It's following EJ. Following the matching marble charm he has in his pocket."

"Oh," I whispered. "Right. The charm." Hope of finding EJ shot through me. "I could take that and track him in animal form."

Hope and then anguish flashed across Big Evan's face. He said, "No. It's tied to me, to my magic. If I had the time, I could modify it and make that work, but . . . we don't have time." The marble went dim and stopped moving. The big witch stank of rage and frustration and helplessness. The entire room stank of fury and guilt and failure, the stench coming from all of us. "The full diameter of the tracking device is only one mile. They just passed that." Evan looked down at me. "He was moving north at speed."

"North," I whispered. *Better than nothing.*

Molly shoved to her feet, raced from the suite, and outside. I pulled myself to my feet and followed, leaning on the wall for support. She was standing on the back stoop. She screamed. Her death magics rippled out, a wavering, half-controlled beam of black light. The three evergreen fir trees nearest the tree line began to wither. To dry. They crumbled. A dozen closer to the sweathouse browned and dropped needle leaves; bark cracked and fell.

Evan set me aside as if I weighed less than his daughter and began to play his flute, the same kind of soothing anti-magic he had made for were-creatures. The Everhart witch clan all appeared, human and witch sisters, gathering on the stoop to huddle behind Big Evan. The witch twins were enraged, magics boiling around them like heat off a hot road. The human sisters were carrying enough firepower to supply a platoon of warriors, and both girls sported bruises. Their eyes look odd. I wondered fleetingly if the vamps had knocked them out getting to EJ.

Angie threw her arms around my hips and I slid down the wall to cradle her on my lap. "It's my fault. The bad guy came in so fast," Angie whispered, tears shining in her eyes. "Brute jumped on him, but the other vampire man got behind the werewolf and hurt him bad. I picked up Cassy. EJ was running to us. But the bad man grabbed my brother. He put a hand over EJ's face so he couldn't scream." Her face crumpled, her tears flowing freely.

My hands fisted. I wanted to hit something, but I had to be calm and controlled. Adult.

Angie said, "I screamed and opened a protection ward over Cassy and Unca Shaddock and me. He . . . he . . . he . . ." Her words stuttered into a sob and she wiped her tear-streaked face before she could continue. "The man said he'd give me EJ if I gave him Cassy. But he was lying. I knew he was lying. He wanted us all."

Her tears were hot on my skin. I stroked her sweaty hair, not knowing what comfort she needed.

"If I let down my ward, we were all gonna be hurt. I didn't have enough magic, Ant Jane. I didn't have enough workings to save us and save EJ and stop the vampire too. I wasn't good enough. My brother is gone. I messed up, Ant Jane. I messed up bad."

"Angie," I whispered, "your dad is right. It wasn't your fault. It was mine. They fooled us. They got past me."

"You gotta save my brother. He's not really a pain." Angie started hiccupping through her tears. "I really love him. You gonna save him?"

"Yes. Yes, I'm going to save him." I pushed away from the wall, carrying Angie back to the bed, where I placed her near her baby sister, and made my way to our bedroom. No one followed. I removed my weapons and packed a small gobag with a cell phone, a charger, my medicine bag, two silver stakes, and a thin T-shirt and pants. I pulled off my gold-nugget-and-mountain-lion-claw necklace and added into the mix a talon I hadn't used recently, one with a tiny bit of dried tissue on the fleshy end. I wrapped the gold chain tightly around the strap of the gobag. Slung it over my shoulder.

Bare-pawed, I went to Alex's desk. He was in an electronic face-to-face meeting, had three text message threads going, and was on the phone for a conference call. He was busy. I handwrote a note and tucked it into his palm. He opened it, scowled, shook his head no at me.

I waved my fingers at him and he scowled some more. He mouthed, *I'll let Eli know.*

I nodded and went to the kitchen, where I raided the refrigerator, taking a small raw steak and a high-calorie, high-protein sport shake.

Without telling anyone else what I was doing, I left the house. Ran through the crusty snow, my breath a billowing cloud behind me, my footsteps crunching as I ran. At the pool, I walked along the downed tree, out over the water, and down to the far shore. I set down my bag and grabbed the end of the log. Lifted it with all my half-form strength and stepped back from the water. The log end on the higher shore slipped and splashed down into the water. Eli would be after me fast, probably trying to talk me out of this. He'd have to figure out another way across the creek, which would give me an extra five minutes. By then I'd be gone. I raced upstream, looking for a good rock, small enough to lift, large enough to take mass, clean and free of moss. This time of year, finding bare rock wasn't hard. I found one, water-shaped into a small rounded boulder, maybe two hundred pounds, balanced on two similar rocks. I shoved it hard, putting my back into it, and it fell, dropping ten feet to rocks below, cracking open to reveal much lighter, rough granite in a paler charcoal color.

Brushing the snow away, I placed the steak on one of the remaining frozen stones. I stripped and laid my clothes on the topmost stone. Sat on the cloth, the cold instantly working its way through to my bare bottom, my paw-feet dangling over the ten-foot drop. I scratched the gold nugget on the rough face of rock, depositing a tiny amount of gold, so I could find it easily again. The nugget I carried worked like a homing beacon to my skinwalker nature, binding the scratch of gold to itself.

I texted Alex four words. *I'm ready. Follow me.*

Adjusting the strap of the gobag to its smallest size, I hung it on a branch at belly level, close enough to touch, and tucked the necklace into the gobag. I took up the talon as shivers shook through me. I fingered the raptor claw. Closed my eyes. Relaxed. Listened to the night. Felt the pull of the waxing moon growing toward fullness, hidden by the snow clouds. I listened to the beat of my heart.

I breathed, slowing my body's functions, my heart rate dropping, my muscles relaxing in meditation. I pulled my knees into a yogi position and breathed, hands on thighs, arms at my sides in the frozen air.

Quietly, inside me, Beast murmured, *Save kit. Even if Jane loses Beast.*

Saving the kid. That's the idea. But losing you is not part of the deal. I'm not losing you. You remember how you saved us in the chasm, when we fell, and the boulders dropped? Like that. Hang on.

I hadn't dropped mass in a long time, and while it wasn't actually difficult to do, it was also the most dangerous shape-shift, to set aside mass to take on the shape of a smaller animal. Dangerous because the frontal lobes of the human brain were completely lacking in much smaller creatures. I had to set aside the essential parts of myself to achieve the form I needed. It was possible that I might forget who and what I was and never return for the parts of me I was leaving behind, but if I was successful and if I remembered, my memories and my mass would be here, on the clean broken rock, waiting for me to take back myself.

Mind slowing, I sank into the talon. Deep inside. Conscious thought slipped away, all but the purpose of this hunt. To find and follow Legolas. To rescue EJ and Soul. Those purposes I set into the lining of my flesh, into the deepest parts of my brain, so I wouldn't forget when I shifted. I dropped deeper. Pulled the Gray Between out from within myself. I began to chant, whispering almost silently, "Mass to mass, stone to stone . . . mass to mass, stone to stone . . ."

I slid deeper, into the flesh on the wider end of the talon, into the double helix of DNA, the snake lying inside the heart of all creatures on Earth. The transition was like water flowing in the nearby stream. Like the snow falling, resting on my shoulders. The Gray Between streamed over me.

My breathing raced. Heart rate sped. My last thought

was of the animal I was to become. The Eurasian eagle-owl, *Bubo bubo.*

Beast thought at me, *Remember Beast. Come back for Beast.*

I promise, I thought back at her.

My bones slid, skin rippled. Mass shifted down, falling to the newly broken stone. Black motes of power sprang along my body, burning and pricking. *Mass to mass, stone to stone . . .* Pain like a knife slid along my spine. Wings formed and lifted out along my shoulders, metamorphosing from arms. I dropped more mass, my body falling away, altering. Golden feathers, tawny brown, sprouted. My nostrils narrowed, drawing deep, filling smaller lungs. My heart raced, a heart meant to power flight. My talons clawed across the stone, scratching, tearing my piled clothing.

The night was alive in ways my Beast never saw it. Everything was brighter, intense shades of greens and silvers, with tiny flashes of red and gold and orange. I could hear everything, everywhere. The movement of tree branches a hundred yards away. The sound of water tumbling in the creek, so loud it was like a waterfall roar. The smell of the steak.

I fluttered my wings and tore into the meat, ripping off strips with my beak and swallowing in greedy gulps. The meat was cold, but my belly was empty and I devoured the meat.

Eyes meant for the night took in everything as I ate, light and shadow, the movement of the wind in specks of energy that tumbled through the trees and bounced off the cold ground only to rise again. Currents were visible to owl eyes as they twisted and shifted up and down, side to side, and swirled back again the other way. When the food was gone, I spotted the bag and . . . remembered. I was Jane. The small human had been stolen. EJ.

I ducked my head through the loop of the strap and let it settle against me. Gathered myself, spread my wings, and leaped from the boulder, out over the stones and the creek. Beating the air with a five-foot wingspan. It had been a long time since I flew, but the memory was stored in the snake of the bird. Instinct that threatened to take over, threatened to make me forget I was Jane. I quivered and swayed off course, stretched into flight. Found a rising current of air and let it carry me up.

My human consciousness merged with the owl's, dispersed into the cells of the *Bubo bubo*. I hunted for the creature that had stolen the chick. The creature would not look like living meat. It would look like frozen meat, but the chick would be warm, alive.

Flew high and leveled out, banking a widening spiral. Bag bumped my chest like prey, pulling against my flight. But bag was important. I needed bag.

Below, I saw the warmth of creeks, like gleaming trails through ice. Saw the body heat of a deer herd. A small wild boar. A large rabbit. And a chick . . . No. Small human. A child. In the arms of a frozen dead thing. Child's heart was beating. Was alive. But child was silent.

Dead thing had long white hair and ran faster than deer. I followed, flying steadily.

Snow started to fall again. Colors of air currents muddied as snow fell through them.

I saw lights ahead. Word came slowly to mind. *Cars.* Lights on.

Memory came, more sluggish than before.

I am Jane. I am looking for EJ.

I folded wings and dove, spreading wings and dipping back, claws outstretched. Settled on top branch of tree. I watched white-haired dead thing run close. Saw other dead things near cars. Saw dead things step behind trees. Making snare of bodies. Waiting for white-haired dead thing.

Thoughts came. *Lego. Legolas has EJ. The Flayer of Mithrans is waiting for him.*

Lego stopped. Lifted his head. Sniffed. Turned and raced into the woods, uphill. Away from the Flayer. Then Lego disappeared. Vanished. To reappear farther away.

It's a trap. Understanding came. *They aren't working together. Lego isn't part of the Flayer's group.*

Lego lifted his hand as he ran. He was holding something clear and shining. I focused owl eyes in tight. It was a crystal. It was . . . *Soul. Lego has Soul. He's learned how to ride time. Or skip time, at least. And for some reason Soul hasn't gotten free, though she had the working that should liberate her.*

I felt magics in my middle glow. Looked down with owl eyes. Saw red magics in pointed shape in my owl middle. I knew this was somehow caused by Lego and by Soul. *I can't lose him. Can't lose EJ.* Magics faded inside my feathers. I leaped into the air. Beat strong wings, caught a shining thermal, soaring higher and higher. Banked, studying the cars. Cold dead things were vampires. They had moved. Some were in cars. Some were in the snow, following Lego. Trap had not been sprung. Lego had gotten away, skipping through time.

I remembered the thing in EJ's pocket. Molly and Evan could track EJ. Remembered cell phone and saying *Follow me.* I was not alone.

I banked and followed Lego and EJ. Warmth was a brightness against the cold air ahead. Squares of light reflected from the windows to the snow. There were houses and cars. Lego put EJ onto snow and raced into the house. From high above, I heard the screams of children and smelled blood. Lego raced out of the house and dropped a large body on the snow. A man. Inside the house, humans screamed. Blood scent rose on the air. The vampire had fed, ripping the man's throat with his fangs. Lego picked up EJ. Opened the door to the car and got inside, throwing EJ onto the seat. Car started.

Vampire is taking EJ. The car moved. Jerked. Moved. Jerked. Stopped.

I heard sound of many cars coming up the road. Looked. Dove. Circled. Saw cars approaching.

Thoughts struggled up from the deeps of me. *I am Jane.* I thought about numbers but I could not understand. My Jane brain was slowing down. My owl brain was taking over. Snow fell. Sleet fell. Owls do not fly in sleet. Ice gathered on my wings, weighing them down. I fluffed my feathers and fought the wind. Watched the ground.

The cars grew close.

Lego ran from the broken car into woods, leaving EJ. But he carried the trapped Soul. She hadn't used the spell to break free. Did the Flayer have a counterspell, or did the fact that Soul was part fish keep her from breaking free?

Other cars stopped. Vampires raced after Lego. Predators. Other vampires stopped and killed the human in snow. Killed the humans in the house. All the humans, all old humans. Was bad. But was much blood and meat.

Frozen human with hard chest and long legs opened the car door. Took EJ.

CHAPTER 18

Sucks to Be You. Lemme Play My Tiny Violin.

My thoughts were confused. I did not know what to do. Follow Lego? Follow EJ? I needed more of myself to decide. I wanted to eat the meat in the snow. Wanted to hunt. Wanted to fly high above the clouds or find a safe place to hide through the storm. I did not want to fight the frozen dead thing that had Soul. The vampire. He ran through the sleet and snow, faster than a deer. I followed and then circled back around. I did not know where EJ was. I was supposed to save EJ, to keep him safe.

Many predators had EJ.

I could not fight many predators.

I could kill *one*.

I folded my owl wings tight to my body. Aimed my killing beak down. I fell and fell and fell, hard and straight. Adjusted my angle for the heavy bag on my neck. *I am Jane. And I am owl.*

I tightened my neck and wings and feet. Vampire-frozen-dead-with-white-hair thing ran fast. Leaping over logs and jumping into folds of the earth, to race up the other side. Skipping time, disappearing and reappearing fast. I focused my eyes on the dead thing's neck. Lego. Lego's neck.

Dropped down hard. *Hit.* Shock whipped through my owl body. Through the dead thing's body. I heard bones in his neck break. Swept feet forward and clawed at neck. Cold blood flew. Taste of blood was rich and strong. Frozen thing fell and rolled. Hunger cut through me. I swept my wings back and hovered/followed/flew after it. Downhill. Through the snow. It stopped.

I landed on the frozen dead thing. On Lego. The bag on my chest hit hard. I hurt. I wanted to leave the bag, but . . . I needed the bag. Did not remember why. I ripped flesh and ate. Ate and ate. Was good food.

I saw the chain on Lego's neck. The chain was important. Did not remember why. But it was in the way of good food. I pushed it away and ate more good food. Belly filled with strong meat and rich blood.

Memory of Jane came back. *I am Jane.*

I heard the frozen dead things coming and hooked my beak under the chain on Lego's neck. The chain did not come free. I hopped to Lego's head and pulled the chain that way. It came free and I leaped into the air, flying to the branches above my kill. Tucked my wings and fluffed my feathers. I made myself small and warm. The meat had been good. Owl was warm and strong.

I am Jane. My memories struggled back to me.

I watched more vampires arrive. Dead things raced around, looking on the ground for the predator who ate Lego. They did not look into the trees overhead.

They picked up Lego and dragged him back uphill. They talked about Jane Yellowrock. Talked about killing Jane Yellowrock. Talked about using EJ to kill Jane Yellowrock. To steal the treasure of Jane Yellowrock. Jane was like crow, stealing shiny things. Hoarding shiny things. *I am Jane.*

I lifted my wings and shook off the snow. Shoved off from the branch and flew high into the air, the bag on my chest and the chain in my beak. I followed the vampires to the cars and then followed the cars to a new human house, one with lights and warmth spilling out everywhere. I circled high, watching vampires go into the house. They carried EJ. EJ was crying. Then there was silence.

I was cold. Was tired.

I remembered the warm place where I had been Jane and had eaten not-frozen meat. Was my nest. I flew back to the stream where the steak was and settled onto the rock. I dropped the chain and pecked at frozen blood. The steak was gone. I looked up and saw a human sitting in the snow. Human moved slow and pulled out meat. Not-frozen meat.

Hungered. Human tossed the meat to the rock. I ate the meat. Was warm. Was good. Human came close, moving slow. Was nest mate. Moved slowslowslow. Touched owl. Pulled bag off neck. Took chain owl had dropped.

"Hey, Janie. Shift back. I got a warm blanket for you." Was Eli.

I am Jane.

I remembered the shape that was my human self.

I changed. Rocks broke and shattered.

I became human.

"Holy ccccrap on a cracker with toe jjjjam," I said, my body curled atop the frozen rock. Shivers shook through me. Eli, whose eyes were looking to the side to give me as much privacy as possible, pulled something from under his shirt and tossed it over me. It was a blanket kept warm by his body heat. I sat up and wrapped it around me. "Ccccccrap, this feels good." I focused on him and said, "I found EJ. I think. Lego took him. But Lego and the Flayer weren't working together. And now the Flayer has him."

"Good work, Janie." Moonlight glowed on the snow, then dimmed as fast-moving clouds hid its face for a moment before freeing the light again. Eli pulled out his cell and tapped in a number. He said, "She's safe. There are definitely two groups of fangheads. Copy. Copy."

He ended the call and said, "That was Bruiser. He's with Molly, using his Onorio gifts to keep her from killing everything in sight."

I pushed up with an arm, trying to stand. Pain slivered through my middle like blades of glass. I gasped and my arm gave out. The pain of my weight resettling stole my breath entirely. Eli didn't move, evaluating, his face as unemotional as a vamp's in the darkness. *Battle face.* He went back to laying fresh warm clothes in my lap. "Stay down. How bad is the pain?"

My plan to race back to the house and get a group together to save EJ was seriously not happening. It took a few breaths before I could reply. "Fifteen, on a one-to-ten," I managed. "You didn't happen to bring the Anzu feather, did you?" Eli pulled the blue feather from a pocket and I stuck it against my belly. The pain faded from fifteen to about a five. Bearable.

Beneath the blanket I touched my belly, finding the hard points of the star tumor. No bigger, but still there. "Still there," I whispered. "I'm gonna give it a name."

Eli opened a thermos but I waved it away, sick to my stomach. He asked, "Give what a name?"

Moving slowly, holding the feather in place, I pulled on warm sweatpants and wool socks. "My tumor."

Eli said, "Interesting. What are you leaning toward?"

I loved that my chosen brother was willing to play along. I pulled the sweatshirt over my head. "Voldemort, Sauron, Darth Vader, Gargamel. Gargamel is the Smurf wizard. You know. Magic workers. Because of magical cancer."

"Um. I like Dudley. Or Basile. Something less powerful. Vaguely emasculated."

"I could go with Dudley."

Eli gave me an evil smile. "While you think of names, you also need to figure out how you're getting back across the creek. Someone threw the tree bridge in the water."

I stopped to catch my breath. "In hindsight that may not have been my smartest move."

He breathed a soft laugh that didn't touch his eyes. "Thank you for leaving a trail in the snow that a three-year-old could follow."

EJ was in the hands of bloodsuckers. "Welcome. I need to shift to half-form."

Eli didn't reply. I pulled on boots, trying to breathe through the pain of movement. When I had them on, Eli handed me the open thermos, steam rising from it. "Try it. It might settle your stomach." I could smell the chocolate and my mouth watered as I raised the metal cylinder and sipped. It was his wonderful brew, with a hint of bitter undertaste.

I looked at him, questioning.

"A double dose of CBD oil. It doesn't stay in your system when you shift."

I sipped some more and my stomach settled. "Thanks. This helped."

Eli gathered up my other clothes, the ones buried under an inch of snow. He helped me into a coat. I picked up the high-calorie-drink bottle I had brought, but it was frozen solid. That wasn't good. Eli ripped open a strip of beef jerky and I took it. Managed to eat and keep it down. I waved away a second roll and the protein bar. No way could I keep that thing down.

I drank my hot chocolate and felt better. I thought about my half-form, but it seemed very far away. *Beast?* She didn't answer. I had shifted into a form she couldn't share. Had I hurt her? It was always a possibility. I closed my eyes and thought about my Beast, thought about my soul home. I could feel her there, in the darkness, but distant. *I'm sorry,* I thought at her. She didn't reply. From my soul home, I could see the star energies in my middle. Oddly, they were moving slower. "I can't shift to half-form right now. Beast is . . . something's wrong with her."

Eli canted his head, acknowledging my words. I finished the cocoa. Eli offered me a hand. I looked at it but I had to clear the air first. "I know how dangerous it is to shift to a smaller mass. I was afraid someone would try to stop me."

"I'm not that someone. Don't play games, Jane. Not with me."

"If I wanted to do something really, really stupid, you would let me?"

"We'd talk over options. Weigh threat levels. Discuss backup. You claim you want family and clan. But when it comes down to the battles we should be fighting together, you go rogue. Bruiser was livid. Molly was furious. I was pissed. Still am." His words were hard, with sharp angles, meant to cut.

I wasn't good at apologies. Or doing things with others. I had run away from my people when I got sick. I had run away when I planned to shift to owl. "I didn't know if I could shift to owl with the tumor in my belly. I was afraid I'd die and you'd be here to have to watch."

"So you ran off alone. Again."

"I told Alex what I was doing and where I was going. I carried the cell phone."

"Not good enough."

Viciously, I said, "I don't want you to watch me die, you idiot. It's tearing you apart watching the cancer eat me."

Eli slanted a look at me, one hard and cutting. "You ran away. You always run away."

I tried to cuss but the words stuck in my throat. I managed, "I'm sorry."

Eli nodded, a tiny dip of his chin. "You should always make use of backup if it's available. It was available and you went out alone. *Don't*." His tone was steely. Softer he said, "However, what you did was brilliant, flying with a trackable cell. It was a good plan. We know where you went. Is the last location you circled for so long the place where EJ is?"

"Yes." I took a few deep breaths. And accepted Eli's hand, which was still out, in offering. He pulled me to my feet and steadied me. The pain swept through me like waves if waves were made of blades and broken glass. "Gimme a minute," I said. I held the Anzu feather hard against me. The pain ratcheted down slowly.

"You're right about one thing. I do not want to watch you die."

"Okay. So I don't die. I stay alive."

"Good plan." Eli opened his cell. Punched a number. He said, "Yeah. We're heading back in. Last coordinates are where she tracked EJ. Shimon has him. She confirmed that there are two groups of fangheads, competing." He listened for a bit and I didn't try to overhear. I was too busy breathing. "Copy." He closed the cell and picked up my gobag and the crystal. "What's this?"

"Soul. I'm pretty sure. We'll need to free her but . . . I don't know how. She's trapped but that isn't her arcenciel form. It's a mermaid form. And I'm pretty sure she isn't sane in that form."

"Yeah. Copy that." Eli studied Soul in the beam of his flash.

"If we find a rift in the dimensions," I said, lying by omission, "we can try breaking the crystal and tossing her in."

"Yeah. We'll do that. Just go out and find a rift. Though I guess a rift isn't any more impossible than anything else we've done." He tucked Soul in his pocket and slid an arm under my shoulder and around my back. Our heights were pretty much the same, but it worked. He flipped on a strong flashlight and shone it across the snow.

"Okay," I said. "Let's do this." I took my first step. Agony like boiling oil passed through my middle. I took a second step. And a third.

It was nearly dawn when we got back to the inn. Eli used his cell continuously, and by the time we got back, a battle plan had been organized. But I still hadn't found Beast. And I wasn't able to fight for EJ. I would be a liability. Which just sucked.

I lay on my recliner with the heated blanket on high, sipping chocolate with CBD oil in it, trying to find Beast, trying to find my half-form. No such luck. I watched the team as they filed out the door, taking the kids with them to drop off with Bedelia and Carmen at Evangelina's old place, the only safe place the witches knew. Gramma, Carmen, and the two human sisters were going to keep watch over them. The café would remain closed for the morning breakfast business. Asheville didn't slow down for a little snow, and the locals without power usually came out to Seven Sassy Sisters Café en masse when snowfall hit. Snow days were big moneymakers. But not today.

Brute, who had been injured in the vamp attack, was

on the sofa, curled around himself, healing with were-creature speed. I smelled vamp blood on him and in him. Once again, despite the hatred between weres and vamps, they had saved him. But he was deeply asleep. On one shoulder lay the grindylow, also asleep.

Outside, as the dawn grayed the sky, the vamps went to their hideouts for the day and the witches and humans took off on snowmobiles to the main road, which was freshly plowed. Box trucks that had been parked at a nearby gas station pulled up and the smaller vehicles were loaded in. I hadn't even thought about needing to get around on plowed and clear streets and then back onto packed snow. "Good thing someone had a brain," I said.

Understanding my comment, Alex said, "Box trucks were put in place by Eli and Shaddock during a break in the weather. Eli also has the helo on standby. And the sheriff's office and Buncombe County Emergency Services have been informed that the Dark Queen's people are searching for the Flayer of Mithrans. Your brother called. He said to let him handle it. I told him to . . . um . . ." Alex's face went red. "I told him to do something anatomically improbable."

My lips twitched into a smile before it faded. Pain brushed through me as if pushed by a broom, and I forgot to breathe. When I could speak, I griped a whisper, "I'm useless in this form. No wonder they left me behind."

"Nah. You're just a lone wo . . ." He stopped as Brute rolled over on the oversized sofa, lifted his head over the sofa arm, and gusted out a sigh that stank of dog breath. "Lone cat," Alex said. "You're just a lone alpha cat trying to lead a pride of alpha cats." He grinned over his keyboard, curls dangling in his face. "Sucks to be you. Lemme play my tiny violin, Your Majesty."

I threw a pillow at him. But I felt a lot better.

It was Alex and me in the house, alone—sleep deprived and ornery on Alex's part; sleep deprived and in serious pain on my part—as the box trucks and then the snowmobiles moved our people around. I was hoping Beast would come back online, reboot herself, and help me into my half-form. If not, I'd have to change to Beast and then I'd be useless until she let me shift into half-form. I hated to admit it, but Beast had as much control over my shifting as I did. Maybe more, since we had spent more than a hundred years in her form.

On the screens and over the comms, we listened to the team travel, which was next to impossible on roads that were mostly but not always plowed and some that were not designed for anything bigger than a pickup truck. It was midday before they were in place. And by then, the cars I had followed as owl were all gone.

The team moved in to find a Halloween fright house complete with scattered viscera and gore, five beheaded vamps, six dead humans, and enough blood spatter to qualify the house as a testing ground for crime scene school. Legolas wasn't there. Neither was EJ.

I could practically feel Molly across the miles, disintegrating. "Alex." I made a cutting motion across my throat. The younger Younger cut the mic so we could talk privately. "Ask Eli on a private channel if EJ's clothes or his marble locator device are on site. If not . . . I have an idea."

"Copy that." Alex opened a private channel to his brother.

I lifted the crystal prison that held a mermaid-predator creature captive. Soul was frozen inside the four-inch-long quartz crystal, her finger-fins wide open, her lips parted, her scaled body trapped in the midst of a twisting motion, like an eel trying to escape. Slavery was evil in every way.

But, for EJ . . . I twisted the chain, sending Soul's body twirling with the decorative quartz.

I would do horrible things to save my godchildren.

I'd even try to ride a trapped arcenciel, one I considered a friend.

I was probably going to hell for the things I had done. I had killed and maimed and destroyed so many sentient beings, all in the name of the greater good. But I'd do it all again to save EJ. I pressed the Anzu feather against my belly. The pain was breaking through even that now. To stay human-shaped, I'd soon have to resort to morphine, and the drug would shut down my brain. So I'd be saying goodbye to human Jane again, but just in a different way.

And then another option occurred to me. I examined it from every angle I could think of.

"Janie," Alex said, sometime later. "No clothes. No marble in a mile-wide circumference from the target location."

"Tell Molly I have an idea how to find EJ. Tell her I need her to stay calm and in control until I see if this works. Tell Eli to clean up the site," I ordered, which meant burning it to the ground. The vamps would burn to ash. The humans would be an unsolved murder case. "Then please find Girrard DiMercy and ask him to come by." Gee loved a good fight. Where had he been?

"Copy that. Relaying."

I worked through my idea as he chattered on the communication system. What might have been a long time later, I woke to find Alex kneeling at my side. "Janie?"

"I smell chocolate." My voice croaked and I cleared it and tried again. "I sm—"

Alex pressed a freshly filled thermos into my hand. I drank until I felt a measure of warmth fill my cold middle. I asked, "Is Gee here?"

"No answer on his cell. Eli says he hasn't seen the big bird."

"Not that I'm surprised." I sipped the chocolate. "I'm going to need your help. You got pics of the circle Big Evan made in the main room?" Alex nodded. "Well, you're going to reproduce it." Alex raised his eyebrows in questioning disagreement. "It'll be fun," I said.

"I'm not a witch."

"Me neither. There's no law about a nonwitch preparing a circle. Besides, I have witch magics right here." I tapped my belly. "They gave me Dudley."

"Uh-huh. Fine. You drink chocolate and CBD oil. I'll get the equipment."

"After you re-create the circle, find Molly's silver shot

glass/chalice. We're going to summon Girrard DiMercy."
Forcibly if necessary.

Alex frowned, thinking it through. "Because he signed
on as part of Clan Yellowrock, you can call him to come
to you."

"That's the theory. Last time I tried it I got into his
head, but he, more or less, told me to shove it."

"This should be interesting." He stood and placed a
hand on my head as if in benediction. It wasn't the first
time he had done that. I had a feeling he was praying for
me. He dropped his hand and left the room.

I looked at Brute, whose odd blue-crystal eyes were
staring at me. "I'm going to try something. If I need help,
are you game?"

Brute closed his eyes and faked sleep. *Stupid wolf.*

I lowered myself onto the pile of cushions at the north
point of the talcum powder circle and made sure the
fringe and tassels on the pillows didn't overhang the talc.
The floor was cold and my body couldn't handle prolonged contact with it, so Alex had gathered pillows from
every room and placed them inside.

Situating the Soul crystal on the cold floor in front of
me, I crossed my legs yoga style and tried to find a comfortable position. There wasn't one, and I still hadn't
found Beast to let me shift into half-form. I knew she was
inside me somewhere, because I could feel her panting,
but she wasn't speaking to me. She probably knew what I
was thinking about doing, the idea spawned by being
owl—though owls didn't spawn.

Animal humor, but Beast wasn't buying it. Not at all.
Silent and distant and I didn't know if it was pique or
damage from taking owl shape.

Alex placed the shot-chalice in my hand, the burning
candle in a candle stand on the floor at one knee, and the
blood-drawing tray near the other, before stepping back
and away. I closed the circle with the last of the talc,
dusted my hands into the air, and wiped the residue onto
my sweat pants. I stared at the talc clouds in the air.
Would that damage the working? I was way messier than

a witch, but then I didn't have talent, power, or craft, and I was as likely to kill myself as accomplish what I wanted. I decided to ignore the dissipating talc fog.

I opened and prepared the blood-drawing stuff and cleaned one finger with alcohol. I held the shot-chalice over the flame and was surprised at how fast the silver heated. "Shoulda gotten a potholder," I muttered.

"Beg pardon?" Alex drawled. There was a hint of snark in his tone, and he was leaning against the wall to the TV room, ankles crossed, arms crossed over his chest, cell in one hand, recording. He wore a hip rig with two nine-mils. He was a pretty good shot. Better than me, these days. He was dressed in hiking boots, tight jeans, and layered shirts. His too-long curly hair fell over his forehead and his eyes looked a brighter green than normal. Alex looked like . . . Well, wow. Stinky the Kid had grown up. He'd gotten buff and tough and kinda cocky . . . and . . . looked like a male model. An unexpected gush of pride welled up in me, though I'd had nothing to do with the transformation.

"If something happens to me, you take care of the others, you hear?"

"If something happens to you, Eli will beat my ass, so make sure that doesn't happen."

"Ouch!" I dropped the silver shot-chalice and it landed on a pillow, upside down, as I shook my burned fingers. The shot glass was sterling, so I figured the shallow bottom was as useful as the deeper bowl on the proper side. I stabbed my finger with the lancet and said a bad word. Alex chuckled, sounding as wicked as his brother. *Dear God.* What was I going to do with two of them? I squeezed my finger over the shallow silver bottom and blood filled it quickly, then started to run everywhere. I applied pressure, but it didn't stop. "Stupid cancer," I said. "Now my blood isn't clotting." And I was breathless and nauseated and . . .

Brute wandered in from the TV room and flopped on the cold floor, head on one ear, tongue lolling, watching me sideways. *Stupid dog.*

"Girrard DiMercy," I said. "By my blood I call you."

The blood in the silver vessel didn't boil, but it did warm a little. For the space of maybe a minute nothing happened. So I picked up the mermaid in my bloody hand and said, "Girrard DiM—"

"By the feathers of Artemis, what are you doing!"

I looked up to see Gee hanging off the wrought-iron chandelier overhead. The chandelier was swinging and looked as if it might fall and hit me.

"Are you trying to kill us all?" he went on in his vaguely Spanish accent. "Do you know how many arcenciels are in the area? Three! Three of the flying goddesses, searching for a juvenile that someone sensed. And the three are in contact with others." He said of the crystal, "Who have you trapped?"

I placed the crystal on the floor. Tucked my bleeding finger into the tight space between thigh and calf and used my body weight to apply pressure to the tiny cut. "Soul, but I didn't trap her. She was captured while stuck in mermaid form and didn't try to free herself and was carted off by a vampire. You missed the battle." I didn't add that if he had been here things might have gone very differently. "I got her back but I don't know how to free her. The arcenciels owe me for reneging on Leo and the Sangre Duello. I want to collect. She's my bargaining chip."

"You want the arcenciels to free Soul?"

Brute snorted as if he thought that was funny.

"Yeah. And then help me rescue my godchild."

"Have you not bothered to inspect Soul?"

I frowned and lifted the chain to study the trapped mermaid. "What am I looking for here?"

"Her left *leg*," Gee said, as if I was stupid.

I held the crystal to the chandelier; something inside caught the light. A silver-toned circle was around Soul's ankle. Fin. Whatever. It was tight, cutting into her flesh. Small blisters ran up the scales of what would have been her calf and knee, then thinned and vanished. "Okay. I see it. Is this why she can't find her dragon form?"

"Yes. No one will help her. No one will save her. No one *can* save her. She was punished by the Arcenciel

Council for multiple infractions; for shifting the timelines
enough to give Leo a faint chance for life, when they had
decided to allow him to die. When she refused to assist
them to go back far enough in time to destroy the Mithrans before they could be born. When she helped you,
against their advice. And when she failed to keep their
age-old enemies, the salamanders, from the Earth. They
decided the infractions had piled high enough and they
punished her."

I didn't know or care anything about salamanders. I
cared about my godchild. "And if I let her go? Break the
crystal right now? Will she go crazy and bite everyone in
sight?"

"She may. Or she may die. Soul has two choices for
recourse. She can help the arcenciels destroy the origination of the bloodline of the Sons of Darkness, or she can
dive through a rift and be saved. She refused the former
option. And there are no rifts available to her."

"Why not?" I knew the answer, but I wanted to hear it
from his lips.

"All the others are buried beneath the oceans, lost in
the deluge that resulted at the end of the last ice age, or
surrounded by Mithrans or they open into the middle of
a mountain. The arcenciels have been cut off from their
world for millennia."

My entire body stilled. Even the pain seemed to pause
for a bright, shining moment. Slowly, I repeated, "'Surrounded by Mithrans.' That's why they want the Mithrans
all dead? Because the vamps have access to a rift?"

"But of course. Why else?"

But of course. As if I had known, as if everyone knew.
Had I bothered to ask why? Had I asked and accepted
some excuse that made no sense? Because this . . . this
made total sense. "'All the others,'" I repeated. Except
the rift *only I knew about.* Well, me and the one arenciel
I had seen come through. Had that one found the others
yet? They were searching for her, so no. She was young
and the young dragons were more interested in sightseeing and playing and hunting than they were in helping
their species accomplish their ends. I frowned, thinking

it through. "So if there was another available rift, then Soul and the rest of the arcenciels would give up on the plan to kill the vamps."

"Not exactly, but a close enough summation. With the goddesses not everything is always so clear."

"Uh-huh." Soul hadn't seemed overly interested in gaining entrée to the rift. But maybe, in reality, she was desperate to do so and had been hiding her need to gain the upper hand in any bargain I might make. I held the long quartz crystal up to the light. "And if I just break it, she might die because she isn't in her dragon form. So she can't help me, and without her to interpret for me, neither will the dragons." And Beast wasn't responding and I might have hurt her. And I had a terminal illness. And EJ was in the hands of the monsters. Somewhere. Time was very, very short.

The Anzu still hung from the chandelier, looking alternately amused and irritated, though at the moment leaning toward amusement. He recognized that we were bargaining for something and considered me inept.

"Don't you owe me a boon?" I asked.

"No," he said. "You utilized my debt to make *me* your Enforcer instead of Eli Younger." His eyes were narrow and he was grinning. Enjoying this.

I was frustrated and in pain and getting close to blowing my cool. Which would not help this negotiation. Not at all. I shoved down on my anger and affected a curious expression. "Mmmm. You're blood sworn to me as my clansman in Clan Yellowrock. Under that relationship, would you consider helping me to track and kill the Son of Shadows, in your Anzu form?"

"My little bird form is outside of that agreement."

"As the Enforcer to the Dark Queen, would you consider helping me to track and kill the Flayer of Mithrans, in your Anzu form?"

"No matter the relationship, my little bird form is outside of that agreement." He pushed back from the chandelier, deliberately making it swing, like a kid on a playground. Yeah. Amused. Enjoying himself.

I shifted on the pile of pillows and the Anzu feather

tickled my bare stomach. So far as I could tell, I was out of options. "Fine. I have something to offer." I stopped. I had to be careful. A lie in the midst of a parley might ruin any outcome or negate the terms of the agreement.

"What have *you* to offer"—the Anzu placed one hand on his chest—"that *I* would desire?" As if saying he was out of my league when it came to things he might want.

I gave a slight shrug. "If you agree that what I have to offer is vitally important, then I want the following: For you to go on a hunt with me, in your Anzu form, for EJ, right away, today, at the close of this agreement. That you will help me locate and rescue EJ, wearing any form you may have, using all the weapons and contacts at your disposal. That such rescue would include fighting Mithrans, humans, witches, Onorios, and *senza onore*, using mundane and magical weapons, workings, and curses. And that you help me get arcenciel help," I added. Not that they had followed through at any other time we had an agreement. "Oh. And you help keep the other arcenciels off Soul's back."

The chandelier stopped rocking. The Mercy Blade to the NOLA Mithrans, and one of my Enforcers, dropped to the floor, a twenty-foot drop, and landed easy, crouched on toes and fingertips, just outside the circle. His hair was longer than I remembered and it flew forward as he landed to make a veil around him. Behind the hair, his eyes glittered. "What have you to trade for such perilous services, services that might mean my death?"

I wanted to blast out to him that this was urgent, wanted to shake him, skewer him for making me parley when all I wanted to do was get on the road. I shrugged, aping Leo Pellissier for nonchalance. "The location of a new . . . rift."

Gee's muscular, compact body tightened all over, giving away his shock.

I let a tiny Eli-worthy smile escape. "One not catalogued by Soul's arcenciels. One not hidden beneath the oceans, or in the possession of the Mithrans, or that opens into a mountain." But known to the one who came through. Not said. Not a lie to break the pact. Not exactly.

"One I found some time ago." To imply, though not to state outright, that I found it long ago. Lying by prevarication.

"I would sell my body into slavery for a thousand years for such knowledge. Every misericord on this planet would."

"Would the arcenciels fight at our sides for such knowledge?"

"I cannot speak for the goddesses, but it is possible that the ones you call Opal and Cerulean and Pearl would assist for this knowledge." He tilted his head, oddly like a vamp, or his lizard. "But if you have found such a rift, you are asking for more than this. Do not play games, little goddess. Not with the location of a new rift."

"A few more things. That you help me find the time circle that's allowing the Flayer of Mithrans to alter his body. Help me destroy the time circle. And help me save any witches still alive."

"Is that that the limit of our bargain?"

"Soul said that stepping into a rift would heal me, if it didn't kill me. After EJ is saved and his captors killed and the boy returned to his parents, I want you to make sure I survive stepping into and back through this rift, safely and not killed, and that I return to *this* world, at the *correct* time, through that same rift, healed, with my Beast self and my human self intact. With no loss of abilities or knowledge and with no loss of time." I didn't want to be returned a hundred years in the future with everyone I knew dead and gone.

"You would have me step through a rift. With you," he clarified. There was something in his tone I couldn't place, but I let it go for now.

"Yes. You or an arcenciel of your choosing, one who will abide by this agreement, if that's what it takes to get me back safely and healed. I have one of Opal's scales," I added, to sweeten the pot, "that I will return as part of this agreement. And lastly, that you will swear this to me by blood."

"I do so swear. But if you are foresworn, and if there is no rift, I will break all oaths of fealty and honor and take you as my slave for the rest of your life."

"I do so swear," I repeated his words back to him.

I blew out the candle. Wrapped my fingers around Soul's chain and forced myself to stand. Pain ricocheted through my body like a musket ball made of lightning, shattering and cutting and burning. I scuffed out the circle, not that magics had risen when I closed it. In fact, I was pretty sure it had all been for show. But the Mercy Blade was all about show, and I had . . . I had acquired his help. Under my own terms. Leo had taught me well.

"When do we leave?" he asked me.

"I have a gobag to pack. Say, fifteen minutes?"

"Yes." He looked me up and down. "Do you remember how to fly?" His tone said he doubted it.

"I do."

"Remove your clothing and meet me at the deck outside your sleeping quarters. We will rescue your little witch, save your buried witches, and heal your illness. Then you will give me the keys to the world."

Keys to the world? I didn't like the sound of that, but there was nothing I could do about it. "Fine."

Gee vanished, like a magician's trick, poof. I looked at Alex, who was still leaning against the wall, his face wearing a half grin, as if I had gotten away with pirate's plunder. Brute was sitting at his side with a grindy clinging to his fur. "He'll kill you when he finds out you don't have a rift."

"I have a rift. I can take him straight to it."

Alex's face went through a series of emotions. "No shit?"

"None at all."

"Daaaang."

I gave him a half grin. "I know, right? So we have one problem. Big Evan has the magical device that can track EJ. He said he could modify it to be used by anyone. If he already did that, then I need to pick it up, so I need you to find out if he succeeded in the modification, then arrange a rendezvous point, and convince him to stand on top of one of the vehicles with his hand in the air, holding up his marble, and let me pluck it out of his hand. In Anzu form. And my control isn't very good."

"So you might claw his arm off?"

"I hope not. But I'm not placing any bets. Now help me to my room so I can pack and strip and jump off the railing outside my second-story window."

"Do I get to watch?"

It was an ongoing complaint that he had almost never seen me shift. "No. You do not get to watch me shift. But I'll let you watch me leap out the window."

"Almost as good."

Alex stood slightly in front of me and I placed a hand on his shoulder as he led the way to the elevator. "Going up. Lingerie, undergarments, and naked bird ladies on two."

CHAPTER 19

Beast Is Inside Stupid Anzu Bird

The team and my clan were still miles away when I settled to the floor of my bedroom with the draperies thrown back and the French doors open wide to the icy, dull day. I was naked and shivering, and my skin was tinged slightly bluish, the way flesh looks when it's oxygen deprived. Or dead.

I pulled the special gobag over my head, situating it to lie beside the doubled gold chain and the gold nugget and the mountain lion tooth. Adjusted the strap for a larger neck. Inside the gobag were a pair of sweats, lightweight shoes, my cell phone (which had a call open to Alex), and a few weapons: a nine-millimeter, two extra mags loaded with silver-lead rounds, one vamp-killer, the arcenciel scale, and six stakes—three ash wood, three sterling. I added three packages of jerky strips and two protein bars. The gobag was heavier than usual, but I needed all the stuff in it, and as far as vamp-killing gear went, I was traveling light.

Vamp-killing. It's what I did, or had done, prior to taking the gig as Leo's Enforcer. I was a rogue-vamp hunter. And no way was I leaving home again without the tools of my trade, even if I was flying. I had done this before and it had sucked, but that didn't matter. I had a job to do and not much time to do it in.

Wrapped safely in a length of bubble wrap and my sweats, tucked into the gobag, was the crystal holding mermaid-Soul. And the Glob. Just in case. Yeah. Just in case.

I dragged the comforter from the bed, over my shoulders, gripped the feather I had taken from a dead Anzu, closed my eyes, and calmed my breathing. Eventually, I felt my heart rate slow. My shoulders relaxed. I slipped into a deeper meditation, where the world was peaceful and calm and there was only soothing light.

I sought the Gray Between. The silver mist of my skin-walker gift rose around and within me. Slowly I fell *into* the feather, into the bit of dried flesh at the base of the quill. Into the deeps of the Anzu, into the snake that lives at the center of all creatures: the double helix of DNA, as understood by the Cherokee of my own time. Except the genetic structure of the Anzu wasn't like a human's. So far as I knew, the feathered Anzu were not native to earth, and had once been worshipped as storm gods, back in Mesopotamia and Samaria, enormous storm gods with claws, wings, a raptor's beak, sapphire blue blood, and a bad attitude.

Their DNA wasn't the double helix of Earth creatures. It was a tangled mass of circular strands, glowing like spun glass, emitting light in pale blues and greens. One ovoid spot was denser and darker. It opened its eyes and looked at me. I flinched, knowing what was coming. Fighting my own tension, my own fear.

The oval slowly unfolded, unwound. The genetic structure was, literally, a snake, one holding its own tail in its mouth. *Ouroboros*, I remembered. The ouroboros focused on me, in the Gray Between, a place where energy and mass are one.

The snake opened its mouth. Let go of its tail. I tensed further but didn't look away. It struck. Snake fangs pierced my soul. Pain zinged through me like lightning, a massive bolt from a major storm. My bones bent. Darkness took me, blazing and icy.

Through the darkness, I heard Sabina's voice, from

the only other time I had taken this shape, when she told me, *"With this action, you walk the sharp edge of a blade between light and dark. You do not cross that edge into darkness, but if you slip, you may bleed."* Yeah, that made it all hunky-dory.

And softer, the words Frenchy and seductive in my memory, Leo Pellissier had written, *May your hunt be bloody. May you rend and eat the flesh of your prey.* Words he had once sent to me about hunting with an Anzu.

I woke. The night was warmer, strongly scented of the synthetics in the carpet, the drapes, and the cleaning supplies that kept the place Eli-sterile. The snow through the window smelled clean and sharp. Distant stinks of exhaust, gasoline, diesel fuel, added a dark twang to the mélange. The light bouncing off the snow outside and reflecting into the room was a magnitude of lumens brighter. Sounds were sharper. I could hear the *dripdripdrip* of melting snow, the crack of warming ice, the patter of a rabbit exactly . . . there, in the front tree line.

I was supposed to call for Alex. I lifted my arms and my right finger-feathers brushed the bed behind me, and spread out to a full twenty-foot wingspan. I rose to my feet and stretched, my head swiveling. I had shifted into Anzu.

I was sapphire and scarlet and some sort of ultraviolet color. The glowing UV feathers were up under my wings and on my chest and belly. A darker shade overlay the tips of finger-flight-feathers and tail feathers, black-light glowing and intense to my Anzu eyes. My feet were ten inches from back claw and rear toe, called the hallux, to the longest front toe claw, and knobby joints were covered with glowing orange skin. My beak matched my orange legs, was pointed and curved, a vicious hook on the end. I inspected my spread wings carefully, sapphire flight feathers, the band of scarlet near my shoulder, and another on the back of my neck.

I shook, folded my wings and settled my feathers, feeling each one as it found its place. Like last time, I wasn't hungry, which was a change from all my other shape-shifts. Usually I had to fuel my shifts with prodigious amounts of food, but something about the soft-lit magic trembling along my wings again suggested that I had pulled the energy from elsewhere.

Beast? I thought, hopefully.

Beast is here. Beast is inside stupid Anzu bird with Jane. Anzu bird is stupid shape, but Anzu shape lets Beast be here with Jane. Beast hunted and killed mooses with claws and strong beak, she thought at me. *Want to hunt cow or bison. In Edmund car.*

Thank God, I thought.

Beast is not god. Edmund is not god. Anzu is not god.

Something like joy flitted through me. *True. And yes, this is good.*

I opened my beak and a warbling cry echoed in the heights of the room as I called out, my bird throat trying to make a word. *Alex* came out as "Aulkxsh."

The door opened and my younger partner entered. "Dang, Janie. You look dangerous."

Beast is dangerous. And beautiful, she thought at me. *More beautiful than stupid bird.*

Dang skippy, I thought back.

I warbled again, trying to say hello. It came out a rippling trill of *L*s.

Alex carefully, slowly, raised a hand to my head and stroked my feathers. "You are . . . This is amazing. I wish—" The words broke off abruptly.

Alex wishes to be skinwalker, Beast thought.

Alex wishes to fly, I thought back.

Flying is stupid. Beast does not like to fly.

It's the only way we'll find EJ.

Beast chuffed in irritation.

I leaned into his hand and let him groom my feathers. Then I caught a flash of color from the open door and I hopped away, out the door and up onto the railing of the balcony. I looked back and said, "Aulkx, callll Evannnn. Remembbbber."

"I remember," he said from behind me. "And as Leo once wrote to you, 'May your hunt be bloody. May you rend and eat the flesh of your prey.'"

With those words, and the memory of the bloodsucking

fanghead foremost in my mind, I gathered myself and
crouched until my knobby toes touched my breastbone, a
position I might achieve in human form—if I broke my legs
first. I leaped and threw out my arms. Not arms. *Wings.* Icy
air caught beneath them and my wings beat down. Tips of
flight feathers hit the earth and brushed through the snow
on the second and third strokes. And then I was lifting,
wind in my face, air thin and icy and very, very wet. I
tucked my feet and angled my body, rising into the air with
each wingbeat. The Anzu Mercy Blade Enforcer flew at
my side.

Over the cell phone, I heard Alex's voice, crackly and yet
crisp in my Anzu ears. "Janie, I am tracking. Head to your
two o'clock. You'll see Asheville in the distance. Copy?"

"Coee," I said in my bird voice, my wings carrying me
onto a high-rising thermal. I tilted my feathers and found
an air current that let me relax, soaring as the wind lifted
me. Below me I smelled people and petroleum products
and felt the power of the mountain ridges as the energies
rose and built and as air currents met and twisted together.

Alex said, "I-40 should be visible beneath you about
now."

"Cokee," I said, trying my bird voice again, trying to
remember how I had communicated last time, how my
mouth worked. It had seemed easier before.

To my side, the air currents underwent a sharp change
and I compensated, looking that way. Gee flew to my side
and a little behind, riding my draft. Letting me do the work
of flying. Useless bird. I caught his eye and he opened his
beak, giving a laughing squawk. I whirled. Batted my wings
at him.

Gee tumbled in the air, all feathers and fluff. I laughed
back at him and got an evil bird-eye in return. Then he
laughed, a peculiar Anzu chuckle. "Urgggglllaaamm-
maaah's body was always beautiful in flight," he said, of
the owner of the flight feather I had used to shape-change.
"Your clumsy antics would make her laugh."

I blew a bird raspberry at him with my beak and spi-
raled hard away. "Alexch? Where?"

"Perpendicular to your right," Alex said, "is the North

Swannanoa River. Upstream, you'll spot the first of two stone quarries, may be hard to spot under the snow. Can you see them? If so, head to the farthest one."

"I ssshee," I said.

"Keep the Burnett Reservoir to your right, at about two o'clock."

"Copy." I found my voice in the guttural and tongue and throat possibilities of the Anzu physiology.

"Wedgewood Terrace wends to your left, with a stretch of road that is actually almost perfectly straight. A house roofed with red-clay tiles is on the right side of the street, new construction, about halfway between two right-angle turns. You see that?"

With my human eyes I'd have said no, the color hidden beneath the snow. But my raptor eyes picked out spots of red beneath the blanket of white. "I see."

"Big Evan is standing in the middle of the road, waiting for you. He has the tracking device in his hand. Quoting him. 'Janie. Bring my boy back. I trust you.'"

Anzu eyes are remarkable. Big Evan was like a beacon, standing on top of a truck in the middle of the road, his magic and his life force a brilliant reddish gold. It was clear that all Anzus knew he was a witch, his half secret even more revealed than he might have known. I half folded my wings and slanted down. There was a vehicle, a garish-painted snowmobile, steam coming from the exhaust, near the truck. I adjusted my approach again just as a flurry of sleet/snow mixture battered down on me. My nictitating membranes flashed closed, changing the world to grays and ochres. A blast of frigid air buffeted me and I raised my wings, flight feathers angled for more drag. Like a fledging learning to fly, I began to tumble. Lost my angle to grab the marble swinging on a macramé strap. The ground came at me fast. Instinctively, my claws outstretched and grabbed the steering handlebar of the snowmobile.

The handlebar gave as my weight settled.

With an unintended squawk, I flapped, flopped, hopped off the handle onto the hood of the small vehicle and gripped a protrusion to keep from sliding off into an ungainly heap in a snowdrift. My eye membranes opened in shock. My claws scored through the paint. "Oopsssh," I said, blinking.

Big Evan smiled slightly as I caught my balance, but the scent of his worry and fear abraded the air like burning sandpaper. "You don't have to carry it now." He climbed down to the snow, landing with a grunt. "Where do you want the tracker?" he asked.

"Tie like jessesssh?" I indicated my clawed foot, holding it into the air.

"Good. Yeah." Evan dropped to one knee in the snow, his body heat a measurable force in the cold air, even through his winter gear. His hands were heated on my leg as he looped the ties of a small bag around my ankle and knotted them off. "I've set it with a soft audible tone. If you get within a mile of my son, it'll make a faint *tinging* sound, like a tiny silver bell. As you get closer, the sound will get louder, more pure in tone, at least to your bird ears. No humans will be able to hear it. It won't be loud enough, I hope, to attract the attention of any daywalking fanghead."

"Mile high or a mile distant?"

"Think of EJ as being on the ground, centered beneath a large bowl, as deep as its radius. The higher you are, the angle of the reading will be less accurate." He paused, testing the thong he had tied to my ankle. "I recommend a height of five hundred to a thousand feet above ground." Big Evan had finished securing the tracker and his big hand rested on my even bigger foot. He met my eye. "If we had been home, we might all be dead. At the inn, we—not you—were responsible for his safety. Losing him is on us. But . . ." Tears gathered in his eyes, fury and fear shifting through behind the tears. "I'll give you anything. Please save my son. Please." A tear trickled down his cheek into his beard.

"Yesssh," I said, discovering that birds couldn't tear up. "Give me your friendship. Believe that I'll alwaysssh put you and yoursssh first."

"So. I've been an idiot where you're concerned. Molly's always said so."

Beast leaned us down and touched his hand with my/our

beak, then slid our head and neck along his hand, scent marking him.

"You really make it hard to hate you."

I chirped. Tried to give a snarky bird grin.

It must have translated because Evan raised his bushy brows. "Alex said the proper blessing for this hunt is, 'May your hunt be bloody. May you rend and eat the flesh of your prey.'"

"People really need to stop quoting Leo to me," I said. The consonants sounded like sharp tocks, but my words were growing understandable. Mostly.

"We have a dozen hamburgers. They're cold but they're yours if you want."

"Thanks. But I think a deer would suit better." I had no idea what hamburgers would do to an Anzu digestive tract. I raised my wings, gently dislodging Evan, sending him lurching into the snow. I sat back on my heels and launched myself at the sky, stretching out my wings, angled for lift, and flapped hard, raising myself into the cold air.

Flying. Healthy. A gust of air flipped me over and I tumbled dozens of feet before I caught my wings under me.

Beast hate stupid bird. Beast hate flying. Beast—

I got it. I got it. Now, hush. I need to listen.

Gee DiMercy angled into my flight pattern and set himself to my right wingtip, still using my energy to soar. Dang bird. Sleet cut through the air. Buried itself in my feathers. I fluffed them out and settled them. Found a height above Asheville at what I felt like was about seven hundred feet. I hoped no local yahoo with a shotgun thought I was a trophy and shot me out of the sky.

To Gee, I said, "I have a bell-chime tracker, and the cell phone is on to Alex for as long as its battery and its minicharger stay active. Starting a grid flight pattern over the city proper, where I-26 meets I-40 and moving east all the way to the edge of the city, then back to starting point and moving west. If we don't find anything in the city, we'll expand, quartering the land along I-26 and I-40 in five-mile segments."

His made an odd bobbing motion, like a pigeon on a window ledge.

Wisely, I didn't say so.

*   *   *

We searched for three hours, silent, listening, and gave up on finding EJ inside the city limits. Expanding our flight pattern, we searched the quadrants from east to south to west to north. We got nothing. Nada. Zilch. I was despairing and my Anzu body was tiring. I was a skinwalker, but like any biological body, this one needed toning and training and its muscles came to me functional but not strong. Snow and ice were building up on my feathers and face. There were good reasons why birds didn't fly in this kind of weather. I was frozen. "I need another break," I said. "Alex, Gee, I need food."

"Can't help you, Janie, but my big bro says the weather is shifting off to the east and the helo can fly. So if you find the kid, you'll have backup."

"That's good," I said, barely stopping my bird beak from chattering with the cold.

"We will hunt deer." Gee banked and dropped below me, swerving toward the Biltmore Estate and grounds and across the French Broad River, speeding toward a leafless, wooded area, near the Biltmore vineyards, where we circled, searching for life in the waning light.

The bell in my pouch gave a soft chime.

I nearly fell out of the sky. "Was that—?"

It chimed again. "Yes! Stay aloft, little goddess. You do not have the gift of cloaking. Their guards will see you." Gee did a whirling, falling maneuver worthy of a fighter jet. Before I could stabilize and level out my flight, he vanished. Completely vanished. Like, poof. Gone.

"Crap. Either Gee transported there, or he went invisible."

Alex said from the cell, "Sneaky bird brain. Working to get your position now."

I circled, waiting, trying to make out landmarks below the blanket of white. The layers of snow made it difficult, though I thought I saw a greenhouse.

Alex said, "You're near the North Carolina Arboretum."

"Copy that," I said. "Gee is reconnoitering from down

there and I'm sightseeing." Minutes passed as I circled, and I identified the tall roof of a greenhouse, a gift shop, flat places that were probably parking lots, a two-story building that looked as if it might be part museum, part visitors' center.

Over one section of the buildings, my tracker gonged much louder. I dropped lower in a smooth, slow soar, and it gonged again, narrowing the location of EJ's marble tracker, hopefully still in his pocket, on his person. My tracker continued to gong, slightly louder each time.

From one section of grounds and building I caught a whiff of smoke, cooking meat, spoiled meat, and old blood. I sniffed carefully with my bird nose, which I discovered was very good at certain scent patterns. I detected human blood. Vampire blood.

Not EJ's blood. "Thank God," I said, the sound a bird-like chirrup.

The tracker bell sounded.

"There's smoke," I said. "Smells like barbeque, maybe pork. Or . . . Oh. *Gack*. Maybe human. Yeah. That's it. Someone is cooking human in a big smoker." I sniffed again.

"Is it—" Alex broke off.

"Not EJ." If it had been EJ I'd have wreaked havoc and destruction on the creatures below. I'd have spared no one. I beat my wings once, hard, and rose through the whispering sleet on the cooking-human thermal. Which was gross and horrific in every possible way. I sniffed again and decided it was truly someone I didn't know. "I don't think so."

I placed where the bell tracker was directing me and focused in with Anzu eyes on the building. The bell was loudest when I soared over the visitors' center or cultural center or whatever they called it, seeing through the distant windows. The building was open space from the lower level to the ceiling two stories overhead, lots of heavily frosted windows, that, in Anzu vision, glowed brightly with light and warmth. The air rising from the heated space smelled strongly of rotten meat/spoiled blood.

"Tell me everything you see, Janie."

I pitched my wings for an oblique angle around the

corner of the building. Hanging from a second-story window, booted feet dangling in space, was a human-shaped, fully dressed Gee DiMercy. His head was the only part of him that might be visible to anyone inside, raised above the lowest part of the glass. He scampered across the outer wall like a monkey in a tree, or like a spider, hanging by his hands on the exterior window sashes.

"Gee is looking in the window of the visitors' center," I said. "The grill is behind that building, and based on the rising thermals, I think they also have a fire in the fireplace in the center."

In Anzu vision, I knew there were no live or undead humans in sight, so I slanted lower over the grounds. There were several SUVs, two vans, and two cars, each glowing in infrared, only a thin layer of melting snow on them. They had been driven recently. "I see vehicles. Including two bloodred Range Rovers. And there's more old-blood scent inside them." In the landscaping below me was an herb garden smelling strongly of rosemary, a garden of what looked like blooming mums, colors fading, but visible even beneath the snow. One garden looked odd, and my empty belly did hungry somersaults at the sight of three deer on the plantings' periphery, but before I could investigate, Gee leaped off the roof and dropped his human-glamoured shape, falling into his Anzu form. I whipped to the side and out of his way as his wings beat down, sweeping hard, rocketing him upward.

I glanced to the west. The sun was setting. We were either just barely in time, or totally out of it.

"You are not cloaked, little goddess. Follow me closely," Gee chirped when he drew level. He folded his wings and dove. I mimicked his movements and followed, sleet cutting through my feathers. I shivered hard as we drew even with the visitors' center, wingtips almost touching. We swept past. I got a good look inside through the windows in the upper story. EJ was sitting on a chair. Sitting in a chair facing him was a dark creature, part human, part . . . other. His exoskeleton was a carapace so black it seemed to suck the light out of the day. His eyes were round and wide at the nose, tilted high and pointed at the outer tips, like teardrops, and glittering with a prism of light and energy. It was the same colors as the rift—blues and greens and shadows that glistened. Once again I remembered that titles had value in Shimon's time. One of his titles was the Son of Shadows. How was he a shadow? Or had Judas, his father, been the shadows?

The Flayer rose from the chair and leaned over the little boy. He picked up my godson and carried him toward the door. They passed a scarlet heap on the floor, all angles and mangled limbs. The Flayer of Mithrans' latest interpreter. The FOM opened a door in the back of the two-story building and carried EJ into the depths. I lost sight of them.

I described what I'd seen. Not that it helped.

"Eli and Bruiser are on the way," Alex said. "Helo has lift-off."

"I thought you said we needed the sleet to be stopped."

"I did," Alex said shortly. "Like they listen to anyone with sense."

Knowing our location didn't get us backup anytime soon. I needed to shift into a primate with opposable thumbs to fight, but I was pretty sure I didn't have time. I followed Gee up and we landed on the crest of the two-story building, my talons cutting through the ridge into the supports below. The tracker continued donging.

"Do you see him?" I croaked. Now that I wasn't expending energy staying aloft in a storm, I began to shiver.

"No," Gee said. "No one left the building. However, there is a circle below us, covered by snow, possibly the circle powering the transformation of the Son of Shadows into whatever he hopes to become, though I must say, it isn't a strong circle. Not a powerful one."

Gee leaped off and beat his wings, one powerful down stroke, to make an arc over the part of the grounds where the deer had stood, and once again, my stomach did a somersault. Not from hunger, but from the weird magics there. I wondered if the cancer had just appeared in my Anzu form, then shoved that thought deep inside. There was nothing I could do either way.

Soaring, I studied the patch of ground, trying to see with Beast thoughts and Anzu eyes and brain. There was a faint ring of magics in a circle on the ground, not nearly strong enough to be witches buried in the dirt, powering a time circle with their life energies. However, human-shaped and sized lumps were in the circle, and the stink of dead vamp and human was strong here. I counted twelve bodies, so the clock concept that we had seen in Natchez was present here. It could be a time circle of some sort.

I swooped lower, into the miasma of death stench and rot, and my bird nose separated out a familiar scent. Legolas. The blond vamp. His blood was here in the circle. A tree had partially fallen near the edge of the circle, and I back-winged over it, catching it in my claws. The tree gave, bounced, and held, roots still in the earth. I folded my wings and sat. Studying. Taking the opportunity to fluff ice off me and to breathe. I needed the rest. Gee settled in a tree above me. I said, "I want to see who and what is powering the circle. If I disturb the circle what will happen?"

"Do not. Your Anzu magics should allow you to see life and death through the snow."

I strained, trying to access Anzu magics the way I did Beast's, but all I saw was the snow mounded in human shapes. "Not sure how to do that, Enforcer. Why don't you tell me. Are the bodies skinned? Are these the handiwork of the Flayer of Mithrans?"

Quietly, Gee said, "Perhaps it is best you not see this, my queen. Yes. They are. Six humans who show signs of torture. Six Mithrans who have been flayed and beheaded. Much power was expended within this circle and little is left. Its working has been completed."

I remembered what Moll had said about the kind of location a time circle might need. "It should have been set up underground, out of the elements, where the power that built wouldn't disintegrate quickly. This is a bad circle, not one made by a mature, capable witch." When Gee didn't respond I said, "We saw the *senza onore* in the illusions. She would be a very powerful witch, and I had assumed she was with the Flayer. But no way an experienced witch created this circle.

"Alex. Contact all the Asheville witches. Make sure no witches have gone missing."

"None are missing. I just got in a call with them. All the witches in Asheville are safe and accounted for."

"The energies are not proper for a witch circle," Gee said. "I do not know what it is. Unless . . ." He stopped speaking and we sat as sleet peppered us hard and an icy wind cut through my feathers.

Worry and fear were just as cold, freezing my heart. The elation of finding EJ alive was gone. Where was he? Where had that *thing* taken him? Visions of EJ dead in horrible ways made my gorge rise, sick and hot. I shivered. "Don't keep me in suspense just for kicks. I'm freezing my butt off here." Shimon still had not appeared and the dinging was still piercing to my Anzu ears.

"What if it is a time circle, but not a *witch* time circle," Gee said, his tone pensive. "For two thousand years, Shimon killed all the witches he came across, perhaps thinking to rise above other magics out of jealousy and anger, to kill all rivals for power." He gave a human-type shrug with his shoulders and wings, uncertain. Gee continued, his words slow, hesitant, like a deer in open land. "Perhaps his knowledge is finite, knowing only that a time circle is possible. Perhaps he even learned this from spies in Natchez, but no one could tell him how to create one. Perhaps that incomplete knowledge is not sufficient to accomplish his ends. Faulty knowledge of time circles might result in a circle built with the energies of other paranormal creatures. That could be why Shimon wants *le breloque*, the crown of the Dark Queen, to help power a circle that is weak at best."

I stared out at the circle, glowing palely through the snow, trying to fit things together, like puzzle pieces. "So we think this is a version of a time circle. Can you tell which body died last? And if that body is a vampire? And if it has white hair? And if it was flayed alive?"

"Yes, little goddess. To all of those things. That one." He extended his wing, pointing. "That Mithran, died true-dead, last. He had white hair."

Sooo. Legolas was dead. That meant . . . "When Edmund was—" I stopped, remembering the bloody body of my friend, and had to force myself to go on.

"When Edmund was being used as interpreter, we know he was possessed. Ed said the Flayer had access to the far reaches of his mind."

"Yes, my queen. He was able to keep little in reserve."

And the FOM had flayed Legolas. "Lego knew a lot about me, about my people, and most importantly, he had known how to time-jump, using the crystal with the trapped mer-form, Soul. Not a smooth walk like I did, maybe a training version, or a version that used the mer-form instead of the dragon-form, but it served the same purpose."

Gee threw another wrench into my thoughts. "What if . . . My mistress, there are no known missing witches. Perhaps the circle is composed of vampires who have been flayed? Perhaps humans who have been spelled?"

"Humans who have . . ." I remembered the bright witch circle over the Shookers' place. I opened my mouth, sucking in air through nose holes and across my tongue, as Beast might do when scenting, double-checking for witch scent. But there was nothing. "Alex," I said, over the open phone line, "what if the Shookers were spelling and powering humans and giving them to the vamps? To be used in this circle. Some witches have a lot of built-up anger over the way they've been treated. Would they—"

"No," Evan said over the connection. I gave a bird grin. Hearing his voice meant that the crew was all back at the inn and safe. "George and I went by there on the way home, the morning we were stuck in town at the church. The Shookers hate fangheads. It was almost palpable in their voices."

"We'll check them out again," Molly said, "but I don't believe it."

"Even if the Flayer has one of their children like he has yours?" Molly fell silent. Evan said, "We saw three adult witches. All there. But we'll check again."

"Okay. I'm trusting your read on them, but something's wrong here. We're missing something."

"The Flayer has a time circle but it's nearly empty of power," Molly mused.

"What if he has another time circle somewhere," I said. "What if he not only learned how to time-jump from Lego but he learned everything Leo knew." A slow fear began to bloom in the back of my mind. The soft *ding* from the tracker marble sent a shock of relief through me.

"What's the helo ETA?" I asked Alex.

"Ten minutes. They're flying above the storm but you should be able to hear it soon."

"Sleet just stopped. Tell them to step on it. Gee, let's fly so we can keep an eye on everything." I leaped from my tree and into the air, straining my tired bird body, searching for height. Gee stayed off my tail this time, for which I was grateful. Moments later, as I circled low over the arboretum grounds, I heard the helo. I needed to shift to half-form. We'd attack the building as soon as the helo landed.

Before I could act on that, the insectoid Flayer of Mithrans stepped from the door into the snow. He was carrying a pack on his back and EJ was draped over his shoulder. Unlike his brother, Shimon was well nourished and strong enough to go outside before dusk, at least when there was sufficient cloud cover, without burning. We hadn't seen him daywalk, but here he was. "Ahhh," I whispered to myself. That was why he had wanted a carapace, so he could gain the light of full day. I circled, losing sight of the Flayer for a half second.

Between one bell tone and the next, the tracker marble fell silent.

I looked back to the ground. The Flayer of Mithrans and EJ were—"What? What happened?" I demanded. "Where are they?"

"I do not know how he did it, little goddess," Gee said, "but . . . I believe he is gone. EJ and the Flayer of Mithrans."

"How? We're right here. No cars got by us. No trucks, no helo, nothing." Shivering, beak suddenly clattering with cold, I understood. "Oh crap. He timewalked. He took EJ with him and he timewalked right out of here. Right under our wings. EJ's gone." But where? Where had the Flayer taken him?

CHAPTER 20

Gack. Ewww. Stop.

The answer was there, in my own last thought. Shimon had had access to the mind and memories of Legolas.

It was a feeling, *only* a feeling, but that was better than nothing.

Gee could follow my Anzu magic, so I didn't have to explain. "Gee, check out the Shookers' place and make sure they aren't doing something with a time circle. Make sure they aren't being forced to assist the Flayer in some way. Then find me." I wheeled and stroked my wings, hard and hard and *hard*, rising, searching for a thermal that might lift and carry me. I was already so dang tired and so very hungry. But I could rest later. Hopefully.

I reached an altitude with a slightly warmer layer of air, one sandwiched between two colder ones, which was just weird. They were things I could actually see with Anzu eyes, sparkling in warmer and cooler colors. Aching, exhausted, I stretched out and soared.

Hoping the cell and charger were still working, breathless, I said, "Alex."

"Yes, Janie."

"Inform Eli to follow my cell as long as it's safe. If the helo starts icing, set down immediately."

"Copy. Wanna tell me where you're going?"

"A place I can't describe and can't explain," I said, stretching out in a long glide. "Tell him it's near the coordinates where he got to play with his new toy, but maybe . . . half a mile away? It's a crevasse in the rock. I'll get there a lot faster than he will and I'll take off the cell phone and hang it in the trees if I have time. If I don't, then he'll have to figure it out from where my cell signal disappears. Climbing gear might be smart."

"Climbing gear. Copy." But Alex didn't sound happy about it.

The daylight died and night fell. I flew into a rainsquall, warmer winds buffeting me, then directly into a crosswind that froze the rain and cut me with sleet. Shivering, wet, starving, and miserable, I was a hundred twenty pounds of wretchedness. I fought to find warmer air and when I finally did, I aligned my course according to the mountain peaks shrouded in the low-lying clouds and by lights from the city behind me. If I was right about his location, and if Shimon had timewalked, he could have arrived at any time. If he even went where I was guessing. And I was only guessing because he'd had access to Legolas. The lovely white-blond vamp who had been injured near the rift. Whom I had left not-true-dead.

"Tell me about Legolas," I said, my bird croak almost unrecognizable.

"I had to go back into some of the older files, Reach's stuff, to find him. He's of Swedish ancestry, turned in 1602. Until a few months ago, he was the MOC of Stockholm, Oslo, Copenhagen, and Helsinki. He decided to make use of the instability among the EuroVamps and attempted to take over Berlin, I'm guessing to get longer periods of night in summer."

Vamps in the extreme North and South had almost no active time six months out of the year, nights lasting only a few hours. "And?" I asked.

"Berlin had just been defeated by the new upstart, Grégoire, Blood Master of Clan Arceneau, the Master of

the City of Paris, Berlin, and assorted other hunting territories. Lego was defeated and barely escaped with his
undeath. His name is Melker, no surname. Apparently he
escaped and came to NOLA. I have confirmed hotel security cam footage of him checking in to the Rose Manor
B and B Inn, a five-star hotel near the river. I also have
footage of a small group of vamps taking Ronald Roland
outside of the clan home. One person in the car seemed
to have white hair, and the car was registered to another
guest at the inn. I'm guessing 'borrowed' for the kidnapping and returned, as it wasn't reported stolen. I haven't
found any record of the others being taken."

"Melker. He doesn't look like a Melker," I squawked,
thinking. What if Legolas had gone back to the place he
had been injured, and backtracked Beast's trail to the rift?
I hadn't looked to see if that had happened. It hadn't
crossed my mind. What if Lego knew where I had been? If
Lego had found the rift, and if its location had been clear
and bright in his mind when Shimon took him and flayed
his body, then Shimon knew about the deep blue pool.
Lots of ifs. But I figured the Flayer knew everything Lego
did. What if the Flayer guessed that the watery opening
into the earth was a rift? What if one of them had seen
another arcenciel emerge from the pool of water?

Crap. Crap, crap, crap.

I crossed hills and dipped out of the near-balmy rain,
into ravines, the colors of night vivid in Anzu eyes. The
mountain ridge I was looking for came into view in my
Anzu eyes, the crests shrouded in clouds below me. I
dipped my flight into the cloud cover. The roads in were
unplowed and now buried beneath more snow, showing
no tracks. To follow the road, I soared lower, into the
layer of freezing rain and sleet. It struck my eyes and buried sharp-edged barbs in my down, gathering and freezing on my wings and the feathers of my face.

"He has the *senza onore*?" I asked.

"That's my best guess," Alex said.

I dropped even lower, skimming the tops of pine and
dead fir, and lower again until I was angling along the
roadway. The turnoff came up quickly and I whipped left,

over the small clearing where we had parked, back what seemed a long time ago. My wings stroked the air higher, now climbing hard to my right, searching for the rift. But tired. So very tired.

The rift had been left unprotected—not that I could think of a way to keep it safe—when I carried Eli back for healing. I had left Legolas arrow-staked and bleeding in the snow, but any vamp, once the arrow was removed and he was healed by drinking lots of blood, would have been able to trace Beast's scent or tracks back to the crevasse. I had been so focused on the Flayer that I hadn't considered where Lego-Melker fit in. I was an idiot.

He had challenged me when he ripped out Shiloh's throat, but before that, he had bled and read her. He had known all about the witches in Asheville from her. He'd had the *senza onore*, the pyro, and somehow he got her to work with him and burned down Molly's house, and yet, even with all he knew, all the alliances he had made, he had still ended up in a circle, flayed and true-dead. Once I took care of the Flayer, I'd track down the woman, the *senza onore*, but first things first.

Ice was building up on my wings. Feathered birds are not built to fly in snow and sleet. The part of me that would have been shoulders had I been human ached with exhaustion, burned with overuse. I was growing clumsy. If I was wrong about my interpretation of events, I wouldn't have time or energy to regroup and search for EJ anywhere else. I needed water and food and—

I glimpsed a glow that disappeared just as fast. I circled that way, the tops of trees brushing along my chest and belly. The glow didn't reappear. But the chasm in the ground materialized below me, black in the snow, as if a huge blade had ripped into the earth.

I folded my wings and plummeted, a heart-wrenching nosedive between branches, to spread my wings just above the earth and align myself above the narrow cleft, looking for the best entry point. Wings providing a slight draft, I slowed and dived into the crevasse.

The air instantly warmed, heated by the earth itself. Little snow or ice clung to the rock face as I dropped into the dark, green ferns clinging to the cracks between rocks, moss in a dozen different shades of green cleaving to the rock itself. Even partially folded, my wings brushed the rock faces to either side. I dodged downed trees that braced across the chasm. Dove beneath fallen rock that spanned the width of the cleft. Gaining speed, too fast. Not easily able to brake and slow.

The air seemed to brighten. The glow reappeared and intensified. Grew closer. The chasm widened and I spread my wings, the temps still rising, the change giving me lift. I was silent, eyes on the bend ahead, the curve where the glow originated. I back-winged. Reached out with my claws. Gripped and settled onto a stub of rock.

The temperature was probably fifty degrees in the microclimate of the rift, but it felt like a sauna after the hours aloft in frozen air. I fluttered my feathers, shook my wings, sending droplets in fine sprays. Another outcropping was just ahead and I hopped, robin-like, to it and perched. I held my wings wide, letting the ice melt and drip off, giving myself a whole minute to thaw. I fluttered my plumage, shaking water off of me, breathing and dripping and trying to gather myself. I ached all over. With all my senses, I searched for Shimon. For EJ. My nose and eyes found nothing except the mineral scent of heated water and the life scents of birds, lizards, mice, and rats, hibernating. Not another thing. No scent of my godchild. No scent of vampire. Nothing new or different from my earlier visit to the crevasse.

I was wrong. EJ wasn't here. Grief boiled up in me, hot and scalding, my eyes full of tears that burned like acid, too long unshed. I didn't know where to go now, yet I had to keep searching. Somewhere.

Exhaustion pulled at my bones and burned through my muscles. Hunger ached inside me from the calorie loss of flight. I didn't know how to draw power from ley lines like a real Anzu, and I hadn't fed. And . . . I had lost my godson.

I screamed out my rage, an Anzu shriek of fury and grief.

He was gone.

Jane will not give up, Beast thought at me. She shoved power into my wings. *Jane will fight.*

Right. I swept down, trying to gain lift. *I won't give up.*

I landed on a third outcropping of stone. A cave rat poked his head out of a slit in the stone. Faster than he could move, I whipped right, struck, and grabbed him in my beak. Yanked him from the slit in the stone. Crunched down to kill him. Tossed the rat into the air and gulped him down, headfirst. He weighed a good three pounds. I needed more food than that to keep searching. Keep flying. I needed twenty or thirty pounds of meat. I'd be forced to hunt deer or boar when I got back to the surface.

And then it hit me. I'd just eaten a rat.

My stomach roiled at the thought.

I pecked at the gobag, which had twisted in my daylong flight. In the deeps of the earth, I had no cell signal, and in my tired, starved flight, I had forgotten to leave it at the rim of the crevice. Gripping the gobag in my beak, I slid it around me, out of the way.

From ahead, I heard soft sounds like sleigh bells ringing, a half tone off pure, both flat and sharp. Not a sound nature made. I sniffed again. Smelled nothing.

I hopped to the next protuberance, a downed log, moss covered. I had forgotten about the tracker tied to my leg in jesses, and the device made a soft *tonk* as it impacted the log. I froze. But nothing changed, nothing happened, and since there had been no reaction to the anzu scream, I wasn't sure why I thought there might be. No one came to look. The bells didn't sound again. I heard only the odd vibration of the heated pool of water rising and lapping. Had another arcenciel come through the rift and made that odd sound, like bells laughing?

I flipped the tracker up around my ankle, once, twice, so it hung higher than my foot on the perch. Satisfied, I hopped to the next spot, this one higher, fluttering my wings. Which freaking hurt. My pecs were aching. My underarms were aching. In fact, everything was aching.

And I had eaten a rat . . . I'd never tell Eli that. *Never.*

Beast chuffed deep inside, amused.

The next outcropping of rock was higher. As was the next. Half winging, swearing inside my head, I made my way from perch to perch. Closer to the bend and the glow of the rift.

I landed, the water of the rift blue and brilliant just ahead. A layer of hoarfrost glittered on the moss above me, in crevices and across the upper side of fallen logs. Below me, heavy mist rose from the surface of the water, to bead when it reached cooler temps and plink back down as if from low-lying rain clouds. The air here was at least another ten degrees warmer. A gust of colder air blew through, carrying the rain made of melted sleet and snow. The drops created a *plink-tap-rat-a-tat-tat* rhythm, the music of nature. The place smelled green and alive, strongly of minerals and water, of warmth. This was a primeval scent my bird brain recognized and knew. A world my Anzu memories and instincts identified by its fragrance. It was something that had been unfamiliar to Beast's brain. This . . . this was the pathway to home.

But. The area around the pool of water was empty. I could have screamed in fury. EJ wasn't here. No one was. And I hadn't seen a vehicle at the parking spot, a fact I hadn't wanted to think about until now. I shook my wings in grief and fury, ready to leap high and fly home. Get food. Change back to my human form, help the clan think of the next move.

The next protrusion was on the far side of the rift, higher, too far to hop. Not a place I had gone when I was in Beast form. Another gust of colder air spun through the crevasse. As it blew through, I raised my wings and leaped, winging across the pool and up, ready to take advantage of the rising warmer air there. I wing-swept down, across to the far side, to a downed log lodged at an odd angle, roots caught between rocks, the tip balanced in a cleft. I landed. Turned. Prepared to shove off and fly home.

Across from me, below where I had perched before my last hop, some twenty feet down, was another opening in the rock. It was a cave mouth, thirty feet high and twenty feet across at the opening. On the floor of the cave a fire burned. My wings folded as if of their own accord. I went still as a vamp.

The smoke was scentless, which was strange with my

improved Anzu nose. From this angle, the cave appeared to be empty, but its floor had been swept clean, and deeper inside, I could make out only a quarter of an arc, perhaps a witch circle on the bare stone, the border made from salt. I spotted a small perch, too small for my feet, but I jumped there anyway. Caught my balance with wings that were too noisy, banging against the stone. Bruising what would be my wrists in human form. Ignoring the pain.

At the edge of the circle was EJ.

Kit! Beast shouted in our mind.

The boy was still. Unmoving. Until his chest rose and fell. Shock slashed a path through me. My heart beat so hard, it felt as if it would fly out of my chest. My godson was only asleep. Drugged or compelled or in stasis. Not dead.

My godchild was alive.

If the Flayer was timewalking, he'd had plenty of time to find this cave, prepare this cave. Do whatever he wanted in this cave. And he could come back and forth through time anywhere. Except for the fire, I had no idea if he was here, now, in this cave. And if he discovered me out here, if he took EJ back or forward through time with him, I'd lose my godchild.

Fear shivered thorough me. I hopped to a better perch, glad for the darkness of the crevasse, glad for the firelight in the cave, which would conceal my presence.

Beside the fire was a flayed vampire, blood tacky on the stone floor, half-dried across her exposed flesh. In the corner lay another vampire, partially skinned, a male. Beside him was a human, female, her wrists and the crown of her head wrapped in silver wire. Her throat was flawless, but her clothing was drenched in dried blood, showing she had been fed from and then healed. A witch? Bled and rolled? Immobilized with null amulets? Over her stood Shimon Bar-Judas. The mouth of his bleeding spokesperson—the female vamp—was moving as she spoke to the witch. I heard nothing, but no matter what words Shimon Bar-Judas spoke, they wouldn't be good.

I couldn't hear a thing, not a peep. There was some kind of energy thingy over the mouth of the cave, not

allowing out scent or sound, but letting in fresh air, if the
flickering flames of the fire pit were an indication. It
wasn't a proper ward, not a proper witch circle, because
it seemed to cover the entrance only, and it wasn't round.
The energies were strange too. This was something I
hadn't seen before. My brain went immediately to *Star
Trek* shields. If the shield let in air, it probably let in sound
too. I'd been anything but silent. A tiny stem dropped
from above and landed on the shield. It made a soft popping noise and gave a small tone of sound, like a dented
brass bowl tapped with a fork. No one inside looked up.
There were dozens of such bits of detritus on the shield,
the noise of their falling having made the people inside
deaf to exterior noise.

A shield meant I couldn't get in.

Unless it was permeable to other things besides air.
Maybe not branches or stems or rain or humans or skinwalkers or weres. But the Flayer had gotten in. Maybe . . .
I studied it closer. The shield wasn't a modern *hedge of
thorns*. In Anzu vision, the energies were orange and
blue, netlike, with ropes of power, thicker in some places
than others. Shields were created to let in and keep out
specific things. Maybe it would let in vamps. Maybe it
would also let in creatures like me. Like an Anzu. But
Anzus had weaknesses, for instance, a lethal allergy to
being cut by iron and iron based metals.

I couldn't see anything made of metal in the cave, no
steel or silver, no athame for a sacrifice. But Shimon had
his own weapons—talons and teeth. If he was here, and if
there was a rift in the possession of the EuroVamps, then
he had to know what the pool at the bottom of the crevasse was. And he might know that arcenciels came
through rifts. And it was likely the Flayer wanted to capture rainbow dragons. Arcenciels, to old vamps, were like
chocolate and diamonds were to humans—there could
never be too many. My thoughts and Beast's came fast,
overlapping.

Had an arcenciel come through the rift and flown by
the vamps Eli had arrow-shot and alerted them? Had
Shimon put the presence of rainbow dragons and me

together and begun looking for the rift? If he could timewalk, then he could have followed me here the first time
I came in Beast form, found the rift, prepared the cave,
gone into the future (or the past?) to the Regal, left himself a message of the location, and then returned to his
own time and place. Somehow or some-when, he had gotten all these people and supplies here. I hadn't seen a car
anywhere when I flew in. Or maybe the Flayer could do
that *Star Trek* thing and transport, using magical energy
and his mind instead of tech. The possibilities and dan-
gers made my head spin.

I tilted, falling, wings flailing. I leaped back to the
other side and settled on the tree.

Only one thing mattered. Shimon Bar-Judas, the Flayer
of Mithrans, the Son of Shadows, was at a rift, was going
to sacrifice EJ for some purpose, maybe to gather power
for a new time circle. He was going to capture a dragon,
and with captured arcenciels, he could do anything, even
perhaps keep the arcenciels from killing him and his
bloodline two thousand years ago.

Maybe.

It was as a good a guess as any other for a magic that
had been created and refined for two thousand years.

The first time I ever saw vampire witches was in a
witch circle with a sacrifice. With EJ and Angie Baby.
Back then the witch-vamps had been trying to bring back
the long-chained. Or . . . Or they had been going to timewalk? Maybe change the past to somehow *save* the long-
chained? Do something special to make their scions'
transition through the devoveo work?

It was important and equally immaterial. I didn't have
time on my side. What I had was the memory of being
Bubo bubo, owl, but bigger and far more formidable.
And I had my own timewalking magic.

Beast?

*Beast is best ambush hunter. Beast bird is best ambush
hunter from sky. Beast will save kit.*

Dang skippy.

Will save skippy too.

I made a *tock* of laughing agreement that echoed

softly in the crevasse. The sound reverberated into silence. Across the way, the Flayer of Mithrans bent to pick up EJ. *We need to timewalk. Now!*

Yesss. Beast tore through the Gray Between. My skinwalker energies burst out and, just as fast, merged back inside, sliding into the star-shaped magics, the scarlet star in my abdomen, visible even in Anzu form. I reached into the Gray Between and bubbled time. Inside the shield, everything stopped: the Flayer had half lifted EJ and was now frozen, unmoving. I had done it!

Pain sliced through me. My bird heart beat fast, too fast, a pounding, racing agony. My wings drooped. My breath strained, not enough to fill my lungs. "Crap," I whispered. I'd been in Anzu form all day, adding Anzu magic to my own, and therefore to any remnants of Dudley. The pain spiked.

Beast dropped time. Inside the shield, the Flayer repositioned EJ on the stone floor.

Jane is sick even in Anzu?

Looks like it. Holy crap on a cracker. This makes it a lot harder.

My skinwalker energies misting around me like a silver veil, I thrust off the tree and flapped my exhausted wings, gaining altitude, banked in a tight circle. Set my eyes on the Flayer of Mithrans. Before reason could suggest I stop, I bent time and folded my wings tight to me. Aimed my beak at the back of the Flayer's head. And dove toward the cave.

Pierced the shield. It shocked across and through me. A blinding glare as if lightning had hit me again, sparking and flashing. Sizzling along my beak and face. Pulling on my feathers in hot tugs of power. Pain like a spear through my middle. And then I was through. Dropping fast. From above.

I dropped the bubbled time.

Slammed into the Flayer of Mithrans. Beak rammed into the back of his neck. At the base of his skull. Perfect raptor kill.

Still moving forward, my wings went out, claws swung

up. Gripped his head. Crushed down. Sweeping him forward. Wings spreading.

I crashed him against the back of the cave. Backwinging, sweeping hard, I hammered his head into the stone. Crushing his skull in claws and rock.

Dropping, I slid down the uneven stone wall, taking him down with me. I landed on the stone floor on top of Shimon Bar-Judas, his body a bloody heap beneath me. Twitching. Still alive. Healing even as I looked. Because the Flayer of Mithrans was truly immortal.

I settled beside him, wings folding, claws holding him steady. Setting my beak in the middle of his neck, I ripped off his head, tossed it high, and caught it in my beak, holding him by one ear. Blood pulsed hard from the ragged stump just above the exoskeleton shoulders, slashing across the cave wall, painting swathes that almost glowed to my Anzu eyes. The body twitched, the hands clenching and unclenching, the feet pointing like a ballerina's. The pulsing slowed and stopped.

I tossed the head against the far wall. Gray matter was visible in the openings I'd made in the crushed skull. The body kept twitching but there was no control, no intent behind the movements. It was like a decapitated snake twitching its tail. I figured it would take a long time for the Flayer's head to heal and figure out what had happened, and—horror movies aside—since his head wasn't attached to his body, I didn't think his parts could go independently searching for each other and put himself back in place.

Hopping around, I checked out the skinned vampire and the witch. The vamp was familiar. I stared at the skinless, unbreathing, but undead corpse. It was Tex. I stopped. Tex had been missing, taken from New Orleans before Shiloh, probably by Legolas-Melker. I hadn't even thought about him, neither him nor Roland, also taken. I needed to find out the whereabouts and condition of all my people. I was a terrible clan leader. I sucked. Later. I'd be a better person later.

The witch was an unknown.

Both of them were silent, eyes empty and haunted.

Neither reacted to the presence of a hundred-plus-pound sapphire bird. Threats eliminated or ineffective, I stared at my godson. He lay in the center of a witch-type circle, sealed with an ongoing working. The dome of the circle was low, and I hadn't disrupted it when I dive-bombed Shimon.

I wanted to race in, breaking the circle working, grab EJ, spread my wings on the far side of it and leap through the shield as we fell into flight. But at some point, Shimon had closed the circle. Because it was still active, it might explode if I broke it improperly. The ward would surely react to EJ trying to get through. Anything I tried or did might kill the little boy.

I didn't have hands to help him, either, and though claws were nimble, mine were huge and I hadn't exactly practiced using them. I was unwieldly on the ground.

I could change form. But if I did, I couldn't get back through the shield. My hindbrain figured out what I had felt when I pierced the outer shield, incoming. The magics of ley lines. Brittle and sizzling and electrifying. Powerful enough to keep me inside the cave, in any form but Anzu. Ley lines and rifts were part of the same power structure, and as an Anzu, I could—clearly—go through them. I should have thought this through before I bubbled time and dove in. Flying by the . . . feathers of my hindquarters, literally. But now, bubbling time again might kill me, and if I was dead, I couldn't save EJ. And in human form, I couldn't get though.

I couldn't just sit here. Help was likely many hours away. Eventually one of the vamps would wake and the mind of the Flayer would take him or her over. I'd have to dispatch whoever it was, even if it was Tex, my friend. And then there was Dudley. The sickness I had felt earlier grew. I had to finish this, had to get EJ out of here.

I needed a safety net and time to figure out my next move, and since bubbling time was out of the question, then gore would have to do.

With wings and claws, I attacked the Flayer's torso and tore through his left shoulder joint. Using the arm, I batted the bashed head farther away, against the far stone wall. I tossed the arm at the mouth of the cave and it flew outside, flashing as it passed through the energies. Interesting. The Flayer could get out without dropping the shield. I hopped atop the body and tore off the other arm, throwing it too, though it landed inside the shield.

I reared back and slammed my beak into the exoskeleton, once, twice, the sharp cracks reverberating through my head. On the third bone-breaking peck, my beak pierced through, stabbing into blood and viscera. I grabbed the exoskeleton in claws and my beak. Straining, I separated it, ripping it along the cracks my beak had made.

Good meat. Strong vampire blood, Beast thought. She shoved me down, hungry. Faster than I could think, she pecked out a lung and tossed it up. Opened her beak and took it all in at once.

Gack! Stop!

Beast ignored me and stuck our head inside the cavity, ripping into the heart and liver, tearing them free and shredding strips off with our beak and claws. One by one, she ate them. With each gobbet of gore, I felt better. And grosser.

Gack. Ewww. Stop.

No. Good vampire blood, Beast thought.

I'm eating rats. Eating sentient beings, and not for the first time. I'm a monster. I'm gonna hurl.

Inside me, Beast flicked her ear tabs and exerted pressure against me, pushing me down, taking alpha place. *Is like Beast giving milk to kits. Will grow back if Jane lets it.* With one eye on Shimon as I ate, I glanced with the other eye at the unknown vamp. The vamp was pretty much out of it. The witch was immobilized. No one was watching me binge-eat an insectoid vamp.

My queasiness faded slightly as I realized that Beast had a point. The Flayer was immortal. He'd grow back all his parts if he got the chance. With one independent eye, I looked over the cave, finding that EJ was still asleep and wouldn't be forever mentally ruined by my dietary habits.

I closed my mental eyes and let Beast feast. When hunger no longer slashed me like knives, Beast withdrew, flopped down on the floor of our soul home, and let me take back over my Anzu's body. Bloody, needing a bath if I stayed in this form, I hopped over to a dark corner and shifted shape, hoping to achieve my half-form this time. The shift took a long time.

It hurt. A lot. And it didn't work like I'd hoped.

I was human—shivering and naked, wanting to toss my cookies. Pain was a deep ache, as if bruised all over; I was weak as a newborn kitten. But I wasn't starving like usual after a shape-shift, just ordinary hungry. Shifting into or out of Anzu used energy from elsewhere, not my disease-ridden body. I guessed the elsewhere was the nearby ley lines, this time, but it was just that. A guess.

The ward flashed overhead, but when I looked I saw nothing. No one. Likely it was a rock or stick dropping from the crevasse above. The cold of the cave pressed into me. Curls of dried blood and blood dust littered the stone around my bare legs.

I had eaten part of the Flayer of Mithrans. *Gack*. Just *gack*.

Holding on to the cave wall, I found my feet and my balance, to study the circle with human and Beast vision. It looked like a simple ward, one a child might create in witch school. I walked across the rough, frigid floor of the cave to the arm of the Flayer and lifted it. Breaking the circle as a human, Anzu, or any other form might have made the circle explode, but I was ninety-nine percent certain that Shimon himself could break it. He was a control freak, and no way would he allow a circle he couldn't manipulate. Still, that one percent chance that I was wrong was a scary one percent. And I might yet kill my godchild.

The exoskeleton was heavy but far more flexible than I had expected. I carried the arm to the north point of the circle and stopped, staring at the sleeping little boy. If I was wrong . . . Dear God, if I was wrong, I'd kill him. But if I waited, the Flayer's reinforcements might arrive and EJ would remain a prisoner of the Flayer of Mithrans. I hadn't prayed much recently, but I said a silent prayer and listened for an answer. There wasn't one.

Carefully, using the strange-looking hand of the Flayer, I leaned in and touched the cold, dead exoskeleton fingers to the edge of the circle. Nothing happened. I pressed into the energies, seeing the spark of magics as I brushed away the salt. There was life enough in the hand that the circle recognized it and fell. There were no explosions. EJ had survived me pants flying. I swallowed past a fear-dry throat and remembered to breathe. I tossed the arm outside with the other one.

I spotted a bundle of discarded clothing in the corner. On top was a length of emerald green velvet that turned out to be a cape, the fabric warmer than my icy hands. That seemed a dangerous sign, not that I had time to worry about the condition of my human body. Staggering, I knelt beside EJ. He was as cold as I was, so, likely hypothermic, spelled asleep, but his pulse was steady and his breathing was even. I hoped that was a good sign. I wrapped him in the emerald velvet and, clasping the hem of the cape, pulled him across the stone floor, close to the fire. It burned in the slight depression of a fire pit, circled with rounded, blackened stones. The stones were warm and I shoved several close to EJ, nestling them around his small body. I had to stop and breathe for a while, and wished I had achieved half-form. But there was that old adage about peasants and horses flying. Or riding horses. Or maybe it was pigs. Whatever.

Sitting on a warm stone near my godson, I added wood to the fire and rested. My legs were skin and bone, and though I hadn't checked my weight, I wasn't certain how I was managing the mass change when I shifted forms. Pain snaked through me. I could almost feel the tumor growing, as if the magic of being Anzu had given it power.

The jesses on my ankle were painfully tight in human form, especially with them slung around to keep them out of the way. I removed the ties and the marble, pulled off the gobag, and dressed in the clothing inside it. The sweatpants and shirt were amazingly comforting. I hung Soul's crystal and the marble around my neck, next to my own golden nugget and lion claw. I pocketed the Glob and pulled on socks and the thin-soled shoes. There was no cell service underground; I'd have been surprised if there had been.

I secured my weapons, such as they were, and hung the

cell in the gobag as close to the cave opening as I could, hoping it would attract the attention of my backup. Weak, sick at the stomach, I ate two protein bars and managed to keep them down. I tore open a jerky strip and bit off a two-inch length, which I tucked into my cheek to soften. I hadn't packed water. Stupid of me. And I saw no water in the cave.

Now that I was human, I grasped the fact that I had no plan for rescue. I had flown in through the outer ward and killed the bad guy, but that wasn't going to accomplish much once the wood ran out or EJ woke up or the Flayer's pals appeared. I needed a part two, a how-to-get-home plan.

The ward flashed again and I gripped my handgun. No one came through. Nothing changed. Weird. I wondered if the ward was set to flash periodically.

To my side, Tex blinked. The skinned vamp took a breath. Let it out. That was too much movement for my peace of mind, what with the Flayer here. I managed to get across the cave, where I staked him low in the belly. He dropped like a marionette in inept hands. My friend was still alive-ish but paralyzed, and I'd not have to kill him true-dead. Hopefully he was also out of pain. I staked the female vamp too, giving me a safety net of time. Shoulda done that right away.

Okay. That was an improvement in the no-plan problem. I was getting there.

I walked to the witch and knelt in front of her. She was young, too young. Maybe fifteen. There were clasps on the silver cuffs and headband, and when I touched the handcuffs, a shaft of pain cut through me. I jerked back. Null cuffs. Great. This was gonna hurt. Steeling myself, I unclasped the headband and the cuffs. Tucked them into my gobag. Slowly she took a breath and her eyes fluttered open. She focused on me. She flinched.

"I'm Jane Yellowrock." I paused, and added, wryly, "The Dark Queen of the vampires. My friends are the Everhart witch clan. Do you understand me?"

She gave an abbreviated nod and shuddered.

"Who are you?"

"Stacey Shooker," she whispered.

Shooker. Of the Asheville Shooker Witch Clan. *Crap.* So much for their reassurances that everything was okay with them. They had lied in the hope that their teenaged witchling might survive contact with the Flayer of Mithrans. Someone needed an education in when to tell the truth and ask for help.

Stacey licked her cracked lips and looked around, her eyes darting. "Where is he?"

"Dismembered. Part of him is out in the gorge. The rest is a mess in the back. I suggest you don't look."

"Oh god. Oh god oh god oh god." A tortured laughter rose in her throat and then choked off. Her breath made little flapping sounds. "Don't look? I've seen shit this week. I don't think you can shock me."

"I get that. Still." I handed her a stick of jerky. "I don't have any water."

"Better than nothing. Thanks." Stacey looked around the cave again as she tore open the jerky, staring at the broken walls and the circle on the floor. "You got the kid out of the circle. Good. But how are we all getting out of here?"

Annnnd we were back to the no-plan part. "Working on that. Besides you, how many witches does he have?"

"Just me."

The ward flashed again, and this time something bright, like glowing charcoal, shifted across the back of the cave. I had seen that before, or something like it. "Has the ward been flashing?"

"No. I never saw it do that."

I made it to my feet and went to the back of the cave, to the Flayer. His exoskeleton was solid, smooth, as if I had never busted it open. And . . . it had arms, which I had tossed out of the cave. That meant that the flashes were to a purpose, likely the result of the arms getting back inside. But how? Unless the horror movies had it right all along and they crawled back without a brain and nerves and muscles being attached to one another.

Huffing through the pain, I picked up a pointed, sharp-edged boulder and brought it down with all my

might onto the chest exoskeleton. The rock punctured
through and I left it in the hole. I pulled the vamp-killer
and brought it down on the Flayer's fingers, separating
them and carrying them to the fire. I tossed them in and
watched them burn, a sizzling fast smell of scorched . . .
scorched something. Not really meat. I had no idea what
scorched insect smelled like. The scent made me want to
hurl. I tossed the arm back out of the cave.

"We have to go," I said to the girl. She was short and
not in shape. I'd be lucky if she could keep up, even with
a sick me carrying EJ. Who took after his dad. Not a tiny
four-year-old-ish kid. "Can you drop the cave shield?"

"It's mine, so, yeah."

I looked back at Shimon's body. A stub was growing at
the neck stump and the rock was being pushed out of the
torso from the inside. Something dark gray flew across the
back cave wall. "Get to it. And hurry. I got a bad feeling."

I made it to EJ and fell to my knees, the pain growing,
and I nearly passed out as I tied the velvet cape around him
to keep him warm and struggled to get him over my shoulder. I didn't make it and he lay on my lap, limbs splayed.

"Shield's down. And no offense, but you look like shit.
Like you're gonna die any second," Stacey said, from
my side.

"Pretty much," I huffed, breathless from even that
much exertion. "Cancer. Can you carry him?"

"Yeah." Stacey got EJ up and over her shoulder, grunting with the effort. She clearly wasn't accustomed to being
hungry, thirsty, or carrying a stout, heavy kid.

At the entrance, we looked down a good fifteen feet to
the floor of the crevice. It was covered with shattered rock
and debris that had fallen from the cave and from overhead. I had no rope. No way could I get down and then
catch either of my charges. *Beast. You gotta give me half-
form.* I looked back over my shoulder. The head of the
Flayer of Mithrans was no longer where I had placed it.
The charcoal shadow moved across the back wall. *Fast.*
Red eyes caught the firelight.

"Holy crap," I whispered, understanding at last. Kicking off my shoes, I demanded to Beast, "Shift!"

"What?" Stacey said.

"I'm a shape-shifter. I—"

Beast opened the Gray Between. A tornado of knives opened with it. I began to shift. As I fell to the cave floor, the Flayer of Mithrans opened his eyes, watching me.

It took way too long and I was beyond starving when I finally settled into my half-form, gagging from the pain, too bony, too skinny, and too sick to move. I was huffing and puffing and feeling as if I had been held down and suffocated with a pillow while being beaten with a baseball bat.

"I put a stake in the belly of Beetle Man, but it popped out and hit me in the head."

I managed to get my eyes open, sort of focused, and looked up at Stacey, who had been talking. "Oh?"

"I tossed his head out of the cave and ten minutes later it was back. And you got fur and fangs, just in case you didn't know."

I managed some kind of a smile. "I noticed." Ten minutes. I'd been out awhile. "And just so you know, we aren't alone in here. We have a ghost, not that I believe in ghosts. But we have one."

"A gho—Oh. You mean the dark shadow."

I shook my head and made it to my feet. Strapped the gobag around me. I tore open the remaining jerky and shoved it in my mouth, which was too dry to soften the dried meat, but the taste was fantastic—which showed me how sick and calorie deprived I really was. I swallowed the leathery stuff whole and said, "I'm going to jump down. You're going to toss EJ to me. I'll set him down; then you jump. I'll catch you."

"No way in hell."

"Fine. Then I'll carry the kid down with me and leave you here."

Stacey gave me a scowl worthy of Molly. I'd have laughed if I'd had the energy. "I don't know you," she said, "but so far I don't like you much."

I tightened the tie at the waist of my sweatpants. "Don't care, but remember this. I didn't come for you. I came for the kid. You're just icing on the cake." I bent to pick up EJ.

"Fine. But if your hair falls out or you grow warts, you can blame me. I'm a witch and I'm pissed."

"Watch your language," I said as I helped her with EJ, adjusting him in her arms. "Kid present."

"He's asleep. And you sound like my mother."

"Good." I leaned out the opening and chose how I'd get down. There were plenty of handholds and toeholds to the crevice floor. I grabbed the gobag holding the cell phone and pivoted my body, taking the first of the steps out of the cave. It didn't take long, but I could feel magic in the air and I knew that the floaty charcoal thing was magical and operated independently of the Flayer. I had a bad feeling that whatever it was, it made Shimon Bar-Judas the Flayer of Mithrans, the Soul of Darkness, the Son of Deception, the Son of Shadows, et al. *Son of Shadows*. Right.

At the bottom I positioned my feet so I could move in any direction. "Toss him."

Stacey tossed EJ over the lip of the cave. Time did that battlefield slowdown where everything happens in slow motion. I saw the cape flutter. Saw EJ's hand flop out. Saw his bare feet. Saw when his body started to spin. I angled myself to the right and caught him, dropping down with him so gravity didn't break his bones against my arms. I carried him across the rocks to the flat floor of the crevice and placed him on a wide, moss-covered boulder, retied the cloak over him, and went back to my place. "Jump."

Except there was no one there. No one replied. And I realized that Stacey had been taken by the Flayer of Mithrans. I raced to the stone and picked up my godson, tossed him over my left shoulder, and rushed back along the crevasse toward the point where I had dropped down in Anzu form.

CHAPTER 21

Tossed the Girl to the Rocks

Stomach rumbling, body quivering from hunger, I dashed along the bottom of the crevasse. Deep in the hole, it was darker than any night I had ever experienced in my lives, both of them. Only with the enhanced night vision gifted to me by Beast did I manage to avoid deadfall, shattered stone, and openings and holes in the rock beneath me. But fear was a tangible presence at my back as I ran.

I kept glancing up, looking for a faster way to the surface, one I could climb three-limbed, holding EJ. I finally saw one, and just hoped the rocks held. Tightening my arm around my godson, I leaped. Caught a rock protrusion. Swung to the toehold and shoved up. Trying to ignore the pain in my belly, I began the arduous climb to the surface.

I fell on the snow, the cold agonizing at the top of the split in the earth. My lungs strained, breath painful. Gasping. When I could breathe, I rolled to my back and saw stars and the moon overhead. The clouds were breaking. I adjusted EJ on top of me for what warmth I could provide to him, and pulled the gobag off my chest. Found the cell.

The call had been dropped, but I now had a signal. I dialed Alex. Felt into my middle. My fingers met something hard and pointed. Dudley. Dang. The tumor had found this shape too.

"Jane!" Alex shouted into my cell.

"I got EJ," I said between hard breaths. "He's spelled asleep but he's breathing and nothing seems broken. At my current coordinates."

"Thank God," Molly said over the connection. And she burst into tears.

"Eli, Bruiser, and team are less then fifteen hundred feet from your current location," Alex said. "But Molly talked to the local witches again and they admitted one of them was missing. The fanghead has a fifteen-year-old witch."

"Stacey. Yeah. I know. Which is why I'm leaving EJ here with the cell and going back down."

"Don't you leave my baby!" Molly growled into the connection.

"I have to buy Eli time to get him away. Only way to do that is to leave EJ and take on the Flayer."

"Jane, don't," Alex said.

"We broke the circle at the Arboretum," Evan said. "Even the humans are flayed. We think he can skin anything for his magic."

Anything. Even me. "Yeah. Okay." Knowing that gave me more incentive to go back down, to get Stacey and to keep my people safe until they could get away. Gathering what little strength I still had, I rolled to my feet and started shuffling through the snow looking for a deep pile of fall leaves. It was dark, but my Beast-eyes had adjusted and the night seemed lighter than it really was. Quickly I found a depression filled with leaves and covered by snow, kicked it around to make sure nothing was nesting in it, then buried EJ, wrapped in his cape, in the leaves. I placed the cell on a branch near him and made sure the Glob was in my pocket and that my other weapons were secure.

"Jane?" Alex said. "Jane! *Jane!*"

I glanced at the cell and spotted Brute in the distance. Timewalking. I wasn't sure how I knew he was timewalking, but he was, and not the way I did it. A grindy was on his shoulder, holding fistfuls of hair. Seeing them meant that EJ would have protection and fast.

Overhead, I heard a soft whirring, and I waved at a flying drone. It tilted itself back and forth at me, acknowledging that the pilot, wherever he was, could see me. Drones with low-light vision. Handy. The drone operator knew my exact coordinates now and my tracks would lead them to the easiest way down.

I turned my back to it and stepped off the edge, into the crevasse. Caught my weight one-handed and swung, like a howler monkey, to another protrusion. Dropping down and down, hands secure on the damp rocks. Plummeting into the dark.

At the bottom of the rock walls, I raced back through the crevasse. It took too long, and I knew Stacey was in danger. Knew Bruiser and Eli would follow, but would need lights and climbing equipment. I'd be on my own for a while, unless the team they led included vampires willing to face the Flayer of Mithrans. And the red-eyed shadow-whatever-it-was that was doing magic all around him.

It seemed to take a lot longer to make my way back to the stone floor below the cave entrance. I was exhausted and starving and wanted nothing more than to stop, lie down, and rest. But when I looked up, I saw the last Son of Darkness, the Flayer of Mithrans, standing at the top of the cave. He was holding Stacey in his arms. Before I could react, he dropped the shield and tossed the girl to the rocks.

I dove for her. Caught her head and shoulders but not her legs, which smashed into the knife-edged shattered boulders. A bone broke with a sharp snap. I smelled her blood. Felt the heated squish of her skinless flesh. She had been skinned. I bent, setting her to the side.

The world tumbled around me.

The Flayer of Mithrans landed on me.

We toppled across the dark stone. I pulled on my skinwalker strength and speed. Beast shoved her own unique power into me. I grappled with the creature, but he was all smooth exoskeleton except for the joints, but any spaces were too narrow for my bony fingers. As we tumbled, my

claws extruded and clamped into his shoulder joint. I
ripped. He got his one good chitinous hand on my vamp-
killer and snapped it free. He stabbed forward, three
sharp blows. Aiming directly into my middle. Pulling on
Beast-speed, I slid left, right, left, fast, and the blade
caught the sides of my waist, slicing instead of stabbing. I
didn't think I'd get away with that one again.

I reached up and found his temple, rolled my hand up
and discovered the rough place where I had broken his
skull. It wasn't completely healed. I shoved my fingers
into the depression and the shell cracked under them. I
shoved my hand into his brain. Clawed through it.

He laughed.

And stabbed me again. Right into the center of
Dudley.

I grunted, a deep, broken sound. My blood gushed out.
My energy pulsed out with it. Surging. Spurting. He'd
sliced the tumor and hit an artery. My hand fell from his
brain. My body went limp.

Shimon dropped me and the vamp-killer, scrabbled
around my neck. Reaching for Soul, trapped in her crystal. If I let him get her, she was lost. If I let him timewalk,
I was lost, and so was Stacey.

His fingers were cold and hard as they fumbled on my
neck and chest. His insect claws couldn't grasp Soul's crystal. He needed both hands and the fingers I had burned.
He hissed in frustration; the stench of his breath was bitter
and caustic, burning my eyes.

A cutting icy pain curled along my right shoulder. Shimon skinned a strip of flesh off of me. Something scrabbled at my skull, thrusting through, pushing on the dark
places of my mind. The Flayer had other titles, the Son of
Shadows. The shadow had to be the thing that had been
racing around in the Regal at our first meeting, and again
in the cave. It didn't perfectly fit the definition of a ghost.
Early on I had gotten the impression that it was a creature, was alive. I turned my magic to see the thing better.

The shadow shaped into a spear point and pierced
into my mind. In a single instant it all came clear. The
memory/vision of the bloody body on the bloody wood as

the Sons of Darkness sacrificed their sister to bring their father back. Biting through her fingers. The Son of Shadows had eaten the girl alive. Black magic. Blood magic. The most heinous of dark magics. And by that rite, he had taken in the soul of his sister. She was the insane shadow in his mind. The trapped soul of his sister.

Had the witch circle given her autonomy? Had the time magics Shimon was using given her extra power too?

Shimon encircled my throat and began to crush the life out of me. Not just suffocate me. But crush my head from my shoulders.

I had one weapon left. I slid my brain-sludged hand down my body, into my pocket. Grabbed the Glob. My star magics stuttered. Twisted. Pain shot through me as my magics, now cut through with the steel blade, tried to realign and sought out the power in the Glob. When it wanted to, the Glob absorbed magical energies, and the shadow was energy. Not a magic I had ever seen, but still, energy. With the last of my strength, I shoved the Glob into the cranial cavity of the Son of Darkness, the Flayer of Mithrans.

Instantly the stone and its components heated, began to suck the power from the Flayer.

Something grabbed my wrist. It wasn't the Flayer.

It was the charcoal shadow. It formed into a vaguely humanoid shape. Female. Small. The shape of a child. The . . . the soul of a child. His sister. She opened her mouth and laughed silently. She touched the flayed strip on my shoulder and slid into me. Inside of me.

She ripped and tore at my mind, her claws leaving flashes of the two millennia of memories, of the slavery that been her life: pain and blood and violence and pleasure and torture shackled to her brother. Quick still shots of torture chambers, of pleasure temples, of dying enemies, of war and misery. Men and women broken on the rack, dead by plague, skinned, dissected while screaming. Dismembered. Roasted to death. Thousands and thousands of humans and vampires and witches and weres she had helped to kill, against her will, at first. But later with glee, dancing on their mangled bodies.

And further back, to the beginning. The sacrifice that

had brought her father back from the dead. Her brothers bending over her as she bled out on the holy trees. Shimon. Eating her alive. Stealing her magic. Stealing her soul.

Her manacles were broken now, her mind a mad, gibbering violence with the freedom to destroy. Her hatred wanted vengeance on the world that had allowed her to suffer so long.

I shoved the horror called the shadow back. Away from my mind.

And we fell into my soul home. Beast and I were suddenly there, in the cavern. With her.

She was human-shaped, naked, spindly, with wild red sclera and huge pupils like a vamped-out vamp, but she had no fangs. She was . . . Not. Not a human. Not a vamp. I didn't know what she was, but I was stunned from the images of her past, and I hesitated a second too long.

She slashed at me with claws that hadn't been there a moment past. Blood flew from my forehead. I dodged. Far too late. Hit the stone floor in a rolling fall.

She was spirit made flesh, here in this place. She was the sister of the Sons of Darkness, sacrificed to bring Judas Iscariot back from the dead. She was the power the Sons of Darkness used to create vampires. She was the beginning. The *Origination*. The title thrummed through her mind and into mine.

She was trapped in my soul home with me. With Beast. Here we could die. But that meant so could she. Too slow, I moved to my feet.

Beast attacked the shadow. Claws and fangs and solid muscle of killing energy. She dragged the wild girl to the floor of the cave and savaged her. Snarling and growling.

The girl grew talons and stabbed them all into Beast's body. Impaling my other half.

Beast screamed.

I tried to move toward them but my feet were stuck to the cave floor. My body wouldn't move. I looked down. Dudley was hanging out of my middle, from the wound given me on the surface. Dudley was a glowing star-shaped tumor. It stank like a charnel house, an open sewer, and rotting fish, all at once. I gagged.

Beast screamed again.

The shadow was killing Beast. If Beast died here, then Beast was lost to me forever. I'd be alone. And I'd die of Dudley. Moving fast, I shoved Dudley back into my abdominal cavity with one hand and held my insides in place. This had the added advantage of stopping the bleeding as I applied pressure. In the other hand, I was already holding the blade I had used to kill a man when I was five years old. The handle was antler, crosshatched, the blade of good honed steel. But like in a bad dream, I was paralyzed; I couldn't fight. I could only hold Dudley and the knife.

Beast screamed again.

Desperate, instinctively, I drew on my skinwalker energies and wiped my blade through my blood. Splatted it onto my feet and legs. A peculiar heat raced through me. Flicking the knife, I flung my blood onto my torso and arms and face. I could move but I had taken too long. Beast was dying. I lurched to the fighting pair and brought down my blade into the throat of the girl. She pulled her talons out of Beast and stuck them into me. I couldn't breathe. I was dying. Beast was dying. In the physical world, the Son of Shadows was wrenching my head. My vertebrae popped. He was killing me. But here in my soul home, we'd take the shadow with us.

Letting go of Dudley, using both hands, I cut through the shadow's throat. Oddly, there wasn't much blood. Her eyes met mine in surprise. As if she hadn't known she could be hurt. She snapped her hands, breaking off the talons. Leaving them inside me. She scrabbled on my hands. Plucking at my fingers.

I levered the blade through her spine. Bearing down. We fell to the floor. My blood puddled over her as my blade ground through. Clinked on the cave floor beneath. The light in her eyes faded, dimmed, and went out. I grabbed the head by the hair and swiveled on my knees to Beast. My Beast was breathing fast and shallow. Her blood ran in hot rivulets everywhere. I pulled Beast's warm body onto my lap, grunting with pain as we bumped Dudley and he fell out of me. Beast's blood drenched me, mixed with mine. The scarlet pool beneath us spread.

"You can't die," I said to her. Beast's eyes began to glaze over. "Hayyel," I called. "Do something! She can't die!"

"Beast killed you, and you killed her, when you took her body that first time," his soft voice said. Hayyel stood at the mouth of the tunnel that led to the underground waterfall. He was beautiful and gentle and glowing. "That first mass change was too great for either of you to survive. But you merged and found accord. You both lived." He stood there, unmoving, hands clasped behind his back, wings folded and invisible. I wanted to kill him for the lack of help he gave.

Beast panted, her breath softer, faster, in time with mine. Her blood stopped running. So did mine. The world swirled and darkened. We were sitting in a sticky pool of her life force and mine, mixed and cooling and growing tacky. We . . . we were both dying. I collapsed to the side, pulling her dying body with me.

"Don't go," I whispered, raking my fingers through her pelt.

The memory of the first time I saw Beast blossomed in the air between us.

I reached in and yanked open the Gray Between.

Tossed the head of the shadow to Hayyel. Startled, he caught it, his eyes going wide. His wings spread and shook. He curled his fingers around the head of the shadow.

I sank into Beast.

Blinked. Tried to focus.

I was in two places at once. I was in my soul home, dying with my Beast. And I was on the cold stone of the crevasse, with the Flayer of Mithrans, dying. He was standing over me, his body broken and bleeding, the Glob still in his brain. My vamp-killer was in his hand. He lifted it high, arm back. Ready to take my head. My throat was crushed, my neck broken. I couldn't breathe, couldn't feel my body. Couldn't do anything.

From the far side, Bruiser leaped at him. The Flayer dropped the blade, whirled, and lifted a defensive claw. In one smooth motion, he ripped out Bruiser's throat.

Bruiser fell to the crevasse floor beside me, his hand near my face. His blood pulsed hard and fast. There was nothing left but vertebrae. No creature except a vampire could survive that. I'd had friends die from this kind of wound. His eyes met mine. His fingers curled once and went flaccid. His pupils went wide, spreading like the night. Bruiser was dying. Beast was dying. I was dying. *This sucks,* I thought.

Bruiser's mouth opened. There was no way he could speak. He had no breath and no larynx. Yet he spoke. In the cadence of the Flayer of Mithrans, he said, "Tribal woman. You will give unto me three things: the iron spike of Golgotha, the crown of the arcenciels, and the heart of my brother. If you do this, your man will live. And so shall you."

I considered it for all of half a second. Considered giving the Flayer the key to time and to control of the arcenciels. The key that might give him back his shadow. Might take him back in time to his own origination, and . . . fix the broken spell that had failed to bring his father's mind back when his body rose from the dead. Suddenly I understood. *That.* That was what the Sons of Darkness had always wanted. Not only to bring back their father's body but also to bring back his mind. With the exception of the Sons of Darkness, all vamps were insane when they rose, even Judas Iscariot. The long-chained were just insane longer. Had Judas been a long-chained? If they had known how to help him, would their father still be alive? Had they killed their father too soon, when he rose as a killing machine that ate his human victims?

If the Sons of Darkness found a way back, they might give vampires the ability to timewalk from the beginning. Might be able to eliminate the ten years of the devoveo altogether.

That was what the arcenciels wanted to avoid at all costs, even to the utter destruction of human civilization.

No. My mouth moved, soundless. *No way. We'll all die first.*

Brute collided with the Flayer. Roaring. Werewolf fangs ripped into him. They went down, snarling, shouting. The smell of blood was strong on the air.

Instantly I was back in my soul home. The Gray Between

was open all around us. And I was inside Beast's body.
"Don't go," I whispered again. "Don't go."

"Beast is best hunter," she said aloud to me. "Beast is
better than *Puma concolor* and Jane." In the deeps of our
soul home, her body healed. Mine did not.

I came to, slowly, smelling Edmund's blood.

I was lying on the ground, eyes open. A heavy mist filled
the air, rising and condensing and falling, dripping, dropping water sounding all around us—splatting on fallen
trees, plopping on stone, plinking into water. A symphony
of nature. A roar sounded, so loud it hurt my ears. The light
changed, so brilliant that pain rammed through my eyes.

Beast?

*Beast is here. Jane must shift. Jane is dying. Beast will
die with Jane.*

Yeah, yeah. Sure. I attempted to shift. Nothing happened. I got a feeble breath. A faint hint of air moved in
my throat, explained by the scent of Edmund's blood. He
had gotten some into or onto me, healing me enough to
be able to breathe. *Go, Ed.*

I remembered the sight of Dudley hanging out of me.
Remembered the talons left inside me by the shadow. Remembered the popping sounds as my neck broke. I was so
screwed. But I did get a second slow breath. There was that.

Beast and I were lying near the rift. Blue water glowed
in the night. In the drips of its moisture, I saw the future
and the past. Options. Possibilities. Some not so horrible,
some . . . dreadful. And none of the possibilities I could
see would prevent this. This moment. This death. Time,
that wonderful weapon, was useless.

Around our body, the Gray Between glimmered.
Waiting.

To my side Edmund worked to save Bruiser. But Bruiser
was pale, too pale, too white with blood loss. I watched as
the man I loved was dying for trying to protect me from the
Flayer of Mithrans. He had come to save me and I was already dead or close enough not to matter. So we both died
for . . . nothing?

Beside him was a skinned vampire, Tex, with a stake in

his belly, waiting for another master vamp to come heal him. Beyond Tex was the female vamp, the one from the cave. And Stacey, the little witch. Also skinned. Dying. Two vampires, a witch, a white werewolf with a grindylow clinging to his back, an Onorio, and a skinwalker on the floor of a crevasse, dying, lying beside the exoskeleton of a Son of Darkness, the Flayer of Mithrans. He was headless, limbless. At his side were his arms and legs, twitching.

This time, the shadow wasn't here to carry his parts back to him. The shadow was dead. Brute had Shimon's head, his jaws clamping down and spreading the crack I had started in the exoskeleton skull.

Eli knelt and put a cervical collar onto my neck, then half lifted me in his arms. I felt the stricture of bandages and sticky tape, and my middle burned. Eli had tried to put me back together. I wanted to chuckle but could only make the feeblest of breaths. But I caught the smell of more vampire blood. Of Kojo and Thema. Tasted them on my cracked, dry lips. They had made me drink their blood. If I had been human, I'd be bound to them and to every other vamp who had fed me to heal me over the last few years. And so would my people.

Leo had bound me and Beast had bound him. But my people, they had never been bound by the blood of the MOC. More important, Beast and I had broken Leo's binding.

Only a master vamp could break a binding, could keep her people from being bound by a strong vampire. Only death or a master vamp could shatter bonds. Or me.

Understanding bloomed, another layer, as if I finally understood all the questions of my existence in this moment of imminent death. I understood that I was the Dark Queen, had *always* been the Dark Queen, from the very beginning, from the moment I first touched *le breloque* and it recognized me as its own. But the words didn't make it past my lips, falling away into silence without enough breath to speak.

Was the Dark Queen the sacrifice that led to a safe future for all the paranormals in the world? Is that what I had always been? A body to die?

"Babe," Eli said gently. "You still with us?"

I grunted, too soft to hear, yet he did. Ranger ears.

"Helo is on the way, but the cleft is too narrow for it to land. Thema and Kojo went to get the helo's rescue litter and scoop stretcher and more climbing gear. We're going to have to haul you out." He hesitated. "It's going to be bad."

I had worked with search and rescue in the mountains before. Being taken out in a rescue litter or a scoop stretcher would be a long, arduous, painful process. And time-consuming. And time was something I no longer had. "Ne'er easssy," I managed.

He laughed, some foreign emotion on his face. Maybe grief. "Now that I know you're conscious, is this a rift?" he asked me.

"Yeessss," I breathed.

"You said that if we ever find a rift, we should break the crystal and free Soul. You want to watch?"

"Ssssure."

"Go ahead," Eli said. He shifted me slightly to see the hot pool.

If I hadn't been dying, I'd have screamed with the movement. As it was, my vision went dark until I managed a breath. Shaddock leaned out over the blue water. Without hesitation, he broke the crystal of quartz and instantly dropped it into the water. He leaped back to safety.

From the corner of my eyes, I watched as Edmund performed cardiac compressions on Bruiser. My heart was breaking. But something wriggled in the back of my mind. Something about the rift. Unlike the other things that had come clear, I couldn't find it, whatever it was. The fleeting memory was gone. Important. It was important.

From the water, Soul leaped high, in partial mermaid form, pearlescent teeth gleaming, her legs ending with huge fins instead of feet, her fish frill wide. She landed with a broad splash. I caught a glimpse of horrible scarring up one leg and all along her body on that side, as if Soul had been hit by lightning or burned. The scarring led to one ankle where a thin braided strip of silver alloy was linked, burning her. I had thought it was jewelry, but it was a prison. Holding her in human and fish form. Soul was still being punished for helping Leo, or trying to. For not letting the arcenciels go back in time. Probably for other infractions that I didn't know about.

Soul broke the surface of the water, her silver hair streaming back. "You freed me from time," she said to Shaddock.

"Reckon I did," he said back. "But you can thank our Queenie for that."

Above the pool, Gee perched in his Anzu form, preening and batting his wings in the rising and falling steam, like a bird. There was a small scarlet-winged lizard on his shoulder. I hadn't gotten around to talking to him about that. One of many things I might never get the chance to do. The lizzie was staring at Soul, his tongue flicking out and in, tasting the mineral and blood-laden air. Gee said, "If the silver cuff were off, she could go through the rift. She would heal."

"How do we get it off?" Shaddock asked. "I could—"

"Wait," I whispered. Shaddock paused. Soul's part-fish, part-human face froze in what could only be called fear. "I claim my boon," I said to Soul. "Heal Bruiser."

She tossed a spray of water into the air and studied the droplets as they fell. Without looking I knew they were moments of time. "You would trade your boon for a single life?"

"I'm nothing but a sacrifice. Right?" I whispered.

"You are what you fight for," the Anzu said from overhead. "Not all sacrifices die. Some suffer and live and make the world a better place." And wasn't that a cheerful thought. The Mercy Blade flipped a wing and a long Anzu feather dropped from him to the crevasse floor. Eli picked it up and pressed it to my middle, over the wound where he had taped Dudley in place. My pain eased slightly. Not enough. But anything helped.

"Heal Bruiser," I repeated, the words barely a breath. "I'll owe you a boon."

"It is too late. His soul is ready to depart," Gee said, "ready to shatter the earthly bonds."

My own soul shriveled inside me.

"With *le breloque*, you could have all the power of the

world," Soul said. "You could go back and keep all this from happening. You could go back to your father's house and save him from the white men who killed him. You could stop the Trail of Tears. You could create the world that could have been. Or you could give it to me. Allow me to rule."

Pain slithered through my insides like a ball of snakes. It took two tries but I managed to say, "No one should have that power. Not even the arcenciels." I breathed in, fighting the pain. "So I'll just take my chances, like I've always done, and pray and hope God's listening." *Or Hayyel . . . Or . . . I'll go to water,* I thought.

The memory surfaced, like a whale rising through the ocean, shoving everything else aside. The rift had been called the Waters of Life. Who had used that phrase? I couldn't remember. But Waters of Life sounded like . . . healing.

The way of the Cherokee was harmony, and to achieve harmony with others and with nature, we went to water. So I'd go to water here, and I'd take Bruiser with me. And Beast. The little witch. Tex. I'd take them all. I told Eli what I wanted to do. What I wanted him to do.

Soul looked us over, thinking. She splashed a fin and studied the droplets of time in them. Her eyes went wide. "You have . . . You might . . . This is a new possibility, one not yet posited or evaluated by the Conseil d'Arcenciels."

From the darks of the crevasse, I heard the clatter of movement and saw lights. Soul slid deeper into the water, half-alarmed, uncertain, as she splashed and studied the droplets my words had changed. The noise of humans grew closer. Liz, the redheaded witch, walked into the small clearing, looking over the wounded and the exoskeleton. She bent her knees, putting one to the earth beside Eli, looking me over. "Dayam, woman, you look bad." She placed a duffel beside Eli and opened it. "Got what you asked for."

Eli reached in and pulled out the small white box holding my medicine bag. His face like stone, he opened the box and lifted the thong over my head, settling the bag on my chest. "Your teeth from when you were five," he said.

Then he removed *le breloque* and placed it on my head. It sealed to me tightly. I raised my eyes to him. I hadn't been thinking about using the crown, but then I wasn't exactly strategizing for an op. "Your crown, my queen," he said, straight-faced, serious.

Shaddock was holding the Glob. "Ugliest thing I thing I've ever seen, and pulling it out of a bug skull wasn't fun, but you know?" He flipped the Glob over and over as if testing its weight. "The power in this thing is mighty amazing. Don't reckon you'd want to sell it?"

"Like the crown, it chooses its victim."

"Mmmm. Dawn's coming. We need to get moving, Queenie." Shaddock placed the Glob in my hand, and when he realized I couldn't hold it, he tied it in place with a strip of cloth he cut from his own shirt. "Your scepter."

Gee flapped his wings and tossed something down. "Your arcenciel scale," he said. "I found it in the rocks, covered with your blood, from the battle with the Flayer of Mithrans." Edmund caught it and Eli tucked it into the sticky wrap holding my bandages in place.

I looked at Gee, perched in the tree overhead. "You said you'd show me the way through the rift and back, so I didn't get lost."

"I would guide you, but the Dark Queen has an angel to guide her, if she lives or dies. Heavenly power is far better than any assistance or pathways I might offer."

I wanted to argue and call him foresworn, as I had Soul, but Bruiser was dying. I whispered, "Put me in the rift water, Eli. If I don't drown immediately, put Bruiser and the others in."

That strange expression was still on his face. "And if you die?"

"Then I'll have screwed up, you doofus."

A faint smile ghosted over his face.

I searched through my memories, through poorly learned protocol, and half-recalled Cherokee words and phrases. I couldn't move, couldn't touch his chest, over his heart, but at least I had the words. "You have been my protector and shield bearer, my brother in thought and deed. *Nvwadohiyada*," which meant "Harmony to you,"

said as a type of blessing to the warrior who had fought
for me. I had already taken care of Eli and Alex and the
Everhart-Truebloods in my will, and I had positioned
them in a place of power in Clan Yellowrock. This last
blessing was all I could do at this point.

Tears gathered in Eli's eyes. His nostrils trembled; his
lips went hard and thin as if he held in a scream.

"Throw me in the pool, Eli. Let's see if I sink or swim."

Gently he slid his arms under my knees and beneath
my shoulders. Even with the Anzu feather, the pain was
a red-hot razor of agony. Eli lifted me and carried me
the few feet to the pool. Soul was on the far side, watching. Silent. Not her usual self, but then she *was* a fish. Or
an aquatic mammal. Whatever. He knelt again and
eased me into the heated water. Instantly my bones
stopped aching. My muscles relaxed. But I started bleeding again, a pale cloud of pink in the water. Dudley was
hurting so bad it was off the scale, even with the new
Anzu feather and spinal damage. I held in a scream,
knowing that if I ever started wailing, I might never stop.
I breathed short and fast as Eli settled me with a rock at
my back and the arm holding the Glob around another
rock. Floating.

Other than that, nothing happened.

Edmund was dribbling his blood onto Bruiser's throat
and into his mouth. Bruiser wasn't breathing, wasn't bleeding. But what had Gee said? *"His soul is ready to depart."*
Not *"His soul has departed."*

I turned my head, able to move that much, healed at
least a little by vamp blood. "Put Bruiser in. Fast," I said.
Edmund lifted my honeybunch as if he weighed nothing
and placed him in the water with me. The master vampire
had to hold Bruiser up by his shoulders or he would have
slid beneath the water.

I had said the word, *Nvwadohiyada*, the word and
meaning lodged somewhere in my brain. The way of the
war woman was not always to lead others into violence.
The war woman could also lead to peace. The way of the
Cherokee was harmony and harmony was peace. To
achieve harmony with our clans, our tribe, with other

tribes, and with nature, we went to water. Water was sacred. Holy.

Some water was more sacred, holy, and healing than others. More of my blood spun into the water, whipped away. I wondered where the water went. It was rising from the deeps of the earth, a hot spring. It had to go somewhere. I looked down into the deep blue of the hole in the earth. It was so dark down there; it was blacker than the darkest night. Darker than my soul home. Darker than the shadow's mind had been.

"Eli? Find a small stick? Something that will float?"

He squatted, holding a six-inch stick, dead and dry. "Hold it down in the water," I said. He frowned at me but he bent over the water and stuck his arm in to the shoulder, lower and lower, until it was as deep as he could push without going under.

The water grabbed the stick. Whirled and spun his hand and arm. Sucked the stick out of his hand and down into the dark. He jerked away, his eyes hard. "You can't—"

"The water comes up and shoots back down," I said. "Don't let go of us."

"Not planning to, Janie. But we need to remove the silver shackle on Soul's ankle. Anyone got an idea how to remove a magical ankle cuff?" No one spoke. Eli gave a tiny shrug, pulled a U.S. version of a Swiss Army knife from his pocket, and unfolded a pair of metal snips. He gestured Soul over. Unsure, she raised her scaled and burned ankle. "When in doubt," Eli said, holding me with one hand and leaning out over the water, "use the training provided by Uncle Sam."

I didn't watch, not taking my eyes off the blackness of the deeps, but heard small clicks, one, two, a third. A moment later, Soul flashed by me and dove into the blackness. Just as she disappeared, she transformed into her rainbow-dragon form. And once again she had promised what she didn't deliver. No arceniel help. No helping me with the rift. Nada.

Yet . . . I had an angel to help me. And maybe angels and arceniels didn't mix?

I angled my gaze up to Eli and smiled. "Mr. Fix-It."

"That's me, ma'am," he said, miming tipping a hat at me.

"Make sure that Shimon is still in pieces," I said. "Keep him away from the water. Put the others in. Hold on to them." I felt the presence of others being added to the pool with me, though I couldn't have said how I knew.

I looked down at the magic within me, motes of scarlet, black, silver, and charcoal, from witch, vamp, Anzu, and skinwalker power, unique among magic users. Now that the magic had been cut and pierced with steel, the star shape was broken. I felt the magic in the corona, old and austere around my head. I thought about the Glob, a thing made of suffering, death, lightning, witch magic, and from my body. There was power here, magic and life. And there was no reason why I couldn't use the magic in my middle to heal myself, to heal us all, if I knew how. Except that if I tried, I was as likely to kill us as heal us.

I pulled on the Gray Between, still open around me. Using my own skinwalker magic and the power of my soul home, I mentally twined the darker magic of *le breloque* with the brighter, newer magic of the Glob. I began braiding the three strands of magic. My own weird power, the Glob's, and the crown's. The braid began to glow, to sparkle, visible in the water to human eyes, which I knew when Eli casually asked, "Janie? Whatcha doing?"

"Changing my life," I whispered. "Changing my magic. Flying by the . . . throne of my power."

I took the long tail of strange new energies and draped it around the others, first around Bruiser, then Stacey, and Tex. My body was above the current only feet below, my neck and chest muscles the only ones still working. "Hold me," I whispered to Eli. I let my head drop beneath the water. Eli's fingers tightened on my shoulder, anchoring me in place. I arched my neck slightly, resurfaced, and said, "I call on *Unelenehi*, the great one, who is the sun." I dipped my head below the water again, tying the braided power off, sealing it in place, and to a purpose. I resurfaced and said, "I call on *Selu*, first woman, the corn mother." I went back beneath. I tried to resurface but I couldn't, not alone. This time I needed Eli's help, his hands strong on my shoulders, lifting me. "I call on *Kenati*, her husband, the first man." I went beneath the water and Eli pulled me back up. "I call on the great female spirit, *Agis-seequa*." I dipped again. "I call on the redeemer, who gives everyone a second chance." I went under a sixth time and opened my eyes, staring at the blue, blue water and the dark hole below me, opening into the earth.

I broke the surface and said, "I accept the power that has been given to me. I accept the cost that will come to me." I whispered to the injured, "Be healed." Magic, the power of the Glob and *le breloque*, sparked and flew from me and into them. Looking up into Eli's eyes I smiled. Without taking my eyes from his, I said, "Let go of me."

"Janie."

"Do it." His eyes went cold, the hard, blank gaze of his battlefield self. He released me. I dipped the seventh time. Snapped the magic braid away from them. The current caught me. Sucked me down. And pulled me into the deeps.

The water buffeted me, boiling up and sweeping down. My body followed the current. But instead of taking me straight down, it swept me under a ledge to the side and swiftly into the dark beneath the crevasse. The light vanished. I crashed into rocks, unable to protect my broken body. Pain shot through me and I figured the rocks had broken me open again and I was bleeding out what little blood I had left. I was desperate to breathe, but my throat seemed to have closed down again too. I was too weak to fight any longer.

The water began to cool. Then grow cold. The underground river rushed me through the mountain. In the cold dark, I opened the Gray Between wider around me, pulling the new magic into me, twining it about myself, about the star magics, about Dudley, tied it into *le breloque* and the Glob. I didn't struggle. Couldn't struggle. The water grew colder and colder. My bodily functions began to close down. I gave in. I let the darkness take me.

CHAPTER 22

Dudley Had Caught Fire

I woke in the dark. I was lying in frigid water, the ground sandy beneath me. The roar of water surrounded me. Mist rose and fell. The sound and smell of this place was familiar. I was in the water below the waterfall in my soul home.

I had no idea if I was alive or not.

A light appeared in the darkness. On the bank over the stream stood Hayyel, his body glowing, his wings spread. He was dressed in white, loose pants and a tunic belted with a vibrant blue. He stepped down, across the rocky drop, the broken boulders looking suspiciously like the rocks below the cave in the crevasse. Which was odd.

He took my hand and pulled me from the water. Lifted me to my feet. I could stand, but I wasn't sure this was real; it might be a vision. Probably was.

Hayyel helped me up the grade to the level floor of the tunnel. There he dropped my hand and turned, walking back toward the main room of my soul home. I was pretty certain that this wasn't real, but something that was happening in my brain as I died. Not that I could change it. So I went with it.

I walked beside him, my clothes wet and clinging, my feet squelchy, in moccasins. I wasn't in pain and when I touched my middle, I didn't feel Dudley. I was wearing the woven cloth pants common to the men of my clan, with a long over-shirt, tied with an even longer scarf. I was dressed kinda like Hayyel, or he was dressed like me. My vision, so my rules? At the thought, my clothes were dry. Yep. This was a vision.

My medicine bag and my doubled gold necklace were both around my neck. The Glob was in my belt. The Anzu feather was tight against my skin at my waist. My hair felt strange, and when I touched my head, I discovered two braids, the strands woven with feathers and beads and bits of ribbon and lengths of leather, which made no sense. The Cherokee didn't adorn their braids often, and certainly not in a spirit dream. The hair was sort of like the vision of the soul. They should represent my spirit, my image of myself. Ornate and pretty wasn't it. The braids swung with each step.

I was wearing the crown. Pulling it off, I threaded my left arm through it, propping the crown on my shoulder to carry. It felt good there.

After a bit, the angel said, "You did not take the path I expected."

"Yeah. Drowning myself. Who'd'a thunk it? Surprised me too. Am I dead?"

"No. Not yet."

"Okay. Sooo. What am I doing here?"

"You are in your soul home," he said, stating the obvious. "The place where you first changed your shape and became *We-sa*. Bobcat. The place where you were welcomed into your clan. Where you fulfilled the genetic call to walk in the skin of animals."

"Wait. No." I plucked the clothing. Dry. Not stuff I owned. "Nope. Not reality. The rift did not take me to the actual cave."

Hayyel chuckled. His laughter warmed me to my toes and rang through the darkness. *Angel magic.* "No," he said. "This is no miracle or loop of time. This is your brain, taking you where you need to go, to your beginning. To your own origination story."

Interesting choice of terms. "Like the origination story of the shadow."

He nodded, clasping his hands behind his back as we walked. The sound of the waterfall fell behind. "Shimon and Yosace sacrificed their sister to bring back their father. Shimon ate her and took in her soul. You and your Beast sacrificed yourselves twice, the first time to survive together, becoming two-souled. And just now, the second time, to keep others alive. It is not exact, of course, but there are parallels. Your life has been one of violence, of death and war and pain. You are dying. And you have chosen a remarkable way forward."

"The beloved woman was adaptable. War women have to be to survive."

Hayyel glanced sidelong at me, amused. "You gave me the head of your enemy. I took her spirit to the other side."

"Hell? Heaven?"

He unclasped his hands and flipped one back and forth. "Judgment is not my responsibility. But your choice was unforeseen."

"I can't see how. What else was I supposed to do with the spirit head of the shadow?"

"I expected you to kill the vampire and feed the soul of the shadow to your weapon."

He meant the Glob, the thing that absorbed magic and stored it. I had no idea where the energies went when the Glob absorbed them. Which was kinda scary. As scary as where the death-magic energies went when Molly used her power. Maybe they went to the same place. I grunted, a sound that might have meant anything.

We entered the main cave, the roof in a dome above us, stalagmites and stalactites rising and falling, the few columns where they met holding up the roof. A fire burned in the fire pit, smoke rising, smelling of hickory and cedar. The fire was warm, which was a surprise. There was a pitcher made of fired clay and a wood ladle. A war drum, like the one from the sweathouse. A basket of dried and fresh herbs rested near the drum. A large, elliptical stone, flat on top, with a long stone channel down the middle, rested beside it, a rounded stone in the groove. It was a hand mill used to grind grain or macerate nuts. To the other side was a much smaller mortar and pestle for grinding herbs. Wood and kindling were stacked in the shadows.

A pile of deer hides were folded nearby. Packs were lined against the walls. Cured-hide water bags hung near the far wall, some wet and dripping. I turned to the fire and saw Beast, lying on her belly, resting, head up, ears pricked, looking into the dark. She wasn't dead, at least not in my vision.

"I'm not sure why I'm here," I said. "I'm even less sure why you're here. And even more so, I'm not sure whose side you're on."

Hayyel laughed, that joyous sound that quavered along my nerves the way vampire laughter did. Odd thought that, a comparison for a later time. "You thought I was a watcher?" he asked.

"I thought you were one of the fallen."

That sobered him fast. "Few of us have autonomy. Guardians are among the few."

"You're saying you're my guardian angel?"

At my disbelieving tone, he gave me that amused expression again. "No. I am guardian to many, including Angelina Everhart Trueblood, but in this place, I am Beast's guardian."

I opened my mouth and shut it. Started to speak again and didn't. I sat and added wood to the fire. Warmth from the flames heated my body. I put my crown on the rock to my left and Hayyel sat to my right. I picked a sprig of rosemary from the herbs and dropped it on the burning wood. The strong scent of the burning herb rose on the air. "Okay. You're Beast's guardian angel. And Angie Baby's. And you fight demons. And save werewolves. And help with vision quests, assuming that's what this is. You're a busy angel. I'm dying. I figure you're here to take my soul to be judged, right?" He didn't reply and my eyes narrowed as I watched the flames climb along the dry wood and char the rosemary to ash. Tone sour, I said, "But you've got something you want me to do first."

Hayyel chuckled. "I have nothing planned for you, *Dalonige' i Digadoli*. This choice is yours, to live or to die, as it has always been. To serve as queen or to slip into the next world." He stretched out his arms, wrapped his fingers around one knee, pulling that leg up. He rocked back against the support, shoulders straining the fabric of his tunic, wings gone again. "I am merely here as an interested observer as you choose your next pathway."

"I let go and got sucked into the water. I either went to another world in the rift or I'm drowning. Oh. And I have Dudley cancer. And the shadow's talons in my body. And I've bled to death. Kinda out of my control."

"Or you bubbled time and are ready to be healed."

"That's what got me in trouble and gave me Dudley in the first place."

Hayyel shrugged. "Live or die." He smiled. "However. You already braided the powers and magics together. It seems a shame to waste them. And you do have the scale . . ."

I sat up straight and reached into the belt wrapped around my waist. In its folds I found the Glob, the Anzu feather, and the arcenciel scale. Once upon a time I had used it as a mirror and untangled some of the mess that was my DNA. "Humph. How about that?"

I looked at my middle, seeing the tangled, twisted, shredded, knotted, doubled, broken DNA. And all that magic from too many species, too many sources. "It would take forever to get that all fixed."

"Magic broke you. Perhaps magic can fix you."

"Or . . . giving up magic." I lifted the Glob in my other hand and held the two magical items close together. In my mind, I found the coil of braided magics in my belly and wrapped them all about the Glob and the scale. It was a messy tangle, much like a present wrapped by a kid. I added *le breloque* and the medicine bags containing the DNA from my five-year-old self into the mix. "If I'm going to do this, I can't do it alone. I need power other than timewalking. I need the power of the beloved woman, the warrior who makes peace. I need—"

Heat shot through me as if Dudley had caught fire. A blistering pain, as if a red-hot branding iron had been dipped into my middle and boiled my juices. It stole my breath, stopped my heart. I tumbled back, off the warm rock to the cold stone floor, and landed hard. Smacking my head. Stars swam in my vision and through me, joining with the star magics in my middle. Whirling and spinning. The Glob sucked up the magic, ripping the spinning energy out of me. It drew in all the magics, all the broken bits of power and shredded DNA. Taking with it the pain. Stealing the tumor, sweeping Dudley into the maelstrom. A tornado of power and intent and purpose.

I took a deep, pain-free breath and sighed it out. The scale and the tail of my braided magics floated inside me. Together they began to unravel the mess that was my DNA. The extra strands disappeared. The shredded strands mended before my eyes. The scale spun and danced along with my own skinwalker magic, and the tail of the braided energies joined in.

Time passed. I had a feeling it was a lot of time. Days. Maybe weeks. I slept. I dreamed. I felt the passage of the moon and the tides and the movement of winds.

I came to slowly, first my hearing, then my sense of smell. I could tell by the ambient sounds and the wet-cave and old-fire scents that I was still in my soul home. I opened my eyes, focusing on the dome of the cave-roof overhead. Tilting my head, I looked down my body, inside myself, studying the energies in my middle.

Dudley was gone. The scarlet mote, the dark taint of blood-witch magics, the black mote left in me by Bethany when she tried to kill me, were all gone. As if they had never been.

I was healed. I sat up slowly, the muscles of my abdomen pulling hard, to find Hayyel sitting on the rock beside me. The fire was out. The cavern of my soul home was cool and dark. Beast sat across from me, her eyes glowing gold. Alive. Thank God, alive.

"Go home, *Dalonige' i Digadoli*," Hayyel said. "It is not your time. You have much work to do."

Instantly I was sucked into a frigid stream of water and pulled along through the current.

I followed the current, warm against my skin, swimming leisurely up through the heated water. I broke the surface, cooler air on my skin. I thought, *Beast?*

I am here. We are Beast.

I opened my eyes. The light was bright after the darkness.

I was at the rift. I was alone. Well, unless you counted the arcenciel in human form, sitting on a rock, her feet in the water. Her silvery-lavender hair had a single lose purple strand over her left ear, the rest was twisted up in a chignon, her diaphanous dark purple gown weighted down by moisture. She had been here a while or was working to give that impression. Having no idea who she was, or if she planned to eat me, I was uncertain what to do next. I looked down to see if I was dressed, and I was. Sorta. It was mostly rags but it covered the important bits. Oddly, I was in my half-form, the shape I had been in when I went into the water, pelt, knobby joints, tiny waist, not my human form, but I could deal with that later.

I floated, watching the arcenciel, keeping my toes out of the current I had dropped into and, seemingly, swum back up through, my body still beneath the surface. After a while, I figured if she intended to eat me she would have tried, so I pulled myself out of the water and sat as she did, clawed feet in the warmth. My hair was loose, wet, and hanging plastered to my shoulders in a long black veil. The smell of mineral water was strong on the air.

I patted my clothes and found the Glob in the belt I had been wearing in my vision quest and, even more weirdly, was still wearing here. The traditional scarf/tie/belt was green like fir trees and was the only thing I wore that wasn't ragged. The new Anzu feather gifted by Gee was gone. *Le breloque* was tied to the ends of the belt, but when I touched it, I could tell the crown was different. Not exactly inert. Not quite empty of magic. But more than just a hunk of shaped gold. I had tied *le breloque* to the Glob with magic. Now it was a timewalking, storm-bringing crown bound to an energy-eating weapon made out of the Blood Diamond, a sliver of the true cross, a bit of the iron of Golgotha, witch sacrifices, witch magics, lightning, and my body. Ducky. Another thing to deal with.

I pulled out the neckline of my shirt and looked at myself. I was skinny as a rail, no boobs to speak of, but no pelt on the boobs I did have, so that was good. I ran my hand over my belly to feel only smooth skin and good muscle tone. I was mostly the size I had been when I was eighteen, when I first discovered my skinwalking gift, before I became Enforcer and the Dark Queen. Before . . . Before Dudley. I retraced my belly.

No magical star in my middle.

No Dudley.

No Dudley.

Excitement pattered through me on tiny paws, pricking my skin into goose bumps. I ran my hand over myself again and there was no pain. I was . . . healed? When I shifted to human again would I be myself again? My heart raced, my breathing sped, as I considered the way I felt. Energetic. Normal. Like my pre-Dudley half-form. I felt healed.

A breeze blew across me. It smelled of warmth and the end of winter. I reached up and didn't encounter the medicine bags. Just my doubled gold necklace and its usual focals—the gold nugget and the mountain lion tooth.

The breeze touched my flesh, drying my clothes, drying me. From somewhere I heard birds singing, chirping, the notes sharp, intense, and raucous. Heard water dripping and falling. I smelled the mineral rift water, the wet of stone and the green of bracken and moss. I smelled the magic of the arceniel. I breathed through my mouth, flehmen response, and tasted pollen, the hairy sensation of squirrel and rat, downy baby birds, delicate flowers of springtime.

My mind and my body felt raw and hypersensitive and very in tune with the world. *Healed* . . .

But what had happened to the others?

I had a lot of questions for the arceniel, but when I opened my mouth, the words wouldn't come. I wasn't sure I wanted to know about Bruiser yet. Or how long I had been gone. Or what happened to the Flayer of Mithrans. All that was too scary to ask aloud when I felt so sensitive, so peculiar.

I blinked at the arceniel. She hadn't moved. Suddenly, I wasn't certain if I was alive or if this was a new vision. Or some kind of dream state.

The air felt warmer than before I fell into the rift, maybe in the midsixties. The breeze smelled different. My body felt stronger, with a denser muscle mass. And healed. I could feel the grit of sand beneath my fingers, the frayed ends of my pants on my pelted legs.

If this was reality, then I was different. And I had been gone awhile. The unknown rainbow dragon and I studied each other to the accompaniment of nature plinking and dripping around us. Reality or a vision?

Eventually, the arcenciel must have decided I wasn't going to speak because she said, "You make strange decisions for such a bloody creature."

"Oh?" That seemed as good as any other reply I could give.

"You freed her from her restraints. You gave her access to the rift. She is free."

Several breaths later I figured it out and guessed, "Soul?"

"As you call her. She is not called that by us now. In your pitiful language, she is called She Who Claims the Rift. She is called She Who Seeks Peace. She is *revered*." The arcenciel didn't seem happy about that.

"Okay."

"But she is still hated and feared by a few of us." Meaning her. Got it. She leaned in to me, watching my face as she said, "I don't like her." The arcenciel sounded young and petulant. Maybe not quite stable. Kinda like Soul when she had been trapped in human and mer-form.

I didn't see a silver anklet on this one, but there might be one elsewhere. Or maybe she was just rude. "Okay."

The arcenciel scowled at me. "I have been assigned by She Who Seeks Peace as emissary to your court. I have been told that your man and your brothers and your court are waiting for you." She pointed a finger beyond me. "They left you that."

Glancing away for all of a single heartbeat, I took in the open area of the crevasse to see a ring of blackened stones and ash, the remains of a fire that had burned a long time. Hanging above it was my large gobag. The arcenciel hadn't attacked, so I pulled my feet from the water, stood, and lifted skinny, pelted arms up, taking down the gobag and setting it at my bare paws.

I opened the bag to find the contents were in large zippered plastic bags. There was a change of clothes and a lightweight jacket in one. Water bottles in another. A dozen chocolate bars and protein bars and turkey jerky were packed tightly in another.

There was a cell phone and a charger in another baggie. Not that I had a signal down here. In another baggie was a brand-new medicine bag. I touched my chest and felt a pang of grief. Both were really gone, my father's and my own. This part felt more real, less visiony.

I hesitated. *Beast?*

She didn't answer this time and my heart beat funny. My fingers went cold and tingly.

Beast is here. Jane chose well.

Relief whooshed through me and I nearly fell, suddenly dizzy. I caught my balance and managed, *Yeah. Beast is best hunter. Jane and* Puma concolor *are always the best hunter, right?*

Yes. Best ambush hunter. But Jane/Beast is skinny. Jane must eat much cow and gain much weight and muscle.

Second thing on my personal to-do list is eat.

Eat dead cow?

Yeppers, I thought. *A big honking steak.*

Steak does not honk. Gooses honk.

I didn't smile. She had a point.

I opened the medicine bag and the scent whooshed out. I could smell Eli on the leather. He had made it for me. I hung the bag around my neck with my gold necklace. I opened the plastic bag holding clothes. I stripped out of the rags and dressed in tight, thick yoga pants, a stretchy, tight tank, and two loose, long-sleeved tops, all in shades of dark blue. I retied the green scarf around my waist and braided my damp hair, fingers moving fast. There were three elastics in the baggie and I tied off my plait with the blue one. There was a pair of rock-gripping climbing shoes in another plastic bag, but they wouldn't fit my pawed feet.

In the bottom of the bag, I found weapons and strapped on the vamp-killer. Left the handguns and the stakes in the bottom of the bag. Caught a fleeting memory of the soul-home vision and wondered how I was supposed to be the warrior who brings peace. I would figure it out. Hopefully. I was tired of winging things. I needed to learn to plan things.

Beast chuffed at that. I ignored her.

In the side pocket of the gobag was an envelope. I opened it and smelled Bruiser's citrusy Onorio scent. Tears flooded my eyes and I gave a single, harsh sob as I realized that the arcenciel had been telling the truth when she said my man had survived. His note read:

My darling Jane,

I don't know if you will ever come back to me, or if you even yet live. I hope you climb from the pool that stole you away, read this, rush to the top of the crevasse, and call me. I hope you still love me as I love you, and I will love you with all of my heart and soul, forever. I miss you more than I would miss the sun if it was taken from me.

But you are Jane and I know you are impatient for news. I come here, to the rift, two times each week, and leave new supplies and a new note, so this one is less than four days old when you read it.

I smiled, and my skin and pelt felt tight and shriveled, my mouth moving in a way that was not-Jane, not-half-form, but something strange and new. I wondered what I looked like, lifted a hand and ran it over my face and head. My jaw was humanish but square and with a cleft. My skin was tight, plastered across my skull. I had Jane hair but was pelted on the back of my neck and shoulders, but not my throat or chest. I had rounded Puma ears. Again I ran my hand over my ribs and skinny belly. No Dudley. No cancer. No tumor. Was I healed in my Jane form? I went back to Bruiser's note.

The Flayer of Mithrans was not eaten by Brute. We burned the body of the last Son of Darkness over the fire, until even the bones were ash. Then Evan and Eli brought in bags of concrete, mixed the concrete with water from the rift, and stirred the ashes into it while Evan wove a music spell. True- blood magically bound the ash into the dried con- crete at the cellular level. If you noticed the fire pit, it has a cement bottom. The Flayer is gone.

I looked at the pit and a creepy feeling came over me, the feeling described by childhood acquaintances as someone walking on my grave. I planned to never spend the night at the rift. I figured I'd have night terrors. His letter continued:

We are all healed. EJ is well, with no memory of the events at the hands of the Flayer. Tex and Shiloh are with us here, and we found Roland, who has re- turned to his anamcharas in New Orleans. Derek is well and human, though as angry as usual. The Everhart-Truebloods, with the exception of Liz, have left the winery, to see how much is left of their homes. Edmund has returned to Europe as the em- peror, where he and Grégoire, the Dark Queen's Warlord, are fighting for control of all European lands. Though they know you have no desire to rule, they hold the land in the name of the Dark Queen, and await your return.

We have gained a new pet. A strange creature that looks like a striped, foot-long, flying, scarlet-winged lizard. Gee says his name is Longfellow, and for now, he sleeps beside Brute and Pea. I have provided a photo on your cell phone. It is quite adorable.

I stopped, turned on the cell, and checked the stored pics. The photo was of the sleeping white werewolf, a neon green grindylow lying on his shoulders, and a scarlet-winged lizard asleep between his front legs, curled under his chin. It looked bigger than I remembered, but yeah. Adorable. I went back to the note.

> *There is one bit of good news. Jodi Richoux and Wrassler are to be married in the fall and have asked that the ceremony take place in the ballroom of the Council Chambers in New Orleans. On your behalf I approved their request. We are expected to attend. Formal attire is required. I look forward to seeing our friends happy and you on my arm, in a beautiful gown.*
>
> *I will be at the vineyard with the Younger brothers, raising vines and preparing for this year's crop. We'll harvest our first grapes late this summer. We have branded the wine Yellowrock Clan, and the first pressings will be a mixed-grape white, and a mixed-grape red, both table wines.*
>
> *Come home to me. Please.*
>
> > *Yours forever,*
> > *Bruiser*

I folded the note and stuffed it back in its envelope. Then tucked it down my tank top, next to my heart.

Looking at the arceniel, who fortunately hadn't attacked me while I was occupied, I said, "What do you want to be called?"

"I am Storm."

"Of course you are." I sighed. "Why couldn't I get a Breeze or a Rose or something peaceful? No. I got a Storm for my court." I tossed her a protein bar and a package of turkey jerky. "I'm heading out of here. You can come if you want."

Shouldering the bag, I began the hike up the chasm, watching for the climbing gear that would be hanging down in place, at some point. I was going home.

Keep reading for an excerpt from
the first book in the Soulwood series

BLOOÐ OF THE EARTH

Available now!

Edgy and not sure why, I carried the basket of laundry off the back porch. I hung my T-shirts and overalls on the front line of my old-fashioned solar clothes dryer, two long skirts on the outer line, and what my mama called my intimate attire on the line between, where no one could see them from the driveway. I didn't want another visit by Brother Ephraim or Elder Ebenezer about my wanton ways. Or even another courting attempt from Joshua Purdy. Or worse, a visit from Ernest Jackson Jr., the preacher. So far I'd kept him out of my house, but there would come a time when he'd bring help and try to force his way in. It was getting tiresome having to chase churchmen off my land at the business end of a shotgun, and at some point God's Cloud of Glory Church would bring enough reinforcements that I couldn't stand against them. It was a battle I was preparing for, one I knew I'd likely lose, but I would go down fighting, one way or another.

The breeze freshened, sending my wet skirts rippling as if alive, on the line where they hung. Red, gold, and brown leaves skittered across the three acres of newly cut grass.

Branches overhead cracked, clacked, and groaned with the wind, leaves rustling as if whispering some dread tiding. The chill fall air had been perfect for birdsong; squirrels had been racing up and down the trees, stealing nuts and hiding them for the coming winter. I'd seen a big black bear this morning, chewing on nuts and acorns, halfway up the hill.

Standing in the cool breeze, I studied my woods, listening, feeling, tasting the unease that had prickled at my flesh for the last few months, ever since Jane Yellowrock had come visiting and turned my life upside down. She was the one responsible for the repeated recent visits by the churchmen. The Cherokee vampire hunter was the one who had brought all the changes, even if it wasn't intentional. She had come hunting a missing vampire and, because she was good at her job—maybe the best ever—she had succeeded. She had also managed to save more than a hundred children from God's Cloud.

Maybe it had been worth it all—helping all the children—but I was the one paying the price, not her. She was long gone and I was alone in the fight for my life. Even the woods knew things were different.

Sunlight dappled the earth; cabbages, gourds, pumpkins, and winter squash were bursting with color in the garden. A muscadine vine running up the nearest tree, tangling in the branches, was dropping the last of the ripe fruit. I smelled my wood fire on the air, and hints of that apple-crisp chill that meant a change of seasons, the sliding toward a hard, cold autumn. I tilted my head, listening to the wind, smelling the breeze, feeling the forest through the soles of my bare feet. There was no one on my property except the wild critters, creatures who belonged on Soulwood land, nothing else that I could sense. But the hundred fifty acres of woods bordering the flatland around the house, up the steep hill and down into the gorge, had been whispering all day. Something was not right.

In the distance, I heard a crow call a warning, sharp with distress. The squirrels ducked into hiding, suddenly invisible. The feral cat I had been feeding darted under the shrubs, her black head and multicolored body fading into the shadows. The trees murmured restlessly.

I didn't know what it meant, but I listened anyway. I always listened to my woods, and the gnawing, whispering sense of *danger, injury, damage* was like sandpaper abrading my skin, making me jumpy, disturbing my sleep, even if I didn't know what it was.

I reached out to it, to the woods, reached with my mind, with my magic. Silently I asked it, *What? What is it?*

There was no answer. There never was. But as if the forest knew that it had my attention, the wind died and the whispering leaves fell still. I caught my breath at the strange hush, not daring even to blink. But nothing happened. No sound, no movement. After an uncomfortable length of time, I lifted the empty wash basket and stepped away from the clotheslines, turning and turning, my feet on the cool grass, looking up and inward, but I could sense no direct threat, despite the chill bumps rising on my skin. *What?* I asked. An eerie fear grew in me, racing up my spine like spiders with sharp, tiny claws. Something was coming. Something that reminded me of Jane, but subtly different. Something was coming that might hurt me. Again. My woods knew.

From down the hill I heard the sound of a vehicle climbing the mountain's narrow, single-lane, rutted road. It wasn't the *clang* of Ebenezer's rattletrap Ford truck, or the steady drone of Joshua's newer, Toyota long-bed. It wasn't the high-pitched motor of a hunter's all-terrain vehicle. It was a car, straining up the twisty Deer Creek mountain.

My house was the last one, just below the crest of the hill. The wind whooshed down again, icy and cutting, a downdraft that bowed the trees. They swayed in the wind, branches scrubbing. Sighing. Muttering, too low to hear.

It could be a customer making the drive to Soulwood for my teas or veggies or herbal mixes. Or it could be some kind of conflict. The woods said it was the latter. I trusted my woods.

I raced back inside my house, dropping the empty basket, placing John's old single-shot, bolt-action shotgun near the refrigerator under a pile of folded blankets. His lever-action carbine .30-30 Winchester went near the front window. I shoved the small Smith & Wesson .32 into the bib of my coveralls, hoping I didn't shoot myself if I had to draw it fast. I picked up the double-barrel break-action shotgun and checked the ammo. Both barrels held three-inch shells. The contact area of the latch was worn and needed to be replaced, but at close range I wasn't going to miss. I might dislocate my shoulder, but if I hit them, the trespassers would be a while in healing too.

I debated for a second on switching out the standard shot shells for salt or birdshot, but the woods' disharmony seemed to be growing, a particular and abrasive itch under my skin. I snapped the gun closed and pulled back my long hair into an elastic to keep it out of my way.

Peeking out the blinds, I saw a four-door sedan coming to a stop beside John's old Chevy C10 truck. Two people inside, a man and a woman. *Strangers,* I thought. Not from God's Cloud of Glory, the church I'd grown up in. Not a local vehicle. And no dogs anymore to check them out for me with noses and senses humans no longer had. Just three small graves at the edge of the woods and a month of grief buried with them.

A man stepped out of the driver's side, black-haired, dark-eyed. Maybe Cherokee or Creek if he was a mountain native, though his features didn't seem tribal. I'd never seen a Frenchman or a Spaniard, so maybe from one of those Mediterranean countries. He was tall, maybe six feet, but not dressed like a farmer. More citified, in black pants, starched shirt, tie, and jacket. He had a cell phone in his pocket, sticking out just a little. Western boots, old and well cared for. There was something about the way he moved, feline and graceful. Not a farmer or a God's Cloud preacher. Not enough bulk for the first one, not enough righteous determination in his expression or bearing for the other. But something said he wasn't a customer here to buy my herbal teas or fresh vegetables.

He opened the passenger door for the other occupant and a woman stepped out. Petite, with black skin and wildly curly, long black hair. Her clothes billowed in the cool breeze and she put her face into the wind as if sniffing. Like the man, her movements were nimble, like a dancer's, and somehow feral, as if she had never been tamed, though I couldn't have said why I got that impression.

Around the house, my woods moaned in the sharp wind, branches clattering like old bones, anxious, but I could see nothing about the couple that would say danger. They looked like any other city folk who might come looking for Soulwood Farm, and yet . . . not. Different. As they approached the house, they passed the tall length of flagpole in the middle of the raised beds of the front yard, and started up the seven steps to the porch. And then I realized why they moved and felt all wrong. There was a weapon bulge at the man's shoulder, beneath his jacket. In a single smooth motion, I braced the shotgun against my shoulder, rammed open the door, and pointed the business end of the gun at the trespassers.

"Whadda ya want?" I demanded, drawing on my childhood God's Cloud dialect. They came to a halt at the third step, too close for me to miss, too far away for them to disarm me safely. The man raised his hands like he was asking for peace, but the little woman hissed. She drew back her lips in a snarl and growled at me. I knew cats. This was a cat. A cat in human form—a werecat of some kind. A devil, according to the church. I trained the barrel on her, midcenter, just like John had showed me the first time he put the gun in my hands. As I aimed, I took a single step so my back was against the doorjamb to keep me from getting bowled over or from breaking a shoulder when I fired.

"Paka, no," the man said. The words were gentle, the touch to her arm tender. I had never seen a man touch a woman like that, and my hands jiggled the shotgun in surprise before I caught myself. The woman's snarl subsided and she leaned in to the man, just like one of my cats might. His arm went around her, and he smoothed her hair back, watching me as I watched them. Alert, taking in everything about me and my home, the man lifted his nose in the air to sniff the scents of my land, the delicate nasal folds widening and contracting. Alien. So alien, these two.

"What do you want?" I asked again, this time with no church accent, and with the grammar I'd learned from the city folk customers at the vegetable stand and from reading my once-forbidden and much-loved library books.

"I'm Special Agent Rick LaFleur, with PsyLED, and this is Paka. Jane Yellowrock sent us to you, Ms. Ingram," the man said.

Of *course* this new problem was related to Jane. Nothing in my whole life had gone right since she'd darkened my door. She might as well have brought a curse on my land and a pox on my home. She had a curious job, wore clothes and guns and knives like a man, and I had known from the beginning that she would bring nothing but strife to me. But in spite of that, I had liked her. So had my woods. She moved like these two, willowy and slinky. Alert.

She had come to my house asking about God's Cloud of Glory. She had wanted a way onto the church's property, which bordered mine, to rescue a blood-sucker. Because there was documentation in the probate court, the civil court system, and the local news, that John and I had left the church, Jane had figured that I'd be willing to help her. And God help me, I had. I'd paid the price for helping her and, sometimes, I wished that I'd left well enough alone.

"Prove it," I said, resetting the gun against my shoulder. The man slowly lowered his hand and removed a wallet from his jacket pocket, displaying an identification card and badge. But I knew that badges can be bought online for pennies and IDs could be made on computers. "Not good enough," I said. "Tell me something about Jane that no one but her knows."

"Jane is not human, though she apes it better than some," Paka said, her words strangely accented, her voice scratchy and hoarse. "She was once mated to my mate." Paka placed a covetous hand on Rick's arm, an inexplicable sort of claiming. The man frowned harder, deep grooves in his face. I had a feeling that he didn't like being owned like a piece of meat. I'd seen that unhappy look on the faces of women before. Seeing the expression on the face of a man was unexpected and, for some reason, unsettling. "He is mine now," Paka said.

When Jane told me about the man she would send, she said that he would break my heart if I let him, like he'd broken Jane's. This Rick was what the few romance novels I'd read called tall, dark, and handsome, a grim, distant man with a closed face and too many secrets. A heartbreaker for sure. "That's a start," I said. In their car, a small catlike form jumped to the dash, crouched low, and peered out the windshield through the daylight glare. I ignored it, all my attention on the pair on my land, moving slowly. Rick pulled out his cell phone and thumb-punched and swiped it a few times. He paraphrased from whatever was on the screen, "Jane said you told her you'd been in trouble from God's Cloud of Glory and the man who used to lead it ever since you turned twelve and he tried to marry you. She also said Nell Nicholson Ingram makes the best chicken and dumplings she ever tasted. That about right?"

I scowled. Around me the forest rustled, expectant and uneasy, tied to my magic. Tied to me. "Yeah. That sums it up." I draped the shotgun over my arm and backed into my home, standing aside as they mounted the last of the steps. Wondering what the church spies in the deer stand on the next property would think about the standoff.

They thought I didn't know that they kept watch on me all the time from the neighbor's land, but I knew. Just like I knew that they wanted me back under their thumbs and my land back in the church, to be used for their benefit. I'd known ever since I had beaten them in court, proving that John and I were legally married and that his will had given the land to me. The church elders didn't like me having legal rights, and they didn't like me. The feeling was mutual.

My black cat Jezzie raced out of the house and Paka caught her and picked her up. The tiny woman laughed, the sound as peculiar and scratchy as her words. And the

oddest thing happened. Jezzie rolled over, lay belly-up in
Paka's arms, and closed her eyes. Instantly she was asleep.
Jezzie didn't like people; she barely tolerated me in her
house, letting me live here because I brought cat kibble.
Jezzie had ignored the man, just the way she ignored hu-
mans. And me. It told me something about the woman.
She wasn't just a werecat. She had magic.

I backed farther inside, and they crossed the porch.
Nonhumans. In my house. I didn't like this at all, but I
didn't know how to stop it. Around the property, the
woods quieted, as if waiting for a storm that would break
soon, bringing the trees rain to feed their roots. I reached
out to the woods, as uneasy as they were, but there was no
way to calm them.

I didn't know fully what kind of magic I had, except
that I could help seeds sprout, make plants grow stronger,
heal them when they got sick and tried to die off. My magics had always been part of me, and now, since I had fed
the forest once, my gifts were tied to the woods and the
earth of Soulwood Farm. I had been told that my magic
was similar to the Cherokee *yinehi*. Similar to the fairies
of European lore, the little people, or even wood nymphs.
But in my recent, intense Internet research I hadn't found
an exact correlation with the magics I possessed, and I
had an instinct, a feeling, that there might be more I could
do, if I was willing to pay the price. I had once been told
that there was always a price for magic.